Amanda Jennings has written six novels, and numerous short stories for anthologies and magazines, and is published both in the UK and abroad. She is a contributor to BBC Radio Berkshire and a long-standing judge for the Henley Youth Festival literary competition, has taught writing workshops, and enjoys appearing at literary festivals. Before becoming an author, Amanda worked at the BBC as a researcher, and studied History of Art at Cambridge University. She lives in a cottage in the middle of the woods in Oxfordshire with her family and a varied assortment of animals.

Also by Amanda Jennings

The Haven
The Storm
The Cliff House
In Her Wake
Sworn Secret

The Judas Tree

Amanda Jennings

ONE PLACE. MANY STORIES

HQ
An imprint of HarperCollins*Publishers* Ltd
1 London Bridge Street
London SE1 9GF

www.harpercollins.co.uk

HarperCollins*Publishers*
1st Floor, Watermarque Building, Ringsend Road
Dublin 4, Ireland

This paperback edition 2022

1

First published in Great Britain as *The Judas Scar* by
Cutting Edge Press in 2014. This edition published by HQ,
an imprint of HarperCollins*Publishers* Ltd in 2022.

Copyright © Amanda Jennings 2014

Amanda Jennings asserts the moral right to be
identified as the author of this work.
A catalogue record for this book is
available from the British Library.

ISBN: 9780008471606

MIX
Paper | Supporting
responsible forestry
FSC
www.fsc.org
FSC™ C007454

This book is produced from independently certified FSC™ paper
to ensure responsible forest management.

For more information visit: www.harpercollins.co.uk/green

Printed and Bound in the UK using 100% Renewable Electricity
at CPI Group (UK) Ltd

For Sian, who brightens life.

Betrayal is the only truth that sticks.
Arthur Miller

PROLOGUE

'Do you remember what else you said that day?'

There was an eerie calm to the man's voice that chilled the dead, stale air around them. He looked up at him, those eyes burning with hatred, mouth twisted into a bitter snarl. Adrenaline coursed through his veins as he fought against the cords that bound him, a desperate rabbit tugging and twisting in its snare.

The man leant forward and whispered close to his ear. Breath hot. Words creamy with intent. 'You don't remember? Shall I remind you? You said, *This will teach you*. Remember now?' Then a soft rumble of laughter as he dangled the penknife in front of his face like a hypnotist's watch.

Later – how long had it been? An hour? Maybe two – he lay on the floor alone and bleeding. He craned his neck to see where the man was, if he was near, but there was no sign of him, no sound. The concrete beneath his cheek was cool and uneven, its musty dampness filling his nose with each breath. It was a smell he'd always liked. In his top three, in fact, along with petrol fumes on a garage forecourt and hot bitumen. His wife thought he was mad to like smells like these, but what did she know? She liked smells that made her fat: vanilla, freshly baked bread, and cake.

He listened to the hum of traffic outside, passing cars and vans, fewer now than earlier, the drivers unaware of him, hurrying home, minds focused on crawling into warm, safe beds. The gaffer tape wrapped around his head and covering his mouth pinched at his skin, and when he coughed there was a strange rattling inside his lungs that pushed phlegm and Christ-knew-what against his sealed lips, making him gag.

Fuck being tied up and left bleeding on the floor of some godforsaken shithole.

He made another futile attempt to pull his hands free. The ropes bit into his wrists and a sharp pain shot up his arm through his shoulder and into his neck.

A broken collarbone. The bastard's broken my bloody collarbone.

One of his eyes had swollen closed; through the other he saw a pool of blood that bloomed on the concrete. What the hell was he doing there, shivering on the ground, beaten, kicked and cut, watching blood quietly seep from his body? Things like this, deaths like this – was he really going to die? – should only happen to two-dimensional characters in ten-a-penny thrillers and crappy TV dramas. But here he was, dying a fictional death, lying in his own blood and piss, pathetic, cold and broken. How long would they take to discover him? Would the police find his killer? Or would he be just another unsolved crime, the murder of a nobody cluttering up their files?

Footsteps approached. His body tensed as a surge of fresh panic jump-started him. His heart pounded as he turned his head towards the approaching noise. The man stopped walking. The knife glinted. He held his breath and waited for whatever was going to happen next. Every cell in his body screamed with pain. He kept as still as possible. Played dead. Would that send the psycho away? Sure enough, when the footsteps started up, they moved in the opposite direction, echoing lightly on the floor.

He lay there some time. He was aware of his body growing colder. He vaguely remembered reading that as an injured body lost blood its temperature dropped. His mind drifted in and out of consciousness, a listing ship on a gentle swell. He tried to listen for the cars, perhaps catch the sound of a police siren, but all he could hear was a faint ringing in his ears.

White noise.

His vision blurred to a hazy mirage and the effort of keeping his good eye open was too much so he allowed it to close. His breathing was steady now and at last his pain began to subside. Perhaps he'd make it after all? All he needed to do was rest, to regain his strength, sleep a bit. Then he would work out how to get help.

His last thought before he finally gave in was of the weather. How on earth could it be this bloody cold in July?

CHAPTER ONE

Harmony lay on the grass and searched the cornflower sky for clouds. There were none, not even the breath of one. The only thing that broke the blue was a fading streak of white from a long-passed plane. The sun warmed her face as she listened to the sound of Londoners all around them enjoying the hot June Sunday on Wandsworth Common.

'He's so good with the boys,' said Sophie.

Harmony sat halfway up and propped herself on her forearms to watch Will and her nephews playing football. Her husband in knee-length khaki shorts and pink shirt, crumpled and rolled to the elbows, and the boys – Cal, Matt and George, aged fifteen, twelve and nine respectively – bare-chested, skin glistening with sweat, tearing about on a makeshift pitch marked out with T-shirts and trainers. Cal went in for a sliding tackle and knocked his youngest brother's feet from beneath him. George scrambled up, indignant, appealing for a foul while glaring at his brother as he geared up for a fight. Will ran over to George and lifted him high before turning him upside down and diverting his attention from the injustice.

'He enjoys their company.' Harmony smiled as Will deposited George back on the ground and ruffled his hair, before hooking an arm around his neck and pulling him close. He whispered something conspiratorial and George's face broke into a smile and he nodded, then the two of them jogged back to rejoin the game, the fight with Cal forgotten.

Sophie looked over at Roger, who sat a little away from them in the shade of a sycamore tree, eyes glued to his phone as his thumb scrolled. 'Why don't you join them?' she called.

'Got an email that needs to go before noon.' He glanced up at Will and the boys. 'They're fine anyway. If I join it'll be uneven.'

Sophie groaned and rolled her eyes. 'He's literally never off that thing,' she said. 'He's worse than the kids.' She reached into the cool-box for the bottle of wine and poured some into her plastic glass, then held the bottle out towards Harmony. 'Want some?'

Harmony shook her head then turned back to watch Will with her nephews. Sophie was right, he was great with them. A phantom pain shot through her stomach.

'He'd be a brilliant dad,' Sophie said, reading her thoughts.

Harmony nodded. 'He would.'

'How are you feeling about things?' Sophie's voice was soft and gentle.

'I'm fine.' She smiled at her older sister. 'It's taken its time though. I'd no idea I'd be such a wreck for so long.' Sophie reached for her hand and gave it a rub. 'And Will?'

She didn't answer immediately. 'It's hard to tell. I mean, I know he's thinking about it, sometimes he seems distant and stuck in his thoughts, but you know what he's like, buries his feelings, makes stupid jokes at the wrong times. He doesn't seem to get it. The awfulness of this thing we've been through. It's as if he's scared of owning up to any emotion. As if doing that is somehow admitting a weakness.' She sighed and shook her head. 'But what can I do? That's Will. Always has been.'

'That's *men*.' Her sister directed a pointed look towards Roger, still staring at his phone. 'We've been married forever and he's totally incapable of recognising the mood I'm in.'

Roger glanced over and smiled. 'You're always happy, aren't you, my angel?'

'See what I mean?' She shook her head in mock despair. 'Yes, my love. Always happy!'

He grinned and went back to his phone.

Sophie looked over at the game of football and burst out laughing as Will faked a fall and all three boys jumped on top of him. Harmony watched her husband fight to escape the pile-on, finally crawling out, blond hair sticking up like a scarecrow, cheeks red from exertion. George shrieked with glee and ran at him again. Will put out a hand and fended off the attack as George lunged in an attempt to bring him down.

'Enough now, mate,' he said with a laugh. 'You've killed me. I need a stint on the bench.'

He jogged over to Harmony and Sophie and collapsed on the picnic rug. 'They're exhausting, Soph,' he said, panting heavily. 'How on earth do you guys do that every day?'

'We don't do it every day. In fact, we try never to do it. Why do you think we invited you to have lunch with us?'

Harmony smoothed Will's hair. His brow was clammy with sweat. 'It would be good for you to do this more,' she said. 'Looks like you could do with getting a bit fitter.'

He turned his head on the rug and lifted his eyebrows. 'What are you talking about? I'm in peak physical condition.' He patted his middle and laughed, then closed his eyes and tilted his face towards the sun.

Harmony heard a small child yell out. She turned to see a little girl in a denim dress with dimpled knees and dark hair in bunches. She was crying, red-faced and angry, as her steely mother fought to fasten her into her pushchair. There was a baby lying on a rug beside them, happily kicking its legs, oblivious to the battle of wills going on between its mother and sibling. The woman finally succeeded in strapping her daughter in and sat back with a weary sigh and a silent mutter. Then she scooped up her baby and kissed its cheek before standing to truss it into a sling on her front.

Harmony leant down to kiss Will. He opened his eyes and smiled at her.

'What was that for?' he asked.

'Just because.'

He turned on his side, shifting himself near enough to lay his head on her stomach. 'This is nice,' he murmured, draping an arm over her.

Harmony combed her fingers through his hair. 'It is,' she said.

She glanced up, conscious of being watched, and caught Sophie looking at them with a smile on her face. Harmony smiled back then lay down beside Will, linking her fingers through his. She stared up at the sky. A single cloud, a wispy white smudge, now drifted silently across the wide expanse of blue. She watched it as it moved, morphing imperceptibly from one nondescript shape to the next, and when it had passed she closed her eyes and listened once again to the noises of the people all around them.

CHAPTER TWO

'Are you all right?' he asked, as they pulled up on the grass beside the long row of cars parked beneath the oak trees. 'You seem quiet.'

'Do I? I'm fine,' she said. 'A bit distracted perhaps.'

'But you're happy?' There was a hopefulness in his voice that stung her.

'I am.'

'I'm glad; it suits you.'

She furrowed her brow. 'I'm not sure being sad suits many people, does it?'

'I didn't mean that. I just meant it's good to see your smile. Your smile suits you.'

Like a shirt or a new shade of lipstick, she thought, as she looked out of the window across the fields that rolled away from the smart estate fencing. The evening was beginning to thicken with dusk and two horses stood beside each other grazing in the last few hours of light, their tails flicking at the midges that hung suspended around them. An ungenerous part of her wanted to tell Will not to be so grateful she was happy, not to seem so bloody relieved, but she bit her tongue. 'I'm certainly feeling more like myself.' She bent to retrieve her bag from the footwell. 'Come on, we should get in there. We're late enough as it is. Emma will never forgive me.'

They got out of the car and Will went to the boot to get his camera bag. Their eleven-year-old Clio looked small and scruffy parked next to the shining army of Range Rovers, Porsches and BMWs. Harmony imagined the people who'd driven them here, high-powered men with glamorous wives dressed in designer clothes and judgemental sneers. 'Do I look OK?' she asked, straightening her dress and arranging a pale pink pashmina loosely over her shoulders.

'You look beautiful,' he said. 'I should have told you earlier.'

'You look good too. Except your tie's on the wonk.' She gestured for him to come to her.

He stepped closer and tipped back his head so she could reach up and straighten his bow tie.

'There,' she said. She brushed her fingers through his hair in a futile attempt to neaten him. His unruly hairstyle had remained unchanged forever, a foppish mess that in spite of the wrinkles which had folded themselves into his forehead and around his eyes managed to keep him looking young for his years. 'That's better.' She brushed a few loose hairs from his shoulders. 'You might have shaved though.'

He grinned and rubbed his chin which was covered in light blond stubble. 'Beards are all the rage.'

She laughed. 'That's not a beard. That's not bothering with a razor for three days.'

He smiled. 'You love me rough and ready.'

'I don't have a choice, do I?'

He leant forward and grazed his scratchy skin lightly against her cheek. 'No, I'm sorry Mrs English, you're well and truly stuck with my scarecrow chic.'

They walked hand in hand up the driveway. The gravel crunched beneath their feet and the still summer air was filled with the delicate smell of burning oil from the flares which lined the way. As they neared the house the noise of the party – exuberant music and a rumble of chatter and laughing – grew. Harmony's stomach pitched with nerves. She glanced at Will. Relaxed and nonchalant as always. Nothing fazed him. She was envious of his ability to walk into a party like this without a worry, confident and at ease, eyes glistening with anticipation, not even a whiff of apprehension at the prospect of a room full of strangers.

'Can you believe they re-gravelled the drive?' he said. 'Christ, imagine having so much money you'd redo the bloody drive for a party.' He laughed. 'When Ian told me the budget for the champagne I nearly choked.'

Harmony wasn't surprised; if you were as wealthy as Ian said he was, re-gravelling the driveway was nothing. 'From what Emma's let slip over the past few months, the drive is the tip of the iceberg.'

Will clapped his hands together and grinned. 'Excellent,' he said. 'Can't wait to get in there and start gawping.'

They reached the entrance to Emma and Ian's imposing Georgian pile. There were three stone steps leading up to the front door on which were scattered a few handfuls of red rose petals. Harmony remembered Emma telling her they were supposed to look like wedding confetti, but seeing them now they reminded her of drops of blood and she was careful not to tread on them as they walked up the steps. The heavy door opened and they were greeted by a man in striped grey trousers and a black evening jacket who balanced a tray of champagne flutes on his white-gloved hand.

He bowed his head in greeting. 'Welcome to Oak Dene Hall,' he said, with theatrical solemnity.

Harmony smothered a smile; she had to admire her friend's attention to detail. Emma hadn't mentioned a butler, almost certainly because she knew what Harmony's reaction would have been. They'd been friends since primary school, but sometimes Harmony wondered if they had anything in common outside a deep affection and shared memories. They were different in almost every way. Harmony loved to travel and devoured books, was dedicated to her work, never went to the gym and rarely wore make-up. In contrast, Emma's world consisted of a few square miles of rural Oxfordshire, the shops of Bond Street and Knightsbridge, and innumerable Instagram pages showcasing pristine beaches, gourmet cooking, and aspirational interior design. Emma had been planning this party – meticulously – for months. Harmony was also turning forty that year and had made Will promise there'd be no celebrations. She didn't even want a card. She'd be perfectly happy if the day passed without mention; like a dirty secret it was best kept hidden, not due to vanity but because of what the milestone symbolised. That she was past her best. That time was running out.

Will thanked the man and took two glasses of champagne. 'I know you're driving,' he said, as he handed her a glass. 'But you should try this; it's one of the best we stock, from a tiny vineyard that doesn't usually supply outside of France. It's very easy drinking.'

She took the glass and they walked over to the circular table in the large entrance hall that held a huge vase of flowers and a bowl of tropical fruit that spilled over the shining mahogany like a nineteenth-century still life.

Will lifted his glass and she clinked hers against it. 'Cheers,' he said, leaning over to kiss her.

She took a sip of champagne. 'It's delicious.'

He grinned. 'I knew you'd like it. I'm glad Ian came to me. God knows what he'd have ended up with if left to his own devices. I'm not sure he could tell champagne from bleach—'

'Shhh, Will.' She smothered a laugh and glanced over her shoulder. 'Someone will hear you.'

He laughed.

'Will?' she said, with a certain reticence. She fixed her eyes on her glass, watching the stream of tiny bubbles race to break the surface of her drink to leave a thin, fleeting foam. It was no doubt a terrible time to raise the subject, but this was the most relaxed they'd been in ages.

'Yes?'

'I've been thinking about things over the last week or so.' She glanced towards the front door but the butler in the grey striped trousers was too busy bowing to be interested in eavesdropping.

'What things?'

Her heart skipped a beat. She was surprised how difficult it was to get the words out. She'd been over them again and again, toying with them like worry beads, but as she spoke they caught in her throat. 'I think . . . I think we should . . . try again.'

'Try again?'

'Yes.' She reached for his hand. 'For a baby.'

His smile fell and his body tensed.

'It's been six months,' she said quickly. 'And, like I said in the car, I'm feeling good, back to normal really. And seeing you with the boys in the park the other day . . . I think we're ready. I know it's taken some time, but I really think we are.' She paused, halted by his expression, a mixture of shock and confusion which said more than words could ever say. Her stomach turned over.

Will glanced at two women who were walking in their direction, full-length dresses trailing the floor, heads tipped together, sharing a joke behind raised hands like Cinderella's cackling sisters.

'This isn't the right place to discuss this,' Will said, watching them as they passed, his features stretched taut.

'Does it need a lengthy discussion?'

'Yes,' he said in a low voice. 'Of course it does. This has come totally out of the blue; I had no idea you'd been thinking about this.'

'It's all I think about.'

'I'm not—'

'Hello, my *darlings*!'

Harmony closed her eyes and swore quietly at the sound of Emma's voice. She should never have brought this up at a party. Stupid and impulsive. They needed time and space, and now she had to put on a show and pretend everything was OK. She turned to face her friend who was dressed in black from shoulder to toe, the taut satin fabric sparkling with what looked like ten thousand beads and sequins.

'Thank God you've arrived!' Emma threw her arms around both of them and kissed each of their cheeks in turn. 'I was beginning to worry you weren't coming!'

'As if we'd miss it.' Will turned his smile on like a light.

'You look amazing, Em.' But her words sounded forced, her mind too full of Will's reaction, the way he'd looked at her as if she'd pulled out a gun.

Emma beamed. 'You do too!' she said. 'It's criminal you spend all your time in jeans and a sweatshirt. I'd *kill* for a figure like yours.' Then Emma leant forward, her face suddenly serious. She gave Harmony a hard stare. 'Darling? Are you OK?'

Harmony nodded. 'Will and I were having a bit of chat, that's all.' She paused for a beat as Emma began to express concern. 'We're fine. Honestly.' Harmony gave Will a tight smile to prove how fine they were.

Will smiled back and put his arm around Emma's shoulders and squeezed. 'All good,' he said. 'I'm just hoping you'll let me have the first dance with you.'

Emma squealed. 'Oh, yes *please*! Now, enough serious talking, let's have some fun! Oh,' she said, touching his arm. 'You've got your camera, haven't you?'

Will patted the bag that hung over his shoulder. 'Of course.'

'Good,' she said. 'It would be great to get some photos of people while they still look gorgeous. Will you take one of Harmony and me now?'

Without waiting for him to answer she stood next to Harmony and put her arm around her waist. 'Christ,' she said. 'You really don't have an ounce of fat on you, do you? My stomach's a horror show, like a hot cross bun with all the flab and C-section scars.'

Harmony smiled weakly then leant in towards Emma and posed for the photograph.

'See you in there,' Emma said, as she trotted down the hallway towards the throb of the party, lifting a hand and shrieking a greeting to another of her friends.

Neither Will nor Harmony spoke immediately. Harmony rested her hand on her tummy – flat, muscular and barren – and her throat constricted. Would these flashes of sadness ever stop? The desperate grief that had come with her miscarriage had been hard to endure. The only time she'd felt anything like it was when her mother died, but at least then the loss had been tangible, an actual known person physically gone, a person of whom she had memories and photographs. It was far easier to miss her mother's hugs or the way she stroked her forehead at bedtime than it was to miss a baby she'd never met. She was painfully aware she was mourning a concept, an unknown foetus barely the size of her thumb – four point one centimetres, the books had told her – no name, no face, even gender unknown.

'I'm sorry,' she said, with a heavy sigh. 'Tonight isn't the right time to talk about it.' She tried to smile. 'I wasn't thinking. It just came out.'

'You don't have to be sorry.' His voice was soft, eyes gentle. 'You've done nothing wrong. It took me by surprise, that's all.' Will reached for her hand then leant forward and kissed her forehead. She rested her head against his lips for a moment and closed her eyes; she felt desolate.

'Come on.' He took a step back from her. 'Let's get back to enjoying the criminal extravagance.'

Harmony hesitated, wondering briefly if Emma would notice if she slipped away, past the ridiculous butler, over the petals on the steps, out to the quiet safety of the car and home. But instead she nodded and followed Will.

The party was in a marquee that butted up to the side of the house. It was accessed through the French windows in the living room, a high-ceilinged room with two huge sash windows, original plasterwork and a number of sofas carefully arranged with gold-tasselled cushions. She gasped as they entered the marquee. It was enormous, covering the entire rose terrace, the neatly clipped box hedging and flower beds incorporated into the design with garlands of flowers and strings of lights and what appeared to be a thousand candles decorating every surface. The navy material which swathed the roof was studded with tiny lights to look like stars. There was a table in front of them that held a cake that was more work of art than pudding with hundreds of perfect choux puffs piled three feet high with hardened glistening caramel flowing down them like lava. Waiters circulated with bottles of champagne and silver trays of geometric canapés. The tent heaved with beautiful people with shining white teeth and loud, confident laughter, vying to be heard over the music.

'Bloody hell,' Will said. 'It's *Made in Chelsea* does *Midsummer Night's Dream*.' He gestured with his glass. 'There's Ian, Oxfordshire's answer to Gatsby.' He started to walk towards Ian, but Harmony didn't follow. He turned back to face her. 'Are you coming to say hello?'

'You go ahead.' She tried to sound as relaxed. 'I'm going to nip to the loo.' She took a step backwards. 'I won't be long.'

'Do you want me to wait for you?'

'No, I'll find you.'

Harmony walked back out of the living room and down the panelled corridor towards the downstairs cloakroom. As she walked she straightened her shoulders and breathed deeply. Will's reaction had unsettled her. They hadn't spoken much about the miscarriage. They both found it hard. Will always managed to say the wrong thing somehow, upsetting her without meaning to, incapable of understanding the maelstrom of emotions she was battling. But was it really that surprising she wanted to try again? Maybe, as was often the case with Will, he needed time to get his head around it.

There was a woman in a short red dress waiting outside the loo. She smiled at Harmony as if she was about to engage in conversation. Harmony turned away, focusing her gaze on the photographs of the Barratt-Joneses displayed on a console table in the corridor. The photographs were all black and white and presented in a variety of silver frames. Some of the pictures – the better ones in her opinion – were Will's. There was one he'd taken in his studio when Emma had insisted the whole family dress in blue jeans and white shirts and pose in front of a white background. Will had tried to convince her to go for something less hackneyed, a little edgier, but she was having none of it. So there they were now, preserved in manufactured perfection, Emma sitting beside Ian, with Abi on her lap, and Josh on the floor, all of them immaculate and smiling and lost in a sea of white. Then there was a photo of Ian and Josh out shooting, Josh a mini-me beside his father in matching flat cap and leather boots, holding aloft a brace of dead pheasant like a trophy of war. Abi in her ballet leotard, leg outstretched at the barre, almost regal in her grace and poise; Emma and Ian arm in arm in front of the Colosseum; Josh scoring a glorious try in an under-nines rugby match. A tinge of envy crept under her skin. Harmony pushed it away. What was she jealous of anyway? Not the money and she certainly didn't resent her having children. She was happy Emma had a family. Maybe it was the way Emma's life had panned out exactly as she'd intended, with no obstacles to negotiate, no trapdoors or landmines to surprise and derail her?

'I'm not going to be poor when I'm older,' she'd told Harmony when she was fifteen. 'Being poor is absolute shit.'

'You can't predict the future.'

'You can make choices, though, can't you? And that's my choice. I don't want to be poor. I'm done with it.'

Every decision Emma had made since then was part of a grand plan that led to this very point: the large house, the wealthy husband, the perfectly turned-out children. Harmony had watched with amused fascination as her friend single-mindedly pursued what she perceived to be happiness. Often she'd been scathing of Emma's undisguised aspiration, but looking at these photos, knowing how much the family loved each other, perhaps she had to admit the planning had worked. She was pleased for her friend. Of course she was. What kind of person would she be if she wasn't?

Harmony glanced over her shoulder at the sound of the toilet door and saw the lady in red disappear inside as another woman came out, smoothing her dress as she passed. She looked back at the photos. Behind the family shots was one of her and Will with Emma and another couple of friends. They were on the beach at West Wittering, where they'd been camping for the weekend, drinking cans of lager and eating sausages cooked on a cheap disposable barbecue. She picked it up and smiled, stroking her fingers lightly over the faces in the photograph. They were all so young, so full of optimism and possibility. She stared at her own face. She was plumper back then, not overweight, but fuller, her face less angular, but even so she still looked masculine, she thought. Will's mother had once described her as handsome and it was a good description. Her face was symmetrical with an aquiline nose, high forehead and pronounced cheekbones. That day her hair was brushed back into a ponytail and she remembered Will kissing the nape of her neck as she bent to blow on the struggling barbecue. When she'd turned to smile at him he'd mouthed: *I love you.* A few hours earlier, holding each other in two sleeping bags zipped together to make one, he'd asked her to marry him. She remembered the thrill she'd felt, lying in his arms in the sun-warmed tent, looking at him with tears in her eyes and nodding.

'But you're so young,' Emma had said as they watched the boys throwing a rugby ball down by the water's edge. 'Why get engaged at twenty-two? I mean, what's the point? How do you know it's right? That he's The One?'

Harmony had laughed. 'There's no such thing as The One! It's a ridiculous notion. What if your The One is in India or Papua New Guinea and you never, ever met? And, anyway, I know Will's right for me. It's not as if we've just started going out; we've been together ages and he's funny and different and kind. And we have *amazing* sex.' She grinned at Emma then turned back to watch Will catch a high ball and fall backwards onto the sand in a fit of laughter, his strong forearms browned by the sun, blond hair falling over his face. 'I love him, Em. I really, *really* love him, so much I feel I might actually explode.'

Then Will's words echoed in her head like a spectral prophecy. *And you're OK with not having children? Because that won't change, Harmony. Promise me you understand.*

'Yes,' she'd said, kissing him full on the lips. 'I understand.'

But she hadn't understood, not properly. She only really understood the day she lost her baby.

'Are you waiting?' The voice startled her. She turned to see a man behind her. He was very good-looking, medium height and slim build with chiselled, tanned features and thick dark hair swept back off his face. He wore a crisp white shirt that was open at the neck, no tie, no jacket. His eyes were dark, almost black, and he looked at her with such directness she felt herself blush.

'Sorry?' she said, putting the photograph back on the table.

'Are you waiting to go in?' He pointed at the cloakroom.

She looked and saw the door open, an array of scented candles flickering inside.

'Oh, yes, I am. But I'm not desperate so go ahead if you'd like.'

He smiled a broad and generous smile. 'No, after you. I'm not,' he paused, amused, '*desperate*, either.'

Harmony blushed again. 'Thanks,' she said. 'I'll be quick.'

'Take all the time you need.'

As she walked into the cloakroom she turned and mumbled another thank you before closing the door behind her. Harmony looked at herself in the mirror and shook her head; had she really just told that man she'd be quick? She was a liability in social situations.

She didn't need to use the loo so instead she rifled through the basket of products that Emma had left beside the basin: a hair-brush, hairspray, a choice of lip glosses, perfume, a powder compact, and even a small case of expensive bronzing powder and a big fluffy brush to apply it. Had it been her own party she'd have forgotten to check there was toilet roll, let alone provide the contents of a chemist for her guests to use. She dragged the brush through her hair and gave her neck and wrists a spray of perfume.

'All yours,' she said, as she came out. As they passed each other their shoulders lightly brushed.

'Will you wait for me?'

'Sorry?' She turned to look at him.

'Wait for me?' His eyes drilled into hers and her heartbeat quickened. 'I'd like to talk to you properly. You're the first inter-esting person I've met tonight and I've been here for over an hour.'

'Oh,' Harmony said. 'Yes . . . OK.'

He nodded and went into the cloakroom. She stood for a minute or two then laughed under her breath. What was she doing? Waiting for a stranger to finish in the toilet because he asked her to?

'If he wants to talk to me he can find me again,' she said under her breath. She began to walk away, but a raucous screech of laughter from the living room stopped her in her tracks beside the console table. She hesitated and glanced back at the cloakroom and as she did so the door opened.

'You waited.'

Harmony blushed and cast her eyes down at the table, pretending she'd been looking at the photographs. 'No, I was enjoying a moment in the quiet actually. I'm not really in the mood for a party.'

'Well, I'm glad you stayed. Everybody else here is extremely dull.'

'Everybody? That's quite a generalisation and incredibly dismissive.' Harmony glanced back at him and lifted her eyebrows. 'Some of those people are my friends, you know.'

'I'm sure the ones that are your friends are fascinating.'

She smiled, pleased she no longer felt girlish and silly.

They surveyed the photographs, side by side, in silence. She was aware of him next to her. It was as if he had a force field that crackled the nearer he was. He leant in close to her ear. 'So what do you think?'

'Of the pictures?'

He nodded.

'They're lovely.'

He shook his head. 'They're not *lovely*. They're staged and smug, with a hint of narcissism that makes them unbearable. They reek of self-promotion.'

A small laugh escaped Harmony's lips. Immediately, she clapped her hand over her mouth, but it was too late, her disloyalty hung in the air around her and she felt grubby with guilt. 'You can't say that,' she said. 'They're a lovely family and very good friends of mine.'

'Not dull then,' he said, with a glint in his eye.

She smiled.

'The one with you is good. Exactly how a photograph should be. A perfect moment, suspended in time. You look beautiful.'

She wrinkled her nose. 'I'm twenty-two in that photo. Youth is beautiful.'

'Perhaps,' he said, though there was an edge to his voice, a reticence, as if he didn't agree with her.

She held her hand out. 'I'm Harmony.'

He shook her hand, his grip firm, holding on a fraction too long. 'An unusual name.'

'My father chose it,' she said. 'I was lucky. According to my mum the final choice was between Harmony and Sunrise.' She laughed lightly. 'He was a bohemian artist type, a bit of a hippie, apparently.'

'Apparently?'

'He left when I was three.' *Like a fart in a storm*, as her grandmother always grumbled. 'You didn't tell me your name,' Harmony said.

'Would you like a drink?'

'No, I have one thanks.' She lifted her almost empty glass. 'Aren't you going to tell me who you are?' She was intrigued by the way he looked at her; his eyes didn't waver but stayed locked on hers.

'Why do you need to know?'

The mocking in his voice grated and the hold he had on her was broken long enough for her to consider walking away from him. 'I don't,' she said. 'But it's fairly standard etiquette in our society. I tell you my name. You tell me yours. We talk a bit then run out of things to say and move on.'

He laughed. 'And by society you mean the masses?'

'So damning of society? Let me guess, society exists merely as a concept and in the real world there are only individuals?'

'Oscar Wilde,' he said. 'I'm impressed.'

It was Harmony's turn to laugh. 'Christ, you can't be impressed by an Oscar Wilde quote.' She gave a derisive shake of her head. 'They fall out of Christmas crackers with paper hats and plastic key rings.'

He stared at her, narrowed eyes flicking back and forth over hers as if trying to read her thoughts. Her cheeks flushed with heat again. She lifted her glass and drank the warm, flat dregs of her champagne to fill the silence.

'You said you're not enjoying the party,' he said. 'Why not?'

'I didn't say that. I said I wasn't in the mood.' She paused and shrugged. 'It's all a bit loud and crowded in there and I'm not great with parties at the best of times. But it's my best friend's fortieth, I'm sure I'll get into it soon.'

'It's not a very good party. Too showy and self-conscious. I'm not enjoying it either.' He paused for a beat. 'At least, I wasn't.'

Harmony lowered her eyes.

He placed his glass on the console table and stared at her, silent for a moment or two, until she finally looked up at him. When she did, he smiled. 'What would you say if I asked you to leave and have dinner with me?'

Harmony laughed abruptly, taken aback by his question. 'Excuse me?'

'Right now, if I asked you to leave the party with me, would you come?'

Her heart began to race as she realised he was being perfectly serious. 'No,' she said, quickly. 'Of course I wouldn't.'

'Why not?'

She faltered. The hairs on her forearms stood proud. Her heart hammered. 'Because I'm married and I love my husband. Who's here, by the way.'

The stranger held her eyes for a moment then gave a deferential nod. 'He's a lucky man.'

As if on cue she heard Will's laugh, unmistakable, generous and full, one of those infectious laughs that set other laughs off in a line of falling dominoes. She turned to look over her shoulder and saw him standing with his back to her at the entrance to the living room talking to a man she didn't recognise. She was filled with a sense of relief as the tension between herself and the stranger disappeared like water through a cupped hand.

'In fact, that's him now,' she said. 'He's probably come looking for me. I should join him before we sit for supper.'

The stranger stared at her and smiled. 'It was nice to meet you, Harmony.'

She held out her hand again. 'Nice to meet you, too,' she said. 'Whatever your name is.'

He took her hand and as he did he stroked his thumb against

her, barely there, a butterfly's kiss of a touch. Her skin tingled. As she walked down the corridor away from him she felt his eyes burning into her back. When she reached Will she kissed him on the lips. The man he was with chuckled drunkenly.

'What was that for?' Will asked with amusement.

'No reason.' She glanced over her shoulder, but the stranger had gone and she felt a surprising stab of disappointment.

CHAPTER THREE

Though Harmony looked for him she didn't see the man again that night. She would have enjoyed talking more to him; he was interesting and so different to anybody else she'd ever met. Intriguing and enigmatic. She recalled him asking her to leave with him, the focused intent with which he'd delivered his question, and despite herself she felt a rush of excitement. She'd half-hoped she might find herself sitting next to him at supper, but instead she was stuck with two men she'd met a couple of times, neither of whom she had much in common with, and she spent most of the meal sitting quietly, toying with her water glass and watching other people as they chatted and drank. Will spent no time at the table. Instead he leapt around the marquee with his camera like a man possessed. Harmony felt a warm glow as she watched him. Taking photographs was his passion and it was good to see him so energised and enthusiastic.

By two o'clock she was shattered. The number of guests had dwindled, but those who remained were opening more wine or knocking shots back or dancing in happy, sweaty groups, and all looked set to see in the dawn. She found Will chatting to a couple she didn't recognise.

'Do you mind if we go soon?' she whispered in his ear. 'I'm tired and we've got to drive back to London.'

Will excused himself from the couple, who wandered off hand in hand towards the dance floor. 'Have you said goodbye to Emma and Ian?'

'No, Em's having far too much fun dancing and I don't want to bring her down. I had a quick look for Ian, but can't see him.'

'He's extremely drunk. Last time I saw him he was clutching a bottle of vodka and stumbling into the undergrowth with only one shoe on.'

'Let's slip away. I'll phone Emma in the morning.'

There were a few people waiting in the hallway for taxis, putting coats on or standing patiently, eyes tired and heavy with alcohol. As Harmony and Will walked down the steps she noticed the rose petals were now crushed into the stone in dirty smears. Most of the flares that lined the driveway had burnt down, the low blue flames of those that soldiered on licking sporadically at the darkness as they clung to life.

Within moments of being in the car Will fell asleep. His head lolled forward, and every so often soft snores escaped him. Despite the time and the soporific hum of the engine, she was wide awake, mind buzzing, flitting between Will's look of shock when she mentioned a baby and the man she'd met. There had been something about him – a powerful sexuality – not the bravado of a self-styled Casanova, but something rawer, more intrinsic. She'd been with Will since she was twenty, and it was the first time since then she'd felt any hint of sexual connection with another man. She knew she should probably expel these thoughts from her head, but it was a breath of fresh air to have her mind occupied with such frivolity. There'd been too much sadness and soul-searching over the past few months. She rested her hand against her stomach as the familiar phantom ache crept into the centre of her, where her baby used to be, as if the scar left when it was torn out of her had opened up again. She glanced at her husband, still asleep, head nodding with the motion of the car.

'I wish you felt this,' she said, her words loud against the quiet in the car.

'What?' he said, his voice groggy.

'I thought you were asleep.'

'Just resting my eyes.' He reached for her hand on the gear stick and stroked it. 'What did you say?'

She didn't reply.

'It's about the baby, isn't it?' he said, with a slight drunken slur.

'Yes, it's about the baby. Our baby.' As she spoke a lump of emotion caught in her throat. 'We need to talk about it.'

'I'm not sure what you want me to say.' His feeble words staled the air.

Yes, said a voice in her head. *I want you to say yes. Yes, you were devastated when we lost our child. Yes, you want to be a father as much as I want to be a mother.*

But again she didn't say anything and they drove the rest of the way in silence.

She turned off the Talgarth Road and into their street and parked in a space a little way up from their flat. She stilled the engine then swivelled in her seat to look at him.

'I just . . .' She faltered. 'It's what I said at the party. I want to try again.'

They sat in the quiet for a minute or two. She willed him to speak but instead he got out of the car and closed his door. She stared ahead feeling empty, hands clasped lightly in her lap. There was a group of girls walking down the street. They were under-dressed and swaying, passing a bottle of alcohol between them and smoking, the ends of their cigarettes glowing orange in the dark as they stumbled, arms linked, in a drunken chain. Harmony rubbed her face hard and got out of the car.

Will was sitting on the steps of their block. His elbows rested on his knees. 'I'm sorry,' he said as she approached. His eyes dropped to the ground and he scuffed the side of his shoe against the pavement. 'I know we need to talk, but right now I'm tired and drunk and need our bed.'

She walked past him and unlocked the door that opened on to the communal hallway. Three flats shared the building and as usual the man from Number Two had blocked their way with his bike. Harmony squeezed past it and descended the four stairs to their basement flat. She unlocked the door and went straight along the narrow corridor to the kitchen and filled two glasses with water. When Will came in she handed him one then leant back against the kitchen worktop. He drank his and put the empty glass on the table.

'Emma seemed to enjoy herself tonight,' he said. She knew he was hoping this would be enough to deflect her.

Harmony tipped the rest of her water into the sink, rinsed her glass and upended it on the draining board. 'She did. I'll see you in bed.'

Will came into the bedroom as she was climbing into bed. She waited for him to use the bathroom and as he was undressing she mustered the energy to try again.

'Losing our child floored me,' she said. 'You don't seem to feel the same and that makes me feel very alone.'

He sat down heavily on the edge of the bed.

'Will?' Harmony asked. 'Did you hear what I said?'

He lifted the duvet and lay down. 'I didn't expect you to want to be pregnant again.'

'Why on earth not?'

He hesitated.

'Please, Will, talk to me.'

'I know how upset you've been and I assumed you wouldn't want to risk putting yourself through it again.' He sighed then reached to turn his bedside light off and the room fell dark, a sliver of city light pushing through a gap in the curtains.

In the silence that held them, Harmony's thoughts drifted back to discovering she was pregnant. A missed period. Then two weeks late. The blue line on the pregnancy test. Such a simple indication of a new life growing inside her. She'd sat on the floor of their bathroom and hugged her knees tightly. As the minutes passed, euphoria and joy took over from shock, and she realised how deeply she must have buried her desire to have children, hidden it from herself, pretended it didn't matter. She'd convinced herself the two of them – evenings out, long Sundays in bed with the papers or making lazy afternoon love, impromptu trips to the pub, to the cinema – were enough. But something awakened in her. Then six short weeks later she found herself on the same spot on the bathroom floor, the same position even, knees drawn in tight to her chest, white-knuckled hands clasping them to her as she lost her baby. Dark blood stained her underwear. Smeared her inner thighs. Disbelief and panic flooded her. Then piercing grief as she'd curled up on the floor and begged her baby to stay with her, just as she'd done with her mother. She thought about her mum then, a skeleton in a pink cotton nightie lying beside her, so brittle and feather-light Harmony worried she might crush her with the weight of her arm. Those rattling breaths that came from her struggling body as Harmony cried silent tears that soaked into the pillow.

'Please, Mum,' she'd whispered. 'I love you. Don't leave me.'
Don't leave me, baby. Please. Don't leave me.
But neither her mother nor her baby had listened.
Both left her.
Harmony turned on her side and tucked the duvet around her.
She had to make him see how important this was for her.
'Good night,' she said into the darkness.
But Will was already asleep.

CHAPTER FOUR

'I can't wait to see these photos, Will.'

Will smiled and kissed Emma on both cheeks. 'They're good. There's a gorgeous one of you – you look like a film star – which you're going to love.'

Emma beamed. 'How exciting! But first,' she said. 'What can I get you to drink? Wine, beer?'

'A beer would be great.'

'Could I have something soft?' Harmony asked.

'I've some elderflower,' Emma said. 'Ian's mother made it. Though I hate to admit it, it's delicious.' She smiled conspiratorially. 'Don't ever tell her I said that.'

As Emma went back into the kitchen, Will and Harmony walked through the living room and stepped out onto the terrace. The sun was high and bright, but not unbearably hot, and a light breeze carried the smell of freshly cut grass. The table was laid with a pressed white tablecloth, a vase of yellow roses, with a large white parasol offering shade over half of it, a slice of Tuscany brought to North Oxfordshire. All trace of the party had gone. The York paving, speckled with moss between the slabs, looked as if it had been vacuumed, and the lawn beyond rolled gently between extravagant flowerbeds in even emerald stripes that reached out like fingers to the strip of woodland that marked the garden's boundary.

The woods had been thinned so individual trees stood like sentinels guarding the view of the undulating countryside beyond. There was a swing that hung from a beech tree, a wooden fort with a slide, and further into the trees was a platform high up in the branches with a zip wire that shot into the wood below. Will heard his father's ghost tut-tutting at these expensive, spoiling toys – *indulge the child and ruin it* – and sat at the table facing away from the woods to silence his disapproval.

He was glad to be out of London and in familiar company. The conversation he and Harmony were still to have was a low, black cloud hovering over them continuously. He knew what he had to say, but couldn't find the words to tell her without hurting her more. Every time he tried, he knotted up.

Will lifted his laptop out of the bag and made space for it on the table. 'I hope she likes them,' he said to Harmony.

'Of course she will. They're great. It was lovely of you to spend the evening taking them.' She tilted her face up towards the sun and closed her eyes in the warmth like a cat.

Emma came through the French windows and put a tray of drinks, a bowl of crisps and a small plate of swollen green olives on the table. She sat in the chair beside Will and slipped her sunglasses down from the top of her head to shield her eyes.

'So who's this nightmare colleague of Ian's you're making us eat with?' Harmony asked Emma.

'God, don't tell him I said that, whatever you do.'

Harmony laughed. 'As if I would!'

'It's his lawyer. He worships the bloody man.' Emma poured Harmony a glass of cordial from a jug filled with ice cubes and freshly cut mint. 'He was asking questions about you.' Emma grinned at Harmony and lifted her eyebrows.

'Me? Really? Do I know him?'

'You met him at the party. Dark hair. Good-looking, if you like that sort of thing.'

'Should I be jealous?' Will smiled and sipped his beer.

'What type of questions was he asking?' Harmony sat forward, her interest piqued.

Emma shrugged. 'It was Ian he was asking. Said something along the lines of him having met one or two interesting people at the party and then described you. Ian knew he meant you when he said your husband had white-blond hair. Anyway, Ian mentioned we were having lunch with you and Will to look at the photos, and as far as I can tell he invited himself along. Like I said, Ian worships the man, so obviously his wish is his command, and, well, here we are.' She reached for an olive then gestured towards the laptop. 'Come on, Will. Show me these photos before they get here and I have to start dashing in and out of the kitchen like a lunatic.'

They were interrupted by high-pitched screaming. Will turned to see the children running across the lawn towards the fort. Josh had clearly stolen something from his sister and was holding whatever it was above his head as she ran after him shrieking at him to give it back.

'For goodness' sake, Josh!' Emma called. 'We've guests. Can you try not to be a total savage for a few hours?'

They both ignored her and disappeared into the woods.

'It's a shame they aren't eating with us,' said Harmony, staring after them.

Will's stomach turned over as he caught her sadness.

'I had to feed them before you got here. If they don't eat before midday they'll eat each other,' Emma said. 'They're basically wild animals. Don't worry, though, they'll be like wasps on jam when I bring pudding out.' She smiled. 'They're Pavlova addicts. You'll be lucky to get any.' She reached for her glass of wine then leant forward to peer at the laptop.

'These are amazing, Will,' Emma said, a few moments later as she looked through the photographs. 'Oh!' she exclaimed. 'I look gorgeous in this one!' She grinned and kissed him on the cheek. 'You're a photographic miracle worker!'

'I tell him that all the time,' Harmony said, without moving her face away from the sun. 'He needs to make time for it. I can't remember the last time you went to your studio, Will.'

'And that's a great one of you, Harmony.'

Will looked at the photo. He didn't agree with Emma; his wife didn't look *great*. Her silk dress skimmed her body in all the right places, but she looked thin, her collarbone pronounced and her cheeks gaunt. She'd lost so much weight since the miscarriage.

Emma continued to scroll through the pictures. 'There,' she said, tapping the screen with her fingernail. 'That's Ian's lawyer.'

Will looked at the screen. The photo showed two people, a couple – Anne and Cliff – whom Will had met a couple of times before. In the background, cast in shadows to the left of the picture, was a figure Will hadn't noticed until then. It was difficult to make him out properly, but he seemed familiar. Will had certainly met him, but for the life of him couldn't work out when or where. There was an intensity about him that cut through the blurry darkness and locked on to Will. As if he was staring right at him. Now Emma had pointed him out it was hard to look anywhere else; his presence held the photo like a curse.

'I recognise him,' Will said. 'But not from the party. I must have met him here before.'

'Not here,' said Emma. 'That was the first time I'd met him myself. I thought he was a bit strange, to be honest, but then I was as drunk as a tequila worm by nine.'

Will stared at the indistinct face and racked his brain to place him. 'Must have been with Ian then.'

Emma didn't answer but clicked to the next photo. 'Oh my God!' she exclaimed. 'Just look at Pete in this one! What kind of face is he pulling? And there's Katia and Steve.' She glanced at

Harmony. 'Such an odd pair,' she mused. 'Do you know them? The world's least suited couple. I mean, look at them. Could they be any more mismatched?' She laughed. 'She's tiny, barely speaks English and is only interested in handbags, and Steve is a six-foot-five oaf who lives in his – frankly vile – cycle lycra. God knows what they have in common.'

'Sex!' came Ian's voice from behind them. 'They bonk like rabbits on Viagra.'

Will turned and saw Ian stepping through the French windows onto the terrace. Tall and slim with ruddy cheeks and hair that was greying at the sides, he was a man whose looks had improved with age and privilege; unfairly – in Will's opinion – given what a git he was.

'Excuse me?' laughed Emma. 'Is that any way to announce your arrival?'

'Sex and shoes. He told me she goes like a steam train every night in return for a pair of Lablahniks once a month. They're both as happy as pigs in shit.'

'Laboutins,' corrected Emma. 'Or Manolo Blahniks. Not Lablahniks, for God's sake. And don't say that pig thing – I hate it.' She peered behind her husband. 'Where's your golf partner?'

'Nipped to the boys' room,' Ian said, as he bent to kiss Harmony's cheek before reaching over her to shake Will's hand.

'Hello, Ian.' Will had to work hard at liking Ian. He was pompous, too pumped up with that ludicrous alpha machismo he'd seen so much of at school and loathed, and, as far as Will was concerned, he brought the worst out in Emma. When they'd met they were plain old Emma Jones and Ian Barratt. When they married they became Mr and Mrs Ian Barratt-Jones. Will and Harmony had laughed when they'd heard about the hyphen.

'She always wanted a hyphen,' Harmony said, stifling her giggles. 'How do you think they chose Barratt-Jones over Jones-Barratt? I mean, how did they decide who got pole position?'

If it wasn't for the fact that Emma adored him, Will wouldn't have given Ian a second look. But he was fond of Emma, who, despite her occasionally grating aspirational streak, was warm, kind, and funny. He'd liked her from the moment Harmony introduced them, aged twenty-one, the three of them picnicking in Hyde Park, sitting on the soft, green grass, laughing until they cried while getting drunk on Jack and Coke.

'How was your game?' Will asked.

'Played like a fucking moron.'

'Ian!' Emma shook her head indulgently.

'Sorry,' he said, taking a couple of olives and shoving them into his mouth. 'Played like a fucking idiot.' He winked at Will, who forced a smile back.

Will's attention was caught then by Ian's companion walking through the French windows, his head slightly bowed as he watched his step.

'He didn't leave you on the eighteenth then?' Emma said, as she walked up to greet him.

The man lifted his head and Will's heart stopped.

It couldn't be.

Could it?

'Oh my God,' he breathed.

Harmony looked across at him. 'Will?'

Will stared at the man who was now kissing Emma on both cheeks, warmly telling her how nice it was to see her again, how much he'd enjoyed the party, thanking her for allowing him to join them for lunch.

'Let me introduce you to our friends,' Emma said genially. 'Harmony, Will this is—'

'Luke.' Will stepped forward.

Harmony looked between the two of them. 'You know each other?'

Will and Luke held each other's stare then Will watched a wide smile dawn on Luke's face. 'Will English. Well, I never!'

Will opened and closed his mouth, his voice sticking in his throat. 'Luke?'

As he spoke his name there was a thump to his gut like a heavyweight punch. He recalled the photo from Emma's party. The face in the shadows. How had he not recognised him?

'You know each other?' said Emma, repeating Harmony's question and looking from Luke back to Will.

'Actually, we do,' Luke said. 'We were at school together.' He stepped forward towards Will, hand outstretched in greeting. 'A *very* long time ago. What a surprise!'

Will hesitated then shook his hand. He was startled by his solidity, a matured masculinity that seemed alien; the Luke he knew was slight and small, a skinny wisp of a child with pale skin and a dusting of freckles. How could he be this fully grown man?

'Yes. I'm . . . it's . . . God, I'm lost for words.' Will's lungs constricted and his thoughts grew foggy as spiking memories bit into him. He'd spent so long trying to erase this boy – this man – from his head, yet here he was, standing right in front of him.

Luke Crawford.

'You were at school together? Really?' said Harmony.

Luke looked at her. 'Yes. At Pendower Hall.'

Will winced.

'You didn't tell me that at the party,' she said.

'I didn't know who you were married to at the party.' He looked at her quizzically and Will watched her cheeks blush.

'What an amazing coincidence!' Emma gave a surprised laugh.

Luke smiled. 'Isn't it?'

'Well, come on then,' she said then. 'Do sit down. Ian, will you sort some drinks out, please? This is now a proper celebration.'

Ian clapped his hands together and asked what they'd like. Will was vaguely aware of saying yes to another beer. Of Ian disappearing into the house. Emma laughing. Repeating the coincidence. He was aware of Harmony, poised in her chair, waiting with bated breath for more information, details and stories of a past Will had purposely shielded her from.

'This is all a bit surreal, isn't it?' Will finally managed to say. 'I was just looking at a picture of you and trying to place you. You've changed.'

'It's been a long time,' Luke said.

'How long?' asked Harmony, her eyes glinting. Will imagined how quickly her brain must be whirring, cogs blurring with speed as she grappled with questions he had no intention of answering.

'About twenty-five years? Wouldn't you say, Will?' Luke leant across the table for a crisp, and Will noticed his wrist, fine-boned still, but strong, skin tanned, a smartwatch so polished it glinted in the sun like a beacon.

'Yes, it must be,' Will said. Luke's eyes had the same intensity they'd had all those years before, dark and earnest, hiding a seething tangle of thoughts and emotions. He was shocked how unnerving he found it. Will glanced at Harmony then back at Luke. Sitting between them was unbearable; two separate chapters of his life, as incompatible as oil and water. 'We were fourteen when we last saw each other.'

'Were you good friends?' Emma asked.

'Yes,' said Luke evenly. 'In fact, we were best friends.'

Will clenched his fist.

Ian reappeared with drinks. 'Don't sit down,' Emma said, grabbing his arm. 'I need you in the kitchen.'

'Is there anything I can do to help?' asked Harmony.

'No, no. you sit there and chat. It's all done.' Emma ushered her unwilling husband back towards the French windows.

Left alone, the three of them fell into silence. The atmosphere was claustrophobic. Will's heart raced; he was finding it hard to keep his breathing steady. Long-buried memories resurfaced: the crisp chill in the dusky October air, the feel of the cold, damp earth, that rich, mulchy smell of fallen leaves beginning to rot that caught in the back of his throat.

'So you were best friends?' Harmony said, clearly hoping for more information.

'Actually,' Luke replied. 'We were more than that.'

'There's something better than best?' Harmony flashed him a playful smile.

'Yes, we were blood brothers. Still are, I suppose.' He held his hand up, palm outwards, five fingers splayed. 'You remember, Will?'

Will's stomach knotted as he saw the white scar that ran from the base of Luke's index finger to the heel of his palm.

'Blood brothers?' Harmony laughed. 'That's all a bit *Huckleberry Finn*, isn't it?'

Will tried to stamp down his unease. He breathed out and forced another smile. Made an effort to keep his voice light and relaxed. 'Yes, of course I remember.' Then he raised his own hand and unfurled his fingers to display his matching scar. 'Blood brothers.'

Luke's smile faltered and he lowered his hand as Emma appeared through the French windows with a tray of food. 'I must say this has made lunch so much more interesting. It's like an episode of *This Is Your Life*. I feel like Michael Aspel!'

Will smiled tightly.

'I've just discovered they're blood brothers, Em.'

'Oh, that sounds exciting. How do you become blood brothers?' Emma asked as she sat down.

'Will had this penknife his father gave him. God, we loved that knife, didn't we, Will?'

Will recalled unwrapping the knife on his thirteenth birthday, the thrill he'd felt as he tore off the brown paper and realised what he'd been given. The inscription on the blade was as cold as the metal itself – *To W.P.E. from your father* – but Will hadn't cared. It was like unboxing treasure; a real penknife, a Swiss Army one, with its magnificent blood-red handle, the mirror-like blade reflecting the excitement in his eyes in flashes as he opened and closed it, opened and closed it.

'There was this tree we used to climb. The school's hallowed Japanese Judas or Katsura, *cercidiphyllum japonicum*. Pride and joy of Pendower Hall. A specimen. One of the tallest of its kind in England, they said. Gifted by a renowned botanist, an ex-pupil, in the nineteenth century on his return from travels to Asia. We loved it, didn't we, Will?'

Will didn't reply. He lowered his eyes and stared at the tiny bubbles in his beer, rising to the surface as if trying to escape.

'It had branches which were perfect for climbing and thick leaves we could hide in. Anyway, one day we went up into the woods, to this favourite tree of ours, and took turns to cut our palms,' Luke continued. 'Then we pressed our hands together, said a few words, and pledged eternal loyalty to each other. That kind of rubbish.' He laughed. The sound jarred and Will wished he could ram his hands over his ears to block it out.

'Ow!' Emma exclaimed.

'Yes, it hurt like a bitch.' Luke's smile fell away.

Will thought of the tree. Its branches fanning upwards like the fingers of a giant's hand. The cloak of leaves and dappled sunlight. The exhilaration he'd felt as they climbed higher and higher, his heart thumping, skin tingling.

Harmony reached for Will's hand and turned it over, then traced her fingertip the length of the thin, raised scar. A tingle ran through him. 'After all these years, I've finally found out.'

Will pulled his hand back then reached for his glass and downed the last of his beer.

'I can't believe you cut your own hands open,' Harmony said. 'Can you, Em? Didn't we just read copies of the *NME* and lust over David Bowie?'

'It seemed like a good idea at the time,' Will said.

'Boys can be very odd,' said Emma.

Emma took each plate in turn and served everybody thick slices of honey-roast ham. They passed bowls of green salad and new potatoes around and Ian circled the table pouring cold white wine.

'Your garden's looking beautiful, Ian,' said Will, keen to keep conversation away from him and Luke. 'You've been working hard.'

Emma snorted with laughter. 'Will, you should know by now, my husband's idea of a hard morning's gardening is napping in a deckchair under the willow tree.'

'Excuse me?' Ian retorted. 'The lawn was mowed this morning.'

'By the gardener!' She furrowed her brow and reached across the table for the bread basket. 'You're such a liar.'

Ian's face clouded over. 'A liar? I'm not a bloody liar!'

Emma was clearly startled by his eruption. 'I didn't mean to touch a nerve. I—'

'You haven't touched a nerve,' Ian interjected. 'Not at all. But *liar* is a pretty strong word to use.' He stared at Will. 'Don't you agree? I'm not sure it's on for a wife to call her husband a liar in company. Or at all, to be honest.'

Will wasn't sure if Ian expected him to agree with him or not. He hesitated, glancing at Harmony for guidance, but she wasn't looking at him. She was looking at Luke. The look on her face was one of focused curiosity. Will had always been cagey about his childhood and she was obviously ravenous for details. He knew she wasn't going to let this go and reliving it all was the last thing he wanted. Perhaps he could just get up from the table and leave? Walk away without saying a word.

'It's OK, Ian. Emma didn't mean anything by it.' It was Luke who spoke.

Emma looked at Luke with visible relief. 'You're right. I didn't. It was a joke, because you implied you did the garden but the gardener does the garden.'

'Well, I pay for the bloody gardener,' Ian blustered.

An awkward silence settled over the table.

'This ham is delicious, Em,' Harmony said, trying to ease the discomfort. 'You're such a good cook.' She turned to Luke. 'I'm appalling in the kitchen. Every time I eat Emma's food I'm reminded just how bad I am.'

As quickly as it had blown up, the exchange with Ian was forgotten as Emma laughed Harmony's compliment off with a casual wave of her hand. 'You're a perfectly good cook when you want to be. You just don't want to be.'

'Shoddy cooking skills is the price you feminist working types have to pay, isn't it?'

As Ian laughed to show he was 'just playing' with Harmony, Will cut into his ham. Luke's composure rattled him. How was he so unfazed? How could he conduct himself with such confidence, remain so unaffected by the crippling discomfort that silenced Will? And how suave he was, leaning back in his chair, casually holding his glass of wine, elbow resting on the back of Emma's chair. He listened intently as she spoke, engaged and interested, so different to the wraith-like boy he'd known, with his darting eyes, coiled like a spring, so thin his bones threatened to pierce his paper-white skin.

Emma finished the story she was telling and they all laughed. Ian stood to refill their wine glasses and as he did so, Luke turned to Will. 'Tell me, Will,' he said. 'What's happened since we last saw each other? Has life been good to you?'

The table fell to a pin-drop silence as they all turned their eyes on Will.

He wasn't sure how much Luke meant him to tell. He was a child when he last saw Luke; everything had happened. 'Yes, life's been good,' Will said at last. 'I got married to Harmony soon after college, we live in London. Things are good.' He smiled at Harmony who smiled back.

Luke nodded. 'You certainly seem happy.' He looked at Harmony, who lowered her eyes and reached for the pendant that hung around her neck.

'And you? Are you married, Luke?' Will asked.

Luke seemed to do a double take, his cool facade slipping for a fraction of a second. He reached for his glass, then sat back in his chair. 'I was.'

'That's a shame,' said Emma. 'But so many marriages fall by the wayside these days.'

'It wasn't quite like that.'

Will saw Ian glare at his wife and shake his head frantically; marital code for shut up.

'And you're a lawyer?' Will asked.

'For my sins.'

'Best corporate lawyer in the whole damn City,' Ian said, like a puffed-up father boasting about his favourite son.

Luke shook his head. 'Nothing great about being a lawyer. We're just successful parasites.'

'And that's how you met? Through work?'

'We met playing golf, actually,' Ian said. 'Luke joined the club last year. Met at the bar and hit it off in an instant. A mutual love of expensive watches and fast cars.' Ian laughed loudly.

'What about you, Will?' Luke asked, ignoring Ian. 'What do you do?'

'I've a wine shop.'

'It's a fabulous place!' exclaimed Emma. 'A real treasure trove.'

'This is one of his.' Ian held his glass up, the liquid within like watered-down honey, sparkling pale gold in the sunshine. 'From one of those mixed cases I bought from you last year at the opening of the shop.'

'It's very good indeed,' said Luke.

The table fell silent again and Will listened to the sound of the children playing on the other side of the house, both happy now.

'He's also a wonderful photographer,' Harmony said. 'Really talented.' Her compliment was delivered with too much enthusiasm and, to Will at least, it sounded insincere.

43

'I enjoy it, that's all.'

'What about you, Harmony?' Luke said, turning his attention on to her. 'What do you do?'

Will watched her fingers fiddling with the gold Tiffany heart at her neck. He'd given it to her on their tenth wedding anniversary and he loved how she played with it gently between her fingers.

'I'm based at Imperial. Well, in offices opposite,' she said. 'I'm involved in business development.'

'What field?' Luke asked.

'I'm a scientist by training. But I work in technology transfer, which is basically securing funding for various university-developed patented compounds.'

'Not just a pretty face.' Emma stood to clear the plates. 'Harmony is the cleverest person I know.'

'Of course I'm not,' Harmony said.

'You are,' Emma said. 'How many of my other friends have a PhD?'

Ian leant towards Harmony. 'Of course, we've got to remember who her other friends are. Not too many PhDs required to book a spa day.' He sat back in his chair and snorted loudly.

Emma ignored him. 'Pudding?'

Everybody nodded and Emma picked up the pile of stacked plates and cutlery then started walking towards the French windows.

Harmony stood and reached for the bowl of salad.

'No, you stay,' Ian said, with dramatised weariness. 'I'll go. If I don't I'll get it in the neck for being lazy.' He winked at Will.

'So, Dr English—' Luke began.

'Dr Hanney,' Harmony corrected, raising her eyebrows.

'My apologies. Dr Hanney. What was your PhD?'

'Functional genomics.'

Will reached across the table for the bottle of sparkling water and poured himself a glass.

'And what area are you currently involved in?'

She laughed. 'Are you sure you're interested?'

'I am. Very.'

'Pharmacogenomics, the bit of pharmacology that deals with genetics and drug efficacy.'

Will watched her run her fingers through her hair then lightly touch the corner of her shirt collar. He turned away and looked across the lawn. Luke's presence was impossible to ignore, impossible to laugh away, and with it came a rush of self-loathing and shame, as familiar as old toys found gathering dust in an attic. It didn't matter how well Luke looked, how in control of his life he seemed, how undamaged, Will couldn't control the jabs of shame and guilt.

'We're looking at the use of gene type to optimise the potency of a drug while minimising its side-effects.'

'Personalised medicine?'

'Exactly.'

A bird screeched above them. Will looked up. It was a circling crow, cawing high in the sky. It wheeled then flew over the house, its wings flapping strongly, with purpose. As it disappeared out of sight he heard his mother's voice warning him about a single black crow overhead. She loved her superstitions and had an impressive catalogue of ominous rhymes for almost everything she encountered. He searched his memory for the one about a lone crow but couldn't recall it.

'. . . what you do sounds incredibly interesting,' Luke was saying to Harmony.

'It is. And, sadly, very poorly paid,' she laughed. 'But you can't have everything, can you?'

'Unless you're Will, it seems.'

Will saw her lower her eyes as a slight smile passed over her lips.

'Yes, I'm very lucky,' Will said.

Luke and he locked eyes then, dogs assessing each other, uncertain and wary. Will gently stroked his thumb over the scar that crossed his palm. He had a vivid image of his blood falling unchecked onto the sun-speckled grass, felt again the tingle of exhilaration as Luke dragged the blade across his hand, remembered his pale skin parting, his blood flowing. A tremor shot through him as he recalled them pressing their hands together, blood and pain combining, wide eyes bolted on to each other, gripping tight.

'We're blood brothers now,' Luke had said with a trembling voice. 'That means we're connected. By blood. Like real brothers.'

'You watch my back. I'll watch yours,' Will replied. 'That's what it means. There for each other. *Forever*.'

Then they smiled and tightened their grip as their mingled blood ran down their wrists and fell like tears on the earth.

CHAPTER FIVE

By five o'clock the terrace had fallen into shade and a chill had descended.

'I think we should head off,' Will said. 'If we leave now we might miss the worst of the traffic.'

'Yes,' said Luke. 'I should also go. You're right, the Sunday traffic into London is dreadful.'

They walked through the living room and into the hallway. Luke picked up his car keys from the circular table in the centre. The spectacular red and orange flowers from the party still held pride of place despite their fading beauty, a handful of petals fallen like the first leaves of autumn.

At the front door Harmony kissed Emma and Ian goodbye and then looked at Luke. She offered her hand. He shook it and her cheeks warmed.

This was pathetic. She was behaving like a teenage girl with a silly crush.

'It was good to meet you again, Luke,' she said. 'And amazing about you and Will.'

He smiled. 'Well, I hope now Will and I have made contact we'll be able to stay in touch.'

Harmony nodded. 'That would be nice.'

Ian clapped Luke on the back. 'Thanks for the game. Shame you played so damn well. I'll give you more of a run for your money next time.'

Luke shook Ian's hand then turned to Emma and kissed her on the cheek. 'Lunch was delicious. Your children are charming and, you're right, they certainly have a passion for Pavlova.'

Emma laughed. 'They do.' She paused and smiled at them all. 'Perhaps we should do this again soon.'

Luke looked directly at Harmony. 'I'd like that.'

She reached for Will's hand and took hold of it. 'We would too.'

The three of them walked out of the house and across the driveway towards the cars, their feet crunching over the silence. They paused beside Luke's dark grey convertible Audi, its alloy wheels shining like polished silver medals. He pointed his key at the car and it flashed its lights in greeting.

Luke and Will faced each other and Harmony was aware once again of the tension between them. Luke held out his hand. Will stared at it and for a moment Harmony worried he might not respond, but thankfully he reached out and grasped it, pressing their two scarred palms together.

'It's good to see you, Luke.' Will seemed to hesitate, then reached into his jacket pocket for his wallet. 'Here's my number,' he said, handing him one of the shop's business cards. 'Why don't you give me a call? Maybe we could meet for a beer?'

'Sounds good.' Luke took the card and smiled.

Will reached for Harmony's hand. As they walked to their car, she could feel Luke watching them. She glanced backwards and, sure enough, he was sitting in his car, door closed, hands gripping the steering wheel, eyes locked on them. He didn't move a muscle. There was no embarrassed look away. No smile. No reaction at all. He just sat there, impassive, watching.

Once in the car, Harmony expected Will to say something to her, but he was silent, his eyes distant, driving on autopilot. Every now and then his brow would furrow as if trying to work something out.

'Seeing him again has thrown you, hasn't it?' she said at last, unable to keep quiet any longer.

He glanced at her then nodded.

'I spoke to him for quite a long time at Emma's party. He's . . . unusual.' She paused, waiting for Will to reply. When he didn't, she pressed on. 'And charismatic. Was he always like that? I mean, when you were friends at school?'

Still Will said nothing.

She turned to look out of her window. It was so frustrating how guarded he was when it came to his past. She loved to discuss things and probe and learn. Her mother used to laugh at her when she was a young girl, always asking questions, determined to know why trees grew upwards and how clouds floated and why snowflakes looked like miniature paper doilies. Facts made life easier to understand. She'd asked Will so many questions over the years and only ever had an array of non-committal one-word answers and dismissive shrugs in return. As far as he was concerned his history was irrelevant. It didn't merit discussion; as unimportant, he said, as a mediocre one-night-stand with a forgotten name. All that mattered, he said, was the present, her and him and their life together. She'd accepted his secrecy because she had no choice, but now his past had been revealed like the tip of an ashen finger in the soil and she was desperate to uncover the rest. The fact that it included Luke was exciting. The man fascinated her. There was something about him that brought to mind her father. *Charismatic*. The word she'd often heard her mother use to describe him. Despite having dredged every corner of her memory for any recollection of her father she had nothing. The image she carried was based entirely on a single photograph she had. She'd found it about a month after their mother's death, when she and her sister finally mustered the courage to sort through her personal effects. They'd wedged a chair beneath the door handle of the bedroom they now shared at their nan's house then put their mother's beloved Ella Fitzgerald on the tape machine. Sitting cross-legged on the floor, her sister holding a bottle of vodka and an expression of grim determination, they placed their mother's precious shoebox between them. They stared at it for a while then in one swift movement her sister tipped the bottle up to her lips, winced, and pulled the lid off the box. Inside were hundreds of letters. All of them were from their father to their mother. Harmony became breathless as she read them. They were beautiful; incredible expressions of love – poetic, ethereal, surreal even. They were written in curling hand-writing with intricate doodles and motifs decorating the white space around words that struck Harmony as the most romantic thing ever. Then, as she picked up one of the letters, a photograph fell from its fold.

Harmony gasped. 'Is that him?'

The photograph showed the most handsome man she'd ever seen. He wore a loose white, unbuttoned shirt and stood on a table laden with wine surrounded by a group of people laughing and clapping, their eyes fixed on him as he played a guitar. Her mother was among those at the table. She stared up at him with adoring eyes, her face sliced in two by the widest of smiles, love radiating from every pore.

'Fuck him,' her sister spat as she snatched the picture away from her.

Harmony was about to protest but kept quiet when she saw the tears coursing down her sister's cheeks. 'I fucking hate him. I hate him.' She grabbed the vodka and drank some more, then scrabbled to collect the letters and shoved them back into the box with the photo. 'We're burning them all, the whole box of crappy, lying shit. He's nothing, a ne'er-do-well and a wastrel. I *hate* him.'

Harmony didn't know what a ne'er-do-well or a wastrel was and wasn't sure her sister did either. They were the words their nan used when talking about him, but as the woman spent her spare time dressing Bentley – her hideous snappy pug – in miniature human clothes, Harmony had sense enough to know not to believe everything she said. While her sister swigged at the vodka and swiped at her tears, Harmony inched her fingers towards the box, removed the photograph of her father, and surreptitiously slipped it into her jeans pocket.

'And I'm changing my name,' her sister said. 'I'm not having that stupid, hippy name he bloody chose a moment longer. I'm Sophie from now on, OK?'

Sophie was her sister's middle name, the name their mother wanted to call her. The piercing look of anger in her sister's eyes made her wonder if she was expected to change her name as well. The thing was she liked Harmony and wasn't keen on Patricia at all.

As she followed her sister downstairs, Harmony tried to work out why everything was her father's fault anyway. Cancer was to blame for taking their mother away from them, not their absent father. He hadn't been around for years and years. Why was her sister freaking out about him now? It didn't make sense.

They found their nan sitting on the sofa reading the *Radio Times* listings to the pug, who wore a hand-knitted pink cardigan with big blue buttons.

'We'd like to burn this and everything in it,' her sister announced. Her attempt to mask her vodka-slur made it sound as if she was pretending to be the Queen.

'What's in the box that you want to burn exactly, Starla?' their nan asked sternly.

'Letters from the wastrel.'

Their nan gestured sharply at the fire. 'Good riddance to bad rubbish.'

'And I'm not called Starla,' her sister said, lifting her chin high. 'I'm Sophie now.'

Their nan nodded then the three of them watched in silence as the box went up in a rainbow of flames in the grate.

Harmony pushed the recollection away and looked back at her husband. 'Will,' she tried again. 'Is everything OK?'

'I'm fine. I wasn't expecting to see him, that's all.'

'Talk to me. Please?'

'There's nothing to say. I knew the guy at school. We lost touch. It was a surprise to see him.'

'It looked like more than that to me.'

They drove in silence for a while then Harmony heard him take a deep breath. 'It's thrown me,' he said. 'I suppose I'd sort of blanked him out of my head, and seeing him like that was . . .' He paused, hesitating, searching for the right words. 'It was like seeing a ghost.' His words rang around them like the echo of a church bell. His brow furrowed and his mouth twitched, as if he was trying to decode his thoughts.

They didn't speak for the rest of the journey. The car was warm and the silence loaded, the air too stuffy to bear. She opened her window and leant her head against the door so the stream of cool wind ran over her face and tousled her hair. Her mind drifted to Luke. She thought of the way he'd looked at her during lunch with that peculiar directness she found so fascinating. She heard his voice, steady and calm, asking her to leave Emma's party with him. What would have happened if she'd said yes? She closed her eyes and indulged the fantasy, watched herself take his hand and follow him down the corridor and into the hallway. Past the butler. Out of the house. She saw herself climbing into his car. The car door closing. His hand reaching over to rest on her thigh.

Harmony opened her eyes and shook her head free of the images as she shifted herself in her seat then glanced at Will, who stared at the road ahead.

When they got back to the flat Harmony went to her small study and grabbed a pen and her reading glasses and the pile of papers from her desk. In the living room she sat down on the sofa and put on her glasses.

'Would you like a cup of tea?'

'I'm fine.' She kept her eyes fixed on her papers.

'Hey,' said Will gently. 'Don't be like that.' He sat on the sofa beside her and took her hand. 'Don't be cross.'

'I'm not.' She leant forward to put her work on the coffee table. 'I wish you'd talk to me about this, that's all. I've never even heard you mention the name Luke before.'

'Look, I'm not keeping it from you for any reason. It's just not important.' He reached out and grazed his fingers down her cheek then pulled her into him. 'I've told you before, those years at school, none of it matters now. I've put it behind me.'

'Put what behind you? What happened?'

He didn't answer immediately. She could tell he was thinking about telling her, weighing it up, but then he shook his head. 'I really don't want to talk about it. Stuff happened. Stuff that's too hard to talk about. It's best forgotten.'

'But Luke—'

'Please, Harmony,' he said, interrupting her. 'You know better than anyone how little time I spend thinking about school. Seeing him like that threw me. Last time I saw him he was a kid. I was expecting a nice lunch in the sun with Emma and Ian. I just wasn't expecting it and it winded me.' He sighed heavily. 'I probably need to work on my acting skills a bit. Perfect the art of hiding shock. That's the second time in a week I've failed with that.'

She sat back and dropped her eyes, focused on her hands, folded in her lap.

'I'm going to grab a beer,' he said. 'You want anything?'

'No, thanks.'

She watched him leave the living room then leant back against the arm of the sofa, turning her head to breathe in its smell; safe and familiar, wrapping around her like a warm blanket. She and

Will had bought it in the sales on Tottenham Court Road the weekend they moved in together. It was the first piece of furniture they'd bought, and as they left the shop he'd squeezed her hand and whispered, 'This is it, Harmony. Our beginning. It all starts here.'

The sofa was delivered two weeks later and put beneath the window in the small living room in their first flat in Vauxhall in front of an upturned packing box they used – for five months it turned out – as a coffee table. They sat on it all evening, drinking wine and eating Chinese from the takeaway a few doors down. Later they made love on it, their wine glasses and empty food cartons discarded on the floor, the ancient television – as deep as it was wide – flickering silently in the corner of the darkened room. Those were innocent, happy times, and the hit of nostalgia made her head swim.

Harmony worked for the next few hours. When the words began to swim, her eyes heavy with tiredness, she put the papers down and stood. She gasped a little at the stiff pain in her lower back and cursed herself for not sitting at her desk. She saw her mother wagging a finger at her, telling her off for working slouched on the sofa, and mouthed a silent *I know, I know.*

Will appeared at the living room door. 'I'm going to go to bed. You coming?'

'Yes,' she said. 'I'm shattered. I'll get a drink and then follow you.'

Harmony filled a glass of water then checked Will had locked the back door. As she did so, she peered through the glazed panel. The garden, which was bathed in the last of the fading light, could have done with their attention this weekend. It was looking neglected and untidy. The garden was pretty much the only reason they'd stayed in the flat, which was dark and poky, with one bedroom, the box room she used as a study, and a living room they squeezed a dining table into. The garden, however, was beautiful and large by London standards, about forty feet by thirty, with a magical feel. It had high brick walls that were carpeted with unruly bottle-green ivy and an area of aged paving, some of the slabs cracked with moss growing between. There were two overgrown flower beds that ran along each of the walls, and at the end of the garden was a stone bench with carved legs behind which was a mature rose bush that seemed to flower for months. It was a hidden gem in the slice of urban grey between Barons Court and West Kensington tube stations. When Harmony found out she was pregnant she knew they'd have to move. Will had been hard to persuade – he loved the flat with a passion – but she persisted, explaining they needed somewhere more suitable for a family, somewhere with a proper bedroom for the baby and a utility room, maybe a playroom too. When she showed the valuing estate agent the garden she had a pang of doubt as his eyes lit up.

'Oh, this is *very* special,' he'd said, purring with excitement. 'Yes. Lots of potential here. It'll fly off our books. Not many places with an outside space like this around here.'

After the miscarriage, there was no reason to move, no need to justify the expense – the conveyancing fees alone were enough to make their eyes water – but rather than feel relieved she could stay in her home, she felt trapped, resentful of the flat now inextricably linked to her loss.

Will was reading in bed. She went to shut the curtains.

'Can you leave them?' He closed his book and laid it on the bedside table.

She hesitated, her hand resting on the edge of the curtain. She didn't like sleeping with them open; she felt exposed, worried about people being able to see in.

'I'd like them open tonight, if you don't mind?'

She let her hand drop from the curtain and climbed into bed beside him and he turned his bedside light off.

She curled up close to him, resting her head on his shoulder. 'Are you sure you're OK?' she asked. 'Everybody around the table today could tell there was something wrong, you know.

Did you and Luke fall out at school? Was he the reason you didn't enjoy it there?'

'No, we didn't fall out. We were great friends. I met him towards the end of the first term when we were thirteen. He left though, was expelled actually, and I didn't hear from him again.'

'Why was he expelled?'

Will turned his head to stare out of the window. 'I don't know.' His voice was edged with sadness. 'He shouldn't have been.'

'Was it dreadful there?'

He didn't answer immediately. Then after a few moments he spoke quietly. 'Not all of it. Most of it was bearable. But, yes, some of it was awful.'

She kissed his chest. 'I can't believe your parents sent you away.' She was unable to keep the blame out of her voice. 'I don't know how people do it. I mean, what age were you? Eight? It's barbaric. Why have children if you're going to send them away?'

'Mum didn't want me to go, though I remember her saying something about it being good to get away from her apron strings. It was my father. He believed it was the right thing to do. He saw it as some sort of rite of passage. Spouted all that nonsense about boarding school turning boys into men.' He paused briefly. 'I suppose it was what people did back then.'

'Not the people I knew.' She thought of her father-in-law, of his holier-than-thou attitude to life, his favouring of etiquette over emotion, the malice in his voice when he talked about immigrants, the way he buttoned his coat before leaving for church and tutted at Harmony as she sat at the breakfast table reading the Sunday papers, his sneering and sniping at Will, his inability to show any signs of affection towards his only child.

Early on in their relationship, Will told her he had only seen his parents on the last Sunday of each month during term time. They'd drive to a pub on the A30, order three portions of scampi and chips, then he and his father would eat their food as his mother chattered mindlessly to fill the stony silence. It was from the odd anecdote such as this that Harmony began to understand Will's unwillingness to talk about his childhood and his loathing of school. They'd driven past the place once, years earlier, on their way home from a wedding in Fowey.

Harmony had been studying the map as Will drove.

'Well, look at that. Tintagel is a real place,' she suddenly said. 'Who knew?'

He laughed. 'You thought it was made up?'

She smiled. 'I never gave it too much thought. I thought it was all just part of the legend. Ladies in lakes and dashing knights and swords in stones.'

'Do you want to visit?' Will cast her a glance.

'Tintagel?'

He grinned and nodded.

'But it's out of the way?'

'So what? Come on, let's go. Walk where King Arthur walked. We can book into a crappy B and B with a grumpy landlady. Get out on the cliffs. Have our chips stolen by sea gulls.'

'What about work?'

'We'll call in sick.'

She hesitated. 'We can't—'

'But we can. Come on. It'll be fun.'

Then she'd nodded, hesitantly at first, then with more vigour. Will's enthusiasm was infectious. Maybe it would be fun to do something on the spur of the moment for once? 'Go on, then. Why not?'

They'd been talking and laughing, energised by their impetuous decision, but then Will had fallen quiet. He pulled over and stopped the car. His knuckles were white as he gripped the wheel.

'What's wrong?' Harmony asked.

'Pendower Hall,' he breathed.

'What?'

'My old school. Back there. We just passed it.'

Harmony turned to look and saw a long grey brick wall, too high to see anything behind it. 'Can I see it?' she asked then. 'Will you show me?'

A look of horror swept over his face. 'Jesus. *Why?*'

'I don't know. I suppose I'd like to see if it's anything like I imagine. It'll help me build the picture of you from back then.'

'That place won't help you build any picture of me.'

'Please?'

For a moment he didn't move, then suddenly, in one quick movement, he threw the car into gear and reversed at speed back to the entrance where two aged stone lions sat bored on pillars either side. They turned up the driveway, long and straight and lined by tall and ancient trees like the bars of a prison, and drove up towards a looming gothic manor.

'It's deserted,' she whispered. A shiver passed through her as she looked up at the windows that punctured the stone like dead, glazed eyes.

'School holidays.'

They pulled up in front of the pillared entrance and Will turned the engine off. 'This is where my father handed me over to that cock of a headmaster,' Will said grimly. 'I can still remember his fingers digging into my shoulders and him saying to Drysdale, "Well, all I can say is he's a little bugger. Do what you must." You should have seen the bastard's eyes light up. Parental permission to make my life a misery.' He drew a laboured breath and exhaled heavily. 'Come on, it's a fucking shithole. Let's get out of here.'

That was the last time he spoke about the school.

'You know,' Harmony whispered, gently moving his head to face her. 'If you'd been my child I'd have kept you with me as long as I possibly could. I'd never have sent you away.'

He smiled, his features lit by the gauzy moonlight. 'Hey, it's

OK. You mustn't worry about me. It wasn't great, but I'm fine. It was just school. Children can adapt to everything and we all found our ways to cope at that place. It's in the past now. Where it belongs.'

CHAPTER SIX

Will couldn't sleep. He lay still as Harmony mumbled quietly beside him, every now and then letting out a torrent of mutterings. This was something she did – talking in her sleep – yelling out as if in surprise then murmuring unintelligibly, her head moving back and forth emphatically, as if arguing intently with a character in her dreams. She settled and he focused his hearing on the noises outside the flat, the occasional car, a police siren not far away, faint footsteps and muffled talking of a group of people as they walked past the living room window. His mind whirred; he was never going to get to sleep. He eased himself out of bed, careful not to wake Harmony, lifted his clothes off the chair in the corner of the room and crept out of the bedroom. He dressed in the hallway, then took his keys off the hook by the door and slipped outside.

Night-rambling, he called it. Walking at night. It was a habit that started when he was about ten or eleven when, one night, unable to sleep for worrying about going back to school, he'd called for his mother. She had sat on the edge of his bed, patted his hand, and told him, 'Enough now. Be quiet and count sheep.' His heart sank as she left the room, closing the door behind her so he was plunged back into darkness. He was pretty sure counting sheep would do nothing to ease the fear which clamped around his heart and stomach and squeezed and squeezed, and he was right. By the time he'd counted a flock of four hundred he was no more sleepy than when he began. It was then, on a whim, that he climbed out of bed, let himself quietly out of the house, and set off on his very first night-ramble. In the years that followed he often found himself creeping downstairs, holding his breath as he stepped over the creakiest floorboards, pausing every few steps to listen for the telltale sounds of adults on the prowl. Back then these nighttime treks would set his pulse racing, send adrenaline pumping into his blood and push his worries into the background. But as he got older the night-rambles became calming, those first deep slugs of night air like Valium.

It was a ramble, or at least the repercussions of one, that first brought him and Luke together. One night in the third week of his first term at Pendower Hall, Will was caught sneaking out by Mr Fielder, a reedy history teacher with a sparse moustache who reeked of coffee and stale cigarettes. Will had eased open the door of the boarding house and walked straight into him. The man sent him back up to the first years' dormitory, his thin voice laced with what might have been regret as he told young Will he'd be seeing the headmaster the following day. Will's stomach had churned with dread for the rest of the night and the whole of the following day until, finally, in the evening after prep, Drysdale summoned him.

'Tell me, English – I'd love to know – exactly why you want to run away from school? Why you'd want to cause us bother? Why you would want to worry your parents? Hm?'

Will's stuttered mix of *ums* and *ers* failed to convince this terrifying man and the caning that followed was brutal. Will limped back to the dormitory bruised and biting back tears, and climbed gingerly into bed. Later, a little while after Matron had turned the lights out and the dorm was still, a boy on the other side of the room – a quiet, small boy whom Will hadn't taken much notice of – crept across the room. The boy stood motionless by Will's bed for a moment or two. Then he glanced over his shoulder and thrust out a closed fist. Will didn't move. Nor did the boy. He stood there, like a statue, his arm held out towards Will. Will furrowed his brow and shrugged, unsure what he was meant to do. The boy sighed theatrically and leant closer.

'Take it,' he whispered. 'It'll stop the bum-sting.' Then he grabbed Will's hand and pushed something hard into it and closed Will's fingers around whatever it was before silently returning to his bed.

When Will opened his hand and saw what he'd been given his heart missed a beat. Two foil-wrapped toffees lay on his palm like gold coins. Will closed his hand and thrust it beneath his blanket. Sweets weren't allowed. Sweets would get confiscated by the prefects, stolen and eaten, your things ransacked if there was even the smallest suspicion there was more. Where had this boy hidden his contraband?

Will sat up in his bed and looked over at the boy, Luke, who also sat up. His pale, thin face was lit in the shaft of fluorescent light from the corridor. He stared at Will, solemn and intense, nodded once then lay back down. Will pulled his grey, regulation blanket over his head and waited with bated breath, heart hammering, until the duty prefect had done his final rounds. When Will was sure it was safe, he undid the golden wrappers, coughing to mask any rustling, then popped both toffees in at once, almost too much for his mouth to hold. He sucked slowly, closing his eyes as the creamy sweetness ran down his throat. Luke was right; for a few glorious minutes his throbbing backside, the desperate homesickness, the injustice and loneliness, was all forgotten.

In the morning, as they walked down the stairs on their way to breakfast, Will caught up with Luke.

'Thanks,' he whispered.

Luke grinned and his face lit up like a flare.

Will walked along the deserted back streets of Fulham. His stride was full and his rhythmic footsteps rang on the pavement. The houses he passed were dark, lights off, curtains drawn, their front doors locked and security chains slid across. He imagined the people who lived in them tucked up in their beds, quietly snoring, sleeping deeply. He heard the startled screech of a cat or maybe a fox and picked up his pace. He allowed his thoughts to settle on the last time he'd seen Luke – the day he was expelled – both of them perched on those hard wooden chairs in Drysdale's office, which stank of old leather, wood polish, and mothballs. He remembered the look in Luke's eyes. The way they'd welled with tears that spilled down his cheeks . . . Thick nausea pooled in the pit of his stomach as he strode onwards.

In the morning, Will left their flat and headed up towards the North End Road, weaving in and out of the people on the busy pavements as he walked to the shop.

'Morning, Frank,' he said, as he pushed through the door to the happy tinkle of the old-fashioned bell that hung on the back.

'Morning, William,' Frank replied brightly.

Will was fond of Frank. He'd known him for years. Frank had worked at the wine merchant's Will got a job at when he finished college. When his father died, leaving Will a small lump sum, he decided to open his own shop and asked Frank to work for him. He was delighted when Frank said yes; he was great company, eccentric in a very British way, with a great sense of humour and an easy-going nature. Frank was a short man, and a little rotund, and always dressed in well-fitting suits with his grey hair slicked back with hair cream that he ordered from a specialist gentleman's shop in Bristol. He lived in Chiswick with two Persian cats called Pie, short for Pork Pie, and Pinwheel and his husband, a writer of moderately successful science fiction, who was as wiry as Frank was portly. Frank loved wine with a passion, and was a walking encyclopaedia when it came to claret and burgundy, but tended to struggle with other types. His cheerful demeanour brought warmth to North End Wines, which nestled in a tired row of shops between the Co-op and a bookmaker's. From the outside the shop didn't look like much, with its chipped maroon paintwork, dirty white walls and security bars on the windows – a legacy from its days as a sex shop – but the rent was cheap. Inside, however, was an Aladdin's cave of beautiful wine. Bottles were shelved from floor to ceiling and wall to wall, all of them carefully selected by Will from a variety of vineyards, large and small, and already, even after only a year of trading, they had a small but loyal customer base who travelled from various corners of London and beyond, battling gridlock to buy their wine.

'So how are you today, young William?'

'All good thanks.'

'Super stuff. The kettle's just boiled.'

'Lovely. Would you like a coffee?'

'Gracious, no. I've had three already.'

'Three?' Will lifted his eyebrows. 'It's not even ten. You'll be bouncing off the ceiling.'

Frank smiled and playfully batted the air. 'I've been up since five. I'm surprised I've only had three.'

Will pushed through the plastic strip curtain, reminiscent of a seventies corner shop, and in the tiny cupboard that passed as a kitchen he made himself an instant and dumped two spoonfuls of sugar in it. 'How are the boys?' he called through.

'Fluffy,' Frank said. 'And as lazy as ever. Poor Pinwheel was a bit off-colour on Saturday but the vet wasn't worried; she said it was probably something he ate. A past its sell-by mouse, I suspect. Greedy toad.'

Will smiled to himself and took his coffee back through the strip curtain. Being at the shop settled him; he felt comfortable here, knowledgeable and well respected, with no pressure to be anything out of the ordinary. He didn't have to be talented or skilful, or, if truth be told, stretch himself. He knew about wine. He'd worked in the business since his early twenties, and he enjoyed working close to home with no commute and no pressure. Frank was independently wealthy and worked because he loved it; if the business ever folded, he'd be unaffected financially. It was easy and pleasant, which is just how Will liked it. He didn't make much money but it was steady, and though there were undoubtedly days when he wished he was out with his camera searching for beauty in the obscure and mundane, they weren't frequent.

'Would you like a custard cream?' Frank asked. 'I've a packet in my satchel.'

'I'm OK, thanks.' Will opened the large desk diary by the till. There was a delivery that afternoon and he was meeting a new restaurant owner on Wednesday, but other than that, it was a quiet week.

'Did you have a good weekend, William?'

Will had a flash of Luke walking out onto the terrace and his stomach somersaulted. 'Fine, thanks. You? Get up to anything fun?'

'Oh, well, you know, this and that.' Frank opened his old, battered bag, so stuffed with god-knows-what that it bulged in the middle, cracking the dry tan leather. He retrieved the packet of custard creams and carefully unwrapped them, took one, then wrapped the packet up and slid it back into his bag. 'I do like a custard cream,' he said to the biscuit. Then he seemed to remember something and waved the biscuit frantically at Will. 'Ooh, yes, yes. Something *did* happen,' he said triumphantly. 'Eric had a death threat through the post. That was rather thrilling.'

'A death threat? A real one?'

'Yes, from a poor woman distraught he'd killed off Princess Aisha in *Far Reaches of Sylion*.'

'Blimey. That must have been terrifying.'

'To be honest, we're used to it. Some of the diehards get terribly upset when he hurts their characters. And Aisha was very popular. Her fans saw it as an unforgivable betrayal that their gorgeous heroine got the chop.' He shrugged. 'I think that was it as far as weekend excitement goes.' Frank put the last of his custard cream into his mouth then brushed the crumbs from his suit. 'And now to work. I was thinking it was all getting a bit untidy in here. How about I give it a dust and a straighten?'

Will smiled; the shop was immaculate as always, but Frank was cursed with a compulsive disorder he wasn't aware of and every Monday and Thursday he dusted and straightened the clean and perfectly straight bottles.

'Good idea,' Will said. 'I'll get on with sorting out the cellar to make room for the delivery.'

'I meant to ask you on Friday, how's your mother?'

'She's doing OK, I think. I spoke to her last week. Though she still seems a bit off with me. I've done something to upset her, but I've no idea what.'

'That's grief for you. It makes everything terribly cloudy. When I lost my dear old mum I couldn't talk to anyone. Not even Eric. The only ones who understood were Pinwheel and Pie. They were such a support. She'll come around. Time's the perfect healer. You should visit her, she'd like that.' Frank took a breath and clapped his hands together. 'Right. Must get on. This shop isn't going to clean itself, you know.' He disappeared through the strip curtain to get his duster and polish.

Will perched on the edge of the stool behind the counter and idly switched on his phone. There was an email notification. He clicked to open it.

Luke's name hit him so hard he felt winded.

From: Luke Crawford
Subject: Following up

Will,

It was good to see you yesterday and lovely to meet your beautiful wife. Though I have to say rather strange bumping into each other like that! A small world, as they say. I was thinking on the way home how close we'd been at school and what a shame we drifted apart. Would be great to catch up properly. I'm away on business next week and pretty busy towards the end of this week, but I'm free tonight or tomorrow evening. Would you and Harmony like to meet for a drink or something to eat? Either at mine or at yours if that suits you better.

How does this sound?

Luke

'Frank, I'm nipping out for a minute or two,' Will said, trying to keep his voice steady.

'Everything OK?' asked Frank. 'You've gone white as a sheet.'

'Just need some air.'

Will's head swam. This wasn't going to go away. He leant back against the wall of the Co-op and covered his face with his hands. Christ. Why had he given him his card? He needed to work out what to do, but it was too hard, his head too mixed up, his thinking blurred.

He turned on his phone and dialled Harmony.

'Hey,' he said when she answered. 'It's me.'

'You OK?'

'I'm good. You?'

'In the middle of something.'

He tried to speak but the words stuck in his throat.

'Is it important?' she said with a degree of impatience. 'I'm quite busy.'

'Luke emailed me.' He felt sick.

'Really?' Her voice softened. 'What did he say?'

'He wants to meet up. Either tonight or tomorrow at ours or his.'

'Do you want to?'

'I'm not sure. He's keen to see me. I think if I say we can't, he'll just come back with another date. I think I should.'

'Do you want me there too?'

'Yes. Yes, if you're happy to be. Yes, of course.'

'Tonight is better for me. I've got a lot of work to do so shall we do it at ours? That way, if the evening runs on, I can excuse myself and get back to it if I have to.'

'So you think I should say yes?'

'That's up to you. But if he's coming you need to sort the food out. I'm up against a deadline at work. Jacob needs to see my interim draft by the end of the week.'

After the phone call ended, Will rested his head back against the wall and turned it over and over in his mind. Seeing Luke, having him over for a catch-up, was the very last thing he wanted, but he knew it was the right thing to do. He just had to say yes and get it over and done with and then they could both move on. He took a deep breath then hesitantly typed a reply.

Hey Luke, yes it would be great to catch up. Why don't you come to ours for 7ish tonight? I'll cook something. Our address is 146a Hanniker Rd, W14.

Will wasn't sure how to sign off. Yours sincerely? Kind regards? Best? He scrolled down to see how Luke had done it and saw a simple *Luke*. Will added his name and pressed send. Then he stared at his phone in his quivering hand and battled a wave of nausea which swept through him.

'I'm glad you're back,' said a worried-looking Frank as Will pushed back through the door. 'A young woman came in asking for a bottle of pudding wine suitable to accompany a chocolate roulade. I panicked a bit.'

'What did you go with?'

'The Estrella Moscatel de Valencia.'

'Perfect,' Will lied. 'I'd have given her the same myself.'

Frank's face relaxed. 'That's a relief. It was a bit of a punt, if

I'm honest.' Then he picked up his duster and Pledge from the top of the stepladder and returned to his spraying and polishing.

At five o'clock Will told Frank he had to leave to meet a client. Frank didn't seem to mind; he said he needed some peace to tidy the cupboard in the kitchenette. Will walked down to the Sainsbury's Local at Fulham Broadway. As he walked up and down the aisles, memories of Luke bombarded him; things he'd forgotten came back as if it were yesterday, like the time they tore pages from their hymn books in assembly and made tiny paper aeroplanes. Later they'd bunked off cadet training and scrambled up the wooded hillock behind the science block, as steep as it was overgrown, where masters on the hunt for errant boys rarely went, and spent an hour flying their hymn-book planes. They'd been in fits of giggles as they launched the flimsy things, which looped and plopped at their feet or flew off in odd directions, both as close to happy as either of them could be in that place that was more prison than school.

Will pushed through the front door of the flat laden with shopping bags and kicked it shut behind him. Harmony's bag hung on the hook in the hallway.

'Hello,' he called, as he walked down to the kitchen. There was no answer. 'Harmony?' He put the bags on the worktop and went back down the corridor to her study. The door was shut. He knocked as he opened it and saw her at the computer, the glasses she wore for close work perched on her nose and her hair tied up in a loose ponytail, revealing the soft, smooth skin of her neck.

'Hey,' he said, putting his hand on her shoulder and bending to kiss her. 'Good day?'

She tilted her cheek towards his kiss but didn't look away from the screen. 'Fine.'

'I didn't know you were working from home today.'

'I came back at lunchtime. I left some notes here which I needed.' She glanced at him. 'My head's all over the place at the moment.'

'Luke will be here about seven.' He paused, waiting for her to say something but she didn't. 'I'll leave you in peace and make a start on the supper. I bought steak.'

'Lovely,' she said, squinting at the screen. 'Let me finish this bit I'm on, then I'll have a quick shower and be with you.'

'No hurry.' Will turned to head out of the study.

'Will?' She swivelled in her chair.

'Yes?'

'We really do need to talk soon. About trying for a baby.' She smiled, and he nodded and left the room.

Before he unpacked the shopping, he opened the bottle of Italian red he'd brought back from the shop. It was one of his favourites. He poured himself a large glass, which he drank as he set about making French dressing and a salad, laid the table, put out salt, pepper, mustard, both English and French. A heaviness, a solemn resolve, had settled over him. He felt as if he were preparing a wake. When he'd finished, he topped up his wine and went outside and sat at the wrought-iron table they'd found at a salvage yard a few years back. They'd planned to revamp it, rub the rust back, repaint it in a vibrant colour, something unusual, but it had never been done. Truth be told, Will liked the rust and the chipped paint, it suited the garden with its rampant weeds that ate up the terrace and overgrown shrubs that threatened to suffocate the small patchy lawn area.

Will sat for a while, nursing his glass of wine, his mind drifting to the conversation he'd had with Frank about his mother. However distant he'd been from his father, he forced himself to remember how lost she must feel without him. He tried to recall the last time he'd seen her. It was months ago. He must call her and arrange to visit.

The sound of the doorbell startled him.

He stood, straightening his shoulders and lifting his chin. 'You can do this,' he whispered. 'Just be pleasant and get it over with.'

He walked into the house and as he passed their bedroom, called in to Harmony, 'He's here.' At the front door he paused and inhaled, then let his breath slowly out, before opening the door.

Luke held a bunch of flowers and a bottle of wine. 'Hello, Will,' he said, as he held out the bottle.

Will took the wine and glanced at the label. It was a Saint Emilion, a good year; he'd spent some money on it. 'That's a very generous gift,' he said. 'Thank you.'

'It's hard to buy wine for an expert,' Luke replied. 'The flowers are for your wife.'

'That's kind of you.'

They stood either side of the threshold. Neither moved or spoke. There was a palpable tension between them, thick with conflicting emotions. They held each other's stare until it became uncomfortable and Will was forced to step to one side and allow Luke in.

'You have a nice place,' Luke said, as he followed Will into the flat.

'We're happy here.' Will cast his eye over the living room which was filled with the assorted bits and pieces they'd collected over the years. It was like a shop of curiosities, cluttered and eclectic. There was a lot of kitsch Americana they'd bought while living in the States when Harmony had taught at Stanford for two years. *Coca-Cola cool* she called it: a battered bubblegum dispenser, an imitation Route 66 road sign, vintage baseball cards pinned along the mantelpiece like cardboard bunting. There were things they'd picked up while travelling in their early twenties: a statue of the elephant-headed god, Ganesh, which they'd bought in Delhi, some Sri Lankan and Balinese throws, a wooden frog from Thailand. Then Will's photographs, which patchworked the walls with arty landscapes, cityscapes, and portraits of Harmony. Luke walked over to one of the pictures of her. It was taken at the foot of a looming Mayan temple. She wore a turquoise vest top and a pair of safari shorts, her hair held off her face with a red and white bandana, a water bottle in one hand, her skin tanned and smooth as caramel. As Luke looked at it Will recalled making love to her later that evening, how they'd talked about the approaching end of the world, the Mayans' prophecy, how he'd kissed her from head to toe, and how she'd tasted sweet with coconut oil and bitter with citronella.

When he finally drew his eyes away from the photo, Luke smiled at Will.

'Can I get you a drink?' Will said.

'Yes, please. A beer if you've got one.'

Will fetched a glass from the cupboard in the kitchen and grabbed a bottle of Becks from the fridge. Back in the living room he found Luke holding a silver-framed photo of them on their wedding day, studying it as if trying to memorise it.

Will poured the beer and handed it to Luke, who thanked him and sat in the armchair by the window.

'So,' Will said, sitting on the sofa opposite, trying to think of conversation as far away from Pendower Hall as possible. 'You were saying at lunch that you work with Ian?'

Luke nodded. 'I'm his lawyer.'

'What sort of thing do you do for him?'

'I shouldn't really talk about it.' Luke fixed his eyes on Will. 'I'm sure Ian will tell you if he feels the need.'

Will looked down at his drink. His hand was trembling and the dark red wine wavered gently in the glass, the reflections from the light overhead dancing on the surface. The living room felt hot and stuffy suddenly. Will stood and went to open the sash window.

'Did you take the photographs?' asked Luke.

Will nodded and sat down again.

'They're very good.' He turned and looked at the picture of Harmony on the steps of the temple again. 'Especially the ones of your wife.'

'She's very photogenic. An easy subject for anyone to photograph.'

'Yes, the camera seems to love her, but the way you've framed them is impressive, your sense of space and balance.'

Will cast his eye over the photographs, which were as familiar as his own reflection; each one he remembered taking with crystal clarity. 'It's my passion.'

'It always was, wasn't it?' Luke stared at Will so intently that Will had to look away. 'You did it professionally, didn't you?'

Will furrowed his brow, taken aback by the question, wondering how Luke knew. He shifted in his seat. 'For a while. It was a few years ago now. I did a couple of weddings and some portfolio shoots. But there were a lot of people – most far more talented then me – doing the same and there wasn't enough regular work to rely on. Hopefully, one day, I might try again.' He smiled and lifted his glass to his lips. 'That's the plan anyway.'

'I remember that Polaroid camera you had at school.' Luke leant forward to put his glass on the coffee table. 'You were always snapping something.'

Will's heart missed a beat as a recollection of that afternoon caught him unawares.

Luke laughed. The noise was incongruous and unsettling. 'Always slung around your neck, that camera.'

The camera Luke was talking about was gathering dust in a box on top of the wardrobe. He hadn't used it since school, but Luke was right, when he was young he rarely went anywhere without it. He'd been given it by a little-known uncle, his mother's bachelor stepbrother, who lived a reclusive life with three boisterous chocolate Labradors in a cottage on the edge of a Scottish loch. They had visited him once when holidaying near Inverness. Will had found the camera on a shelf and been fascinated by it. The uncle apparently never used it and sent it home with Will. From the very first photo he'd taken – a picture of his mother at the kitchen sink filling the kettle – he was hooked. Those images developing from ghostly white to brilliant colour in front of his eyes was actual magic. There was something about preserving a fleeting moment for eternity that bewitched him. His mother had encouraged him, and on those days when his father was in one of his black moods, ready to fly off the handle at anything Will might do or say, she'd pack him a bag with some lunch – a cheese sandwich, an apple and, if there was some in the battered royal wedding biscuit tin, a piece of fruit cake – and send him off to take photos. On one of these trips, not far from the stream that ran through a wooded glade about half a mile from their house, he found a dead shrew. The wretched creature was half covered with leaves and had been dead some time, its body stiff and dry. Its eyes had rotted away or been eaten by insects and were just empty hollows, brown velveteen fur frayed around the sockets like ragged fabric. Its feet were curled into tight balls. Its mouth was open to reveal sharp yellowed teeth. Will had taken a photo of it then sat cross-legged in the long grass and watched the picture emerge like a mirage from the whiteness. When it did he smiled; it was a brilliant photo. Everything was captured. There was even a mini-insect crawling across the shrew's shoulder that he hadn't noticed when he'd taken it. He sat beside the animal and stared at its death portrait, the sun warming him in dappled patches as it shone through the trees. Eventually, when the rumbling in his tummy became too loud to ignore, he said a solemn goodbye to the tiny corpse and walked home. He couldn't wait to show his mother the photo.

But when she saw it she'd recoiled in shock. 'I hope you didn't touch it! Good God, child, you'll catch rabies or bubonic plague or something! Go and wash your hands and make sure you scrub under your nails with the soap and brush.'

His father had come up behind him and grabbed the photo before Will had a chance to hide it. Given the mood he'd been in at breakfast, Will had half-expected a hiding, but instead he rested a heavy hand on his son's shoulder. 'That's a good find,' he said.

Will remembered the astonishment he'd felt at the note of pride in his father's clipped words. 'Did you bring the thing back with you?'

'No, sir.'

'Well, run and find it,' he barked. 'We'll leave it in a box in the shed to rot down then I'll show you how to bleach its skull.' Then he patted his shoulder and gave it a slight squeeze. It was one of the only times his father had touched him with any breath of affection.

'Oh, Philip!' his mother cried. 'That's revolting. I don't want him doing any such thing.'

His father then looked at him with a brief flash of collusion and Will felt as if he might explode with pleasure. He dumped his rucksack and camera on the kitchen table and charged out of the house like a greyhound from the traps. His heart hammered against his ribcage as he ran. He scrambled over the fence at the bottom of their garden, ignoring the sting of brambles as they tore at his legs. When he reached the glade, out of breath, lungs burning, he dropped to his knees to look for the shrew. But there was no sign of it. Will searched the ground, snatching at the grass and leaves in desperation, patting the earth frantically.

'Where are you?' he wailed, tears stinging his eyes.

After half an hour of searching he fell back on his haunches, sweat streaking his dusty face, and looked up at the darkening sky through the trees. He would have to go home empty-handed. He pulled the Polaroid out of his pocket and stared at the picture of the shrew for a few minutes before ripping it into tiny pieces and throwing them into the undergrowth, where they settled on the vegetation like confetti.

'How are your parents?' Luke asked, breaking into Will's thoughts. He picked up a frame from the small table beside him. Another picture of Harmony, this one taken about ten years before. Her hair was kissed golden by the sun, fine grains of sand decorated her eyelashes and dusted her cheek, and her eyes matched the sky behind her perfectly. She smiled back at the camera, back at Will, and he recalled the sound of her laugh just before he had taken the shot. He'd told her a joke. A bad one.

'You fool,' she'd said through her giggling.

Then *snap*, *snap*, *snap*: three photos, one of them the best he'd ever taken. Will wished Luke would put it down; the way he looked at it unnerved him.

'My mother's well. My father died last year.'

'I'm sorry,' Luke said, as he rested the photograph back on the table.

'We weren't close.'

'I know,' he said. 'I remember. I remember it all.'

Luke stared at him with unfaltering eyes and Will wondered if the discomfort he felt was from Luke's implied judgement or his own overwhelming shame.

CHAPTER SEVEN

Harmony stood in her towel, damp and warm from the shower, and looked in the mirror. Her heart sank a little. Age had crept up on her, sallowed her skin, folded fine wrinkles and creases around her tired-looking eyes, dotted her hairline with grey. She sighed and rubbed some tinted moisturiser over her face, dabbed Vaseline on her lips, then applied some mascara. She went back into the bedroom and opened the wardrobe. She had no idea what she should wear. Why did she even care?

She was surprised at how jittery she felt knowing Luke was in their flat. She reached to open her top drawer then paused, hesitating, her fingers resting lightly on the drawer handle. She glanced at the bedroom door and listened. She could hear the men talking in the living room, their voices low, words indistinct. She reached into the back of the drawer and felt for the cardigan. When her fingers found the soft wool her stomach knotted. She pulled it out and held it up, brushing her thumb over the little brown teddy bear stitched to its front, before bringing it up to her face and breathing in its smell, closing her eyes as she did so, pretending for a few moments her baby was still growing inside her. This cardigan was the only thing she'd bought for her unborn child. She wasn't superstitious; she was a scientist and knew better. She walked beneath ladders and thought nothing of black cats crossing her path, but even so, something had stopped her buying things for her baby. Emma had turned up a few days after Harmony told her the news, her car jam-packed with baby paraphernalia, tears of joy in her eyes. But Harmony insisted she take everything back with her; she didn't want any of it in the house. Just in case.

'I'm sorry,' she'd said, trying to ease Emma's disappointment. 'But it feels wrong until the baby's here safe and sound.'

Emma rested a hand on Harmony's arm, her head tipped forwards with concern. 'There's nothing wrong about being prepared. You've got to channel the inner Girl Guide when it comes to babies. What if it comes early? Take the Moses basket and sling at least.'

But Harmony stood her ground and a disgruntled Emma had driven everything back to Oxfordshire.

Then one day she weakened. It was a crisp winter morning with a royal blue sky and sunshine that glinted off the shop windows and illuminated the clouds of vapour as they formed on her breath. She was happy, the type of happy that fills a person up and spills over the edges. As she walked, stroking her hands lightly over her tummy, she couldn't keep her smile from beaming. Before she knew what she was doing she'd turned into Jojo Maman Bébé. The tiny cardigan caught her eye immediately. The wool was soft and warm and she could so clearly picture her baby buttoned into it and lying in her arms. It had seemed such an innocuous thing to do, buying the cardigan that day; so easy and inconsequential. But after her miscarriage this piece of clothing seemed to possess an almost mystical hold over her. It represented everything that should have been and though she'd tried on numerous occasions she couldn't bring herself to throw it away.

She breathed in its smell one last time then carefully folded it and slipped it back in the drawer. As she closed the drawer, the bedroom door opened.

'Harmony?' Will said, poking his head around the door. 'Are you nearly ready?'

'Yes, sorry. I'll be two minutes.'

He nodded and disappeared, closing the door softly behind him.

They had to talk soon. She'd make him, later, after Luke had left. He couldn't keep avoiding the subject.

When she walked into the living room Luke stood and smiled at her. His presence overpowered the room. There was a luminosity about him, a magnetism she imagined A-list actors possessed. He was out of place in their living room and she felt strangely uncomfortable.

'Glass of wine?' Will asked her.

'I'll have one with supper,' she said. 'Maybe some orange juice if we have any?'

'We do,' he said. 'Luke? Another beer? Or would you like to move on to wine?'

'Wine would be great,' he said.

Will left the room and Harmony and Luke stood in an awkward silence until he cleared his throat and gestured at the mantelpiece. 'I've been admiring these beautiful pictures of you.'

Harmony felt her skin flush. 'My husband's a great photographer. He can make anyone look good.'

Luke laughed. 'He said they were only good because you were a great subject.'

'He's too modest.' She sat on the sofa as Luke sat back down in the armchair. 'It's impossible to compliment him. A bit more self-belief would do him no harm at all.'

Will came back into the room and handed Harmony her juice and put a glass of wine on the coffee table in front of Luke. 'Do who no harm at all?'

'You,' she said. 'I'm talking about your photography.' She watched him bristle uncomfortably. 'I was saying it would be good if you believed in yourself a bit more.'

'Well, I am who I am, I suppose. Luke bought you some flowers,' he said, changing the subject. 'I wasn't sure which vase to use so I put them in some water in the sink.'

'Thank you,' Harmony said to Luke. 'I love cut flowers.' He was looking at her in that way again, like he was studying her for an exam, taking in every detail, every eyelash, every mole.

'So,' said Will, as another silence took hold of them. 'How about I get the steaks on? I mean, if you're both hungry.' Will looked at Luke. 'How do you like your steak?'

'Let me guess,' said Harmony, with a smile. 'You like your steak rare.'

'Yes. Always rare.' He leant forward and took hold of his glass of wine, his eyes locked on to hers. 'With the heart still beating if possible.'

She wrinkled her nose and shook her head.

'I presume from your face you like yours burnt to a crisp, with all the guilt and flavour cooked out of it.'

'Nothing wrong with having a conscience.'

'Nothing wrong with liking your food to taste good.'

'Think we'll beg to differ on this.' Harmony smiled. 'I was a vegetarian for years and still can't get my head around the idea of eating bleeding food.'

'And you marched against the Iraq war and you believe immigration is the basis for economic growth and cultural advancement?'

'Of course I marched.' Her smile slipped from her face as she saw the challenge in his eyes. 'Everybody should have marched. It was an illegal war based on fabricated motive. It was an utter disgrace and yet another blot on our country to add to the catalogue of blots that litter the history books.'

Will, who was standing behind the sofa, rested his hands on her shoulders and gave her a steadying squeeze. 'Harmony has an impressive moral compass,' he said to Luke.

'Don't patronise me, Will.' She shrugged his hands off her and turned to glare at him.

'I didn't mean—' Will didn't finish his sentence. 'I wasn't patronising you.'

'There is no shame in standing up for what you believe in, in making yourself heard and sticking to your principles. In fact, there is considerable shame in not doing so.'

Will drew in a sharp breath as if she'd stabbed him. 'I need to get the steaks on,' he mumbled as he backed out of the room, unable to escape fast enough.

'He seems on edge,' Luke said after he'd gone. 'Do you think it's something to do with me?'

'No, of course not. At least I don't think so.' She hesitated. 'Will hasn't mentioned you before. He never talks about school. Actually, he doesn't talk about anything from his childhood. Maybe seeing you again is bringing stuff back that he doesn't want to think about.' She sighed. 'I can see he's finding it strange, unsettling even. I shouldn't have snapped at him.'

'I shouldn't have come.'

Harmony shook her head. 'No, you should. It's great that you and Will have met up again. I think it's a good thing for him. Maybe it will help. It can't be healthy to keep so much bottled up.' She stood. 'Are you all right for a minute or two? I think I should give him a hand in the kitchen.'

'Of course.'

'Hey,' she said, as she walked into the kitchen.

He was blotting the fat-marbled steaks with some kitchen roll. He was a great cook and she loved to watch him doing it. He made it seem so effortless. When she cooked it was stressful; she was far too concerned about measurements and timings, and had no natural affinity with flavours or seasoning. Will was flamboyant and experimental, loved unusual spices, and always sloshed an extra glass of wine in. But as she watched him drying the meat she noticed none of his usual enthusiasm. He was being deliberate, methodical, his face set in concentration as he pushed his fingers

83

against the steaks. He glanced over his shoulder and tried to smile at her but didn't quite manage it. His skin had paled and he blinked at her slowly.

'I wasn't trying to patronise you,' he said. 'I'm sorry if it came across that way.'

'I overreacted. I don't know why. Work's been difficult today, but that's no excuse.'

'No, you didn't. I shouldn't have said that thing about your moral compass.' He wiped his hands on the tea towel which was draped over one shoulder then reached for the pepper mill. 'Just ignore me when I say stupid things like that.'

'Don't be daft.' She paused. 'Are you OK?'

'Just need to get these steaks on.'

'No, I meant—'

'I'm fine.' He threw a couple of pinches of salt onto the steaks. 'Do you mind going back and keeping Luke company? I'm nearly done.'

She glanced back towards the living room and hesitated.

'I won't be long.'

'Everything all right?' Luke asked as she rejoined him.

'Yes, all under control.'

'I was looking at your wedding photo. You both look so young. Did you meet at university?'

'We were at different places but, yes, we met while we were both students. He was studying photography and media studies at East Anglia and I did natural sciences at UCL.'

She thought back to the day she met Will. He was so very different to the boys she'd been out with before; he drank wine, not beer, had floppy blond hair, wore faded blue jeans and a crumpled pink shirt, and his well-bred accent was softened with a laid-back confidence. She'd have written him off as a vacuous posh boy if it hadn't been for his smile – wide and open and honest – which drew her in from the very first moment.

'We bumped into each other. Literally. He was listening to music, not looking where he was going, of course. I was late for a lecture and we collided.' Harmony smiled. 'My stuff went everywhere and he helped to pick it up. He asked if I wanted to go for a drink and I just said yes. Which was very unlike me. But I felt immediately relaxed in his company. He was gentle and easy to talk to.'

Luke nodded in agreement, as if this was also his experience of Will.

'My mother would have loved him,' she said softly.

'She died when you were young?'

'I was twelve.'

'Losing someone you love is incredibly hard.'

'Have you lost someone close?'

He nodded, visibly wincing with remembered grief. 'My wife. Eighteen months ago.'

'I'm so sorry.'

He looked at his glass, swilled the wine around it, lost for a moment in sadness. 'She was killed in a car crash. She swerved into oncoming traffic and hit a lorry. He said she came from nowhere.'

'Oh my God,' breathed Harmony. 'How awful.'

He looked back at her and smiled briefly, before his face reset, lips drawing tight, thoughts turning over and over in his head. Grief did that. It hit out of the blue, the slightest trigger bringing unwanted recollections: a turn of phrase, a song, a smell. Sitting there watching him quietly process his emotion, she found herself thinking of her mother's death. She remembered climbing the stairs that lunchtime, carefully carrying a bowl of soup, which was all her mother could eat by then, trying not to let it spill. She set the bowl on the bedside table and rested a hand on her mother's bony shoulder.

'Mum?' she whispered. 'I've got your lunch.'

There'd been no movement or response, and as Harmony stared at her mother, perfectly still, her lips parted as if about to speak, she realised something was different. A serenity had settled over her like a silk veil. Her face was relaxed, with none of the pained tautness she'd grown used to. Harmony took hold of her hand and turned it over, tracing her finger along the crease that crossed her palm, her lifeline, strong and pronounced, no breaks at all, no warning she'd die at the age of thirty-six. A dishonest line. Then she laid her cheek on her mother's upturned hand.

'Is she dead?'

Harmony lifted her head to see her sister in the open doorway with her arms crossed.

'Yes,' Harmony said. 'I think so.'

Her sister nodded and walked over to the bed. She bent and kissed their mother's forehead, pausing for a moment, her eyes tightly closed, then she reached for the bowl of soup and without saying a word she took it back downstairs.

Harmony looked up at Luke. 'Death is hard however it comes. We were expecting my mother's for a long time. She was in so much pain, and had been for months, that in a way it seemed kinder for her to slip away. I miss her every day, even after all these years.'

Just then, Will came into the living room carrying three plates like a silver-service waiter. 'Supper,' he announced with exaggerated brightness. 'Burnt, bloody and somewhere between.'

Harmony pushed her mother's death from her mind and stood. 'That looks delicious,' she said, as she approached the table.

'This is very kind of you,' Luke said, as he came to the table and placed his wine down. 'And what a treat to have steak.'

Will wiped his hands on the tea towel, still slung over his shoulder, then pulled his chair out to sit. 'I hope it tastes OK.'

Harmony could see how hard her husband was working to appear relaxed, how rehearsed his words were, as if he'd been in the kitchen practising until he could recite them without tripping up.

'So how did you two meet?' Harmony said, as she cut into her steak. It was just how she liked it, cooked through with the slightest blush of pink in the middle.

'You know how.' Will furrowed his brow. 'At school.'

'Yes, but I wondered how you actually became friends. You seem quite different. It would be interesting to know what drew you to each other, I suppose.'

'We just met,' Will said. 'We shared a dormitory with thirty other boys. No special story.'

'Harmony's right though. There was a moment that we came together, that cemented our friendship. It's quite a story, isn't it?' Luke finished his mouthful then sat back in his chair. He smiled broadly and reached for his wine.

Harmony saw Will swallow. 'It was a long time ago,' he said. 'I'm not sure we need to talk about any of this. It wasn't the happiest of times for either of us.'

Luke laughed. 'It certainly wasn't. But what do they say? What doesn't kill you makes you stronger?'

Harmony felt Will tense as he cut vigorously at his meat. 'The steak's a bit tough,' he said. 'I'm sorry about that. I should have let it rest a while longer.'

'Mine's perfect,' said Luke.

Will raised his head. His face was stony, his eyes hooded, and Harmony was shocked to see how angry he looked. He put his knife and fork together then pushed his plate away. 'I can't do this anymore.'

'Will?'

'It's a charade, Harmony.' Then he turned on Luke. 'How can you just sit there without a care in the world? How can you act like you're interested in my photographs? Laughing it all off like it doesn't matter?'

Harmony looked between the two men, Will's face reddening, his breathing heavy, hands clutching the table with white knuckles.

Then Luke, impassive, his body relaxed, registering no surprise at Will's outburst.

'You want me to tell you the story he's laughing about?' Will said to her, his voice hard and unyielding.

'No, I—'

'You want me to recount the details in all their unpleasant glory?' But then Will stopped speaking. He shook his head, and thrust his hands up to his face, jamming the heels of his palms against his eye sockets.

Luke leant forward, resting his elbows on the table. 'We knew each other,' he said, his voice quiet, his eyes bolted on to Harmony's. 'From the dormitory and from lessons. We'd spoken a bit, but we weren't good friends, not until the day Will rescued me.'

'Rescued you?'

'I didn't—'

'I was tied to a fence,' he said. 'Naked, of course. This *was* boarding school, after all.' He moved his glass an inch to the right, sliding it across the table with his index finger. 'A group of boys grabbed me after supper, took every scrap of clothing off me then tied me to the fence in the garden of our boarding house and left me there.' He spoke with no emotion, his face blank, intonation flat; he could just as easily have been discussing the weather forecast.

'That's appalling,' breathed Harmony. She looked at Will, who shook his head slightly, eyes closed.

Luke ran a hand through his hair. 'The best bit,' Luke said with a smile, 'was when the headmaster found me and told me to stop mucking around and get back up to the dormitory, "And when your housemaster asks why you're late, tell him you've been playing silly buggers and need a caning."' Luke started to laugh. The noise was disconcerting against the uneasy silence in the room. 'So there I was, naked as a newborn baby and tied to the fence, unable to move, with this crazy man shouting at me to get back to the dorm.' Tears of laughter formed in the corners of his eyes.

Harmony shifted in her seat. She glanced at Will, his face set in an iron grimace as he pushed a piece of steak fat towards the edge of his plate with the tip of his knife.

'Then Will comes along,' Luke continued, his laughter fading, 'and unties me. Then he asked my first name. I remember that so clearly.' He looked at Will. 'We called each other by our surnames, you see, so him wanting to know my Christian name felt special.' Luke smiled and looked back at Harmony. 'Will was my hero from that moment on. I'd have done anything for him.'

Will looked up at the ceiling and she noticed a hint of exasperation or perhaps impatience in his expression. 'A hero?' he said. 'For Christ's sake, I was just a boy who thought another boy stripped naked and tied to a fence could do with some help, that's all. I didn't do anything heroic. I just untied him.'

'Will, I think—'

'For crying out loud, Harmony! Please stop it will you? Just leave it alone.'

CHAPTER EIGHT

The steak sat like concrete in the pit of Will's stomach. He remembered the panic that had coursed through him as he fought with the ropes, knots so tight he worried he'd never loosen them. All the time his heart pummelled his chest. All the time ready to run if the boys or the headmaster showed up. How could Luke talk about it with such casual disregard? Will flinched as he recalled Luke's eggshell skin marked with bruises from where the older boys had manhandled him, his pathetic nakedness, the tear tracks that cut through the dirt on his pinched cheeks, and how, as Will battled with those hellish knots, Luke had gazed up at him as if he was the loveliest thing he'd ever seen.

'All I was going to say is I can't believe those boys would do something like that,' Harmony said with lilting sympathy that stung Will.

'Alastair Farrow's an accountant now.' Luke spoke matter-of-factly.

'Alastair Farrow?' Harmony asked.

'One of the boys who tied me to the fence.'

Will's gut twisted as anxiety flooded him and a hatred he tried to keep at bay reared up from the depths of him.

'I found him on Facebook,' Luke went on. 'Wife. Two children.'

Will closed his eyes and swallowed. Then he shook his head and stared at Luke. 'Why are you here?' he said. 'What do you want? I don't understand. Do I owe you an apology? Is that what you've come for?'

'I don't want that.'

'Then *what*?' Will shouted, banging his hand against the table. 'What is it you want?'

'Will, don't,' said Harmony, reaching out to rest her hand on his.

'I should go.' Luke stood and wiped his hands on his napkin.

'Yes, I think you should.' Will pushed back from the table and strode out of the room. He walked into the kitchen and out of the back door, into the garden, and breathed deeply. He kicked the ground and swore. He hated that he'd lost control. He couldn't let this get to him. He sat on the edge of the terrace, elbows resting on his knees, his chin in his hands. Why had he confronted him like that? All he needed to do was be pleasant, cook steak, share a bottle of good wine, endure an hour or two of small talk, and then close the door on it all again. He shuddered at the memory of Luke tied to the fence, that look of adoration in his desperate eyes, the horror of what followed.

A few minutes later Harmony appeared beside him and sat down, her body pressed up against his. At first neither spoke. Then she put her hand on his leg and stroked him.

'He's gone,' she said.

He looked down and nodded slightly.

Harmony leant forward and picked a daisy from between the blades of unkempt grass and began to pull off each petal one by one. He imagined her chanting a childish rhyme: *Will he talk? Won't he? Will he talk? Won't he . . .?*

Will rubbed his face and concentrated on easing his racing pulse. When he'd collected himself he took a deep breath and blew sharply out as he tried to find the words he needed to explain what he was feeling. It was impossibly hard. It all took place so long ago. He'd buried it – or tried to – but right now it was all as clear and raw as if it happened yesterday.

'The bullying was pretty bad,' Will said. The sound of his voice surprised him, as if his words had become impatient and barged out of his subconscious without his consent.

Harmony took his hands in hers.

'Luke was one of those boys who should have stayed quiet and kept his head below the parapet. But he had this temper on him. Christ—' Will shook his head. 'He went mental sometimes, you know, if people teased him. And they found it hilarious. So of course they teased him about everything – his dad being a vicar, his clothes, being small, his name, anything and everything – and each time he'd fly off the handle. It was a cruel and vicious cycle. The more he reacted, the more they went for him.'

Will was quiet for a moment or two, remembering the speed with which Luke's anger would ignite. Sometimes the slightest jibe would set him off, screeching, stamping his feet, slamming his fists into walls.

'I saw him smash a window once. A boy in the year above sniggered as we walked past, about nothing much as far as I could tell, and before I knew what was going on Luke grabbed this boy's text book, tore it in half and threw it through the glass. Two prefects had to hold him down until he finally calmed.' Will had watched, first in horror as Luke raged and kicked and screamed, then with relief as the anger left him like an exorcised spirit, his balled fists relaxing, his breathing slowing to normal, eyes refocusing.

'I should have kept away from him. Being Luke's friend was social suicide. But I was there, hiding in the bushes, watching them as they took his clothes and tied him to that fucking fence. All of them laughing and jeering, howling like a pack of dogs on a rabbit. When—' Will paused to draw a steadying breath. 'When they left, I was about to go to him, but the headmaster turned up. I was relieved, happy that he was going to get help. But the bastard didn't help him. Instead, he started shouting. Told him to stop mucking about. To get himself back to the dorm. It was the unfairest thing I'd ever seen.' Will recalled his horror when he saw the look of spite on Drysdale's face, leering down at the pale, skinny boy, vulnerable and defenceless. 'He was so scared he could barely breathe.'

'I can't believe it,' she whispered.

Will scuffed the ground with the heel of his shoe. 'Word got out it was me who helped him and then I became fair game.'

'What you did was the right thing to do.'

Will didn't reply. Yes, of course, she was right; at the time it was the right thing to do, the only thing to do, but if he could go back in time he knew he wouldn't do it again. He'd have left him tied to that fence so they never became friends, never pushed their bleeding palms together, never went to play by their favourite tree on that crisp October afternoon.

'I'm glad you did what you did. It sounds like Luke needed a friend.'

'Yes,' he said at last. Then he sighed. 'But, you know, he was great. I wasn't just friends with him because he needed me. He was fun and we clicked. He was incredibly bright, which didn't help, of course. Even the masters seemed to hate him for that, hated how he mucked around in class then got full marks in everything. It drove them mad. And he was funny. Really funny.' Will gave an involuntary smile as he allowed himself to remember the laughs he and Luke had. 'He was different to everyone else; there was something unpredictable about him. I envied him in many ways. He never felt as if he had to follow the crowd and he questioned everything. He was ballsy.' Will looked at Harmony. 'He did amazing impersonations of our masters. He used to have me in stitches.'

Will smiled again as he remembered the genius of Luke's impressions. He'd have Will bent double and almost throwing up from laughing at his *Drysdale and the Magnificent Exploding Cane* sketch or his *Professor Thomas the Chemical Car Crash*, pretending to break test tubes and set the lab alight with a Bunsen burner as he bumbled blindly around. He even managed to turn his face puce like Mr Frood, their Glaswegian RE master, about to lose it because of forgotten homework.

'You forgot your PREP?!!' Luke would screech, mimicking Frood perfectly, his skin turning redder and puffing up like a toad. 'If you FORGOT your *PREP* then we MUST all ASSUUUUME, including sweet Jesus HIMSELF, that you HAVE mushy PEAS for BRRRAINS. You. Are. An. IMBECEEEELE!!!' And then Luke would fall to the floor writhing and twitching, chanting *mushy peas, mushy peas, mushy peas* over and over while Will creased up with laughter, tears streaming down his aching cheeks.

'I was pretty good at taking shit, kept my cool, didn't react, and by the end of the year they'd eased up on me.' He glanced at her and kicked at the ground again. 'Bullies try and get under your skin. I found that if I built walls it helped. It's probably why I don't talk about any of it. As far as I was concerned, if I let them get to me I let them win. I also made sure I wasn't seen out and about with Luke too much. We'd hang out on our own in the woods behind the school instead. There was this den we made, hidden away in the trees. We went there. Sometimes in the refectory I sat with other boys to eat.' Will felt a sudden swell of guilt as he heard those words out loud, recalling Luke's downcast eyes, resigned and abandoned, while Will sat with other boys in his year, boys he didn't like as much, but boys he could be seen with without risk. Luke took it on the chin. He never mentioned it, never asked to join them. It was as if he was just pleased to take whatever companionship Will was willing to give him, as if he deserved no more.

'Will?'

'Yes?'

'Why did you ask if he wanted you to say sorry?'

Will's stomach knotted.

'Maybe talking about it will help,' she said. 'You can tell me. I'm your wife and I want you to trust me. You don't need to keep secrets from me.'

'I can trust you. I do. My . . .' He paused, searching his head for the right word. ' . . . reticence to talk about it has nothing to do with you.' He took hold of her hand in an attempt to reassure her.

'He doesn't seem angry or upset with you,' she said. 'He doesn't seem to have any bad feelings towards you at all. He seems fine.'

Will put his arms around her and buried his face in the warm, sweet-smelling curve of her neck, breathing her in as if she were a drug. His skin prickled. He lifted his head and kissed her. He wanted to lie her back and, right there on the terrace in the dying warmth of the day, make love to her. He wanted to lose himself in her. His desire, their sex, erasing Luke – and everything that came with him – from his head.

They sat like that for a while until eventually she made a move to stand. 'We should go in; it'll be dark soon.'

Harmony cleared the unfinished supper away and scraped the food into the bin while Will scrambled some eggs, which they ate leaning against the kitchen worktop. In bed, she pushed herself into him, her back to his chest, his arms enfolding her so he felt she was part of him. He kissed her shoulder, gently lingering, parted his lips and brushed the tip of his tongue across her skin, the slightly salty taste arousing him, the desire he'd felt in the garden returned.

'I love you,' he whispered.

He ran his hand along her arm and over her breast. Then he kissed her and she kissed him back. When she touched him, he moaned quietly. She stroked her hand upwards and over his stomach and chest, then ran her finger over his lips and his mouth. He closed his lips around her, running his tongue around her fingertip. They made love for the first time in a while. It was comforting and safe, each of them knowing their role to perfection, instinctively doing what the other liked, the familiar, satisfying sex of a twenty-year marriage. He adored her body, every curve, imperfection, scar and mole. The touch of her skin excited him, and the smell of her, the real smell of her beneath the creams and lotions.

Afterwards they lay beside each other, fingers lightly laced.

'There's something I need to tell you,' he said.

'Mmm?'

His stomach churned as nerves gathered. He hesitated, the words knotting in his throat. 'It's to do with this baby thing.'

'This baby *thing*?' she repeated, with a small laugh.

He turned his head on the pillow and looked at her in the light coming in from the hallway. 'Nothing's changed, Harmony. I wish I felt differently, but I don't. I . . . I still don't want a child.'

Her face fell. 'But why? You've never explained why.'

The words of the poem he'd memorised at fifteen echoed in his head, as poignant now as they'd been when he first read them. It was the first time a poem had touched him, the words chiming as if the writer inhabited Will's own headspace, the headspace of a boy with no relationship with his father, who had been taken from his mother, his childhood blighted at home and at school. He'd stumbled on the poem while searching for something by Wilfred Owen for a First World War history essay. It was by a man he hadn't heard of before. Philip Larkin. Standing alone in the library that smelt of old books and wood polish, he read the words over and over, angrily swiping at the tears they provoked. The words were stark, sweary, and spoke to him directly, chiming in a way none of the poets he was usually forced to read ever had.

It was there in black and white.

The truest thing he'd read.

Don't have children, Larkin warned him. Don't ever have children.

Will reached over and stroked his hand down her cheek, tucking a tress of her hair behind her ear. 'There's something I've kept from you. I should have told you months ago.' He hesitated.

'What is it?'

'I don't know how—'

'Just tell me.'

'I . . .' He hesitated again. 'I had a vasectomy.'

'What?' Barely spoken, no more than a breath. 'I don't understand.'

'A vasectomy.' He reached for her hand that clutched at the duvet. 'I had a vasectomy.'

CHAPTER NINE

As his words sank in, she stared at his face and caught the full weight of his pained expression and how his eyes wouldn't meet hers.

'Harmony?'

She didn't move. He reached over and turned his bedside light on. She closed her eyes against the brightness, against him. His words tumbled around in her mind.

Had she heard correctly?

Disbelief muddied her thoughts and vision, drunk on his admission. Her head swam and as she forced herself out of bed her knees threatened to buckle.

'A vasectomy,' she said. 'You had yourself sterilised?'

He didn't answer and she turned away from him and walked to the bathroom, closing the door behind her. As she stood in the centre of the room, unsure what to do, her body began to shiver. She reached for the towel on the rail. It was damp from her earlier shower, but she wrapped it around herself like a cape, then closed the loo seat and sat down.

Will opened the door. He'd put some boxer shorts on, which gaped unattractively. She felt nauseous and looked away from him. He crouched beside her. Rested his hand on her knee.

'Don't touch me.'

'Harmony, I—'

'I said, *don't touch me*, Will.'

He withdrew his hand and as he dropped his head, she closed her eyes against a wave of nausea.

'Let me get this straight.' Her voice was quiet, her words strained, and she was unable to look at him. 'You went to a hospital and had a vasectomy without telling me?'

'Yes.'

She concentrated on her breathing, focused on the air passing in and out of her body. Did he have any idea of the damage he'd done? As she sat there, her shock turned to disbelief. She fixed her eyes on him, her brow furrowed, her head shaking from side to side as she grappled with what he'd told her.

'Have you any concept of how serious this is?'

He didn't respond, just crouched there, motionless, struck dumb.

'How could you do something like that without talking to me?'

His face showed all the shame, all the guilt, of a scolded child. His lips were pursed and his gaze was fixed on the floor between them.

'Why would you?' She forced the words through gritted teeth.

'You know why,' he said.

'No. I don't.'

'I never wanted children.'

For a moment she was silent. Processing his statement. She thought of the cardigan tucked into the back of her drawer. 'But we were going to have one,' she whispered. 'I was pregnant. I thought that changed things?'

His eyes flicked back and forth across her face, his head shaking almost imperceptibly.

'But you seemed OK with it. Happy even,' she said. 'When the baby died you must have felt something, some sort of loss? Surely that changed things?' She was pleading with him, pleading for him to admit some sort of emotional response, something that would reassure her he wasn't a heartless monster.

He sighed heavily, rubbed his face, then stood up and walked over to the bath. He sat on its edge. 'That's the point, I didn't. I didn't feel the things you wanted me to feel. I wasn't happy when I found out about it and I wasn't sad when you lost it. I tried to be there for you because I love you and I care about you, but you can't expect me to mourn something I never felt attached to.'

A swell of anger rose up inside her. 'How can you be so callous?' she whispered.

'You don't understand what I'm saying.' Will paused, his face twisting as if in physical pain. 'When it died . . .' He hesitated. 'When it died I felt . . .' He stopped himself.

'What, Will? Tell me. What did you feel?'

'I felt relieved.'

The word hung between them, poisoning the air.

'Harmony, I didn't—'

'Fuck you.' She dropped her head, struggling to process everything she was hearing. Relief? How? She lifted her face and stared at him and as she did she pictured his heart, black and shrivelled in his hollow chest.

'Why are you so shocked?' he asked then. 'We've talked about it. Talked about it until we're blue in the face. When we got married – no, when we met – we talked about it. Christ, Harmony, from the start, you knew the score.'

'Knew the *score*?' She spat the words from her mouth as if they were battery acid.

'I never wanted children. I still don't.' He squared his shoulders and looked her directly in the eyes, faced her, primed to defend himself. 'So I had a vasectomy.'

Raw hatred swamped her then. A hatred born of a wound she never imagined him capable of inflicting.

'What the hell is wrong with you?' she shouted. 'How could you? You and I might have talked about it years ago, but things changed. We got pregnant.' She was crying now, hot tears coursing her cheeks. 'You knew how I felt about our baby. You knew from the start. But then you go . . . and . . . and have a vasectomy? Without even telling me?' She paused and shook her head, pressing the edge of the towel that covered her against her eyes to blot the tears. 'I mean, shit. Is it even legal to do that without my consent?'

'Your consent?' He looked genuinely surprised and she fought the urge to slap him.

'Yes,' she said. 'My consent. As your wife. Given that what you did affects me profoundly.'

'You're missing the point. This goes beyond the vasectomy. It reaches far deeper. None of this is based on a whim. It's fundamental to who I am. I don't want children. I'm not capable of being a father. I'm not capable of caring for another human being—'

'Don't be ridiculous,' she interrupted, looking at the ceiling to try and stem her tears.

'I'm not being ridiculous.' Then he got up and walked back into the bedroom. 'I don't want to have children.'

'But I do!' she shouted after him. Then she started to shake, as the shock of their row and what he'd told her took hold of her body. She felt cold suddenly and tightened the towel around her. 'Oh God,' she breathed. 'Will, what have you done to us?'

When she stood, her legs were shaky, her heart racing. She made herself walk when all she wanted to do was collapse on the floor. She dropped the towel from her shoulders and took her dressing gown off the hook on the back of the door. She put it on, tying the cord tightly, then stood in the doorway and leant against the frame. He was sitting on the bed, his back facing her, shoulders hunched.

'When did you do it?'

He didn't reply.

'Will? I asked you a question. When did you do it? When I was dealing with the pain of losing our baby?'

'Not then.'

'When?'

'I went to see the doctor not long after you found out you were pregnant. I was all over the place. We had this child on the way and I didn't want to make the same mistake again; I didn't want more children.' He shifted his position on the bed to look at her. 'I didn't want to take any more chances.'

'But you would have been unwell – there's swelling, isn't there?'

Again he didn't reply.

'For God's sake! Tell me when you did it!'

He shook his head wearily. 'At the beginning of December. I told you I was sick with flu.'

Her mind whirred, thinking back to the week he spent in bed, tucked up in a darkened room, curtains drawn, an extra pillow. Chicken soup. A hot water bottle. 'But I looked after you,' she said. 'I phoned Frank and told him you were too ill to go into the shop.' She put her hand on her forehead. 'I gave you ibuprofen. I cared for you . . .' Her voice trailed to nothing.

'I didn't know how to tell you. I was going to, at one point, but I kept putting it off, avoiding it, and then you had the miscarriage and, well, I didn't want to upset you any more than you were.'

She laughed bitterly and fixed her eyes on the wall. 'Well, thank you for not wanting to upset me. Thank you for your consideration. For your thoughtfulness.' She shook her head again. 'You get the prize for most caring fucking husband of the year!'

'Don't shout.'

'Why the hell not?' A sense of finality mushroomed inside her. It was like he'd fired a machine gun at their marriage and it now lay in bloodied tatters at her feet. As she stared at him she had the strange illusion of him turning into a stranger. His features grew unfamiliar. The set of his face became that of someone she vaguely knew, a man with a resemblance to Will, but a man she couldn't place.

'This is nuts,' he said, with a note of anger. 'You're looking at me like I'm the devil, like I've torn your heart out, but you knew if you married me you wouldn't have a family. It was a sacrifice – I know that – but you made it. I was there when you agreed to it, standing beside you in the registry office, holding your hand and slipping that band of gold onto your finger.'

'Don't you throw that at me! This is way beyond will we or won't we have a child. Way beyond our marriage vows. If you want to bring marriage vows into it, how about love, cherish, honour – a marriage built on honesty? You've made a mockery of everything that day stood for, every promise you made me. And yes, you're right, I *did* love you enough to make that sacrifice, and it was a sacrifice, it was the hardest decision I've ever had to make. But this isn't about that day anymore, can't you see that?' Tears sprang in her eyes and fell unchecked down her cheeks. 'What you've done is despicable.'

Will stood and walked over to her then. He reached out towards her, but she recoiled and stepped back from him.

'When I felt our baby inside me,' she said, 'I . . . felt . . . like I was complete. Then, when I . . .' Her stomach twinged with an echo of the pain of her miscarriage. 'When I lost it, it was as if my world had ended and, in the months that followed, all I wanted for was that *mistake*, as you call it, to happen again.'

She saw him swallow and his shoulders dip as guilt took hold, or perhaps regret.

'I wanted you to have felt it too,' she said, fighting the lump in her throat. 'I wanted to think you'd imagined being a father and holding your baby and that something inside you had awakened. And I wanted you to feel as bereft and as cheated as I did.' She searched his face for signs of comprehension, of an empathy she now feared he didn't possess. 'I see how foolish it was now, but I just hoped you'd changed your mind.' She blotted her tears on the back of her hand. 'You *have* torn my heart out, Will. Doing what you've done, making that decision without me, taking away the option of me ever having a baby without even talking to me. You've torn my heart out and trodden it into the dirt.'

He moved towards her again but she shoved him back. 'Leave me alone. You can sleep on the sofa. I don't want you anywhere near me.'

'We need to talk.'

She snorted bitterly. 'Oh, *now* we need to talk?'

'Harmony—'

'I said leave me alone.'

For a moment he looked as if he might try and approach her again. She walked past him, careful not to touch him as she did, and got into bed. She stretched across to turn the light off and then lay there, arms either side of her on top of the duvet, willing him to leave the room.

She heard him take a breath to speak.

'Go, Will.'

Then he left.

She listened to his footsteps as he walked down the corridor. Heard him go into the living room. Heard the door close. Then it was quiet. So quiet. The silence rang in her head. She felt as if she'd been driven over, stunned and confused, her head pounding at the temples. It scared her to feel this level of hatred towards her husband. She thought of her mum then, of a conversation they'd had when Harmony was about seven. She'd been crying in bed and crept downstairs and sidled into the television room where her mother was watching the news. Her mother had opened her arms and Harmony had climbed onto her lap and curled herself into her, burying her face in her soft wool sweater.

'What's the matter, petal?'

'Stupid Stevie Graham says my dad left because he didn't love me.'

Her mother had tightened her arms around her. 'Well, what does Stupid Stevie Graham know about anything anyway?'

Harmony had shrugged.

'Nothing, that's what.' She kissed the top of her head. 'Your dad loved you all the way to the moon and back.'

Harmony turned in her mum's arms and looked up at her, her fingers idly reaching up and stroking the balding patch on the side of her head. 'Why did he go then?'

Her mother hadn't answered immediately, but had taken a deep breath then finally smiled. 'Some people are like birds,' she said. 'You can't keep them caged. He needed to fly, that's all. I hoped he wouldn't fly too far, but sadly for us he did.'

'Do you hate him?'

'Hate him?' Her mother laughed softly and rested her chin on top of Harmony's head. 'No, I don't hate him. I could never hate your dad. I love him and you can't turn love on and off like a tap. There's nothing he could do – even leaving – that would make me stop loving him. Just like he still loves us, whatever he does, wherever he is. You remember that next time Stupid Stevie Graham says anything daft about your dad.'

Harmony's memories were interrupted by a sudden wetness between her legs as Will's semen seeped out of her. She cringed as she remembered their lovemaking. Less than an hour ago, when she'd been happy, when she'd felt close to her husband. She recalled the way he'd kissed her, so tenderly, so full of love, but all the time he knew what he'd done and was concealing it. Concealing the stake he'd driven through the heart of their marriage. She shifted her body against the discomfort she felt, pulled the sheets between her legs to dry herself. The thought of it turned her stomach; she was revolted by the dead and useless liquid tainting her body with its deceitful sterility. It was like venom inside her, and suddenly, violently, she wanted all trace of him out of her.

She got up and went to the bathroom and set the shower to as hot as she could stand, and there, in the quiet darkness, she stood beneath the scalding water and scrubbed herself clean of him.

When she'd finished, she wrapped herself in a dry towel and walked back into the bedroom. Then she went over to her drawers and opened the top one. She reached in and felt for the cardigan, closed her fingers tightly around its softness and pulled it out. For one last time she buried her face in it, breathing deeply, and allowed herself to cry. When she finally stopped, she walked over to the bin in the corner of the room, the pain in her stomach making each step unbearable, and dropped the tiny cardigan into it, then turned away from it.

CHAPTER TEN

Will lay on the sofa and stared at the ceiling, picturing the cracks that crept across it, invisible in the darkness. He thought about the moment she'd told him she was pregnant. It was a Thursday morning. She was about to leave for work. He remembered it clearly, even what she was wearing – a dark navy skirt and jacket, a white shirt, her Tiffany heart, trainers on her feet, her smart-heeled 'meeting' shoes that gave her blisters in her bag to change into when she arrived.

'I'm pregnant.'

She'd said it just like that. Out of the blue. She was packing her briefcase with her notes, her reading glasses, an apple, but then she paused, both hands resting on her bag, and said it.

I'm pregnant.

There had been a quiver in her voice and when he looked at her he saw she was trembling, but her eyes gleamed and there was the promise of a smile that lit her face and turned the corners of her mouth up ever so slightly.

'I'm pregnant.'

His heart stopped. 'But how? How can you be?'

'I don't know.'

'Did you miss a pill?'

Her smile fell. 'You think I did it on purpose?'

'What? No.' Will shook his head, confused; he hadn't even considered she might do it on purpose. But then: 'Did you?'

'Of course not! I wouldn't do that and I didn't miss a pill either. I've not missed a pill in eighteen years.'

'Then how?'

'I've no idea. I suppose the stats say it's only ninety-nine point-eight per cent effective. I guess we're the point-two per cent.'

Then Will watched the wonderment dawn on her face.

'Oh my God,' she breathed. 'I'm pregnant!'

Now, lying on the sofa, Will rested his palms on his face. He could smell her on him and his loins stirred inappropriately as he remembered moving inside her. He heard the shower start in their room. She was awake still. Should he go back in and try to talk to her? He thought about what he would say. How could he convince her he was sorry? He should have been honest from the start. He should have told her that Thursday morning. It had been a mistake to let her believe he was OK with it. Let her assume he was looking forward to having a child. He could see his mistakes so clearly now.

Why had he lied?

'What are you thinking?' she'd said on that Thursday, placing the flat of her hand against his cheek.

Will had noticed her other hand resting on her tummy, as if forming a protective barrier between him and it. Protecting it from what? From his reaction? From his coldness? He should have said something right then, as her hand rested lightly on his face and there was understanding in her voice.

But he didn't.

'I know it's a shock,' she said. 'But . . . ' She stopped without finishing her sentence and her face broke into the widest of smiles. 'It's a good thing, isn't it? Don't you think? This will be good for us. Having a family. It's fate.'

Fate? She didn't believe in fate. She was a scientist. Fate was like fairies and ghosts; it shouldn't exist for her.

'I mean, I know we weren't planning it, but you're happy, right?' She rubbed his shoulders and asked him again. 'Please say something, darling. Tell me you're happy.'

He looked down at her, her face tilted up towards his, her eyes shining, and lied.

'Yes. I think so. A bit shocked, that's all. But I'll be fine. I probably need a day or two to get my head around it.'

And as these lies eddied around them, as they filled her eyes with joy, he smiled and kissed her and held her tightly when she threw her arms around him.

'That's good enough for now,' she whispered into his ear, before pushing away from him, her face childlike in its excitement. 'Oh, Will! We're having a baby!' Then she jumped back into his arms and kissed him again.

Would telling the truth have helped? She'd never have got rid of the baby. Maybe she'd have left him. Anger and upset inevitable, whether back then or now. He thought about the vasectomy, the phone call he'd made to the private hospital, the way they'd run through the details, the price, the ease of the operation, the approximate time it would take him to recover. At the time it had seemed rational. Obvious. He'd been annoyed he hadn't done it years earlier. He remembered feeling suffocated, the walls of his world inching in from all sides, the cold sweats, that agonising mistrust of himself. Those damn words – Larkin's words – ringing like a tolling bell in his ears. He'd spent every waking moment of those first few weeks trying to imagine himself with a child. He tried to be positive, told himself it might well be a good thing, an opportunity to right the wrongs of the past, something he should embrace. But he hadn't convinced himself and his anxiety had mushroomed until he found it difficult to eat or sleep or breathe. Yet all that time he'd worn a ridiculous mask of happiness. He smiled when she told him how wonderful it was. He pretended to listen when she read aloud from baby magazines, told him how large the foetus was, which bits of its body had developed that week, how her ankles would swell soon, how her stomach would grow until her tummy button turned inside out . . .

He was a coward.

He always had been.

CHAPTER ELEVEN

Harmony woke later than usual. Her eyes ached from crying and lack of sleep, and she felt cold and shivery. She washed her face and dressed in black work trousers and a thick grey winter sweater. As she walked along the corridor to the kitchen, her heart pounded. Remnants of last night's fight came at her like shooting pains and her body trembled.

He was sitting at their small kitchen table wearing last night's boxers and a sweater he'd taken from the laundry basket. His hair was all over the place and she could tell from his puffy, tired eyes he'd had no more sleep than she had. She wondered briefly how long he'd been out on the streets pacing the pavements. As she approached him he stood. They faced each other like nervous teenagers, both knowing they were supposed to say something, neither having the faintest clue what.

'Would you like some coffee?' he asked at last. 'I made a pot.' His eyes searched hers, worry written all over his face.

She nodded. He poured her a cup and added milk from the carton then handed it to her.

'Harmony, I'm—'

'Don't,' she said, her eyes welling with angry tears. 'Not yet.' Her stomach churned and her throat tightened as the kitchen grew unbearably claustrophobic. She opened the back door to let some air in. The day was duller than the last few days with a slight chill and maybe the promise of rain. She breathed in the freshness and stared out across the garden to the flats beyond their wall. She watched as the shadow of a figure walked past one of the windows.

'Do you ever ask yourself if this is it?' She turned to face him. Her voice was calm and level. She looked at his face intently, trying to find signs of the man she was supposed to love.

'What do you mean?'

'I mean this. Us. The flat, your shop, my work?'

'No, I never think that; I have everything I want.'

She narrowed her eyes, feeling herself fill up with spite. She wanted to hurt him. 'Well, I do. I look at this place and I see a dead end.'

'Our flat?' His brow furrowed. 'But you love it, don't you?'

'No, Will. I hate it. I didn't always hate it. For a long time I thought it was perfect.'

'It is.'

'It isn't. It's as far from perfect as it can be. We had all these plans. You remember? We were going to redecorate. Apply for planning to build over the side return.' She turned and looked back across the garden. 'And then there's the garden. We were going to turn it into an oasis, but look at it. It's a mess.'

'I thought you liked it wild and overgrown. You said it's romantic.'

'No. *You* said it's romantic. But it's not romantic; it's untidy and uninspiring. I don't want to sit out there in the evenings with a glass of wine and each other for company, and I should, shouldn't I? That's what it's all about, isn't it? Looking forward to simple pleasures like that?'

She heard him draw a breath as if to speak.

'I am trapped here,' she said, before he had the chance.

'Because of what I've done?' His voice was full of reticence, as if he didn't want to hear her answer.

'Yes. What you did – the timing, the secrecy, your lack of understanding of what I've been through, the finality – it hurts. It really hurts. And now I feel like I'm stuck here with no future. Trapped somewhere I don't feel safe. Last night I was thinking about it all. About why I'd been so excited about the pregnancy and why I was so desperately lost after the miscarriage. Being pregnant lifted me out of a rut, it gave me a new focus, something to feel uplifted by. The miscarriage pushed me right back down.'

'You were that unhappy before the pregnancy?'

She let the question tumble around her head. She'd never thought of herself as unhappy before the baby. Had she been? She trawled her mind, trying to pin down exactly what it was she'd felt. Had she been bored, maybe? Or unfulfilled? Lacking purpose? Were these feelings real or merely a reaction to the bombshell he'd dropped on her?

'All I know,' she said, picking at the edge of her thumbnail, 'is that for much of the last six months I've felt alone and uncared for, and at times as if I'd been abandoned, floating alone in the middle of an ocean. Then hearing what you did, knowing you could do something like that . . .' She shook her head and left the sentence unfinished. She looked at him, eyes burning into him, willing him to reply. Willing him to tell her it was going to be OK. That everything was all right because they had each other and because he loved her and he would somehow repair things.

But he said nothing.

'I need to leave,' she said. Her stomach turned over at the sound of her words. 'I can't be here.'

'What do you mean?'

She began to chew on her lip, unsure what was unfurling, unsure if she believed the words that hovered on the tip of her tongue. 'I need to leave,' she repeated. And as the reality of what was happening took root, she felt another stab of pain in her stomach. She walked past him, unsteadily, then out of the kitchen and back to their bedroom. He appeared in the doorway and watched silently as she bent to pull a suitcase from beneath the bed and gathered clothes which she rammed into it.

'Where are you going?'

'I'm going to work then I'll stay with Sophie tonight.' She went into the bathroom and filled a wash bag with the things she would need. 'I need some space to think,' she said, as she came back into the bedroom. 'And I can't do that here.'

'You can't leave. This is crazy.'

'Stop it, Will!' She turned to face him, hands on her hips. 'Did you not listen to a word I just said? It isn't crazy. You hurt me more than I can say. If our marriage has a chance in hell of surviving I need some time away from you to think clearly.'

He walked up to her, grabbed her upper arms and held her firmly, almost too hard. 'Don't do this.'

She noticed his eyes prickling with a suggestion of tears and her stomach clenched. Will didn't cry. He'd told her once he'd given up crying when he was a child; he said crying only made things worse and was a luxury he'd learned to live without.

'Don't do this,' he said again.

'I haven't done this,' she whispered. 'You have.'

She watched his expression change from distress to panic. His eyes grew wide, darting back and forth over her face.

'I need space and you do too,' she said. 'Maybe you should go and see your mum.'

'My mum? What's my mum got to do with this?'

Harmony growled with frustration as she angrily zipped up the suitcase. 'I don't know! I just know that you're not doing the right thing by those of us you're supposed to love.'

Harmony found it impossible to concentrate on work. The words swam on her screen as she read or wrote. Her thoughts kept drifting back to Will, her mind on a roller coaster as she tried to clarify her thoughts and feelings. She lifted the phone and dialled her sister.

'What's wrong?' her sister asked, as soon as Harmony had said hello.

'I'll explain later,' she said, glancing up as a couple of colleagues walked past her desk, deep in conversation. 'Can I stay at yours tonight?'

'Of course you can. You sound awful. Do you want me to come and get you? Are you at work?'

Harmony's eyes welled. She dried her tears on the back of her sleeve. 'Thanks, but I've got stuff I need to do here.'

'You sure?'

'Mm-hmm.' Though Harmony wasn't sure at all. She would give anything to be with her sister right now.

'OK. I'll see you later. I love you.'

When the clock finally hit six Harmony walked down to South Kensington tube station, battling through the crowds of commuters and camera-toting tourists with her case. The tube was hot and stuffy. Her head pounded. She reached into her bag for her bottle of water. The woman in front of her glared at her suitcase and muttered under her breath. Harmony closed her eyes. She hated the underground, especially in the summer, crammed shoulder to shoulder with sweaty, tired bodies, sticky skin brushing sticky skin.

Harmony wondered if she was making a mistake. Should she be going home to talk to him? Was going to Sophie's just shoving her head in the sand? She thought of Will as she'd left him that morning, standing on the steps of their block of flats, hands in pockets, grim acceptance written on his face as he watched her leave.

When Sophie opened the door of her sprawling Wandsworth home she wrapped Harmony in a tight embrace before leading her through to the kitchen. It was reassuringly chaotic, with discarded school bags and gym kits scattering the floor, shoes kicked off, piles of homework littering the dining table, a pan bubbling away on the hob and the noise of the boys playing football in the garden.

'It's nice to be here,' Harmony said. 'I've missed you all. I'll only be a here a night or two.'

'Stay as long as you want.' Sophie crossed the room towards the fridge. 'Wine?'

Harmony nodded and her sister opened the fridge and pulled out a bottle half-full of white wine, cork pushed into the top. Harmony got two glasses out of the pine dresser that had belonged to their nan. The sight of it reminded her of happier times, before their mum died, when they'd visit their grandmother's house and the four of them ate Sunday tea together, the smell of old wood and furniture polish wafting out of the cupboard when they were asked to lay the table. Sophie sat down, tucking one leg underneath her. She wore tight-fitting jeans that hugged her long lean legs and a smart blue polo neck high against her chin, her mousy-blonde hair tied up in a loose bun, a few wisps loose and falling over her face.

Sophie leant forward and rested her hand on Harmony's. 'So what's happened?'

Ever since Harmony could remember, Sophie had been like a mother to her. She'd tried so hard to ease her grief and, even now, just being near her was comforting. After their mother's funeral, when they moved from their flat on the outskirts of Reading to their nan's terraced house in a small village south of Leeds, Harmony lost everyone and everything she knew almost overnight. Sophie became parent, sister, friend and carer, all rolled into one. It was Sophie who'd borne the brunt of their mother's long-drawn-out illness, looking after her while she recovered from her bouts of chemo, and then, in those final long months, when she was unable to do anything for herself, it was Sophie who cooked and cleaned for them, who made sure Harmony did her homework and ate breakfast and left for school in clean uniform. Their nan had been of little help; she was elderly and irascible, needed care herself, and this, too, had fallen on Sophie's shoulders. It was Sophie's grit and strength that had held them all together.

'I don't even know where to begin.' A couple of tears tumbled down Harmony's cheeks. She laughed helplessly. 'I'm a mess.'

'Sweetheart,' Sophie said, squeezing and rubbing her sister's hand. 'You've been through such a traumatic thing. Losing a baby is incredibly hard. It takes time to get over something like that.'

'He had a vasectomy. Without telling me.'

'He did *what*?'

Harmony dried her eyes with the edge of her sleeve and nodded.

'And you didn't know about it?'

Harmony shook her head.

'Jesus.'

There was a noise from the hob and they both turned to see the pan boiling over, water sizzling as it hit the gas flames.

'Shit,' cried Sophie. 'The pasta.' She jumped up and ran to the hob, snatching the pan off the heat. She took the colander and drained the boiling water off. Harmony watched her sister open a cupboard above her head and rummage around amongst the chaos within for a jar of pasta sauce. She opened it, spooned some into the saucepan, then tipped the steaming pasta back in. Then she abandoned the pan on the side and came back to the table.

'Why the hell did he do it?'

Harmony shrugged. 'He's always said he didn't want to have children.'

'Yes,' Sophie said with forced patience. 'I get he doesn't want kids. You explained that to me when you got together – some dead, half-drunk poet told him not to or something ridiculous – but what I'm struggling with is why on earth he got himself done without discussing it. What was he thinking?'

Harmony had a flare of loyalty for her husband, as she often did when her sister was quick to pass judgement on him. 'I don't think he was thinking rationally. He said he panicked when I got pregnant and didn't want to risk it happening again.'

'I never really understood his fear. He's always been amazing with the boys, even when they were babies. And, anyway, you told me he was excited about having a child of his own.'

Harmony shook her head. 'I thought he was.' She recalled all the times she'd watched him with her nephews, seen how happy and at ease he was, wondering if maybe he'd changed his mind. 'He loves your boys,' she said, tracing her finger around the rim of her glass. 'But you have no idea how many times he's told me that when he sees them with Roger he feels inadequate. He was adamant he'd be a dreadful parent and nothing I said could convince him otherwise.'

'He can join ninety-nine per cent of all other parents in the world then. We're all dreadful. You just get on with it as best you can. And he's silly to feel inadequate around Roger. Roger's totally crap most of the time, he just puts on a show when there are people around.'

'Roger's a wonderful dad and you know it.' Harmony drank some wine. 'I hate how Will doubts himself like he does. Not just parenting but with everything. It frustrates me so much. I blame his father.' She shook her head. 'That arsehole has a lot to answer for.'

Just then they heard angry shouts from the garden. Harmony looked out of the window and saw two of her nephews rolling around on the grass exchanging hefty punches.

Sophie tutted. 'The monsters need feeding. Let me get the pasta inside them and then we'll talk. Help yourself to more wine.' She went to the back door and called her sons in.

Harmony smiled as they piled in through the door and ran to their mother like starving animals. 'Did you say hello to Harmony?' Sophie said.

The boys looked over at her and all three grinned. Cal came over to hug her.

'Hey, Cal. How's things?' she said, wrapping her arms around her oldest nephew. He was now half a foot taller than her and had filled out since she last saw him. Harmony patted his bicep. 'Been working out?'

Cal flushed pink and shook his head.

'He has!' screamed George, who leant against Harmony by way of a hello.

His older brother shoved him hard. 'Shut up, dickhead.'

'Language,' warned Sophie.

Harmony kissed the top of George's head, then smiled at Matt, who'd made it over to her at his own laid-back pace. He gave her a hug too and whispered in her ear. 'He has been working out. Every day before breakfast. Doing dumbbells in his room.'

'It's because he's got a *girl*friend!' sang George.

Cal lunged for his little brother but missed him, instead sending a pile of books tumbling off the table and causing George to erupt into loud giggles. Cal chased him around the kitchen island and punched him in the arm. George screamed as if he'd been stabbed.

Ignoring them completely, Sophie expertly manoeuvred around them to get plates out of the cupboard and cutlery out of the drawer. 'Do us a favour and take your dinner next door,' she said, stabbing a fork unceremoniously into each mound of pasta. She pulled open a bag of ready-grated cheese and dumped a handful on each.

Harmony watched as Sophie busied about, calm amid the chaos, systematically sorting out the things they needed: ketchup, water, a few slices of cucumber. All three boys jostled and pushed and fought, and finally, loaded up with food, they went through to the playroom. A few seconds later the television switched on and it was quiet again.

'It's like a tornado blowing through,' Harmony said with a laugh. 'Can you imagine what Mum would have said if she saw the chaos here?'

Sophie laughed and grabbed a bag of crisps and a bowl. 'She was lucky. She had two neat and tidy daughters. I have three apes who aren't even house-trained.' She put the bowl of crisps on the table between them and sat down.

Harmony rubbed at a felt-tip pen mark on the table. 'I'm so angry with him, Sophie. I'm so angry I can't even look at him.'

'That's natural. Anyone would be angry in the same situation. It would be odd if you weren't.'

'Do you think my marriage is over?' Harmony asked quietly, looking up at her older sister.

'Only you and Will can decide that.' Sophie stroked her hand. 'But one thing's for sure – whatever he's done, whatever his failings – he hasn't done any of it because he doesn't love you.'

'Mum loved Dad but that wasn't enough to keep them together.'

'That was different,' Sophie said, removing her hand and stiffening. 'Our father was a bastard.'

Harmony was used to the vitriol Sophie directed at their father. She'd never heard a fond word for him from her sister's lips. 'Are you sure he was such a bastard? I mean, now you're married yourself, do you think there was a side to his story that might explain him leaving like he did?'

Sophie narrowed her eyes. 'Yes, I'm sure he was a bastard. And you know what? Now I'm married and have the boys I hate him even more. It makes him leaving even harder to understand. I can't imagine walking out on my children. I can't imagine wanting to live my life without them.'

Harmony looked down at the table.

'Oh, God, I'm sorry,' Sophie said. 'That was incredibly insensitive. I didn't mean—'

'It's never going to happen, is it?' Harmony covered her face with her hands. 'I'm never going to know what that feels like. How could he do this? I feel like I don't even know him.'

CHAPTER TWELVE

Will couldn't find the photograph he was looking for. He searched the living room, behind the chest, under the sofa. He was like a dog who'd lost the scent of its prey – fixated, growing more and more agitated as he searched. It was one of his favourites, taken on their wedding night on one of the small disposable cameras they'd left on the tables for their friends and family. When they'd had the films developed, most of the photos were out of focus, off-centre shots of drunk friends gurning at them with over-exposed ghostly skin and demonic red eyes. And then there was the picture of Harmony. He'd taken it in their hotel room right after they made love. They were laughing about something, he couldn't remember what, and he'd reached for one of the disposables that had come back with a bag of bits and pieces from the reception and pointed it at her. She'd complained, put her hands over her face to hide herself, and just as she lowered them he took the shot. Then he threw the camera back on the floor, laughed and kissed her neck.

'I love you, Mrs English.'

'Mrs English?' She made a face. 'God, that makes me sound like your mother!'

Grainy and a little out of focus, the picture was perfection, her eyes vague with wine and tiredness and sex, her hair mussed up, mascara smudged, love and lust for him pouring out of her. There was a decadence about it, a raw sexuality, that stirred him each time he looked at it.

The flat was dark and lonely without her. He sat on the sofa and stared ahead at the mantelpiece, their paraphernalia strewn over it, the postcard bunting inappropriately cheerful. He felt as if he'd been scooped out, emptied, left hollow to his core. He closed his eyes to rest his mind but as soon as he did so Luke was there. Glaring memories of that fateful afternoon invading his mind – the last afternoon they'd spent together before Luke was sent away – the damp blanket of leaves beneath their feet, the sun's last light breaking through the canopy above. Then Alastair Farrow's face as he and his friends stumbled upon them. His eyes burning with intent. The sense of dread that grew as Will realised they were in trouble. He saw the boys who stood with Farrow, fists clenched at their sides.

Will opened his eyes and shook his head to banish the memory then walked down to the kitchen. He opened the fridge door, leaning on it as he stared at the contents. There was a large chunk of cheddar that he'd bought from the deli counter in Sainsbury's for the supper with Luke. He cut himself a chunk of it, spooned some wholegrain mustard onto the plate, and poured himself a small glass of wine from the corked bottle on the sideboard. As he watched the wine fill the glass he thought of Farrow again. What was it Luke had said? He'd found him on Facebook. A wife and two children. An accountant. Will couldn't imagine him grown up, with a life, somewhere out there, going about his day-to-day business like a normal human being. Will needed to see his face. Farrow wasn't going to leave him alone. Seeing Luke had brought him back to haunt him.

Will took his supper through to the study and waited for the computer to heave itself into life. When it did, he brought up Facebook. He logged on, closing his eyes to help him remember his password. He rarely used the site. Frank had set it up for him, horrified he didn't use social media – a 'dinosaur', he'd called him. Will had seven Facebook friends; one was Frank and another was Harmony, who was no better than Will when it came to using it, though her aversion was on principle rather than technophobia. Will had three attempts at the password before finally getting it right. He took a deep breath and typed *Alastair Farrow* into the search box. Eleven faces appeared. Will cast his eyes over the list and halfway down, his heart skipped a beat.

There he was.

Alastair Farrow.

He'd put on a lot of weight and lost some of his hair, but Will would recognise him anywhere. He clicked on the entry and Alastair Farrow filled the screen. No privacy settings had been used, and his whole life was on view: photos, comments, personal information.

Alastair Farrow. Born 1968. Lives in Surrey. School: Pendower Hall. Married. Works at Hammerson Frith Accountancy.

Will clicked on a photo album. Holiday snaps, taken somewhere in the Mediterranean, Will guessed. He was with his children, or at least Will assumed they were his children. The first photo showed him in a swimming pool, a young girl with dimpled knees on his shoulders. Next to him was a boy, a few years older, with chocolate ice cream all over his face holding hands with a woman with a toothy smile and an ill-fitting bikini. The next picture showed Farrow and his wife raising orange cocktails overladen with colourful paper umbrellas and slices of pineapple towards the photographer. They were sunburnt, the light reflecting off their reddened faces to give their tight-looking skin a polished sheen. Will stared at the faint scar that ran from Farrow's cheekbone to his jaw. He felt sick as he heard the blood-curdling scream echo in his head. He wondered what story he'd told his wife to explain it. He'd bet all the money in the world he hadn't told her the truth.

Will tore his eyes off the scar and began to read Farrow's timeline, the vacuous everyday status updates of a normal man, with a normal family, and a normal life.

Kids and wife badgering me to get a dog. I don't want a dog. Will they settle for a goldfish instead?

Rugby with the lads on Sunday. COME ON YOUU BASTARDS! Bring it on!!!

Son turned five. Party on Saturday with twenty kids and a bouncy castle in the garden. A&E expect a visit!

And so it went on.

Will drained his wine then spent the next few hours poring over Alastair Farrow's albums, reading about his wife, opening the pictures of each of his friends, reading their details, piecing together his life. It was all so anodyne, so conventional. Over the years Will had pictured Farrow as a towering demon, a ten-foot nemesis, the epitome of evil, but here he was, a pudgy balding father of two, with a jolly wife and a modest home with a neat front garden in suburban Surrey.

Will moved his cursor over the *Add Friend* button and hovered there.

'No,' he said aloud, his voice stark against the stillness of the study. 'Don't.'

But then, as if someone had moved his finger for him, he clicked. *Friend Request Sent.*

'Bloody hell,' said Will, as he sat back and rubbed his face. 'Why did you do that?'

Will sat in the dead silence and closed his eyes. He saw the silhouette of Alastair Farrow's face burnt onto the back of his eyelids, a ghostly retinal scar. He opened his eyes quickly then leant forward and turned the computer off. As he did so, his mobile rang, piercing the silence and making him jump. He snatched it up.

'Harmony?' he said urgently.

'No. No, it's not Harmony, William. It's Frank.'

Will's heart sank. 'Hi, Frank. Is everything OK?'

'Um, well, that's the thing,' said Frank, his voice shaky and faint. 'I don't think it is. You see, Eric's away, being important at a writer's retreat or something, and . . .' He broke off and Will heard him take a steadying breath. 'Well, it's Pinwheel. He's had a little accident . . .' He didn't finish his sentence.

'Do you need me to come over and help?'

'I don't want to put you to any trouble,' said Frank, so quietly Will could barely hear him. 'But the poor darling is in a bit of a state, and I, well, I think he needs a vet. It's his leg. Oh dear, I'm not very good at coping with things like this.'

'I'm on my way,' said Will. 'Sit tight. I'll be as quick as I can.'

Will grabbed his keys from the hook by the door and went out to the car. Frank and Eric lived in Chiswick, about fifteen minutes away without traffic, in a pretty mews house with lilac-painted woodwork. When Will pulled up outside he saw Frank, hovering anxiously on the doorstep, pale-faced and jittery.

'I'm so pleased to see you,' Frank said, as Will got out of the car. 'He looks very poorly. I'm so sorry to drag you out.'

Will's heart went out to him. 'Don't be silly. Harmony's out tonight. I wasn't busy. Let's have a look at him, eh?'

'Yes, yes, thank you. I'd appreciate that,' he said, with a slight hesitation. 'The vet has an out-of-hours surgery. I should probably have called a taxi and gone straight there rather than bother you.' Frank smiled weakly at him.

'It's no bother at all. Now where's the patient?'

Will followed Frank as he walked slowly into the kitchen. 'Eric normally deals with this sort of thing. He's absolutely super in traumatic situations. He knows just what to do and has this amazing sense of calm about him. I get in all of a dither. I hope my boy is going to be all right. He seems terribly quiet.'

Frank led Will to where Pinwheel lay wrapped in a soft blue towel on a cushion on the kitchen table. The cat's eyes were open but he wasn't moving. At first, Will thought he might not be alive, but as he bent close he heard his laboured breathing.

'He was on the side of the road,' whispered Frank. 'I was calling him in for his tea, but he didn't come and that was a warning sign. He's usually there when he hears me open the door; he's terribly greedy, you see.' Frank had one hand against his mouth and he nibbled on his thumbnail as he spoke. 'He couldn't get to me, because, well, he's hurt his leg.'

Will lifted the edge of the towel and winced. One of his hind legs was badly broken, blood and dirt matted its fur. He laid the towel back on the cat and gently ran his fingers over his head. Pinwheel blinked slowly.

'Poor thing,' Will said under his breath. 'Let's get you to a vet, shall we?'

Will carefully picked Pinwheel up. The cat mewed and his small body tensed. 'It's OK, sweetheart. We're taking you to the vet. You'll feel better in a bit.' Then Will looked at Frank. 'You'll be able to phone the vet and tell them we're coming in while I drive?'

Frank nodded.

Frank directed Will to the vet's surgery, but other than that they didn't talk. Will glanced over every now and then to see Frank cradling Pinwheel like a baby, his eyes shining with a film of tears, bending to plant little kisses on the top of his head. He parked at the back of the surgery in the small, scruffy car park filled with rubbish and overflowing wheelie bins, and aggressive signs threatening clamping for unauthorised cars.

A young girl answered the door when they rang. 'Is this Pinwheel?' she asked.

Will nodded. 'We think he's been hit by a car.'

'Take a seat.' She gestured to some wooden chairs in the window. 'Stephanie will be with you in a minute.'

They sat and waited in the reception area. It was quiet and still and smelt of animals and surgical spirit. The shelves were crammed with sacks of pet food, plastic animal toys, leads and collars and muzzles, and the noticeboard was pinned with photographs of past patients who'd made fabulous recoveries and a large information poster on the life cycle of fleas. Will looked at Pinwheel; his eyes were closed but he was still breathing.

'Would you like to bring Pinwheel through?' said the vet as she came into the waiting room.

Will stood but Frank didn't move.

'Come on, Frank,' Will said gently.

As soon as the vet looked at Pinwheel, Will knew it was serious. She was quiet as she checked him over, her face betraying no sign of either hope or despair. Frank was white throughout. Will put his arm around him and gave him bolstering squeezes. When the vet had finished examining him she smiled kindly at Frank.

'I'm afraid the leg isn't looking good. I'm going to keep him in and do some X-rays. I won't know for sure until we've seen inside, but I'm almost certain we'll need to amputate if he's to make it.'

Frank's eyes welled with tears. 'I just want you to do anything you can to save him.' The pain in Frank's voice cut right through Will.

The vet nodded and smiled. She explained that Frank should call in the morning.

'Can't I stay?' he asked quietly.

'You should go home and get some rest. You can call first thing and we'll give you an update.'

Frank nodded and leant close to Pinwheel, pushing his face into the cat's fur, and whispering words Will couldn't hear. A few moments later he lifted his head and looked at the vet and nodded.

'Come on then,' Will said gently. 'I'll take you home.'

On the drive back, Frank stared out of the window, his face stitched up with worry. Will pulled up outside the house and turned the engine off and for a moment they sat in the stillness of the car.

'Have you ever had a pet, William?' Frank's voice was distant, lost in his worry.

Will didn't answer straight away. It was something he'd never talked about, not even with Harmony. 'A long time ago,' he said. 'A cat. But I didn't have her for long.'

'They burrow right into your heart, don't they?'

Will stared at his hands on the steering wheel. He had a flash of the kitten's face looking up at him and his stomach knotted. He'd found her in a disused farm building amongst some rotten straw bales. He'd been out with his camera and heard her faint mewing. He'd followed the noise and discovered her behind the bales, her tiny paws pressed neatly together, big blue eyes looking up at him. When he gingerly reached down and stroked her soft head she started to purr immediately. He remembered how he'd laughed as she batted his fingers and pounced on his shoelace when he waggled it on the ground like a snake for her. He'd looked for her mother but there was no sign. There was no way he was leaving her there alone – she was far too small and helpless and fluffy – so he tucked her into his jacket and took her home.

His father loathed animals and couldn't fathom why anybody would have one in the house. But a few days earlier his mother had been muttering about mice in the pantry, and his father had hated vermin more than any other creature, so as he walked home he practised his sales pitch: a cat was perfect for keeping mice away. Never in a million years did he expect his father to agree.

'She can stay?' he said, his voice shaking with the thrill of it.

'In the shed. If I see her in the house then there'll be hell to pay.'

'But what if—'

'If you argue, I'll change my mind and she'll be at the bottom of a bucket of water.'

His mother found a cardboard box and Will cut the front out so it looked like a basket and they lined it with a couple of old towels. Will named her Socks because of her little white feet and she was the best thing that ever happened to him. She would wait for him by the garden gate if he went out and as soon as she saw him she'd scamper up and wrap herself around his legs, purring like an engine.

But then things went wrong. The early days of the January after he found her were so bitterly cold the river froze over. After supper, he'd run out to the shed to say goodnight to Socks. She was curled up tightly in the corner of the box. Usually she would get up to greet him, but she stayed curled into a ball, her eyes flicking upwards at him, a single mew the only noise she made. It was arctic in the shed. Swirls of thick frost coated the inside of the window pane and the water in her bowl had turned to solid ice. When he breathed, plumes of vapour hung in clouds in the damp, stale air.

'It's too cold for you, isn't it? Don't worry, I'm here now.'

He picked her up, then hesitated – his father would hit the roof if he found her in the house. But then he caught sight of the frozen water in her bowl and without giving it another consideration, he tucked her under his jumper and walked back to the house where his mother had joined his father in front of the television.

'I'm quite tired,' he said, as he walked past the living room. 'I'm going to go up to bed. Goodnight.' Then he went up the stairs, keeping his eyes to the floor, praying his father wouldn't notice anything unusual. Once inside his bedroom, he closed the door.

'Right, you,' Will said, lifting his jumper up and putting Socks on his bed. 'Not a peep, OK? You can sleep under my duvet tonight. It'll be like a den for you. You'll be toasty warm.'

He stroked her head and she stood up on her hind legs to meet his hand, purring, and rubbing her nose and cheek against him. He undressed, put his pyjamas on, then, needing to use the bathroom, he opened the door to his room. He jumped out of his skin to see his father standing outside it. He pulled the door shut behind him and, keeping his hands on the door knob, looked up at him. His father blinked slowly and stared, his mouth twitching at the sides.

'Is everything all right?' Will asked, trying to keep his voice light.

'What are you hiding?'

'Nothing.' He dropped his hands from the door handle. 'I'm just going to clean my teeth and then I'm going to bed. I'm not feeling very well.'

'You're hiding something, William. Don't you lie to me. If you lie it will only make things worse.'

Will swallowed, his stomach churning. What should he do? Lie? Or tell the truth? If he lied, and his father subsequently discovered Socks, he'd turn apoplectic. 'My cat,' he stammered. 'She was so cold. I bought her in to warm her up.'

His father stared at him as if he was speaking a foreign language.

'Her water was frozen solid.'

Then without a word his father pushed past him and opened the door. Will ducked in front of him, putting himself between his father and the cat, who was sitting on the bed, licking her paw and cleaning herself.

His father turned fiery eyes on Will. 'What the hell is that animal doing up here?'

'She was cold!' Will stood in front of his father and opened his arms wide to protect her, but his father pushed him aside and grabbed Socks by the scruff of her neck. He held her up, pushed her towards Will's face aggressively. She squirmed in his grasp.

'I will ask again. What is this animal doing in my house?'

Will tried to speak but his voice failed him.

'Answer me, you idiot! I asked you a bloody question!'

Will watched his father's hand slowly squeeze the cat. Socks screeched.

'Stop it!' Will shouted. 'You're hurting her. It was freezing in the shed! I didn't want her to be cold. Please stop. You're hurting her.'

'You shouldn't have brought it in!'

His mother appeared at the door. 'Philip?' Will watched her face take in the scene, shock replaced by a calm intake of breath.

'I told him not to bring this bag of fleas into my house!' With each word his father shook the cat, who writhed in his hands, the whites of her eyes showing.

'I'm sorry! I didn't—'

'It's all right.' His mother interrupted Will's pleading. 'William's sorry.'

Will looked at her in panic and she widened her eyes, trying to communicate, nodding with purpose. 'Aren't you, William?' She continued to nod at him slowly. 'You're sorry and you'll take the cat back to the shed straight away.'

Will shook his head. 'But it's too—'

'Won't you, William?' Her voice barked with a level of sharpness he seldom heard. She stared hard at him, willing him to take her lead. 'We all know it's best that cats live outside.'

Will glanced at his father. Thankfully, he'd finally stopped shaking Socks, who now hung in his grip like a rag doll.

'I'm sorry,' Will whispered. 'I shouldn't have brought her in. Please, *please* don't hurt her.'

His mother walked over to his father and held her hands out. 'I'll take the cat, Philip.'

'It needs to go. First thing tomorrow. If not – if I find out it's here – I swear to God, I'll put it in a bag and drown the thing.'

His father pushed Socks towards his mother, who took hold of her and cradled her gently, thumb stroking the soft fur behind her ear.

'Get rid of it.'

As soon as his father had left the room, Will looked at his

mother and pleaded with her. 'Please don't let him send her away. I love her.'

'Then you should have left her in the shed.'

'But—'

'There are no buts, Will. If she stays, he'll drown her. He wasn't joking. Do you want that?'

Will didn't answer, instead he stared at Socks, who had started to purr, eyes closed, chin tilted up as his mother stroked her.

'Where will you take her?'

'There's an animal shelter in Peterborough. Someone will give her a new home.'

'They won't love her like I do.'

'Maybe not. But at least she'll be safe.' She turned away then and as she did so he saw she was crying.

It was the first time he'd ever seen her cry.

Will got out of the car and walked around to the passenger side to open the door for Frank. 'Do you want me to sleep on the sofa tonight, Frank? I'm more than happy to.'

'Bless you. I'm fine, though. I've got Pie to look after me.'

While Frank got ready for bed, Will heated some milk in a pan and made hot chocolate. He carried it upstairs and found Frank already in bed with Pie curled up and purring beside him.

'Do you think he'll be OK?' Frank asked.

'Yes,' Will said gently, unsure if he should answer with such certainty when in all honesty he had no idea at all if Pinwheel was going to be all right. He placed the mug on the table beside the bed. 'I think he'll be fine. Probably being spoilt rotten by all those lovely veterinary nurses.'

Frank smiled gratefully and gently ran his hand along Pie's back. The cat stretched his paws out in front of him and yawned happily. 'Thank you, William. I'm in your debt.'

'Of course you're not. It was nothing.'

'It wasn't nothing. You were there for me tonight. I couldn't have done that on my own.'

Will smiled. 'You can call on me any time. Now try and get some sleep.'

As Will drove home he battled those memories of his father. Painful images of him shaking Socks. His cold and glassy eyes when he said he'd drown her. Will had never got over how close Socks had come to being killed and it was his fault. He'd known full well his father would go mad yet he still brought the cat inside. He made the wrong decision and it nearly cost her life.

The memory was a timely reminder; nothing was safe in his care. Not a cat and certainly not a child.

CHAPTER THIRTEEN

Harmony watched the clock limp around to six to signal the end of another unproductive day. She leant forward and wearily turned off her computer then packed her papers into her bag in the vain hope she'd manage to get some work done later. Will hadn't called since Tuesday evening. Before then he'd been calling every few hours. In the end she'd texted to ask him to give her a bit of space. She'd hesitated before sending it; she knew she couldn't hide forever, but she was still so hurt, and struggling with fresh feelings of loss. She felt utterly betrayed by him.

'See you tomorrow, Alice,' she said to the department PA, who was cleaning her gold-rimmed glasses on the sleeve of her cardigan.

'Will do. You make sure you try and get an early night tonight.' She smiled kindly. 'You look shattered.'

It wasn't any wonder she looked shattered. She was currently trying to sleep in George's begrudgingly vacated bed, surrounded by Lego constructions and *Star Wars* figures, which was nearly impossible with her mind racing the way it was. She couldn't stay at Sophie's for much longer.

She had to face Will.

As she walked down the stairwell and into the building's reception area, she saw a man sitting on the sofa in the entrance lobby, reading a newspaper. As she neared him, he lowered the paper and smiled at her. Her heart skipped a beat.

It was Luke.

'Oh my God, hello,' she said, unable to conceal her surprise.

He stood up, still smiling broadly.

There was an awkward few moments during which she wondered if they were supposed to kiss or shake hands end she did neither.

'What are you doing here?'

'I had a meeting in Knightsbridge that finished early and it's too late to go back to the office now, so I thought I'd pop in and say hello.' He paused then smiled again. 'It's nice to see you.'

She blushed and glanced at the man behind the reception desk, who seemed oblivious to their exchange. 'It's nice to see you too.' She furrowed her brow. 'How did you know where I work?'

'You told me. At lunch.'

'Did I? I don't recall. But how did you know I was here today? Sometimes I work from home or have meetings off-site.'

'Well, I decided to pop in on the off-chance. Then I asked this gentleman if you were in today and he rang up to your office and was told you were just leaving,' he said with wry amusement. 'It's no more sinister that that; you don't have to look so worried. The cab drove past Imperial on my way to the meeting and I remembered you worked opposite and thought it might be nice to go for a drink.'

She tried to smile.

'So do you have to race home or can I steal you for a quick drink?'

'I should get back.'

He leant closer to her. 'I'd like you to come.'

She caught the smell of him, shampoo and a hint of aftershave, an unfamiliar washing powder, and her pulse quickened.

'And it's Friday tomorrow. Nearly the weekend. An after-work drink to celebrate?'

'I'm staying at my sister's. She's expecting me back.'

'Your sister's?'

Harmony didn't say anything.

'Look, I'm here now. Just a quick drink? I'd like to talk about Will. He seemed uneasy when I came for supper. It would be good to have your take on why.'

She hesitated and looked at her watch. It was ten past six; it would be chaos at Sophie's when she got there; the boys would be midway through eating, they'd be fighting, the television would be blaring, then Sophie would be battling to get them to do their homework, shouting as all three did their best to avoid doing it.

Luke saw her indecision and seemed to take that as a yes. 'Good,' he said. 'There's a great restaurant a few minutes' walk away. It's smart but very laid back. You'll like it.'

'You said a drink, not dinner.'

Luke laughed. 'I did.' He smiled and gestured for her to walk in front of him.

What are you doing? demanded the voice in her head as she followed him down the steps and onto Exhibition Road. *Go back to Sophie's, ring Will, sort your life out.*

But she ignored the voice and walked with him. They didn't talk. She was conscious of him glancing at her a couple of times. She wondered if the people they passed assumed they were together as he guided her through the crowds, close beside her, every now and then touching her shoulder. She turned to give him a casual, friendly smile to reassure herself she was doing nothing wrong. Just a drink with a friend of Will's. Someone, perhaps, who could shed some light on his hang-ups and secrecy. Luke nodded and smiled back. A simple, easy smile. Nothing untoward at all.

'Here we are,' said Luke. The restaurant was on a side street and had a few tables set out on the pavement. Each table held a menu, a glass bottle of golden olive oil, and a small white bowl of sea salt.

Luke held open the door and allowed her to walk into the restaurant first. She knew of the place, but she had never been before. It was expensive – the haunt of minor celebrities, MPs and glamorous trust-fund-confident twenty-somethings – not for people like her. A waiter with jet-black hair and doleful eyes welcomed them, nodding his head in exaggerated hospitality, his greeting almost unintelligible beneath a thick Spanish accent.

The main restaurant was dark and cosy but steps at the far end led down to an airy conservatory-style bar area. The walls were covered in murals of curling vegetation and oversized flowers and exotic birds. Harmony was a button in a box of nails beside the animated men and women, talking and laughing, dressed in expensive clothes with glistening hair, a world away from her knee-length black skirt and ponytail secured neatly at the nape of her neck and make-up free face. The opulence unsettled her. She felt both insignificant and insecure. Though she and Will were more than comfortably off, and she was used to hanging out with Emma and Ian, wealth was still a foreign country to her. Somewhere to visit but not home. Before her mum died they'd lived in a cramped second-floor flat on the Park Green estate in Reading. Her abiding memory of the place was the threadbare carpet with its garish seventies pattern of black flowers on a red background. When their mother became too weak to get out of bed, she'd occasionally ask them to 'tidy the carpet', and the two girls would get down on their hands and knees and colour in any new patches of wear with black felt-tip pens.

'I don't see why we have to do this,' Harmony once grumbled, as she lay flat on her tummy, legs kicked up behind her, searching for hessian strands to blacken. 'I mean, it's not as if anyone ever comes to visit. You'd think Princess Whatshername was coming for tea.'

'Di,' her sister said, as she concentrated on colouring.

'Yes, her. Princess Di. She's not coming though. Nobody comes. Only the nurse and I don't think she'd care about the carpet.'

'Mum's *dying*, Harmony. She wants lots of things, like soup instead of beans on toast and three sugars in her tea. If she wants the carpet coloured in then that's what we'll do.' She pointed at the floor beneath Harmony's elbow. 'You missed a bit.'

'Table for two?' the waiter asked Luke in his Spanish lilt.

'We're not eating,' Luke said. 'We've just come for a drink.'

'Certainly, sir. Would you like to sit at the bar?' He gestured to the other side of the room where there was a dark wood bar with mirrors behind and a row of empty leather stools.

Harmony asked the barman what white wines he had by the glass. He recommended a white Rioja with enthusiasm. She thought of Will, who wasn't fond of Spanish whites.

'That sounds lovely.'

'And I'll have a beer,' Luke said.

They were quiet as the barman prepared their drinks. Harmony shifted in her seat, glancing up at Luke to give an embarrassed smile as she tried to think of something to talk about. The barman put their drinks and a dish of almonds on the bar in front of them.

'Thank you,' Luke said. Then he lifted his drink to her. 'Cheers.'

Harmony clinked her glass against his. She noticed how long and slim his fingers were, his nails cut short and clean. They reminded her of her father's fingers, or at least how her mother had described her father's fingers – long and graceful like those of a concert pianist.

'Your dad had the most beautiful hands,' she heard her mother's voice saying.

Luke smiled at her, his eyes burning through her to the point where she had to look away. As she did so, she noticed the woman on a table nearby staring at Luke while the man she was with stared at his newspaper. When she realised Harmony was looking she glanced away, the skin on the back of her neck reddening as she stirred her drink.

'So are you and Will OK?' he said, taking a small handful of almonds.

'Will and I?'

He nodded and put an almond in his mouth.

'Yes,' she said, trying to keep her voice light. 'Yes, of course. Why do you ask?'

'Things were strained the other night, and just now you said you're staying at your sister's. There's also something about you today. You seem . . .' He hesitated. 'Sad.'

Harmony was aware of her body tensing. She lifted her chin and shifted her weight on the stool. 'That doesn't mean there's anything wrong with us. I'm staying with my sister for a few days; we're close and I haven't seen her for ages.'

'I see. I've drawn the wrong conclusions. Forgive me.'

She was about to agree but something stopped her. She sighed. Maybe it would help to talk to this man. What did she have to lose? 'No, you're right.' She picked at the edge of the scallop-edged drinks mat that sat beneath her wine glass. 'We're having problems. It's been a difficult six months.' She paused, glancing up at him. 'I was pregnant, but we lost the baby. It's hard to deal with for both of us for different reasons.'

'I'm sorry,' he said. 'Losing a child is devastating, sadly I know what it feels like.'

'You do?'

His expression closed down, clearly not wanting to explain further. 'You and Will must be going through all sorts of emotions.'

A lump rose in her throat as she tried to push back the memory of Will saying he was relieved when their baby died. She dropped her eyes.

He touched her knee lightly. 'Hey, it's OK. Let's not talk about this. It's painful for both of us. Let's talk about you, instead. You fascinate me.'

'Me?'

'I can't stop thinking about you.'

Harmony looked over her shoulder, conscious they could be overheard. 'Luke, I don't—'

'Do you ever get the feeling you're supposed to be with someone? That it's an imperative?' He leant forward so his face was only a few inches from hers. 'Because that's how I feel about you. I can't get you out of my head.' His eyes dug into her. 'I want to know what it feels like to fuck you.'

Harmony felt as if he'd shot her with his words.

She drew back from him, her heart pounding. Was he joking? Surely he was. But the look on his face was deadly serious. She was overwhelmed by the need to escape; any comfort she'd felt in his company had evaporated.

'You can't say that,' she managed to say. 'I'm married.' She glanced again at the woman who'd been staring at Luke, but she was now occupied with her phone, the man she was with still absorbed by his paper. Harmony reached down for her bag. 'You told me you wanted a drink.' Her voice was shaky.

'I wasn't being entirely truthful.'

'I'm married.'

'But not happily.'

'We are happy.'

'You literally just told me you're not.'

'I have to go.' Harmony stood, angry at his presumption, angry that she couldn't snap back and tell him how wildly happy she and Will were. 'I should never have come.'

Luke grabbed hold of her above the elbow.

'Let go of me.'

'I know you feel it too. You felt it that night at the party. And at lunch. At the way you reacted when you saw me on the sofa back then. I know it from the way you look at me and the way you act around me. I can read you like a book.'

Harmony didn't know what to say. Her cheeks were hot and her mouth dry. She was embarrassed – no, *mortified* – she'd been that obvious, that she hadn't done more to hide whatever kind of schoolgirl attraction she unwittingly felt.

He leant close to her ear. His breath was hot against the side of her face. 'You're inside my head.'

He eased his grip on her. She felt faint. Her head pounded with a mix of emotions, nerves and vulnerability and anger vying with unwelcome excitement and a feeling of empowerment, the like of which she hadn't felt in years. The noises of the bar and restaurant – the chatter and laughter of other people, waiters shouting orders, the clatter of plates – all of it faded into the background. Heat pulsed through her. All she needed to do was move her face a fraction closer, lift her chin, and press her lips against his.

Will's face flashed into her mind.

'I have to go,' she whispered.

'Don't.'

His eyes locked on hers. She felt herself weaken for a fraction of a second.

No! the voice in her head screamed. *For God's sake what are you doing?*

She closed her eyes and lifted her hand, placed it flat against Luke, briefly felt the hardness of his chest, the heat of him beneath his cotton shirt, then pushed him away from her. 'I have to go,' she repeated.

'Because of Will?'

'Yes,' she said. 'Of course because of Will. Because I am married to him and I shouldn't be here.'

'Desire is proof you're alive, Harmony. You don't have to feel guilt. Without desire we might as well be dead. God knows how short life is. Never ever deny yourself pleasure. Pleasure is like gold dust.'

Harmony felt her chest tightening as if a vice was slowly squeezing the air from her lungs.

'Look at them,' he whispered. He turned her head gently in the direction of the couple at the table near them, the woman on her phone, the man with his newspaper. 'They're not old,' Luke said.

'They're married but they've run out of things to say to each other. They're at a table in this beautiful restaurant, and she's looking at other men, bored and disappointed, wondering why she's there, while he reads *The Times* obituaries, idly flitting through it in case a familiar name catches his eye. He's wearing a grey suit, has grey skin, grey hair, sitting with a wife he's not interested in, wondering if the men he went to school with are dead yet. Is that what you want? To be too scared to make changes that would make you happier? I want you, Harmony. I want to hold you, taste you. I want to be with you in a way other people can't be. I want you very, very badly.'

Harmony breathed heavily, light-headed on his words, every syllable weakening her. Will's face came into her head again. She closed her thumb on her wedding ring, felt its solidity against her skin. 'Christ, what am I doing?' she whispered.

Then she grabbed her bag and ran through the restaurant away from him, pushing out through the door and onto the pavement. She walked quickly down towards the Cromwell Road, shaking her head, cursing herself for accepting his invitation, for putting herself in that position.

She heard footsteps and looked over her shoulder to see him striding after her.

'No, go away,' she said, picking up her pace. 'Leave me alone.'

He drew up beside her and took hold of her arm to turn her to face him. 'Harmony—'

'No, Luke. I'm *married*.'

Luke looked up at the sky, annoyed, frustrated, even. When he fixed his eyes on her again, they narrowed. 'But you do feel it too.' He stared at her. 'I'm right, aren't I?'

'No, you're not *right*. Who the hell do you think you are to say all this shit?' She was cross with herself. Cross for opening herself up to him, for indulging such juvenile feelings of lust and attraction, for falling for his playboy looks like a pubescent girl with a crush on a teacher. She'd met him three times and there she was, tempted to do something stupid, a kiss that would seal the fate of a marriage that already hung in the balance.

She turned away from him and started to walk back down to the main road. When she reached it she looked left and right for a taxi. There were none and she swore. 'I need a cab,' she whispered. 'For God's sake, I need a cab.'

'Don't go.'

He was beside her.

She turned and they faced each other.

'I know you're lying. To me and to yourself,' he said. 'I know you feel it too.'

She noticed then a fragility about him, an innocence, that belied his boldness.

She threw her head back and stared at the sky above, then looked at him again and sighed heavily. 'Yes, I feel it, OK? I feel it. But that's all it can be. A feeling.' She paused and shook her head. 'Nothing will ever happen. People can't help being attracted to each other, but they can help acting on it. I'm married to Will.'

He didn't reply.

'Do you understand? We can never be anything more than friends.'

'That isn't enough. Being friends doesn't interest me.'

Harmony didn't know what to say. His sudden raw intensity both scared and excited her. Until this moment she'd only ever truly desired Will. It was a desire woven into her love for him. Knotted into the way he made her feel – as if she'd come home – and the way he made her laugh and lifted her spirits, the way his happy-go-lucky attitude brought her out of her shell. But the way this man, this stranger, looked at her was potent.

'We have one life,' he said. 'Fate brought us together – fate and circumstance – and I'm not going to apologise for how I feel. Tell me one more time to leave you alone and I will. You can walk away. We never need to see each other again. It's easy.'

Her body screamed at her to kiss him but she stepped backwards. 'Leave me alone,' she whispered.

There was a taxi approaching, its orange light switched on like a beacon. Relief swept over her. 'Taxi!' she shouted, stepping off the edge of the pavement, into its path, desperately waving her hand in the air.

'Harmony—'

'50 Greenslades Road, Wandsworth, please,' she said to the driver through the window.

Luke was right behind her. 'You're making a mistake.'

'No,' she replied. 'I'd be making a mistake if I stayed.'

She got into the taxi and closed the door without looking at him again, and as they pulled away she laid her head back on the seat. She thought of how close she'd come to kissing him, then thought of Will. She couldn't hide from him any longer. Being tempted by Luke had clarified her thoughts. She had to talk to her husband.

She leant forward to tap on the glass screen between her and the driver. 'I'm sorry,' she said. 'I gave you the wrong address. Can you take me to Barons Court instead?'

CHAPTER FOURTEEN

In the wine shop, Will was trying to focus on the website of a little-known producer from the southern tip of Italy who had just won a prestigious award at a regional wine festival in Naples. He hated being in the flat without Harmony and had stayed in the shop until late every night since she left. But it was impossible to concentrate. His thoughts constantly drifted back to her, reliving the moment she walked away from him, her gait uncertain, her small suitcase bumping along behind her. He was desperate to speak to her but every time he telephoned she either left the call unanswered or spoke in flat, single-word utterances that left him bereft. At night it was worse, her side of the bed so empty and cold, the bedroom quiet without her restlessness, his stomach a roiling sea. He'd spent most of each night pacing the pavements, consumed by anxiety.

He forced himself back to the Castella de Valde webpage, trying to read words that blurred on the screen. When the bell on the door jangled, he looked up with a start.

'Harmony?' He jumped off his stool and came out from behind the counter.

She stood in the doorway, the evening sun behind her casting her face in shadow. He combed his fingers through his hair, aware of his dishevelled appearance, cursing himself for grabbing yesterday's shirt off the floor that morning.

'Are you back? Are you coming home?'

She tucked a few stray strands of hair behind her ear. 'I'm not sure what I'm doing.'

'I've missed you.' He approached her carefully, as if she were a wild horse and likely to bolt.

She didn't move. Her eyes flicked over his face, her hurt as raw as it had been the day she left.

'Shall we go home?' he said. 'We can't talk here.'

She didn't answer.

'Harmony?'

'I think I'd prefer to go for a walk. I'll go back and change my shoes and put some jeans on. Meet me outside the flat in ten minutes.'

He watched her walk out of the shop and stayed frozen to the spot. His stomach churned. Had she come back to tell him she was leaving for good? If he could he'd have sold his soul to turn back the clock to before the vasectomy, before the miscarriage and the pregnancy, back to when their lives weren't strapped to this horrendous, out-of-control emotional roller coaster.

Will closed up the till and shut down his computer, then switched the lights off and locked the door behind him. He turned into their street as she emerged from the flat, her work clothes swapped for jeans and a sweater, her hair free of its ponytail. He started to jog and reached her as she stepped onto the pavement. They stood in front of each other, apprehensive and awkward.

'Where shall we go?' he asked.

'It doesn't matter.'

'The river?'

She nodded.

They walked in strained silence, passing groups of friends enjoying the warm evening, standing outside pubs, spilling onto the pavement, laughing and joking, others rushing to get home or heading to the park for an evening kick-about.

Without warning she stopped in her tracks. 'You know, I never once questioned you.' Her voice was tempered with anger. 'I never once asked you to tell me why you were so against having children. I just accepted it because I loved you.'

The past tense stung him.

'I want you to explain it to me. You might not think I have a right to know, but I think I do. I want to understand.'

He thrust his hands deep in his pockets and thought for a moment or two. How was he going to formulate his mush of reasons into a coherent answer? There was nothing he could say that was going to help. The argument they were about to have was unavoidable. 'I have no idea how to be a father.'

'But that's ridiculous. Who knows how to be a parent until they become one?'

'The thought of it scares the shit out of me. I learned nothing from my father. Nothing at all. How on earth can I think of becoming a father if I've nothing to fall back on?'

He saw his family then, the three of them – him, his mother, and his father – standing in the car park outside the halls of residence. His mother had fussed around him, reminded him to do his laundry, kissed him, told him to call when he could. His father hanging back, his face devoid of emotion. And Will, full of excitement for his new start, his first step into adulthood, free to get on with his life. He'd looked at his father, given him a moment to step forward, but the man made no move towards him.

Be the bigger man, Will had told himself. *You must be the bigger man.*

So Will had walked up to him and offered his hand. His father shook it briefly, grasping the other too firmly, before Will let go and straightened his back.

'I guess I'll see you at Christmas,' he'd said, unsure what else to say.

'I'm sure we'll see you before then,' his stony-eyed father replied. 'You're bound to cock it up. You always do.'

Will looked at his wife, her questioning eyes burning with livid incomprehension. 'I'd get it wrong. I'd make mistakes and I know what that does to a child. I'm not like you. I'm not strong like you. I'm not strong enough to raise a child.'

'I'm not strong.' She started walking again, her eyes focused on where she was going, her mind working overtime.

'You are,' he said, drawing parallel with her. 'It was the first thing I noticed the day we met. You'd seemed vulnerable and sweet scrabbling around on the floor for your books, then we got talking and I was blown away by how determined and self-assured you were. How independent. Full of fight. You hadn't had things easy, but you were gutsy and secure, and so optimistic.'

My anchor in a storm, Will had thought, after they'd made love for the first time, squashed together in her narrow bed, basking in the glow of sex. She was his salvation. She was everything he wanted to be: principled, brave, focused on the future and not shackled by the past.

'I'm not like you. The way I've coped isn't to fight, it's to box the shit up and pretend it doesn't exist. Not let it affect my life.'

'But that's not true, is it?' She threw her hands up in frustration as she marched. 'You can't *pretend it doesn't exist* because it does. You say you don't let it affect your life but it's the opposite. Whatever it is you're hiding affects everything. Your past, this thing you're trying to block out of your life, *is* affecting everything.'

He shook his head. 'This isn't a nice world. Children are vulnerable. I'd want to be there all the time to make sure nothing could hurt our child, but that's not possible, is it? If you have a child you have to accept that at some point they'll get hurt. I mean, look at us. Your dad leaving, your mum dying, my dad being a cunt, crying myself to sleep in a room with twenty-four other eight-year-olds, all of us trying to keep our sobbing silent so we didn't get the shit kicked out of us. I don't want a child of mine to feel any of those things.'

Her eyes welled and she snatched angrily at the tears with the back of her hand. 'But our child wouldn't have felt those things,' she said. 'Our child would have been loved and cherished. Our child would have been happy.'

'You can't guarantee that.'

'I could have guaranteed it enough to the best of my ability. We'd have loved him or her with every breath in our bodies, and if you couldn't have managed that, I'd have loved it enough for both of us.'

'I think you're being naive.'

'*Naive*?'

'Yes,' he pushed on, trying to ignore her anger. 'Sure, things at home would be good, our family would be content, but what about the bastards out there?' He shook his head and looked up at the sky, trying to repel the image of Alastair Farrow, eyes glinting with spite, lip curled up in an evil half-smile.

'If we all thought about the dangers out in the world, none of us would leave the house. You've convinced yourself the world is an evil place, but it's not. It's an amazing place with amazing things in it – knowledge, laughter, love, friends – all these things make life worth the risk.' She shook her head in frustration. 'If every person thought like you the human race would cease to exist. And why? Because of fear? And, yes, I get it, you and I have experienced pain. We've shed a lot of tears as children, but we went on and found happiness, didn't we? Doesn't that outweigh the bad stuff?' She didn't pause long enough for him to answer. 'I think it does. I think the happiness I've felt makes the grief bearable. You saying that life is so awful it's not worth existing, belittles everything we have together.'

'You're twisting my words—'

But she stormed ahead, not waiting for him to finish his sentence, her feet slamming into the pavement, hands balled into fists at her sides. He followed, turning over her words, recognising the truth in them, wanting to formulate a response that would communicate his complicated feelings. She came to a stop at the railings which ran alongside the Thames. He stood beside her. The tide was low, and the pebbles and rubbish revealed on the shoreline were covered in thick, dirty silt. Will waited for Harmony to say something, but she stayed quiet, leaning over the railings, watching the listless, muddy water pass by.

'I'm going to say something which is going to sound harsh.' He gripped hold of the metal railing, still warm from the day's sun, for strength. 'And I know it's going to upset you, but . . .' He stopped himself then, wary of the words he was preparing to say.

'For fuck's sake, just say it.' The slight breeze brushed her hair across her face and she swept it back.

'I've felt this way since I was eighteen. When most people were struggling with politics or religion or trying to get laid, I was dealing with this. The decision I made, not wanting to be a father, is fundamental to me and, rightly or wrongly, it makes me who I am. It makes me the man you married. If you don't understand that then . . .' He paused and took a breath. 'Then maybe it's your love in question here and not mine.'

She turned on him then. Fire in her eyes which brimmed with tears. 'You think I don't love you?' she whispered bitterly. 'You really think that? If I didn't love you, Will, I wouldn't be here. I wouldn't be standing here desperate to repair our marriage.' She shook her head, tears spilling down her cheeks. 'You know what? Maybe it's beyond repair. Maybe there's nothing we can do. Neither of us can give the other what they need. I needed you in what was a really dark time for me. But you weren't there for me and worse than that you lied to me.' She swiped at her tears and turned away from him, walking away from him a second time.

'Harmony!'

But she didn't reply, instead she walked faster, head down, arms wrapped around her body.

He slammed his hands against the railings, swearing under his breath.

When he got back to the flat she was sitting at the kitchen table. As he approached her she lifted her eyes to look at him. They were red from crying, the skin beneath them puffy, a raggedy tissue clutched in her fingers.

'I heard what you said.' Her voice was quiet but calm. 'About being a father. I can't change how you feel, I know that. And it's not fair of me to ask you to. I know that too. But I can't forgive what you did. It was dishonest and hurtful, and affects my life as much as it does yours.'

'I'm sorry.'

'A sorry isn't going to make this better.' She sighed and exhaled slowly. 'You lied to me. When I lost the baby, when I needed you the most, you gave me no support. You didn't care. But it's not just that. It's the secrets. Everything you keep hidden from me. I know there's something you're not telling me about Luke. I can see it. Why won't you open up to me? I hate how easily you keep things from me. You should be able to trust me. I should be able to trust you. Without trust what's the point? Right now, right this minute, it feels like we've wasted the last twenty years investing in this relationship.'

'Don't say that.'

She lowered her eyes, her fingers shredding the tissue so it fell in bits like snow.

'Harmony, listen to me. You're wrong.' He pulled out a chair and sat opposite her. 'It's not easy keeping things from you. It's harder than you can imagine, but I do it because that's how I deal with things. I don't want to spend time discussing school with you. Luke, Alastair Farrow, the caning and bullying, it's not worth talking about. I don't need your sympathy or pity and I don't want that shit in our lives. It's irrelevant.'

'Of course it's not irrelevant. Your past, that intricate jigsaw of experiences, makes you the person you are today.'

'No,' he said. 'I put it behind me so I was able to become the person I am today. But I hear you. And, yes, maybe I should share more with you. When it comes to the vasectomy there's nothing I can say to defend it. It was a huge mistake not discussing it with you. I can see that now.' He paused. 'With all this crap in my head, I don't always think clearly. I'm not like you. I can't put feelings into words like you can. When you lost the baby, I knew how upset you were but I didn't know what I could say or do to help. Whenever I thought about what to say it sounded insincere or dismissive.' He shook his head. 'You say I didn't care, but that's not true. I did care, I just wasn't any good at showing you.'

Her eyes filled with tears again and she balled up the remains of the tissue.

'Everything I did or said seemed to make things worse. I went onto the internet and read up about it – about losing a baby and what I should do to help – but nothing I found seemed right, and . . .' He paused, finding it difficult to speak. 'And of course I'd had the operation and felt so bloody guilty. The more upset and withdrawn you got, the harder it was to know what to say. In the end I convinced myself that if I just got on with it, tried to keep positive, eventually we'd be OK. But I know I got it wrong.' Then he leant forward again and placed his hands on hers. 'I love you. Please, let's go back to where we were. Let's make things OK again.'

She stared at him, her face still, her eyes as sad as he'd ever seen them. When she spoke her voice was quiet. 'A part of me wants that. But there's another part of me that's still hurting. Maybe I should try and be better. See the bigger picture. Tell you it's OK and move on. But if I'm honest, I don't think I can. I'm hurt and I'm angry, but worse than that, sitting here opposite you, it's like you're a stranger. Like I don't know you. So where does that leave us? What do I do? Go through the motions of being a couple and hope those feelings just go away?'

'They will go away. I promise.'

'I'm not sure they will.'

When she left the table, he didn't follow. There was nothing more he could say. He walked into the garden. It was peaceful and still. Dusk had seen off the heat of the day and there was a suggestion of rain in the air. A movement from behind the study window caught his eye. He watched Harmony sit down at her desk, her shadowy figure moving slowly. He saw her put her glasses on then become still as she stared at the monitor in front of her. He wondered if this was what the rest of their lives might look like, two separate beings tied together in marriage, detached and resentful, circling each other warily. Would that be better or worse than her leaving?

He sat at the table and picked at the flaking rust. Would it have been different if he'd shared everything with her? If he'd described that first horrendous night at prep school? All those homesick eight-year-old boys curled up in uncomfortable beds, abandoned, the sound of stifled crying intermingling with the creaks and groans of ancient timbers and pipes. Should he have described how he'd lain awake wondering what he'd done to upset his parents so much they would send him away? Should he have described the smell of that scratchy grey blanket, heavy with damp and disinfectant, and how he'd hidden from the smell by pushing his face into the teddy he'd brought. Should he have told her the teddy was itemised on the uniform list sent out before the beginning of term?

One small soft toy (if required).

It started to spit with rain. Will turned his face upwards and closed his eyes, waiting for the tiny specks of wet to hit him. He pictured Harmony's face when she'd told him about the miscarriage. How puffy her eyes had been. How her pale skin had been blotched with deep pink. How her chin had trembled when she said the words.

'Our baby died.'

She'd looked up at him, tears coursing her cheeks, her breath coming in short snatches.

'A miscarriage?'

She nodded and her shoulders began to quiver.

He'd sat beside her and pulled her into him, his arms around her, his chin resting on her head. 'I'm sorry,' he whispered, kissing her hair.

His thoughts had been a jumble. He hadn't known what else to say. Everything that came into his head sounded trite and insincere. His emotions were all over the place. The relief he felt shamed him, the unexpected sadness shocked him.

'Do you need to see a doctor?'

She sat back and shook her head, pushing her palms against her red-rimmed eyes. 'I've already been. I went this morning.'

'I should have taken you.'

'There was nothing you could do,' she said through her tears. 'I didn't want to worry you if nothing was wrong.' She sniffed. 'I was hoping she'd tell me it was OK, that the bleeding was normal and the baby was fine. But when they scanned me there was no heartbeat. Nothing at all.' Then she started to sob again. 'Oh, Will, it was awful.'

The drizzle turned to rain. He sat there for a while, but soon the drops became too heavy and too cold. Inside, he took his wet shirt off and threw it in the direction of the washing machine. He was surprised to see it was nearly ten o'clock. He peered into the bedroom and saw Harmony was already in bed, the covers pulled tightly over her shoulder, her back facing him. He knew if he went to bed now he would only lie staring at the ceiling, battling his thoughts, and it was too wet to walk. He went through to the study and turned the computer on, shivering slightly as his damp skin cooled. He pulled Facebook up, wondering if Alastair had accepted his friend request.

God knows why he would. Will imagined him sneering at the thought of it.

But when the page loaded he saw there was a notification.

His stomach turned over.

Alastair Farrow hadn't just accepted his request. He'd sent him a message.

Will English? My God, you haven't changed a bit! What a blast from the past. It's been a long time. Are you still in touch with any of the lads from school? I was glad to hear from you – surprised too – I was a bit of a cock at school! I notice you're in London. I'm not far away, near Camberley in Surrey. Married to Diane. Two ankle-biters, a boy and girl, Charlie and Bea. We should go for a drink. It would be good to meet up again and hear your news. In fact, another friend from school (Toddy – not sure if you remember him) mentioned hooking up for a drink soon. I'll let you know if we do. If you can join us that would be great. Cheers (and no hard feelings) Al

Will's first response was a burst of spontaneous laughter. He leant closer to the screen, his hand rubbing at his chin, head shaking slowly in disbelief. He reread the message a couple of times. Had Alastair really written that? Had he really dismissed his behaviour in that offhand way? Called himself a 'bit of a cock', introduced his children, then signed off with *no hard feelings*?

Will sat back in his chair and stared at the screen.

Alastair Farrow.

The seventeen-year-old who recurred in Will's nightmares now wanted to meet up to laugh about all the bit-of-a-cock-things he'd done, buy him a drink for old times' sake, let bygones be bygones, catch up on all the news. Will stared at the message until Farrow's words blurred and his back had stiffened.

Harmony was asleep, or perhaps pretending to be, when he finally crept into bed. He lay beside her, drumming his fingers against the duvet, his mind whirring. He should ignore Alastair's message. He should unfriend him. He had enough to worry about with his faltering marriage without wasting anxiety on Alastair bloody Farrow. He should forget all about him. Erase him. Push him back into the dark shadowy corners of his mind where he belonged.

But the more Will thought about the flippant tone of the message the more angry he became. How could Farrow pass off what he did with such glib, throwaway comments? Did he seriously expect Will to have *no hard feelings*?

He thought back to that afternoon.

You're pathetic, English. Get the fuck out of here.

Will climbed out of bed, careful not to disturb Harmony, and went into the bathroom. He closed the door quietly then leant over the basin, turned the tap on, and splashed water on his face. He lifted his head slowly and stared at himself in the mirror, his face lit only by the muted moonlight, his skin in shades of blue and shadowed. It was hard to decipher his features. He appeared indistinct, as if fading into nothingness.

A nothing man.

He bent and splashed his face again.

You're pathetic.

CHAPTER FIFTEEN

Talking to Will hadn't helped. If anything it had made things worse. She now realised there was nothing he could have said in the kitchen that would have made his actions easier to comprehend; hearing him apologise was as bad as hearing him justify it. She imagined him making the decision – booking the procedure, travelling to the hospital, signing the operation papers – all without a thought for her. And then there were his secrets about school. Whatever it was it was partly to blame. She hated that he'd never felt able to open up to her. Even after she told him about her mother's death, her father leaving, the difficulties she and Sophie had faced growing up.

The phone on her desk rang, the flashing red indicating an external call. She rubbed her face then reached for the receiver.

'Dr Hanney?' she said as she picked up.

'It's Luke.'

Her heart stopped. She glanced around the office instinctively, but her colleagues were moving about their business as normal, oblivious. 'I told you not to contact me,' she whispered, lowering her head.

'I want to apologise. My behaviour yesterday was inappropriate. I'm—' His voice broke for a second or two. 'I don't know what came over me. Losing my wife . . . It's not an excuse, but I'm sorry.' He sounded distraught.

Harmony had a flash of him leaning close to her, his hand brushing hers, his whispered intent hot on her skin. She pushed the thought away, flicking at her wedding ring with the tip of her thumb.

'Please will you let me see you? Just to say sorry. I promise I won't behave in any way that will make you feel uncomfortable.'

'Luke, I don't think—'

'*Please*? I can't stop thinking about how I behaved. Let me make it up to you. I know you wanted to talk about Will. We can do that. I can tell you about him when I knew him. Back then.'

She thought of him leaning in to kiss her and a flash of heat rose up her neck.

'Please, Harmony. Just a coffee.'

'Look, you have nothing to apologise for.'

'I think I do, and I do want to be friends. I want to reconnect with Will. That part of my life was fairly hellish, but Will was my friend. He was important to me. I want to get to know him again.'

The sincerity in his voice was striking and she'd be lying to herself if she said she wasn't intrigued by the thought of getting to know Luke and hearing about him and Will. Would it help her understand her husband? Would it help her process the anger she was feeling towards him? It certainly couldn't hurt and if it shed some light on what was going on beneath his surface then that could only be a good thing. 'Yes, OK. I've got time for a coffee.'

The relief in his voice was palpable. 'That's great. Can you take a break now?'

She cast her eyes at the pile of papers she had to work through. 'Sure.'

After she put the phone down, she sat and stared at her screen amid the office of people chatting softly, reading, writing papers, preparing for presentations, and recalled his smell as he'd leant close to her and the way her skin tingled when he'd touched her. She dropped her face into her hands and breathed in the hot, trapped air. Her skin tingled.

Was she making a mistake?

'Are you OK, Harmony?'

She swung around to see Alice standing behind her. She gave her a strained smile. 'Oh, yes. Yes, I'm fine.'

Alice furrowed her brow. She'd worked in the department for a long time and was a few years older than Harmony. She had, as was agreed by all, a heart of gold and took the health and well-being of her colleagues very seriously.

'You look flushed. Do you have a temperature?'

'No, nothing like that.'

Alice didn't believe her.

'Honestly, I'm feeling fine. Thank you for asking.'

Alice still didn't look convinced. Harmony smiled as broadly as she could manage and Alice reluctantly returned to her desk. Harmony thought of Luke coming to the office and swore under her breath. Why the hell had she agreed to meet with him? She rubbed her throat with her hand, catching Will's Tiffany heart with the edge of her finger, unsure what to do.

No, that wasn't true.

Of course she knew what to do.

She opened a new email.

Actually, work crazy. I can't leave office at the moment. It's all fine. No harm done yesterday and look forward to Will and I getting together with you another time.

Did that sound right? Was 'look forward' too much? She hovered her fingers over the send button for a moment or two then pressed it.

She imagined him in his office, maybe a large open-plan area on the top floor of a glass and steel building, or a private room with an antique writing desk and leather chairs and shelves of leather-bound law tomes. She saw him opening her email, his hair falling over his forehead, his intense eyes locked on her words, and had another flash of the way he'd looked at her, as if he wanted to consume her whole.

She sat back from the computer and looked around again. Her breath caught in her throat. She took her bag off her chair and walked down the corridor towards the ladies. She kept her head low, and hurried past Alice's desk without making eye contact. She shut herself in a cubicle, closed the seat of the toilet, and sat down to check her phone for a reply.

Nothing.

Her heart started racing again. This time with panic.

Luke, I can't leave work at the moment. Can you email me back to say you've got this message?

She stared at the phone, willing an email to appear.

'Shit,' she breathed.

Was he already on his way?

Her stomach knotted with nerves as she opened the cubicle door. When she got back to her desk she tried to focus on her report, editing her words with a red pen, glancing at her screen every few minutes hoping to see an email from him.

Her phone rang. An internal call. She picked up.

'There's a Luke Crawford in reception for you.'

She swore silently.

'Shall I tell him you're on the way down or send him up?'

'Don't send him up. I'm coming down,' she said, quickly. She had a vision of Luke waiting for her downstairs and chewed the edge of her nail.

As she waited for the lift to arrive, butterflies gathered in her stomach.

'Just tell him you can't meet him today,' she said under her breath.

She had an unbidden image of him leaning in to whisper in her ear. The way he'd told her he wanted her.

The lift doors closed and she pulled her ponytail out and shook her hair free.

When she stepped out into the lobby, however, there was no sign of him.

'Hi,' she said to the man on reception. 'You said there was a Luke Crawford here to see me?'

The man gestured out of the doors. 'He said to tell you he's waiting in his car. The silver one just there.'

She stepped outside. It was a muggy day, the summer sky a yellowy-grey, heavy with the promise of rain. She ran up to the car, polished and gleaming, which was parked on the double-yellows directly in front of her office, and tapped on the window.

When he lowered it, she started to speak. 'I'm really sorry, but something's come up.'

Luke leant over the passenger seat and opened the door. 'Can you get in? I'm badly parked.'

As if on cue a cyclist swerved around the car and glared angrily at Luke.

The voice in her head told her not to get in the car, but then he asked again. 'Harmony?'

Seeing him made her legs weaken. She had a vivid image of kissing him, right there and then, not saying a word, just leaning into the car and pushing her lips against his. She pushed it away. She had no idea what was going on in her head.

'Luke. I . . .' Her voice caught in her throat. 'I can't . . .'

'Will you get in?'

There was a note of force in his voice she wasn't expecting. She glanced over her shoulder, half-hoping Alice or another colleague was there so she'd be compelled to send him away and go back to her desk. But there was nobody there to witness it, so she climbed in and closed the door.

'I haven't got time for a coffee,' she said, avoiding his eyes. 'Sorry.'

He turned in his seat to look at her. A heavy silence held them, wrapped in the heat of the car, its smell – new leather and the scented air freshener that hung off the rear-view mirror – sickly sweet. 'Then we won't have coffee.'

She turned her head to look at him. His expression was steady, his eyes boring into hers. She took a breath.

'You said—'

Then he leant forward and kissed her. Lightly. Quickly. His hand on the side of her face.

She pulled back. 'No.'

He smiled. 'No?'

'You told me you wouldn't.'

'I told you I wouldn't do anything to make you feel uncomfortable. Which, looking at your face, I haven't done.'

'You said coffee and a chat.'

'Both of us knew it wasn't going to be that.'

She shook her head. Her heart was thumping.

'Don't lie to yourself. If you didn't want this as much as I do, there's no way you'd have put yourself within half a mile of me.'

Was he right? Had she lied to herself? Was this a way to hurt Will back? Was this how she knew her marriage was over? People who wanted their marriages to survive didn't get into the car with someone they were attracted to. Someone who'd recently so brazenly propositioned them.

'It's OK to do this,' he said softly. 'Life is for living. We get one go and filling it with regrets is a waste.'

'It's not that simple,' she whispered.

'It's extremely simple. I want you. Very badly. And you want me. Nothing more than that. Denying it is way more complicated.'

He leant closer, his mouth only inches from hers, tilted his head, raised the backs of his fingers and grazed her cheek. 'Nobody needs to know but us.'

Then he pressed his lips against hers and this time she kissed him back.

When they broke apart, she felt weak with guilt. 'I've never done anything like this before.'

'It doesn't matter what you have or haven't done.'

'But I haven't. It's important you know that.'

'Why?'

She didn't know why. She wondered whether it was herself she was talking to. Whether she was trying to excuse her actions, convince herself of her own good character. One stain on a lily-white record.

'I'm sorry,' she said. 'I can't. This isn't me. I don't understand what's going on.'

'I'll tell you what's going on,' he said. 'You and I met through a mutual connection. I have a past with Will and you have a present with him. I am as interested – no, fascinated – in his present as you are in his past, and this has drawn us to each other.' He reached out and traced her lips with the tips of his fingers. She tingled where he touched her, lifting her eyes to meet his and as soon as she did he smiled again – a gentle, unthreatening smile. 'Added to that,' he said, 'unless I'm reading the signs wrongly, we are both undeniably attracted to each other and our attraction is so strong it's impossible to ignore. I know you're having problems with Will. I saw it immediately when I asked you if you were happy. There's nothing wrong with wanting to connect with another person. Sometimes, when a marriage is struggling, it helps. Pushing our attraction underground won't make it go away, it will only make it grow. You'll be thinking about me. I will become a fantasy. How will that help your marriage? Maybe this is what you need. Did you think of that?

Maybe feeling free will give you the space you need to make things work. I have no desire to break the two of you up. I don't even want a relationship. I just want to have you. Give me one afternoon and I promise, after that, I'll walk away.'

Harmony tried to speak, but no words came out.

'Is that fair?'

His question reverberated in the stillness of the car.

Fair? On who? Not on Will. It wasn't fair on Will in the slightest.

'I can't do this to him.'

He took her chin between thumb and forefinger and turned her face towards him. He slid his hand down over her jaw and throat. He leant closer to her, his face centimetres from hers, the smell of him filling her. His eyes were fixed on hers. 'How will he ever find out?'

She closed her eyes and gave in to it with a slight nod. She had never done anything like this before. How much of this was revenge on Will? A way to hurt him as he'd hurt her. A way to break his trust. A way to prove to herself that she didn't need him, that she was her own person, and that if he was able to keep things from her, she was able to keep things from him.

'I'm going to kiss you again,' Luke said. 'Then I'm going to drive you to my flat.'

He moved closer to her so his lips brushed hers and sent electric pulses shooting through her body. She knew then it was too late. There could be no more protesting. No more denying the inevitable. She was going to sleep with him and her head swam with the illicit thrill of it. She turned in the seat, the skin of her thighs sticking to the hot leather, and wrapped her hand around his neck. Her fingers knotted into his hair and she pulled him to her. Their lips met and she was overwhelmed with desire. It erupted inside her as if she was taking her first breath of oxygen. He kissed differently to Will, harder, more insistent, his tongue forcing its way into her mouth, exploring her, tasting her.

He drew away, his lips glistening with a sheen of saliva. 'You consume me.'

She trembled with adrenaline, her hands quivered, her lips tingled. 'You don't even know me,' she whispered.

The shadow of a smile passed over his face. 'I know all I need to know. I knew it the moment I first saw you.'

Luke turned the engine on and pulled away from the kerb.

'You believe in love at first sight?' she asked as he drove.

'Love at first sight?' he repeated with amusement. 'I never talk about love. It's a fatuous, overused word that's impossible to quantify. How long does it take to fall in love? Minutes? Years? Love means different things to different people and it's a one-way street. One of every pairing always loves more than the other. Love is cruel. What I'm talking about – attraction, desire, chemistry – these are the things that matter. You can love a car or a film or a food, but sexual desire is much more specific. Do I believe in desire at first sight? Yes, of course I do. Chemical desire is instantaneous.'

She knew what he meant. She'd felt it too. Outside the cloakroom at Emma's party she'd felt their instant attraction. Perhaps that's when the future was etched in stone. Perhaps it was inevitable at that very moment that she would sleep with him. Perhaps it had nothing to do with her disintegrating marriage or Will's dishonesty or her lost baby, but everything to do with a raw attraction for this man she didn't know.

She was hit then by a realisation. She didn't want to know more about him. She didn't want him to be anything more than an enigmatic ghost from Will's hidden past. She didn't want to see his home, she didn't want to look at the books on his shelf or see the pictures he chose to hang on his walls. She needed him to stay a stranger. If she kept him unknown then she could distance herself from what she was doing. When they walked away from each other it would be over.

'I don't want to go to your flat.'

'Why not?'

She hesitated. 'I can't explain. I just don't want to.'

'Where, then? A hotel?'

She imagined having to walk into a hotel reception and face the knowing eyes of the person behind the desk. A person who'd handed over keys to countless couples with false names who were chasing a few clandestine hours of sordid sex. 'No,' she said, then glanced into the back seat of the car.

He smiled briefly. 'Absolutely not.' He paused. 'What about the photography studio?'

She did a double take and furrowed her brow. 'How do you know about that?'

'Will told me about it. He said he never goes there. He said he hadn't set foot in it for over a year.'

'Did he?'

'Yes, when I came over. I asked him if he still enjoyed photography. How else would I know?' he laughed. 'Is it locked though?'

'There's an entry pad. I know the code.'

Harmony thought about it. They couldn't. Not in Will's studio. But the more she considered it, the more she wondered if it might be perfect. It was safe and anonymous. She didn't feel connected to it in any way. And, yes, it would hurt Will if he knew, but no more than if he knew what they were doing. She felt a stab of guilt, but then, as if in reply, she heard Will's voice.

When it died I felt relieved.

Fuck Will. Fuck Will and his callous relief.

'Yes,' she said. 'We can go there. You're right, he never goes there, and definitely not mid-week as he's always at the shop. Head down towards Battersea. It's a few roads on from the power station.'

She felt for her wedding ring and began to turn it in precise quarter revolutions as she recalled the moment Will had slid it onto her finger. His eyes had sparkled and he'd laughed, standing there in his light blue seventies-style suit, flowery open-necked shirt, scuffed leather shoes and mismatched socks.

'Who's going to see my socks?' he'd said, as they dressed together, bucking tradition and driving to the registry office in the same car. But his trousers were a couple of inches too short and when he sat down they rode up his legs, revealing the black sock on one foot and the striped one on the other. After they exchanged rings he leant forward and told her he loved her, three whispered words that had made her heart sing.

'I love you too,' she'd replied.

Just meaningless words? Was Luke right? Was love an unquantifiable concept as unstable and ever-changing as a sand dune?

'Take it off.' Luke's voice jolted her from her thoughts.

'Sorry?'

'The ring. If it's bothering you, take it off.'

'It's not the ring that's bothering me.'

'If you're having second thoughts, you need to tell me. I'm not going to force you to do something you don't want to do. If this is too much for you, I'll drive you home. Do you want me to do that?'

Harmony thought of the flat, dark and cramped and filled with sadness. She thought about Will and her moving around each other in their separate spheres, her avoiding being in the same room with him, those loaded, bitter silences.

'I don't want to go home.'

Harmony directed Luke to the small yard where Will's photographic studio was located. They parked up and got out of the car. Nerves and doubt began to curdle inside her. This was starting to feel seedy and as they walked over the small, unevenly paved forecourt, full of weeds and potholes, she fought the urge to bolt. There were four small warehouse-style buildings, prefabricated and boxy, that bordered three sides of the yard. One was vacant and dilapidated; another was used as a private storage facility; the third belonged to a motorcycle mechanic; and then there was Will's studio. It was smarter than the others. She and Will had spent a few weekends painting it back when he bought it, the walls in white emulsion, the window frames and door in navy gloss. They'd painted the inside as well, pulled out the rotten carpets, replaced the broken panes of glass in the window, and cleared away the rubbish. She remembered Will eagerly screwing the stainless steel sign to the door then stepping back to read it aloud.

'Will English. Photographer,' he'd said, wrapping his arm around her shoulder.

Harmony and Luke walked up to the door and with a shaking hand she punched the numbers into the keypad.

1209.

Will's birthday.

She stalled as another paralysing wave of doubt bowled into her. Luke bent down and lightly kissed her neck. She pushed Will from her mind and slid the handle back to open the door. It was dark inside and they were hit by a wall of stale, cool air, heavy with the smell of the damp concrete floor. Harmony reached to the side to turn on the lights, and a moment or two later the fluorescent strip lights flickered into life. She stared at the large empty room, the sofa to her left, the white wall in front of her, lighting stands and spotlights to the right. Will's space. She saw him then, tinkering with his camera, glancing up at her, smiling as he focused the lens on her.

Luke opened his mouth to speak.

'Don't say anything,' she said. 'Just kiss me.'

As she said the words, she was filled with self-loathing. She bit back tears. Who was she? She didn't recognise herself. What had happened to her?

His eyes searched hers, flicking almost imperceptibly back and forth, then in one movement he grabbed hold of her shoulders and pushed his open mouth onto hers. One hand went to the back of her neck and the other moved over her breast, pushing hard against her. And in that moment, everything she was feeling – the confusion, the hurt, the betrayal and anger – fuelled an overwhelming need for him. Every part of her ached for him to erase every bit of emotion. As she lost herself in what they were doing, the pain she'd been carrying for so long now began to fade. The more it faded the more she wanted him. She grabbed at his waistband and fumbled with the button and zip. His fingers dug into her. He pushed her backwards against the wall as his hand went to the hem of her skirt, pulling it up and over her hips. His fingers felt for her underwear. She broke away from him to take them down. He dropped his head and buried his face in her chest, she pitched her head backwards, raking her fingers across his back. As he lifted her against the wall, she wrapped her legs around him. He kissed her neck, her chest, her stomach, and ran the flats of his hand up her sides and the insides of her arms, pushing them above her head and clenching her wrists against the wall. She noticed then a roughness about him, a mounting aggression, and when she opened her eyes she was taken aback by the look on his face. Not lust or tenderness, but a reflected anger, his eyes glazed over, mouth twisted into a grimace. His fingers tightened their hold on her wrists as if she were trapped in a vice. He pushed his body hard against her so her shoulder bones grazed the wall.

'Be careful,' she whispered. 'You're hurting me.'

His fingers loosened immediately and he breathed into her neck. 'I'm sorry,' he said. 'I didn't mean to.' His breath came in short, gasping bursts.

She put her hand against his cheek to calm him. When she felt him relax she whispered into his ear: 'Do it now, Luke. I want you to fuck me.'

He pushed himself inside her and cried out, then bit down on her lip. She winced, tasting the metallic tang of blood.

'I've wanted this so much,' he said hoarsely.

As he drove into her he seemed to retreat, become distant from her, as if he was somewhere else. It was over quickly and his head collapsed into the crook of her neck as her body slid down the wall. She loosely draped her arms around him and they both breathed heavily. He stepped back and she pushed her skirt down as Luke pulled up his trousers.

He took hold of her hand and led her to a side room off the main area. It was small and contained a tattered chaise longue that Harmony had fallen in love with from the Portobello Market, a coffee table, and an old chest filled with unusual items – a bowler hat, a silver-topped cane, beads, a plastic pot plant, a large Chinese fan and the like – that Will used as props in portrait shoots. His old camera and camera case and a long lens lay on the table, beside a coffee mug with a thin layer of dried mould.

'He never puts anything away,' she muttered. 'It drives me mad—'

'Don't think about him.'

She held her tongue, resisting the urge to tell Luke it was impossible not to think about Will. He was there with them. This was as much about Will as it was about her.

'Why were you angry just then?' she said.

'What do you mean?'

'When we had sex.'

'I could ask you the same question.'

'I asked you first.'

'It's complicated.'

She nodded. 'For me too.'

'I want to look at you.'

She smiled. 'You are looking at me.'

'No, I want to look at you properly.'

He reached out and began to undress her. His face was blank. He undid each button on her shirt methodically. Ran his hands down her shoulders to slide it off her. Undid her bra. Gently lowered the straps down her arms. He bent to undo the zip of her skirt then eased it down over her hips.

Luke stepped back and stared at her. His dark eyes took her in. Unease settled over her. Having him study her like this, naked and in full light, made her feel vulnerable, as if he was inspecting goods, looking for imperfections. She became aware of her body, those bits of herself she didn't like; her bony hips, the appendix scar on her stomach, the large, dark mole on her stomach, the broken veins on her thighs. She felt dirty. Worthless and cheap. A husk of herself, her morals and goodness sucked out. She lifted her arms to cover herself.

'Don't.' His voice was firm; the sound of it made her heart skip a beat.

'I don't like it.'

'Don't like what?'

'The way you're looking at me.' Harmony was conscious of how quickly she was breathing, how shallow and hurried each breath was. 'Being naked like this, with you dressed, you staring at me. I don't like it.'

He touched his fingers to her mouth to quieten her. Then he reached for his shirt buttons and started to take his own clothes off. They had sex on a rug on the floor. This time there was no rushing or desperation or anger. He was gentle. She should have enjoyed it but she didn't. Without the rush of anger and intensity she was left with the very painful feeling this wasn't her husband. It was as if a witch's curse had been lifted. As if scales had fallen from her eyes. With his every touch, with each moan of pleasure he made, she wanted him less. At one point she put her hand to her mouth to stop herself crying out. Guilt and shame engulfed her. As he kissed every part of her, slowly and deliberately, all she could think of was Will. Everything about this other man felt wrong now, alien, unpleasant. His smell and the feel of his skin. His hard, muscular body. Luke whispered unfamiliar words into the curve of her neck. When he stroked her she wanted to recoil. She closed her eyes and took herself away.

You stupid woman, the voice in her head said. *You stupid, stupid woman.*

Afterwards she lay beside him, not quite touching. He turned on his side and lifted a hand to smooth her hair. As he did so, she caught sight of the thin white scar that cut his palm in two.

Blood brothers.

'Are you thinking about him?'

'No,' she lied.

'Good. You can't think about him when you're with me.'

'It doesn't work like that.'

'It does. When you're with me, I don't want him anywhere near you.'

'This isn't happening again.'

He sat up, eyes burning into her.

'I want to go,' she said, reaching for her shirt and hurriedly putting it on. 'I want to get back to Will.'

Luke didn't move immediately. But then he grabbed his clothes and started to dress, his movements staccato with obvious annoyance. She knew she should say something, perhaps even apologise, but instead she waited quietly for him to dress. She felt sick and drained, and numb with guilt.

She followed him out of the studio. Still he said nothing. He unlocked the car and she climbed in. She reached into the back for her bag and rummaged for her phone. There was a text from Will. She flinched at his name.

Are you coming home? If so what time? X

'Can you drop me at Fulham Broadway?' she asked, chewing lightly on her lower lip.

Luke nodded stiffly and turned the engine on as she typed a reply to Will.

Yes. About six.

She hesitated, then added a kiss.

They were silent on the drive back through London. At one point he reached for her hand and her body tensed. She pulled her hand away. His touch felt wrong now, not exciting but duplicitous.

'I'm away on business for a week from tomorrow,' Luke said, as he pulled over to let her out not far from the tube station. 'I'll get in touch when I'm back in the country.'

'No, Luke,' she said. 'It was only today. It's over now.'

'I'm not sure it is.'

'It is. I'm sorry if that's not what you want to hear.'

'I'll call you when I'm back.'

'You don't have my number.'

'It's on the footer of your email.'

'Please don't call me. And don't text either. If you have to contact me use my email, but I'd prefer you didn't.' She slipped her bag onto her shoulder and reached for the door handle. 'I need to sort my life out.'

His jaw clenched with displeasure and his eyes flicked away from her.

'Please don't make this harder than it needs to be.' She opened the door and got out, then turned to look at him, but he avoided her eyes, staring out of the windscreen as if fixed on something in the distance, his fingers tapping rapidly on the steering wheel. Finally, he looked at her and nodded, and she closed the door. As soon as she did so, he shifted the car into gear and screeched away. She watched the car weaving aggressively between traffic lanes, and when she could no longer see it, she turned and headed in the direction of the tube station.

She arrived home a little earlier than she'd said. She stood in the entrance hall of their building for a few minutes, breathing deeply, trying to gather herself before opening the door to their flat. When she tried to unlock the door, she fumbled with the key, as images of her and Luke bombarded her, each sending a pulse of guilt along her veins.

'Hi!' called Will from the kitchen.

His voice cut into her. Familiar, the most familiar voice in the world. He'd only said one word but she could hear the note of excitement in him. How could he be excited? What on earth was there to be excited about?

He appeared at the kitchen door and smiled. 'I wasn't sure if you were staying here or at Sophie's.' He smiled again. 'I'm pleased you've come home.'

Her stomach seized. 'I'm just going to take a shower.'

'I'll be in the garden. Come out and join me when you're ready. I've something to show you.' He turned away but then stopped and looked back at her. 'Oh, and Emma called. She asked if you could ring the second you got in, her words. She sounded a bit stressed, just to warn you.'

'I'll shower first.'

She walked into the bathroom, legs like jelly, and slid the lock shut. She ran the shower, undressed, made sure she pushed her clothes deep into the laundry basket, then stepped under the water and cleaned herself thoroughly, trying not to think of Luke's hands and mouth on her. When she was finished, she wrapped herself in a towel, and as she did she caught sight of herself in the mirror. There were red scratches over her chest and neck. She stepped closer to the mirror and stared at her face. Her lip had a small cut on it. She lifted her fingers and ran them lightly over it. She recalled the way he'd cried out as he pushed into her and a wave of sadness swept through her. She was a different person now. Just two short weeks ago she was one half of a long-term marriage, a loyal partner, whose only want in the world was to conceive a baby with the husband she loved to take away the pain of losing one. Now she was someone completely different. A woman who'd had extra-marital sex with a man she barely knew. A liar and a cheat. She hated this new version of her. She hated her with a passion. She turned away from her reflection and walked into the bedroom and sat on the edge of the bed. She felt unwelcome. The room telling her she had no right to be there. This wasn't her space. She didn't belong there.

'Oh God,' she whispered. 'What on earth have I done?'

CHAPTER SIXTEEN

First year dormitory
Pendower Hall

Dear Mother and Father,
I hope this letter finds you well. School is fine. I've been doing my best and if you saw how hard I was trying you would be proud of me. The only thing I can't do at all is rugby. I know this will disappoint you, Father. I'm just a lot smaller than everyone else and also not very fast at running. I will keep trying though! I quite like swimming, but it's very cold and the water is quite green. If you are in the swimming team, you get to wear swimming trunks, but if you're not then you have to swim naked, nothing on at all. When I said that I didn't think that was fair to the PE teacher, he sent me to the headmaster for a caning. I'm learning the hard way that it really is best to keep your complaints quiet. Though I find it very hard! I've been saying my prayers every night and asking God to help you do your work. I hope the new church is built now and the villagers are happy they have love in their hearts at last. It's sometimes quite hard here. Lots of the boys are unkind. There is one boy, a prefect if you can imagine, who is awful. Mother, you'd say he has the Devil in his eye. I never knew what you meant by that until I saw him. Now I know just what you

mean. I'm teased every day but I do try to do what you said and ignore it, though it does get annoying and makes me very cross sometimes. Things are better now because . . . wait for this . . . I have found a friend!!! His name is William (Will) and he's great. We like all the same things like adventure stories and the Beano, and we play this game where we pretend we are marooned on a desert island with cannibals who'll eat us alive if they catch us. I know you will think this is a very foolish game but it's really fun! Will is tall and quite strong for his age (our age, I mean!) and he thinks I'm very funny. It's great! When I hear him laugh it makes me feel so happy I could burst. I feel like he is the only person in this whole place who understands me and likes me for being me and it is very comforting. As you know I have found it very lonely here but now I have Will things are looking up! We talk about everything and I can tell him what I'm thinking and even what I'm feeling deep inside. He has a camera so I'll ask him to take a picture of us together and send it to you. You'll see what good friends we are (you'll just be able to tell)!!

The food here isn't great apart from the puddings. Mother, you would love the jam sponge! They serve it with custard which is as yellow as the African sun and thick like glue but they must put a sack of sugar in it because it's so sweet it makes my teeth hurt! The showers are stone cold and take your breath away but I'm used to those now. One bad thing here (there are a few but I won't tell you them all!) is the morning runs we have to do on Tuesdays and Fridays. They make us get up at five-thirty in the morning and run up and down this hill four times. The hill is nicknamed The Killer and at the top you have to touch this tree and a prefect gives you a tick on a piece of paper when you do. It's very steep and there's another prefect who stands at the bottom and basically has the job of shouting. I am always one of the last to finish however fast I try and run. The masters are quite scary but they seem to know their jobs and I am certain I am getting a very good education, which I know is what you want for me. I miss the heat of Africa. I wonder if I will see you at Christmas or if I will be going to Aunt Grace's? It would be nice to come home if you will let me. I'm not sure Aunt Grace likes having me under her feet all the time . . .

I am doing well in Latin and with my oboe. I'll take Grade Six in January and Mr Granger thinks I should get a merit at least and a distinction if I'm lucky. I must sign off now as the bell is ringing for supper. (It's right outside the study and is so loud it deafens you!) If I did have one wish it would be that you came and got me but I know this isn't possible so I will not think about that anymore.

Please send my love to Nairobi. I miss it. I will try not to get cross or do anything that will make you embarrassed and I will keep trying at rugby, Father. Maybe God will help me with that one!

I know God loves you and the important work you do and I hope He loves me too.

Your loving son,
Luke Matthew Crawford

CHAPTER SEVENTEEN

Will's stomach buzzed with nerves as he waited for her. He began to pace, eyes fixed on the back door, fingers drumming his thighs. When he saw her coming into the kitchen he ran up to the back door so he could see her expression as she came into the garden. She stopped on the back door step, her hair wet from her shower, skin flushed and glowing, and took it all in. The surprise on her face dawned gradually, her eyes jerking from one thing to another, her head slightly shaking in disbelief. He wanted her to love it and he crossed the fingers on one hand behind his back.

'I did the garden.'

'I can see,' she said, giving him a brief smile before returning to survey his work.

'I know it doesn't make things better, I know it's not as simple as that,' he said. 'But I couldn't stop thinking about what you said, about it being neglected and scruffy, and well, once I got started, I couldn't stop. I had no idea I would love gardening so much.'

She stepped out onto the terrace, which he'd cleared of weeds and leaf matter, and he watched as she slowly absorbed the changes.

'Do you remember how excited we were when we walked out here when we were buying the place? That estate agent droning on about how close the flat was to the tube station and the patisserie that sold the best custard tarts in West London and all we could do was grin at the garden?'

'Did you have any help?' She glanced at him before walking over to look at one of the flower beds. 'So much has been done.'

'No, but I started first thing this morning. I called Frank and told him I wouldn't be in and as soon as you left I got going.'

He'd made himself a sweet, milky coffee, then dressed in a pair of jeans and an old T-shirt and set to work. He dug out an assortment of garden tools from the narrow lean-to shed, including an electric mower which hadn't been used in over a year. He got a load of rubbish bags from the kitchen and a big blue tarpaulin to use for collecting leaves and weeds and debris. The more he worked the more driven he felt, moving in a frenzy of digging and cutting and weeding. Sweat poured off him as the close, tight heat pressed down. This was his way of showing her the future. He didn't stop to wonder if this was something she wanted, he just knew he needed to tidy it up, that whatever the outcome – whether it helped or made no difference at all – it was symbolic in some way.

At just past one o'clock he took a break and went inside. He made himself a glass of orange squash which he drank in one beside the sink, then he opened the fridge, cut a chunk of cheese and rolled up a slice of ham, which he ate as he went back outside to assess his morning's work. The place resembled a wasteland with rubbish, piles of weeds, clods of earth and clippings littering the whole area. He heard his mother's reassuring voice saying things always looked worse before they got better, and for the first time in months he missed her. If she lived closer he'd have called her to come and help. She was a fantastic gardener, one of those sleeves-up kind of people who got jobs done quickly with no complaining. He wiped the back of his hand across his sweaty forehead and went back indoors to send a text to Harmony to ask what time she'd be back. She was usually home anywhere between five and seven, and today, the later the better. He wanted to have it perfect. He tidied up what he had done then spent an hour and a half turning the soil to reveal moist, deep brown earth, which made a world of difference.

'Flowers,' he said to himself.

He checked the phone for a reply from Harmony, but there was nothing. It was three o'clock. He'd taken a chance and driven to Homebase, the nearest place he knew that stocked plants. There he filled two large trollies with a variety of herbs, flowers and shrubs. He also picked up a couple of terracotta planters, a huge shiny blue urn, a fully developed specimen rose bush with flowers of such a deep red they could have been stained with blood, an Indian-style parasol with tassels and embroidery in a rainbow of threads, a small cast-iron barbecue, and some citronella candles to keep the midges away.

He checked his watch. He'd be home by half past four. He had wanted to cook her supper as well but he knew he wouldn't have time. When he got home he put a bottle of Pouilly-Fuissé in the fridge and checked there was enough ham left. There were some olives as well, and right at the back of the cupboard, he found a jar of roasted peppers. Enough for supper. He went outside and began to position the pots and plants on the beds and terrace. He didn't quite have time to dig them in, but at least it gave a good impression of what it would look like after another day or two working on it. At quarter past five he finally got a text from Harmony to say she'd be home at six. He didn't have long. He ran inside and rinsed the dirt, sweat, and grass clippings from his skin and changed into clean clothes, then grabbed a few bits. He laid a rug on the freshly cut lawn, leant the parasol at an angle over it, lit the citronella candles and placed them around the rug. His heart began to pound with excitement; he couldn't wait to see her. He couldn't wait to start trying to make her love him again.

His heart sank a little when she went straight in for a shower.

He was like a child impatient for Christmas morning. When she appeared ten minutes later her face seemed softer, still sad, but without the underlying anger. But maybe that was wishful thinking.

Now, standing in the garden, her eyes filled with tears. 'Hey,' he said. 'It's not supposed to make you cry.'

'It looks great.' She wiped her eyes as she walked across the small area of mowed grass to the opposite flowerbed. 'You've done so much. The plants are lovely,' she said.

'I didn't have time to get them in the ground.'

'It doesn't matter. I'll help you tomorrow. Do you know what they all are?'

'I've kept the labels. I'm going to try and learn their names.' He walked over to her, then took her hand and gently pulled her up to the top end of the garden where he'd put the rose in the large blue pot. He touched its petals gently. 'This rose is called Danse du Feu. Isn't that lovely?' He turned to her. 'It reminds me of the time you and I went to Anglesey, and we lit a fire on the beach.' He stared at her, waiting for her to nod, but instead she avoided his eyes, seemingly hypnotised by the brilliant red petals of the rose. 'We danced in the sand beside the fire. Do you remember? When I saw the name it made me think of that. Now it's in the garden and every time I look at it I'll remember that night. We were so happy then, weren't we?'

She nodded and smiled sadly. 'That seems a long time ago.' Her arms were crossed, hands clasping her elbows tightly. He could see the whites of her knuckles. He tried to fight his disappointment. He didn't know what he'd been expecting from her but this passive sorrow was heartbreaking.

'Harmony,' he said with a deep breath. 'I'm not asking you to forgive me. I just heard what you said, that's all. The garden needed doing and I wanted to do it for you. For us.'

She didn't say anything, just looked at the ground, and hugged herself more tightly.

'You stay here. I need to grab a few things from the kitchen. I'll be back out in a sec.'

He ran inside and opened the fridge to get out the wine, which he put into the clay wine cooler she'd given him the day North End Wine opened for trade. He put it under his arm then picked up the tray he'd already filled with the food, two glasses, and a corkscrew.

Harmony was sitting on the seat at the far end of the garden, her hands loosely clasped and resting on her knees. He put the tray on the rug on the lawn, then knelt down, smarting a little at the pain in his lower back. He thought of his mother again, of all the times he'd seen her out in their garden, pausing to stretch her back as she weeded on her knees for hours at a time.

Harmony came to join him and he handed her a glass of wine then leant over to put the bottle back in the cooler. She looked pale and drawn, her lips tight, as if she was in some sort of pain. 'Are you feeling OK?'

She sat on the rug, knees pulled tightly in to her chest. 'I'm tired, that's all.' She glanced at him again. 'I love the garden. You've worked so hard and it looks beautiful.' She gave a thin, watery smile that didn't hold.

'Well, you were right,' he said. 'When you said it was neglected. There was no reason for it and it's my fault.'

She shook her head. 'It's both our faults. You've transformed it.'

'All of this wasn't about the garden,' he said. 'I don't give a shit about the garden. I did it for you. To show you I care and that I'm going to do everything I can to make things better.' Still she wouldn't meet his eyes. 'I love you.'

She picked a single blade of grass and ran it through the tips of her fingers. Why wasn't she speaking? Why wasn't she telling him she loved him too? Dread sat in the pit of his stomach like lead. 'Harmony?' He paused. 'Do you want to try and make this work?' He regretted the question as soon as it left his mouth. What would he do if she said no?

Finally, she looked at him. She was chewing on her lip and he noticed a small red graze. 'I'm confused, but I know I love you too. But I'm worried it's all too late.' She looked like a child, her eyes large and wet with tears, vulnerable and exposed.

'I wish we could turn back the clock and do things differently.'

'I wish that too.'

'Hey,' he said with a smile, 'don't worry. We have plenty of time to talk. Are you hungry? Would you like to eat?'

'Yes,' she said, softly. 'I am a bit.'

He was filled with a sense of relief, as if her accepting supper in the garden was a step in the right direction. Though they talked as they ate, they avoided anything of importance, and conversation was stilted, as if they were on an awkward blind date, sticking to neutral subjects, small talk, safe subjects, which had the effect of magnifying the cracks in their relationship rather than helping heal them. She asked him about the garden. How much had he cleared? How hard was the earth to dig? He described the stag beetle larvae he'd found, two fat white grubs resembling a pair of albino slugs, which he'd reburied because he read somewhere they were endangered. And he told her about Frank's cat, Pinwheel, who was hit by a car and lost a leg.

'Poor thing,' she said. 'Can he walk OK?'

'Frank says he hops about as if born with three.'

The sky eventually grew dusky and with it came a chill. Harmony rubbed her arms.

'Are you cold?' Will asked. 'I can run and get you a sweater?'

'I think I'll go in,' she said, standing. 'I might take some work to bed; I've some notes to read through.'

He stood too and they faced each other.

'We'll be OK,' he said.

His sentence hovered in the still air as if unfinished. She folded her arms across her stomach and looked at the ground. He had a sudden feeling she was floating away from him, that if a heavy gust of wind blew she'd be carried away with it, and reached out for her instinctively.

'You meant it when you said you loved me, didn't you?'

She lifted her trembling hand and placed it flat against his cheek. 'Because if you do, that's enough.'

'Is it?' She dropped her hand from his face. 'I'm not sure.'

'Of course it is. Nothing is more important than that. If we love each we can work it out.'

She bent to pick up the tray and carried it back inside.

Will blew out the sickly-sweet citronella candles. He closed the parasol and threw the last olive into the bushes, then picked up the glasses and gathered the rug and followed her in. He suspected their marriage was over. It was there in her eyes. She was distant from him; she had been since the miscarriage, but there was something else there now, something he couldn't pin down. She hadn't been able to look at him, the only touch she'd given him was when she'd placed her hand on his cheek, and that gesture held more regret and sadness than he'd thought possible. It was as if she were saying goodbye. Helplessness gave way to anger, which blew in like a sea wind, bringing with it images of Alastair Farrow, leering at him with malignant eyes.

Will didn't go to bed. Instead, he sat in the living room and stared mindlessly at the television, desperate to keep his mind off Farrow. He watched the news, then a poorly written Australian drama with jerky camera work, then a repeat of a satirical comedy show, replete with canned laughter and a smug presenter in a shiny suit. But as much as he tried to keep Farrow from his head, he was there. He thought about the message on Facebook.

No hard feelings.

He walked through to the study and turned the computer on, logged on to Facebook. He reread the message – Farrow's pudgy, balding head beside it – and a bilious wave of anger tore through him.

'You shit,' he said, his voice loud against the quiet. 'You absolute piece of shit. This is all your fault.'

Then he pressed reply.

Hi Alastair, Good to hear from you. A drink sounds great. It's been a long time. I happen to be coming over your way for work next week. Are you able to meet up for a quick one, maybe Tuesday or Wednesday? Thursday would work at a push. Let me know. Will.

He jammed his finger on the return key and his message etched itself into the computer screen.

CHAPTER EIGHTEEN

Emma Barratt-Jones walked into the kitchen and dumped her shopping bags on the black granite worktop that shone like a mirror. She sighed. It was quiet. Too quiet. She didn't like it when the house was this empty, just her rattling around between school drop-off and pick-up. Nearly all her friends moaned about the school holidays, about the children under their feet, the mess, the constant *I'm-bored-mummy* whining. Not Emma. No, Emma loved the holidays. The house came alive when Josh and Abi were around. Listening to them playing and tearing around, cooking for them, chatting with them, laughing together, was bliss. The children gave this vacuous, often lonely, life of hers meaning. While they were at school the house was dormant, a museum; the only noise she could hear over the silence was her own breathing and the incessant ticking of the clock in the hall.

As she unloaded the shopping bags, she caught sight of the worktop around the sink and oven. The sunlight streamed in through the windows, highlighting a fine layer of otherwise invisible dust. She left the shopping and took the J-cloth from where it hung, folded and damp, over the rise of the expensive designer tap. She wiped the surfaces, making sure every speck of dust was lifted. Then she rinsed the cloth and refolded it over the tap. She returned to the shopping bags and thought about Ian. She'd tried to call him that morning but he'd been too busy to talk to her.

His secretary was vague, as if she was hiding something, and Emma suspected she was lying when she said Ian was in back-to-back meetings and unavailable all day. Nothing was right with him at the moment. It worried her. She was usually very good at knowing what was wrong with him and how to soothe him. She was a good wife. She knew that. She kept an immaculate house. She listened to him. She didn't shop as much as Ian would have their friends believe. In fact, she prided herself on being frugal by nature, something that came from her upbringing. Watching her mother make herself sick with the stress of trying to feed their family of six on next to nothing had stayed with her. Emma never wasted food and always shopped in the sales and took advantage of special offers. She was confident she was upholding her side of the marital bargain. But over the last few months Ian had drawn away from her and nothing she did seemed to bring him any closer, or provide him any relief or comfort. She felt redundant and helpless.

After putting the last of the shopping away, she folded the canvas bags neatly and put them into the drawer then turned the kettle on. She waited while it boiled noisily. When it clicked off, and the rumbling boil ceased, the kitchen was plunged back into dreary quiet. She went through the ritual of making a cup of tea, despite not wanting one. What she wanted – no, what she needed – was to talk to someone; the god-awful quiet was eating away at her. She leant back against the worktop and reached for the phone.

'Hello?' said Harmony.

'Hi,' she said. 'Am I disturbing you?'

'A little, but don't worry. I'm sorry I didn't call you back yesterday.'

Emma could hear the tightness in her voice and knew Harmony was deep in her work. 'It's OK, I know how busy you are. Sorry to disturb you. I hope you weren't in a meeting or anything.'

'I'm working from home today.' Harmony sighed heavily. 'My boss sent me a pretty blunt email last night asking for some changes to a report I'm writing. I'm finding it hard to focus, though.'

'Anything wrong?' Emma leant on the worktop on her elbows, chin resting on her hand. Harmony seemed to hesitate. Emma ran her finger back and forth over the granite and waited for her to speak. She thought she heard Harmony sigh again.

'No, not really.'

'Have you got time for a chat?'

'Yes,' Harmony replied. 'I could do with a break.'

They talked about this and that. Emma could tell there was something wrong. Harmony wasn't herself, she sounded tight and withdrawn, and she wondered if she'd done something to upset her, though for the life of her she couldn't imagine what.

'Are you sure you're all right?' she asked.

There was a pause. Another sigh. 'Oh, Em. It's not great, to be honest. Will and I are having a bit of a tricky time.'

'You and Will?' Emma exclaimed. 'I don't believe it. What's happened?'

Harmony didn't answer.

'Harmony?'

'It's complicated and . . .' She paused. 'And, oh God, it's got so messy.'

'Look, you've had an incredibly tough time. Having a miscarriage is a difficult thing to cope with. You need time to get over it, that's all.'

'I think, I somehow blamed him for it. But that wasn't fair, was it? It wasn't his fault. I'm always too hard on him.'

Emma furrowed her brow. 'Too hard on him? No. I don't think you are at all. Why do you say that?'

'I don't know. I just wonder whether I'm understanding enough. Sympathetic enough. I mean, like when he gave up his photography. He was so disappointed, had the wind knocked out of him and . . . oh . . . I don't know . . . I just can't remember if I was kind to him.'

'You weren't *un*kind. Not as far as I was aware anyway. I've never known you be unkind to anyone or anything in your life.

Least of all Will. You're very practical and logical about things. The photography wasn't working, he decided to give it up, you supported him in his wine venture.'

'Maybe that's what I mean. I was so focused on the idea of him setting up the shop and didn't sympathise enough about him giving up his dream. I think I always thought he should do something with wine, having worked in the industry for so long. The photography sideline seemed like a distraction. I should have been more encouraging and more understanding when it didn't take off.'

'You're being very hard on yourself,' Emma said. 'Someone has to think about the money coming in. He seemed to realise, certainly when Ian and I spoke to him, that businesses go under all the time. He said he always knew it would be hard to make the photography pay. But, look, it's worked out brilliantly with the wine shop and he seems to enjoy it.'

'I know,' she sighed. 'I just wonder if we're all too dismissive of other people's dreams.'

'Listen, I've known you a very long time and you aren't that type of person. Look at you now, worrying about it. You take everything very seriously. It was a few years ago anyway and he always seems so content and relaxed. I . . .' She was stopped in her tracks by a sudden wave of emotion, knowing she wouldn't be able to say the same thing about Ian. 'Sorry,' she managed. 'Give me a sec.'

'Are you crying?'

Emma moved the phone away from her face and pressed her sleeve into her eyes to hold her tears at bay. 'No,' she said, bringing the phone back. 'Not really.'

'What a pair we are,' Harmony said gently. 'What's wrong?'

'Probably nothing.' She paused. 'I've had one of those weeks, that's all.'

'Go on, talk to me. I can hear you're upset.'

'I am a bit.' She paused again. 'Are you sure you have time? You should be working, shouldn't you?'

'Don't be daft. Of course I've got time.'

Emma dried more tears with her sleeve. Then she rubbed at an invisible mark on the worktop. 'There's something up with Ian.'

'What type of something?'

Emma hesitated, shaking her head again, grimacing at the sound of the words out loud. 'I don't know,' she said, her voice unsteady. 'He's not himself. He's working late and drinking so much more than usual. He looks exhausted and is irritable with all of us. The children have noticed it. I know there's something wrong, but he won't tell me. He keeps saying he's fine. I know he's not.' She paused. 'I'm so worried.'

'Do you have any idea what it might be?'

'I'm not sure. It could be all sorts of things. He's just so tense.' She gave a frustrated groan. 'I keep catching him on the phone talking quietly or taking a call then shutting himself away in his office to talk. I asked him about it last night but he got so angry. He shouted at me and he never shouts. He told me there was nothing wrong and he just wanted me to leave him alone. But . . .' She hesitated again. 'Oh, God. I think he's having an affair.'

She paused, waiting for Harmony's reaction, but she was silent.

'Harmony?' she said. 'Did you hear me?'

'Yes, I heard you,' she said. 'I . . .' Emma could tell she was struggling to speak. 'I'm sure he's not.'

'Are you? I'm not sure at all. In fact, I'm convinced. I can't think of anything else. He worked late twice last week but when I called his direct line there was no answer. He's secretive and won't look me in the eye.' She sighed. 'He hasn't wanted sex in over a month and you know what he's like. I mean, it's Ian, he's usually all over me like a rash.'

Harmony was quiet again. Maybe it was the wrong time to bring up her suspicions about Ian. 'I'm sorry, I know you probably have enough on your plate worrying about you and Will without me adding more marriage problems into the mix.'

'I'm sure he isn't having an affair,' said Harmony, so quiet Emma could hardly hear her.

Emma had hoped Harmony would scoff at the idea. She wanted her to tell her not to be so ridiculous, then reassure her Ian wasn't capable of such a thing. That he loved her and was probably just dealing with problems at work. But there was a reticence in her voice. She was holding something back. It was almost as if she suspected Ian herself.

'I always imagined I'd be one of those wives who wouldn't get her knickers in a twist over this sort of thing. You know, husband gets a mistress, one less job on the to-do list, but, well, truth is I do mind. I mind a lot. I mean, God, I just cried. I don't cry. I mean, when do I ever cry?'

'Never.'

'Exactly. Last night I cried proper buckets. I had to hide in the larder, sobbing my eyes out. The children thought I was eating secret chocolate biscuits.' She breathed out heavily. 'I don't want to lose him, Harmony. We've been together too long. He's my husband and I know he's no angel – he's a bloody pain most of the time – but I love him.'

Harmony was quiet again.

'And, oh God,' she said, her voice weak. 'The children? If he leaves us . . . how will I tell them?'

'He's not going to leave you.'

Emma sniffed. 'At the moment he can hardly look at me.'

'Have you asked him about it?'

'No!' she exclaimed. 'I don't want him to tell me he's fallen in love with someone else. Honestly. I don't want to know. I just want him to get it out of his system and come back to me.' Emma stopped speaking then, overwhelmed by tears. 'I'm sorry,' she managed through sobs.

'Do you need me to drive down?'

Emma knew from her voice that she didn't really want to. Not that she'd expect her to. 'That's sweet of you to offer, but it's too far and you have work. I'll be fine. I just needed to share it with you. You're probably right. It's bound to be me overreacting as usual. I know he's got lots going on at the office.' Emma laughed through the end of her tears. 'I'll cook him a steak and kidney pie tonight. Remind him why he loves me.'

Emma nodded, bolstering herself, then took a couple of breaths and exhaled slowly. 'Right. I am absolutely fine. Everything is absolutely fine. I'm sure there's a simple explanation.'

CHAPTER NINETEEN

William waited in his car outside the pub. Rain hammered at the windscreen and, despite it still being early, the black clouds that hung low overhead darkened the sky. He'd answered Alastair's chirpy message which suggested Tuesday in a similarly enthusiastic style. He'd ended with a cheery 'looking forward to it' and had a quickly returned reply saying likewise.

Will continually questioned his motives: as he pressed send on the messages, as he grabbed his car keys and walked out of the flat, as he drove to Camberley. Yet despite all the uncertainty, despite almost turning around a hundred times, there he was, in the car park of the Dog and Duck, there to meet up with Alastair Farrow.

He took a breath, patted his hands against the driver's wheel, then unclipped his seat belt. 'Come on, you can do this,' he whispered, though as he walked towards the pub, he wondered what it was he actually wanted to do. He had no idea.

The pub was low-ceilinged, with a brash tartan carpet and horse brasses that hung on black-painted beams, and cheap dark tables with wooden chairs with green PVC seat pads. It smelt of old beer, last Sunday's roast, and the faint tang of bleach. Will walked up to the bar and smiled at the heavy-set barman who was wiping a cloth over one of the beer taps.

'Yes, mate,' he said, balling the cloth and dropping it onto the counter.

'What do you have in the way of red wine?'

'Large or small?'

'Is there a wine list?'

The man shook his head. 'Choice of two. Merlot or Cab Sauv.'

Will nodded. 'A large Cabernet Sauvignon and a bag of ready salted, please.' He kept his eyes on the bar and focused on the voices behind him in the hope of picking out any that might be familiar. He hated how anxious he was. It was ridiculous; years had passed. He forced himself to turn around to check the pub properly. He spotted Alastair immediately. Having studied his photographs on Facebook for a considerable amount of time, he recognised him easily. He was sitting at a table in the corner, scrolling his phone, thumb working rhythmically, expression unchanging. He wore a green sweater with a pink shirt, a gold watch on his right wrist, brown cord trousers and tan leather shoes with a stripe of red sock just visible. As he studied him Will felt his knees give way. He reached for the bar to steady himself, breathed slowly and evenly as he allowed the memories of that afternoon to play out, not fighting to block them as he usually would. He felt the thump of fists into his sides and back. He remembered Farrow's smell; cigarettes, school soap, alcohol. He felt his full weight on him as Farrow held him down and pushed his face into the dirt, struggling and panicking as that weight squeezed the air from his lungs.

'That'll be six-fifty, mate.'

Will took his eyes off Alastair and slid his credit card out of his wallet.

'Want to start a tab?'

Will nodded absently, his mind focused on trying to hold things together. He handed the barman his credit card, which the man put with the till receipt into an empty pint glass behind the bar.

Will thanked him and picked up his crisps and wine, took a moment to compose himself, then walked towards the table.

'Alastair?' he said, as he drew level with him.

The man looked up in momentary surprise, as if he'd forgotten he was there to meet someone, then hurriedly put his phone down and stood. He held out his hand.

'Will English! Well I never.'

Will shook his hand. A shiver ran up his arm as their hands touched. 'Alastair.'

'Call me Al. Nobody calls me Alastair these days, except for my mother, but only when she's cross with me, of course.' He guffawed with laughter. He was plumper than he'd been in the photos, his hair cut close to his head to make light of the baldness. His skin had that reddened quality which betrayed a fondness for plenty of booze. His eyes were surrounded by deep laughter lines and his lips were so dark they were almost the colour of purple plums.

Will gestured at Alastair's pint glass which was three-quarters full. 'Do you want another before I sit down? I've left a card behind the bar.'

'I'm good for the moment,' Alastair said genially as he sat down. 'Don't want to get into trouble with the wife.' He winked at Will, who managed a tight smile as he sat down opposite him, heart racing. This was even harder than he'd imagined it would be.

'So what's it been?' asked Alastair brightly, showing no nerves at all. 'Twenty years? Must be. At least.'

Will plastered his face with a smile. 'Yes,' he said. 'At least.'

'So go on then, what do you do?'

'I've a wine shop,' he said. He stared at Alastair's face, eyes drawn to the scar that ran down his cheek.

'Ah, wine. Nice. I'm a bit of claret man myself. Do you sell much claret?'

'Yes.' Will dragged his eyes from the screaming scar. 'Quite a bit. How about you?'

'Accountant, I'm afraid.' He smiled at Will. 'Bit of a buzz-kill, that one. Yawn yawn.' He lifted his beer and drank. 'Married?'

'Yes, I am.'

'She's all right, is she?'

'All right?'

'A good catch?'

Will stared at him for a moment or two then Alastair laughed loudly. 'Mine's a bit of a dog, if I'm honest. I bet yours is lovely. Lucky bugger.'

Will moved his wine glass to the side and leant forward. 'I need to talk to you about what happened.'

Alastair looked puzzled.

'At school,' Will said. 'You see, when I read your message the other night, I thought it was strange you weren't more apologetic.'

'Apologetic? For what?'

Will laughed in astonishment. Indignant rage flared inside him.

'For what?' Will repeated. 'For being a fucking cunt, that's what.'

Alastair's joviality fell away and he glanced nervously over his shoulder. 'Steady on,' he said, keeping his voice low. 'That's a bit much.'

'A bit much?' Will needled his eyes into Alastair's puffy face. 'You're joking, right?'

'This is about school?'

'Of course it's about school!' Will shook his head and stared at the man, unable to comprehend how he wasn't getting it. He sat back in his chair. 'You do remember what you did, don't you?'

Alastair's face broke into a smile. 'Will, come on, chap. We were at public school. That kind of thing happened all the time. It's just banter. Mucking around.' His smile broadened. 'You know that. That's what went on. Still does today. There isn't a boarding school in the country that isn't the same. There's no need to get worked up about it. Like I said in my message, I was a bit of a cock at times, I know that. But that's the way it was.' He reached for his beer and drank. 'It was just banter.'

Will's blood boiled with over two decades of bottled-up rage. He wanted to punch him. That would wipe the stupid smile off his fat, ugly face, wouldn't it?

'Banter?' he said instead. 'No, banter is joking around, playing. It doesn't hurt anyone. What you did – beating up young boys, scaring the shit out of them, and doing . . .' He hesitated. ' . . . doing God only knows what – you can't call that banter. It's bullying. Bullying at best, abuse at worst.'

Alastair's features hardened and Will saw a flash of the boy who had terrified him, beaten him and pushed his face into the ground until he thought he might suffocate, and an old fear rose up, a fear he hadn't felt in a very long time.

'You're wrong,' Alastair said, his voice cold and low. 'I *can* call it banter. Because that's what it was.'

They stared at each other. Then Alastair ran his hand over his head and rubbed the back of his neck. He leant forward, turning his face so his scarred cheek faced Will, and jabbed his finger hard against it a couple of times. 'You see this? You see it?' he said, through gritted teeth. 'Am I moaning about this? Am I begging for an apology? No, I'm not. Because it was just mucking around. It was banter.' He sat back and gave a dismissive shake of his head. 'Jesus Christ, English, grow some bloody balls. That stuff is what went on. At Eton, at Harrow, at Gordonstoun, and at bloody Pendower Hall. And it bred *men*. Real men who took it on the chin and grew stronger. Bloody hell, some of this country's greatest leaders would have seen the back of an older boy's hand. Do they sit there like you, licking their wounds, feeling sorry for themselves, and asking for bloody *apologies*?'

Will couldn't believe what he was hearing. It was like listening to his father all over again. All that repellent claptrap about how boarding school bred real men, men who ran the world, men who built the sodding Empire, men for whom this type of thing was character-building and expected.

'It happened to all of us,' Alastair continued. 'It happened to me when I was in the bottom years, and the boys who had their fun with me had the same done to them. Yes, some got it worse than others, but that's survival of the fittest. You might not like it. It might not stand up against all that namby-pamby, woke rubbish we're forced to suck on today, but that's the way it was. Some of us are on top of the pile and some, like you, at the bottom. Like it or not, the system works.' He reached for his drink, sniffing loudly, then rolled his shoulders a couple of times as if limbering up for a boxing bout. 'You got children? A son, maybe?'

Will stayed silent and didn't move a muscle. It was like being stuck in a parallel universe, surreal and nightmarish. He thought of Harmony, of how lovely it would be if he was sitting with her, sharing the packet of crisps that sat unopened on the table, chatting about everything and nothing. He pictured her smile and the way she toyed with her necklace, the look in her eyes before she kissed him.

'I've got a son. Good kid. Bright. Tough. He'll go far. He pulls the legs off beetles and the wings off flies. He punches his friends and they punch him back. For fun. For exercise. Because that's what boys do to amuse themselves. And it's not just Charlie. They all do it. How old were you when you started at boarding school?'

Will didn't answer.

'I was six. Thrown in at the deep end with twenty other six-year-olds. No parents anywhere near us. It was Lord of the bloody Flies and you know it. Most of the masters were wankers. They knew what was going on and it amused them. Those that didn't like it turned a blind eye.'

Will pictured Drysdale then, that sick look of pleasure which settled over his face as he flexed the cane a couple of times to 'loosen her up'.

'And now here you are, sitting there like a saggy-titted feminist wanting to . . .' He bent his voice into whiney sing-song, ' . . . talk about what happened.' He leant forward, mouth turned down, eyes narrowed and cold as ice. 'You want to know what happened?' he spat. 'I'll tell you what happened,' he continued, not allowing time for Will to answer his question. 'Nothing. Nothing bloody happened, you pathetic, whiny little shit.'

Will stared at his round face, polished puce beneath a thin sheen of sweat. 'No, Alastair, something *did* happen.' He kept his voice low and calm. 'You know what you did.'

Alastair Farrow's face darkened like a storm cloud. Will's heart started pumping again as the terror he'd felt on that late afternoon began to creep up on him. The noise of his panting breath loud in his ears as he'd turned to run. The jeering. Luke's screams echoing in the trees.

'I was there, *English*.' Alastair stared hard at Will. 'I was there when you told Drysdale nothing happened. Don't go making stories up now because your life isn't quite what you'd hoped and you want someone to blame.' He shook his head, reached for his glass and drained the remainder of his beer. Then he picked up his phone and made to leave. 'I don't know why I agreed to meet up with you,' he said, with poisonous contempt. 'Forced to listen to you bleating on and on. You know how it was back then. It was kick or be kicked, and keep your mouth shut.' He looked at Will then like he was shit on the bottom of his shoe and gave a derisive laugh. 'No wonder wankers like you got the crap beat out of them.' Alastair shook his head again as he looked down his nose at Will. 'Moaning and complaining. Full of self-pity. *Poor me, what a shitty time at school I had*, cry, cry, cry. I bet you think about what your life might have been like if only you'd skipped happily through childhood getting cuddles and love. You know, English, if you and those other wastes-of-space had just played the game, showed some bloody backbone, then maybe you'd have had an easier time. Maybe it was your fault all along.'

'Played the game?'

Alastair smirked and stood. 'It was good to catch up,' he said. 'Don't bother trying to contact me again.'

Everything inside Will erupted then. Every part of his body inflated with angry loathing. His hand shot out and grabbed Alastair by the neck. Alastair fell against the table, knocking both glasses over. One rolled and smashed on the floor. There was a loud shout from the barman. Two men nearby jumped to attention; one of them rested a hand on Will's arm, the other told him to calm down: 'Easy now, take it outside.'

But Will squeezed harder, a red mist blurring his self-control. Alastair's eyes widened and he lifted his hands, trying to free himself from Will's grip.

'I could fucking *kill* you. You're the waste of space. *You*, Alastair. Not us.'

'Come on now, mate,' said the man beside them. 'Let go of him. We're all having a nice quiet drink here. Nobody wants this.'

Will glanced at the man, and caught sight of the barman walking over with a set grimace. Others around them looking concerned, unsure whether to step in and help or let it unfurl.

Christ. What was he doing? What was this achieving? Nothing. People like Alastair Farrow could never be changed. Their morality – their immorality – was written into their DNA. This man would never admit he'd done anything wrong because he didn't see it as wrong. Attempts to make him see that were futile.

Will let go of Alastair with a final push and he fell back onto the chair, rubbing his neck and swearing under his breath. The barman and one of the men nearby grabbed hold of Will.

'You OK, Al?' the barman said, his fingers digging into Will's arm.

Alastair nodded. 'I'm fine. Just a misunderstanding. My friend's leaving now.'

'People like you make me sick,' Will growled, shrugging the two men off him.

'You're pathetic.'

The words cut into him. No. It wasn't him who was pathetic. It was Alastair. Alastair Farrow, a pathetic bully with an over-inflated sense of self-importance living an empty, pathetic life. Will glanced at the two men either side of him who were poised and ready to grab hold of him if they had to. He turned back to Alastair and shook his head.

'You're not worth it,' he said, through gritted teeth.

Will turned and walked out of the pub. He jogged through the rain and climbed into his car. He closed the door and rested his head against the steering wheel. He shook as he thought of Alastair's smug face and his incomprehensible lack of remorse. There were so many things he wished he'd said to that snarling, nasty piece of work.

'Fuck!' he shouted, lifting his head and banging his hands against the steering wheel. 'Don't do this to yourself!'

He saw himself back in the prep room, desperately trying to concentrate on his English essay. Saw his housemaster, Mr Fraser, walking over to him. Mr Fraser, a short man with tufts of grey hair that fringed a shiny bald pate, who though firm was decent and popular with the boys.

'English, you need to come with me.' His voice was quiet, almost apologetic, and his eyes seemed unable to meet Will's. 'Mr Drysdale needs to see you.'

Will's stomach had turned over. 'Why, sir?'

The housemaster seemed reticent. 'Best just get to his office.'

'Am I in trouble, sir?' Will asked as he closed his exercise book and put the lid on his fountain pen.

Mr Fraser had rested a hand on his shoulder. 'Tell the truth and you'll be fine.'

Mr Fraser had lied.

All he'd ever wanted was to bury Alastair Farrow and the rest of it, but he knew now it would never happen. He sat up, turned the engine on, pushed the car into gear, and drove out of the car park without a backward glance. Will sped along the roads, his mind full of Farrow's barefaced denial, and his unshakeable belief that what happened was acceptable.

When he got to the main road he pushed his foot to the floor, feeling the engine strain, feeling like he wanted to drive faster and faster. The windscreen wipers worked overtime against the heavy rain. As he gained speed, his anger and frustrations boiled over and he began to shout, loud and guttural, banging the steering wheel with one hand as hard as he could, until it stung. When, finally, he couldn't shout any longer and his pent-up rage had begun to dissipate, he eased off the accelerator and breathed heavily, emotionally spent and desperate to be at home.

He walked into the flat and closed the door and found Harmony on the sofa, watching the news, feet up, hugging a cushion. She was wearing a pair of leggings and an old baggy T-shirt, her hair loose, a little straggly. She gave him a weak smile when he came in.

He sank heavily into the armchair opposite her. He wanted her to pat the sofa beside her like she usually did, gesture for him to sit with her, but she didn't move. He closed his eyes, resting his head against the back of the armchair. He was exhausted; his limbs felt cast in concrete, as if he'd never be able to move them again.

Just then her phone rang. He opened his eyes and watched her pick it up. She turned it off without answering it and put it back on the coffee table. Her mouth twitched like it did sometimes when she was angry. At that moment, the pressure of keeping everything inside him finally became too much. It was like he was about to explode into a million pieces.

'I saw that guy earlier today. The one Luke mentioned. Alastair Farrow.' His voice cracked as he spoke.

'The one from your school?'

Will nodded.

She picked up the remote and turned off the television; her eyes had softened and she fixed them on him, waiting.

'Oh God. It was awful.' He pushed the heels of his palms against his eyes. 'I lost my temper. I shouted at him in the middle of a crowded pub. Christ, I grabbed him by the bloody neck.' He sighed heavily and looked at her. 'I thought he might show some sort of remorse, might at least seem ashamed, but he couldn't have cared less.'

'What did he do to you?' she asked softly. 'At school, I mean. Why did you expect remorse?'

Will hesitated. It felt alien to be talking about this. He'd made such an effort to keep it buried. But what good had that done? 'He made people's lives hell. For fun. He was – is – a vile bully.' He broke off. He knew he had opened the box now, that he was going to tell her everything.

He took a deep breath and braced himself.

'There was this one afternoon,' he said, starting slowly. 'The day before Luke was expelled. He and I were in the woods, up by that tree we used to climb. It was late October. We'd had supper and were supposed to be in prep, you know, doing homework. But we'd crept out, bunked off. I had my Polaroid camera and was taking photos of stuff and Luke was trying to make a harpoon with the Swiss Army knife my dad gave me, but these older boys, proper nasty bastards in the sixth form, found us. Farrow was one of them.'

The incident he described had been stored away for twenty-five years, but as he recounted the story to Harmony, every single detail played out in his mind as if it were happening there and then.

'They asked what we were doing in their smoking room, said this part of the wood with the Judas tree was for sixth form only. They said we were trespassing.'

Will recalled the malice in Alastair Farrow's voice. He was much older than them, a senior prefect and captain of cricket. He was popular and respected in his peer group and the staff room.

He had brown hair that flopped over his eyes and that air of confidence that came from a combination of good looks and sporting prowess. But there was a look in his eyes, the Devil's look, Luke called it. He had a way of staring at the younger boys, nostrils flared, lip curled, as if he wanted to slice them up into bits. When the group had found them, cigarettes clamped to their mouths, cans of lager clutched in their hands, Farrow's eyes glinted in a way that turned Will's stomach, in a way that told him he and Luke were in serious trouble.

Farrow and the others had laughed and jeered as they drew on their cigarettes and drank from their cans.

'Look at the little prick!'

'Thinks he's David *fucking* Bailey with that camera.'

'What a wanker!'

'How many of them were there?' Harmony asked.

Her voice broke into his thoughts. 'Five,' he said.

Will had looped his camera over his neck and looked desperately around for an escape route. He'd glanced back at Farrow, who smiled unpleasantly and shook his head slowly. Will felt sick. He turned to look at Luke. His eyes were set like stone, staring at the boys like he wanted to kill them, his lips twitching, fists clenching and unclenching at his sides like beating hearts. 'Don't do anything,' Will had pleaded silently. 'Please don't do anything.'

He kept telling himself they were OK, it was just Farrow and his friends having a laugh, messing about, that soon they'd get bored and leave them alone. He willed Luke to keep calm, willed him to keep his temper in check, but he could see him seething.

'Alastair told me to give him my camera,' he said to Harmony. A vivid image of Farrow flew into his head. The older boy putting his arm around his shoulders, drawing him close.

'So who do we have here? David fucking Bailey and Puke Crawford – Bible Boy – hiding out in the woods like a couple of homo-hobbits.'

Will recalled the smell of his warm, sour breath laced with cigarettes and lager.

'He said if I didn't give him the camera they'd beat the living daylights out of us.' He glanced at Harmony. 'Those were his words. The living daylights.'

Harmony shook her head, lips parted, eyes reflecting her horror.

'I didn't want him to have it so I took it off my neck and threw it as far as I could into the bushes. I don't know what I was thinking, looking back on it. It was only a stupid camera, but it was my favourite thing in the whole world, and the thought of him breaking it or stealing it was unbearable.' Will sniffed and clasped his hands in front of him. 'Anyway, Alastair Farrow didn't like that too much.'

The older boy had angered like a wasp.

Go and get it.

But Will had stood his ground.

Farrow shoved him so hard he went down on his knees. Then a kick to the stomach. Luke began to scream.

'Don't hurt him! Get off him! Get off him!'

Will tried to tell him to be quiet, but was too winded to speak.

'Alastair was . . .' Will hesitated and glanced up at Harmony, who looked horrified. 'He was hurting me. The others were laughing. Luke was screeching at them to leave me alone and all I could think was: *shut up, Luke. Shut up. Stop screaming at them, you idiot. You're making it worse.*' Will paused and laid his head back against the chair. 'The next thing I knew Farrow was on top of me, had my face pressed into the ground. I had all these leaves and dirt in my mouth, and he was punching my head and body again and again.' An unwelcome memory of the earth and grit in his mouth passed through Will and made him want to spit.

'Oh my God.' Harmony whispered the words. 'I'm so sorry.'

Will didn't want her sympathy. His skin crawled with guilt.

'Luke began to make this awful sound, like some weird war

cry, and he ran at Farrow and the next thing I knew he'd pushed him off me. Then I heard Alastair scream. When I looked up I saw his face was covered in blood. Luke had sliced his face open with my penknife.'

Dread filled Will as he watched Luke standing there, panting, eyes crazed, hand tightly clasping Will's knife. The silence that fell around them was terrifying. All he could hear was the slight rustle of the wind in the leaves of the Judas tree that towered over them. Farrow's eyes glinted. A sheen of bloodied saliva coated his lips. One side of his face was scarlet, blood flowing from a cut that ran from his eye to his chin.

You fucking bastards.

Will closed his eyes as he recalled Alastair's words. He'd stared, horrified at the blood on the older boy's face and the fury blazing in his eyes, lips curled back to show gritted, bloodied teeth.

'It wasn't me. I didn't do it! Don't hurt me. It was him!'

Will felt sick as he recalled the look on Luke's gaunt face. Bewilderment and shock. Will's hand flew up to his mouth, but it was too late, the words were out.

'You're pathetic, English. Get the fuck out of here.'

'No, Will. Don't leave me!'

Luke and Will had locked eyes.

'You watch my back, I'll watch yours. Remember, Will? You remember what we promised?'

Then he lifted his right hand like a Red Indian to show Will the scar that crossed his palm.

Farrow began to laugh and he shoved Will backwards.

'You're pathetic.'

Will remembered Luke screaming for him to help him as Farrow set upon him like a ravenous lion on a deer. But he just stood there, frozen to the spot in fear.

'They hurt him. Badly.'

Nausea swept through Will.

Harmony stood up and walked over to him. She sat on the side of the armchair and stroked his head. He leant against her, his eyes squeezed closed trying to block out the memory of Luke's screaming.

Her phone buzzed, the ringer on silent, the vibrations making it dance on the tabletop.

'Sorry,' she breathed.

She got up and turned the phone off then went back to Will and smiled softly.

'Take the call if you want to,' Will said.

'No, it's not important.'

'I should have told you years ago. But it's so painful thinking about it. Alastair is a bastard, but I promise you, I'm fine. He did what he did, he's a nasty piece of work, but there's nothing we can do about it. Some people are just arseholes.'

She nodded then wrapped her arms around him, resting her chin on the top of his head. 'I'm so sorry that happened to you.'

Will woke in the middle of the night and felt for her. She wasn't in bed and the duvet was neatly pulled up on her side, the pillow untouched. Then he heard a soft cough from her study. He checked the time. It was quarter past two. He lay still and listened. She was talking to someone. Though he couldn't hear her words there seemed to be a level of urgency, as if there was some sort of problem. He got out of bed, walked down the corridor, and opened the door to her study. She wasn't on the phone, which was beside the keyboard, but her computer was on. She sat at her desk in her dressing gown and slippers. She jumped when he said her name.

'You scared me,' she said, with a nervous laugh. 'Have you been there long?'

'No, but I heard you on the phone. Is everything all right?'

'It was Emma. What she's doing calling at this time, I don't know.' She was tense; something wasn't right. 'She said she couldn't sleep. She's pretty upset, but I told her I'd call back in the morning.'

'Anything serious?'

'Problems with Ian. Sorry if I woke you.'

'You didn't. Are you coming back to bed?'

'I don't think I'll get back to sleep at the moment. I've got so much on with work so thought I'd do a bit until I feel sleepy.' She glanced at him with a tight smile. 'I've got a small problem I need to sort out.' She put the tip of her thumb to her mouth and chewed on it gently.

'Can I get you anything?'

'No, thank you,' she said, turning back to her computer screen. 'I won't be long.'

'But then you'll come back to bed?'

'Yes,' she said. 'When I've dealt with it, I'll come back.'

CHAPTER TWENTY

Harmony walked into the restaurant and scanned the place for Luke. It was a huge, airy room with modern furnishings. It bustled with noise as conversation fought to be heard above the sounds of the open kitchen where a dozen sweating chefs could be seen cooking and yelling orders. She watched a flame leap a foot out of a pan, the chef turning his head and leaning back to avoid it then heaving the pan upwards a couple of times, expertly tossing the food into the air. He swept his arm across his brow and called out in rapid Italian to someone behind him. It was reassuringly busy, every table filled, and nobody noticed her as they talked avidly, laughed and ate. Her stomach buzzed with nerves. Luke had called seven times yesterday and sent a handful of texts, each of them incriminating should Will happen to see them. When he'd called as Will was telling her what happened at school she knew she couldn't ignore him any longer. She'd waited until Will was asleep then crept into her office. She'd panicked when she heard Will getting out of bed.

'I'll call you in a minute,' she whispered hurriedly. 'Don't call me back.'

He said he was desperate to see her. He couldn't get her out of his head. He was going insane.

She couldn't believe she'd got herself into this mess. She'd let her anger at Will muddy her thinking. She would give anything to turn the clock back and stop herself getting into Luke's car. But she couldn't. And now she had to put an end to it.

She'd spent the morning at the British Library rather than in the office. Libraries calmed her. Row upon row of stacked shelves, insulating her, holding her safely. She'd always felt at home with books. While Sophie had spent any rare free time attempting to cook up half-decent dishes from the meagre supply of store-cupboard ingredients her grandmother kept in stock, Harmony would curl up on the sofa and read. She read anything from Ray Bradbury to Stephen King, Jane Austen to Jilly Cooper. There was always a dictionary beside her. If she came across a word she didn't know she'd stop and look it up. Sophie teased her and called her a nerd, but Harmony didn't care. Stories were an escape from her fatherless, motherless world, a security blanket for whenever she felt vulnerable.

'Can I help you, madam?' asked a man dressed in a spotless black polo shirt, the name of the restaurant stitched across his left breast.

'I'm meeting someone,' she said. 'I'm not sure if he's here already.'

'And the name of the reservation?'

'Luke Crawford,' she said. 'I think it was for one o'clock. I'm a bit early.'

The man looked down his list then nodded. 'Mr Crawford hasn't arrived yet. Shall I show you to your table?'

The table was near the back of the room and as she sat down she felt immediately less conspicuous and her body relaxed.

'Would you like something to drink?'

'Iced water, please. Tap is fine.'

He smiled at her and placed two leather menus on the table. 'I'll send someone over with your water. Can I get you anything else?'

'No, thank you. I'll wait until my friend arrives.' The man left. Harmony wished she hadn't used the word friend. It sounded too intimate, too telling; she should have said colleague instead.

When Harmony saw Luke walk in through the double glass

doors her heart missed a beat. She reached for her water and had a sip, lifting her eyes over the rim of the glass to watch him talk to the waiter in the polo shirt. She saw the waiter point. Luke smiled and nodded in her direction. She cast her eyes downwards so as not to catch his gaze.

As he approached the table she looked up. 'Hello, Luke,' she said, her voice shaking.

He leant in and kissed her cheek. 'I've missed you,' he said. He sat down and immediately gestured to a nearby waiter.

'Yes, sir?' said the waiter, hurrying over.

'We'd like to order some wine and some sparkling water.' He looked at Harmony. 'Red or white?'

'Not for me, thank you,' she said, trying to keep her voice level. 'Just the sparkling water.'

She resisted the urge to thank the waiter, who didn't seem to mind Luke's brusqueness.

'I've haven't stopped thinking about you,' he said.

'Shhh.' She looked nervously around her.

'Why?'

'I don't want anyone to hear.'

He laughed loudly. 'Who's going to care?'

'Me.' She picked up the menu and fixed her eyes on it. 'I gave you specific instructions not to call or text me.'

'Specific instructions?' he repeated with amusement.

'Yes.'

'I was desperate.' He leant forward and laid his hand on her lower arm. 'I can't think about anything else.'

She laid the menu on the table and looked at him. 'I told you not to call me. Will was with me when you did last night. I can't believe you did that.'

Luke fell silent, his disappointment plain. She recalled Will telling her last night about the incident with Farrow and the older boys and felt a pang of pity for him.

She lifted the menu. 'So what's good?' she said, wanting to avoid the hurt in his eyes.

'It's all good but if you like seafood, the salt and pepper squid is fantastic. If you don't, the carpaccio is delicious. Their pasta dishes are excellent.'

'I dislike carpaccio,' she said. 'Remember? The well-cooked steak and the liberal's conscience?'

'With all the guilt cooked out of it.'

She nodded, lips pursed. His eyes were fixed on hers, but he looked at her differently to the way he had before their illicit afternoon. The desire had gone. The playfulness. There was a coldness there now and the hairs on her arms and back of her neck prickled.

'Luke, I came here to—' She was cut short by the waiter who arrived with a bottle of sparkling water. He opened it and poured each of them a glass, then retrieved an electronic notepad. Harmony hadn't even looked at the food, so hurriedly scanned the menu and ordered the salt cod soup and a fennel risotto. Luke then asked for the carpaccio and a seafood linguini.

'You ignored my recommendations?'

She closed the menu without replying.

Luke leant forward, his forearms in front of him.

Harmony stared at his hand on the white tablecloth, those long fingers and perfect nails, gentle moons of white at the base of each one. She recalled his fingers on her skin, grasping her hair, inside her. He moved his hand so the tip of his middle finger rested against hers. She drew away from him. 'How was your business trip?' she asked, her eyes fixed on the table in front of her.

'All I could think about was you, so it was both a waste of time and frustrating. Did you think about me?'

She paused, took a deep breath and lifted her eyes to look at him. 'What we did was wrong.'

'Wrong?' he said, his brow furrowing in confusion. 'Nothing about it was wrong.'

'*Everything* about it was wrong, Luke.'

He sat back in his chair and folded his arms. His features had set hard, eyes narrowed, burning now with the same angry intensity they had when they'd had sex.

'I'm married and having sex with another man is wrong.'

'Your marriage isn't working.'

'My marriage is fine.'

'If your marriage was fine you wouldn't have come looking for me.'

'I didn't come looking for you,' she said, making an effort to keep her voice down. 'We met at the party and then you . . .' She paused as the waiter appeared with a basket of bread, continuing only when he left. 'Then you pursued me.'

He lifted his eyebrows. '*Pursued* you? Is that what you think?'

She reached for her glass and drank some water. She didn't want to rush, didn't want to say the wrong thing, something that would lead him on. She needed to keep her head straight. 'You made your feelings pretty clear at the party. Then you came to my work and took me for a drink and then asked me, in no uncertain terms, to sleep with you. Then you said you wanted to apologise. We were supposed to go for coffee and . . .' She tailed off, leaving the rest of that afternoon unspoken.

'And you got into my car. You let me kiss you.' He reached for some bread, then tore a small piece off it. 'Then you directed me to your husband's photography studio, unlocked the door, took me inside, and we fucked.' He put the bread in his mouth.

'Keep your voice down,' she whispered.

'Is it easier to believe I chased you? That I made you do it?'

'Yes,' she retorted. 'Of course it is. If I think too hard about what I've done, I feel sick.' She drew another deep breath. 'But there were reasons. Things have happened in the last six months that left a chasm between Will and me.' She hesitated, wondering if she should be opening her and Will up to Luke like this. 'Neither of us dealt well with losing our baby. He wasn't able to support me and I felt very alone. I was angry at him.' She paused. 'And there was this numbness around me, like all my anger and resentment and sadness was forming a wall around me. Then I met you and I seemed to feel something again. Something powerful and it was confusing and, yes, exciting. And I lost control of myself and—' She stopped herself, aware she was talking too much, drifting away from her objective of finishing whatever this was and trying to justify it.

'And what?' he said. 'I want to know.'

She took a moment to compose herself. 'Will and I might be going through a rough patch, but I love him. Deeply. What we did should never have happened.'

'But it did happen.' He reached beneath the table and laid his hand on her knee, slowly moving up her thigh, stroking her gently.

His touch sent tingles down her spine and for a split second she let it start to carry her away. But then she caught herself. She pushed his hand away. 'No.' She reached for her water again and found she was shaking. 'I love Will.'

'Do you?' He sounded accusatory rather than curious.

'Just because a marriage has rough patches or people make mistakes, doesn't mean you stop loving each other.'

He let out a contemptuous sigh. 'That word. God, that pointless word. *Love*. What does love even mean?'

'Don't try and belittle what I'm saying. You know what it means. Or, I don't know, maybe you don't. But I do and I know I love him. And,' she hesitated, not wanting to be disloyal, 'he needs me right now.' She glanced at Luke. 'Lots of things he's tried to forget have resurfaced since he saw you. Yesterday he met one of the men who bullied him.' She watched his face for a reaction, but there was nothing.

'Who?' he asked.

'Alastair Farrow.'

'Farrow,' he repeated. 'Why did he see him?'

'I don't know. I think they contacted each other through Facebook. Anyway, Will was in a state when he got home. I think he wanted some sort of closure which is why he met up with him. But they ended up fighting. He got angry and made a scene. Threatened the guy. When he got back he was upset. It really shook him.'

Luke was silent but his mind was whirring, his fingers tapping the table rapidly.

'Will needs me right now.'

'And so you're staying with him because he has unresolved issues?'

'That's a simplistic way of looking at it. I've been with him for over twenty years. His issues clearly have roots in a difficult childhood. He's internalised what went on. All this time he's told me his past doesn't affect him, but it does.'

Luke blinked slowly and sat back in his chair. 'It's difficult to articulate what damage can be caused by people like Alastair Farrow. We deal with bad experiences in our own ways – whatever ways we think will work best – but there will always be times when we can't control our emotions, when we are at a low point. But you shouldn't stay with someone because of some bad things that happened to him twenty-five years ago. You have to stay with him because you want to stay with him.'

'I want to stay with him.'

'That's not what it looks like to me.'

'I was angry with him. So angry it clouded my judgement. It was a mistake. He's my husband. You were married,' she said, glancing at him, unsure if mentioning his wife might upset him. 'You must understand what I'm saying. There are times you are close and times you drift apart. It's not as simple as falling in and—' She stopped speaking suddenly as a group of men came into the restaurant. 'Jesus Christ!' she hissed and dropped her head, lifting a hand to shield her face from them. 'It's Ian.'

'Really?' Luke glanced over his shoulder. 'I know he likes this place.'

She turned on him angrily. 'You brought me to a place that you know my best friend's husband goes to?'

'I didn't know he'd be here.' Luke seemed unconcerned.

'Hide your face!' she said, as she began to panic. Her eyes darted around as she looked for the nearest escape from the restaurant. 'He'll think there's something going on between us.'

'He'll be right.' Luke smiled.

'Oh my God. Please tell me you didn't do this on purpose. Did you know he was coming here? Shit. Are you wanting Will to find out?'

He didn't say anything.

'Jesus,' said Harmony, glancing over at Ian's group.

'Calm down. We're just having lunch,' he said. 'We bumped into each other. It's perfectly innocent.'

'Emma will know that's not true. I'm never in this part of town. What reason would I have to be here?'

'Ian won't tell her.'

'Of course he will,' she said, through gritted teeth. She glanced up again. Ian and his companions were settling themselves down at a table on the other side of the restaurant.

'He won't because I'll tell him not to.'

'And, what, he'll just do what you say?' She shook her head in disbelief.

'Yes, exactly. I'm his lawyer, remember?'

She shielded her face, while keeping her eyes bolted on Ian, who was sitting with his back towards her. 'I'm not staying here. I don't want Ian to know we're having lunch together.' She was filled with such genuine fear then, she knew for certain that she wanted to do anything she could to fix her marriage.

She stood. As she did so Luke grabbed hold of her wrist.

'Will doesn't deserve you,' he said. 'He takes things for granted, Harmony.'

Luke's fingers dug into her skin.

'Let go of me,' she said firmly. They locked eyes for a moment or two before his fingers loosened. 'This?' She gestured to the two of them. 'Whatever it was? It's over.'

'No.'

She leant in close to him. 'Yes. Leave me alone. You and I are finished.'

'We haven't even started.'

'Then there's nothing to finish, is there?' she hissed.

She straightened then glanced in Ian's direction again. He was deep in conversation with one of his companions. She took a deep breath and started to walk towards the door, her head angled away from his table, eyes on the floor. Her heart thumped as if it might break through her chest. At any moment he was going to spot her. At any moment he would call her name across the restaurant.

When she reached the door, she pushed out into the sunshine and walked as quickly as she could past the window. As soon as she was clear of the restaurant, safe from Ian's view, away from Luke, relief washed over her. She looked over her shoulder, back towards the restaurant, but thankfully there was no sign of Luke. She broke into a jog to put as much distance between them as possible.

CHAPTER TWENTY-ONE

His aunt sat in the driver's seat and clipped her seat belt in. He sat in the back seat and stared at the back of her head.

'Your father,' she said, as she turned the Morris Minor's engine on, 'is *speechless*.'

Luke studied her hair, the way it clumped together in greasy, grey whorls. The rosy pink skin on the back of her neck was patched with some kind of flaky skin condition that left a sprinkling of dandruff on the shoulders of her heavy black coat.

'Did you hear me?' She shook her greasy head and then turned to look at him for a moment, her lips pursed together as if she'd tasted something nasty. 'I asked him: "Simeon, do you have a message for your boy?" He said: "I do, Grace. Tell him he has let us down. Tell the boy he has let us all down."' She shook her head again and he saw flakes of dandruff falling on her coat like snowflakes on a coal face. 'Expelled!' she shrieked so suddenly he jumped out of his skin. '*Expelled* from school. And I had to look that headmaster in the eye. I've never been so humiliated in all my days! I feel quite faint. I won't be surprised if I have one of my turns. Oh, the *shame* . . .'

As she droned on, Luke rested his forehead against the cool of the window and watched the world pass as they drove down the long driveway, through the dappled shade of the towering trees, past the stupid lions on their stupid pillars, leaving Pendower Hall behind. The injustice of what had happened overwhelmed him. He imagined his father in the stark whitewashed room he called the Meeting Room, the African sun squeezing its way through the small high-set windows. He could see him sitting in his straight-backed mahogany chair, the cushionless seat curved with a polished dip where three generations of Crawfords, all of them men of the cloth, had sat and passed judgement on the sins of others. He imagined him shaking his head, his grey eyes ashamed and disappointed, his hands clasped and lying heavily on the Bible that rested on the empty desk in front of him. He heard him preaching about love. God's love and human love. His father, the expert on love. But he knew nothing. The closest he and his mother got to love was taking hold of each other's hands as they walked into the hut they called Church every Sunday morning to preach to the 'uncivilised heathens'. His father knew nothing about love. Nothing about opening your heart so wide to another person that you'd weep if you thought about it too carefully. He knew nothing about the impact that love could have. He knew nothing about betrayal.

The antithesis of love.

Luke stared at the scar on his palm, still red and angry even after so many months. But it was healing. It didn't hurt or itch anymore. The skin was repairing, knitting itself together. He clenched his fist closed, his fingernails raking against the scar. He wouldn't let them win. None of them. Not his father, not Drysdale, Aunt Grace, Will, Alastair Farrow, or any of them. They knew nothing. They were idiots. They knew nothing about anything. But he knew. He knew about love.

Love was out there.

Somewhere out there in the putrid, unjust world, love flourished.

CHAPTER TWENTY-TWO

'Mum, it's me,' Will said, as she answered the phone.

'William? Gosh, I wasn't expecting a call from you.'

'I'm sorry I haven't called for a while.'

'I'm sure you've been busy.'

'I should have called.'

'I'm fine,' she said.

'I thought I might come to see you. Today, actually. If you're around?'

'Oh,' she sounded rightly surprised. 'Well, there's a few things in the diary, but I suppose I could cancel them. Are you sure you want to make the journey? It's such a long way.'

'It's not that far, and I . . .' Will hesitated. 'I'd really like to see you.'

'Then that would be lovely. Will you stay the night? I could buy a chicken to roast.'

'Great. Yes. Let me talk to Harmony first. I haven't talked to her about it yet. I'll call you back when I have.'

Harmony was dressing when he went into their room. 'I've just spoken to Mum.'

'How is she?' Harmony sat on the edge of the bed and pulled her jeans on.

'She sounds OK. We didn't talk for long. I suggested going to see her. She asked if we'd like to stay the night. Are you able to?

I know you've got a lot of work on at the moment. The forecast is for hot weather. We could take her for lunch at The Horseshoes.'

'I can't. I'm sorry, there's some work I need to finish. I'm so behind.'

'Oh, OK.' He couldn't hide his disappointment. 'I need to go still. She sounded happy I was coming.'

'I bet she was. Look, how about I get some stuff done today then catch the train down. Get there in time for dinner?'

Will wished things were back to normal. Both of them were still so tense around each other. Tip-toeing about warily. Harmony seemed so distant, lost in a place he didn't have access to. He needed her near him. Now he'd begun to open up about his past, he felt a desperate urge to keep her in sight at all times in case she disappeared into thin air like a magician's dove.

'If you're sure. I'll take the train and leave you the car. That way you're not tied to timetables and can come when you done.'

He left her to finish getting dressed and walked through to the kitchen to call his mother. After they'd spoken he unlocked the back door, and breathed deeply, enjoying the early morning air. There was a dewy dampness to it that made everything smell more vibrant. He went out into the garden and turned the hosepipe on and began to water the plants. It was a simple job but he found it peaceful, meditative almost.

'You're enjoying the garden, aren't you?' said Harmony, from behind him. He looked back towards the house and saw her leaning against the doorframe with a cup of tea cradled in her hands.

'I am,' he said, smiling. 'Who'd have thought it?'

She smiled back and his heart leapt. He put the hosepipe down so the water ran into the flower bed and walked over to her.

'Harmony, I know there's lots wrong and I know I've made mistakes. Really bad mistakes.'

She dropped her eyes and shook her head. 'It's not just you. We both have.'

'I want you to know that I'm sorry. Truly. And I've been thinking about it all. I would do anything I can to make our marriage work, but I can see how unhappy you are. It's hanging over you like a cloud.'

'It's not—'

'No, let me finish. What I'm trying to say is, I don't want you here just in body, living together but not really together. I don't want you here if you'd prefer not to be. If we're going to stay together, I want you to want to be with me. I can't imagine life without you, but stepping around each other on eggshells is unbearable.' His voice began to crack. He knew these things had to be said, but the risk of her nodding, agreeing she could never be happy again with him, was terrifying. 'Being together but worrying you don't want to be here isn't how I want to live my life.'

Harmony nodded and forced a tight smile. 'I want to be here.' She stopped there, but Will could see there was so much more she wasn't able or willing to say.

He ended up spending longer in the garden than he'd intended. He had discovered he found gardening restful, a chance to let his mind drift, and before he knew it, it was nearly lunchtime. He went inside and packed his bag, then opened the door to her study to tell her he was going. She was staring at her phone. She looked up at him, face pale and pinched, and placed her phone face down on her desk.

'You OK?' he asked.

She nodded tightly.

'So I'm heading off. I told Mum I'd be there by three.'

Harmony chewed on her lip and he saw her eyes had filled with tears.

'Do you want me to stay?'

'No, you must see your mum. It's been far too long. You need to spend some time with her.' She gave him a weak smile. 'I'll try and get down tonight. But if not, then tomorrow.'

Her phone began to vibrate on her desk. He saw her tense. She glanced at it, but didn't pick up.

'Are you going to answer it?'

'No,' she said. 'I'll call whoever it is back when you've gone.'

As he left the flat, he wondered if she would make it down to Cambridge the following day, and if she didn't, whether she'd be there at the flat when he got home.

At King's Cross Will bought his ticket, then went to the newsagent to buy a can of Coke and a newspaper. As he waited on the platform for the train, he felt regret that he'd left it so long to see his mother. He hadn't been to her house since his father's funeral, which was back in May of the previous year, and the last time she'd been up to visit them was at Christmas. Six months was a long time not to see her; talking once a week on the phone just wasn't the same. When she'd stayed with them at Christmas, she'd still been lost without his father, wandering from room to room, unsure where to put herself, offering to help but not knowing what to do. Harmony had been kind to her, given her easy and uncomplicated jobs to occupy her. She'd asked her to peel the potatoes then quietly removed any bits of skin she'd missed, her loss distracting her, without comment. She'd made her cups of tea and talked to her, sat and stroked her hand, and reassured her she'd be OK. Will, on the other hand, had observed his mother's grief with mild irritation. He couldn't understand, Christmas or not, how she could still be so broken seven months after his death. He'd bitten his tongue on numerous occasions to stop himself telling her she was better off without him, that after years of living with his overbearing, authoritarian nonsense, she was finally free to enjoy her twilight years. But he kept those words inside him. It hadn't been a good Christmas. Sophie and Roger were in Scotland with his family, so it was just the three of them in their flat for four days. It had rained and sleeted non-stop, and his mother hadn't wanted to do anything or go anywhere, so they'd sat in the living room, watching television in numb silence, occasionally playing cards without enthusiasm. On Christmas Day, Harmony's morning sickness had meant she'd barely eaten anything, and when he lit the brandy on the pudding and the blue flames leapt up to dance, she fled the table with her hand over her mouth, leaving him and his mother waiting at the table listening to the sounds of her throwing up in the bathroom. When she'd returned to the table, skin tinged green, he'd passed her a portion of pudding.

'Half that amount,' she said weakly.

So there they were, three silent people with paper hats gamely balanced on their heads, sitting in front of Christmas pudding with pregnancy-friendly brandyless butter slowly melting its sugary innocence over their best china plates. Harmony had tried to smile as he stood to clear the plates.

'It will be a lot noisier next year, won't it?' she said to him and his mother. 'I mean, with this little one.' She patted her tummy. 'And we'll be with Soph's lot too.' She looked at him, her face falling for a second. 'Maybe we should stay here if we've got the baby. We might prefer to be at home rather than at Sophie's. God, how on earth will we all fit in?'

Will had walked away from the table with an unkind shake of his head.

'The baby isn't even born yet. Can't we just get through this difficult Christmas without worrying about the next?'

No wonder she couldn't look at him.

The train pulled into Cambridge and he lifted his holdall off the luggage rack. His mother and father had moved from their rectory outside Ely to the terraced house on the outskirts of town as soon as his father was diagnosed with colon cancer. His mother was heartbroken leaving the house and garden. His father showed no emotion whatsoever, though in fairness he had more pressing things on his mind. He'd lived another two years, battling his illness with a stoic bravery that Will had begrudgingly admired.

He'd been in and out of the oncology unit at Addenbrooke's on what seemed to be a weekly basis. Chemo, radiotherapy, surgery – he'd had it all. Each time his mother would call to say it looked like the latest treatment had worked and the cancer was 'on the retreat', and each time Will had to muster the enthusiasm she needed to hear. It wasn't that he'd wanted his father to die, more that he had an indifference to the inevitable.

Will thanked and paid the taxi driver, then walked up to his mother's front door and rang the bell.

'Hello Will,' she said, when she opened the door. She kissed both his cheeks and then peered behind him. 'No Harmony?'

'She's up to her eyes with work at the moment. She mentioned maybe getting here for tonight, but if not then tomorrow. You look well.'

'Thank you,' she said. 'I feel well.' She lifted a hand to her greyed hair, cut as it always was in a neat bob with a blunt fringe. She seemed to have put some weight on, which suited her, and her face was less taut, less ravaged. She was dressed in a white shirt, black trousers, and a dark pink cardigan. 'You look tired.'

He smiled at her honesty. As long as he could remember there'd never been any unnecessary bolstering or false compliments; a spade was a spade and if you didn't like spades, then tough.

He followed her through to the kitchen and they sat at her small table with its white plastic top. Their old oak one had been too big to fit anywhere and was sold to a neighbour for £50 and four bottles of homemade quince wine. She passed Will a cup of tea in a commemorative mug that celebrated the wedding of Prince Charles and the then Lady Diana, their young, hopeful faces worn away with time and the dishwasher. He played his fingers over the smooth surface, fighting the sudden and unexpected urge to let go of the mug and watch it smash on the floor.

'How have you been?' he asked.

'Busy, actually.'

'What have you been up to?'

'I've got a job.'

'Really?' he said. 'That's surprising.'

'Why?'

He shrugged. 'I suppose because you've never worked before and most people your age are retiring, not starting a career.'

She gave him a fleeting smile. 'It's hardly a career. I help out at a local café, tend their window boxes and a small patio garden they have at the back. You know, pick up leaves and weed, dead-head the roses. They give me a couple of pounds every Monday, Wednesday and Friday and I potter about for three or four hours.' She took a sip of her tea. 'It's better than sitting around the house.'

'If you enjoy it, that's great,' he said.

'I do. One thing I've learned, is life is what you make of it. Too many people sit in the dark waiting for life to find them when they ought to be out finding life.'

'Very wise,' he said. 'You've become a philosopher too.'

'I'm old. It's easy to see sense when you're old. Harder when you're young.'

'I need a bit of wisdom. I'm making so many mistakes.' He paused then reached for her hand. 'I'm sorry I haven't called you much.'

'Don't be silly,' she said, matter-of-factly, withdrawing her hand and patting him. 'I haven't called you either. I should have done. Especially since you and Harmony lost the baby.' She paused. 'How is she coping?'

'Things aren't great for us at the moment.'

'Most marriages go through a rough patch or two. You have to work through them. If you love each other most problems have solutions. Do you want to talk about it? Not that my advice would help. Advice is one of those gifts that should be given in moderation and generally ignored.'

He smiled ruefully. 'I'm not sure I'm very good at taking advice. I'm not sure it was ever a strong point of mine.'

She smiled.

'Are you still missing my father?' he said, after a pause, and avoiding her eyes as he asked the question.

'I am. It's lonely and sometimes feel sorry for myself. I try to fill my days so I can't think too much. I've got this job and I'm playing bridge again, on Monday and Tuesday evenings. Then I've got the WI on Thursdays. They're a ragtag group, and I'm not sure I like all of them, but it keeps me off the streets. There's a horticultural society I've joined which meets once a month, and I've even been to a few of the lectures at the university, some of which have been extremely interesting.'

'I'm impressed.'

'I spent months sitting alone in this house, which I don't really like, staring at the television and moping, then one day I thought: how ridiculous to be wasting my time. That's another thing you start to value as you get older, the time you have left.' She smiled. 'So in answer to your question, I'm feeling better about losing your father's companionship, though I will always miss him.'

Will nodded. 'Can I ask you something?'

'Of course.'

'Do you wish you had a grandchild?'

'Goodness, I wouldn't presume to have an opinion on something like that. That's between you and Harmony and has absolutely nothing to do with me.'

He nodded and looked down at the table. 'Do you ever wish you hadn't had me?'

'Why on earth would you ask that?'

He hesitated, then shrugged a little. 'I know I made things hard for you. I know my father fought with you about me and you had to intervene all the time. And I know you wished I'd have been easier and not so provocative.' He sighed. 'I suppose, looking back on it, having me must have been exhausting and difficult for you. I don't remember making your life any fun.'

She leant forward and patted his hand. He looked down at hers – liver-spotted, veiny, her thin gold wedding band dull with the years. 'You were my whole life, William. You're my child. The most important thing that has ever happened to me, the most wonderful gift. Life without you would have been unthinkable. And do you know what? Having said all I've just said about grasping opportunities and experiences in old age, I'd swap the rest of my life for just twenty-four hours with you as a baby in my arms, to smell you and kiss you and have you look up at me as if I was the most beautiful person in the world. That was quite simply the most magical time of my life.'

Will nodded. 'I'm sorry I was such a shit to you.'

She laughed, a gentle peal of laughter that he realised he missed. 'Gosh, you were at times. I'd look forward to you coming home from boarding school so much, then you'd shut yourself away in your room, music so loud the walls shook. That awful long hair that I know you only grew to annoy your father. All those damn cigarette ends you threw into the guttering which I had to scoop out at the end of every holiday. But, you know, most of the time you were lovely. You were such a joyful child when you weren't so cross. You made me laugh and I missed you so much when you were away at school.'

'Why did you send me away?' It sounded more like an accusation than he'd intended, so he softened his voice. 'I mean, if you missed me, why did you send me to boarding school?'

'It was hard with . . .' His mother stopped before finishing her sentence.

'Go on.'

She hesitated as she tried to formulate her words. 'It was hard with your father sometimes.'

'He wasn't a good man.'

'You're wrong.'

'I'm not.'

She sighed and looked upwards, as if the right words might be glued to the ceiling. 'Your father,' she began, then she hesitated. 'Your father found it hard to show his emotions. He had a difficult time growing up. His father—'

'I don't care, Mum,' Will said, interrupting her, anger bubbling up inside him. 'I don't care what happened to him when he was a child. I don't want to hear it. Lots of people have crap upbringings or have things happen to them as children and they don't all turn out bad. You can't make excuses for him.'

'I can and I will,' she said, her voice hardening. 'He was my husband and I loved him.' She got up and took their cups to the sink, then turned the tap on and started to wash them aggressively. When she'd finished she turned the tap off and stared out of the window over her small, immaculate garden. 'You broke his heart, you know.'

Will shook his head; that bastard didn't have a heart to break.

'His heart and mine.'

'How did I break your heart?'

The fingers of one hand pulled at the sleeve of her sweater. She fixed her eyes on him. There was an intensity to her stare he found difficult to bear. 'You should have made your peace with him before he died.'

'What do you mean?'

'I mean exactly that. You should have made your peace.'

'Is this why you've been angry with me?'

She didn't answer him.

'But it was him with the problem. Why was it my responsibility?'

'Because he was *dying*. Because you needed to repair your relationship. Because it would have meant the world to him. And maybe left you happier too.'

Will laughed, a bitter laugh born from years of wishing he and his father had a relationship, years of trying to get his approval, years of being desperate for his love. 'That man never gave any sign he cared about me in the slightest. He was cold and detached and went out of his way to crush any self-respect or confidence I might have had. You can't mend that damage with a death-bed heart-to-heart or a meaningless final embrace. It doesn't work that way. We had no relationship; there was nothing to repair.'

Will recalled the one or two trips he and Harmony had made towards the end. His father lying in bed, weak and frail, with yellowed skin, clinical paraphernalia surrounding his bed, his body wasting away before their eyes. Will had never told anyone, not even Harmony, how little he'd felt when he took the phone call from his mother to inform them of his death. There wasn't even an emotional release. Just nothing.

The night of the funeral, a few hours after the last person had left the stuffy wake and the food and drink had been cleared away, the three of them sat in front of the fire, staring silently at the flames licking the pile of logs in the grate, clutching mugs of tea.

'You should have told him you loved him,' his mother had said in a flat, monotone voice, the light of the flames dancing in the shadows on her face and reflecting in her grief-stricken eyes.

'I didn't.'

Will closed his eyes as he recalled the way she'd crumpled, the mug of tea falling to the floor. Harmony had leapt to her side, her hand rubbing his mother's back, his mother collapsed in frightening sobs Will didn't comprehend.

Will pushed thoughts of that night from his head and opened his eyes. 'I don't want to talk about this,' he said. 'It was over a year ago and there isn't anything we can say to change what happened. He's dead. I didn't make my peace and I'm OK with that.'

'He was your *father*.'

'In blood.' Will said, doggedly clinging to the argument, ignoring the voice in his head that told him to tell her what she wanted to hear: that he regretted it and would never forgive himself. Instead he ploughed on. 'In my book you have to earn the right to be a father. You have to earn respect, not demand it. And you have to want to be a father and do your best.'

His mother crossed her arms and stared at him, her eyes prickling with angry tears. 'You are a selfish, *selfish* boy.'

Will opened his mouth to speak, but she didn't let him.

'Did you ever stop to think about how much it would have meant to me? I know how difficult he was – good God, I put up with enough of his rubbish myself – but he was dying.' She untucked a tissue from the sleeve of her cardigan and pressed it against her eyes. 'Did you think how I might be feeling? I wanted him to pass away having had some sort of reconciliation with my son. With you.' She paused. 'You're right, it was difficult being in between you both, listening to your constant fighting, seeing the hatred for him grow in your eyes. I loathed it. It was exhausting. We don't get to choose our parents, but we don't get to choose our children either.' She paused and balled the tissue and closed her fist around it. 'Do you know what my most wished for wish was?'

Will looked at his hands and stayed silent.

'That the three of us could sit down in front of the fire and play a game of gin rummy or Scrabble and chat like a normal family. That was it. Not much to ask, was it?' She shook her head. 'But you're right. He's dead and gone now. It's done so there's no point dwelling on it.'

His mother straightened her shoulders and took a deep breath. Will saw her battling with the regret and sadness that haunted her, trying to paper over it and put on a stoic face. He stood and went over to her and put his arms around her. 'I'm sorry, Mum. I understand what you're saying and I get it. You're right. I didn't think of you. I was only thinking about myself.'

When they separated she looked up at him and nodded. 'It's good to see you,' she said softly. 'I've missed you. I let my feelings over this get in the way of what matters.'

'No,' he said. 'It did matter. It mattered to you and I should have worked that out on my own.'

She smiled and rubbed his hand and at that moment he'd never felt closer to her and a rush of warmth spread through him.

'Hey,' he said, jumping away from her and moving back towards the hallway. 'I've got something to show you.'

'Oh yes?' She pressed the balled tissue against each eye for a final time then tucked it back into her sleeve.

Will grabbed his bag from the hall floor and then came back into the kitchen and got his camera out. 'You might need your specs.'

'What is it, then?' she said, as she reached for her glasses from the kitchen worktop.

Will found the pictures he'd taken of the garden. He stood close to her so he could scroll through them. 'I've started gardening.'

She smiled at him, then put her glasses on and looked back at the camera screen. 'Well, I never,' she said. 'Doesn't it look beautiful?' She touched her finger to the small screen. 'That right-hand wall looks so much better now the ghastly hawthorn's gone.' She smiled again. 'Good for you. It looks lovely.'

'I should have done it ages ago.'

'Better late than never.'

As he put the camera on the table, a movement caught his eye at the door. He turned to look and saw a grey tabby cat slinking its way into the room.

'Why is there a cat in the house?'

His mother bent to stroke the cat, who rubbed herself against his mother's legs and began to purr.

'She's called Penny,' his mother said, tickling the cat's cheek. 'When she came to me she was called Sylvia, but I didn't think it suited her, so I renamed her. You like Penny better, don't you, poppet?' The cat lifted herself off her front feet and pushed her cheek against his mother's hand. 'She was abandoned by an awful person who just went off on holiday and left six cats locked in a top-floor flat in Peterborough. The RSPCA officer who found them said there was no food or water and the place stank to high heaven.' She looked at Will and raised her eyebrows. 'The poor creatures had been left for six days and only survived by drinking water out of the loo.'

Will reached out to stroke the cat. 'When did you get her?'

'A couple of months after your father died,' she said. 'I was terribly lonely and needed something to look after. And, well, I never forgot taking that dear kitten of yours to the shelter and I thought I'd somehow try and make amends. Anyway, she's been an absolute gift, haven't you, angel?'

Will had a flash of his father shaking his cat like a soft toy and closed his eyes against a familiar surge of hostility. 'How did you live with him?' he whispered.

She took her hand away from the cat who sauntered through the room and into the hallway. 'He was my husband and I loved him and, whatever you think, we were happy. Nobody knows what makes a good marriage. People have these ideas of marrying the ideal person, the love of their life, but in reality it rarely happens. Marriage requires care and attention and hard work, like a garden, in fact. There's no such thing as the perfect marriage, but if you love someone enough to marry them then the very least they can expect is your loyalty and support.'

That night he slept in what his mother called the spare room, which was essentially a small storage room, stacked high with boxes of things she and his father couldn't bear to throw away when they moved to the smaller house. He closed the door and sat on the edge of the bed. There were piles of his father's clothes, laid carefully on hangers over the boxes. There was a tweed jacket on the top that his father had worn for as long as Will could remember. He placed his hand on it and pictured his father standing in their old living room, one hand on the mantelpiece, the other on his hip, as if posing for a Victorian photograph.

He reached across and turned the light off. The room was lit by the street lamps outside. He thought of his mother next door. She'd taken Penny upstairs with her and Will had smiled as he caught sight of them when he passed her door, the animal curled up on his father's side of the bed, nestled beside her, contentedly cleaning itself. He imagined how angry his father would be if he was able to see it, and how happy his mum was, lying in her button-up nightie, covers neatly tucked in around her, her fingers idly stroking the cat's fur as she read.

Will was woken from a heavy, dreamless sleep by the buzz of a text. He grabbed for it sleepily and glanced at the time. It was a quarter to one, earlier than it felt. He blinked in the light of his phone and saw the message was from Harmony.

His heart skipped and he sat upright.

I'm parked outside. Are you awake?

CHAPTER TWENTY-THREE

The night before Will left for his mother's, rather than go to bed, she'd sat on the floor of her study, knees pulled into her chest, back against the door in case Will tried to come in, weak with worry as she stared at her phone as it buzzed incessantly. She was in over her head. Luke hadn't stopped calling or texting since she'd walked out of the restaurant. She'd stopped answering or replying. She'd even stopped reading them. All he said, over and over, was life was too short, they had to be together, that he could make her happy. Begging and pleading to be with him. She had hoped each ignored call or text would be the last and that he'd eventually get the message.

But he didn't stop.

At around four in the morning, as dawn crept in on the darkness, her mind had become bleary with exhaustion and panic, she answered.

'Why are you doing this?'

'You know why.'

'Please, Luke.'

'I need to see you,' he said. 'I'll leave now and be with you in half an hour.'

'Christ, don't come here,' she whispered desperately. She took the phone away from her face and looked up at the ceiling. Then exhaled slowly, before returning to the phone. 'Please, don't come here. If you do, I'll call the police.'

'I have to see you. I need to make you understand. You're not thinking straight.'

This had to stop. Harmony squeezed her eyes shut as she thought about what she should do.

'Harmony? Are you there?'

'Fine,' she said, keeping her voice quiet and steady. 'We'll meet. But not now. I'm tired and need some sleep. I'll text you when I wake.'

In the morning, as Will watered the plants, she sat at the kitchen table, nursing a cup of tea she was too nervous to drink, and picked up her phone.

What time and where?

His reply came through immediately.

I'm free all afternoon and evening. We could meet for lunch or an early supper?

She didn't want to be seen out with him. She wanted to be free to shout at him. Cause a scene. Tell him in no uncertain terms to leave her the fuck alone.

No. I'll come to yours. 3pm.

She hesitated before pressing send. Her chest tightening. Was that the right thing to do? Would it be better in a public place? She remembered how she'd panicked when she saw Ian in the restaurant and how not being spotted had taken priority over making sure Luke knew it was over. He wasn't going to hurt her. He was obsessed with her and she needed to do whatever she had to to make this go away. She pressed send.

He sent the address. She turned her phone off and walked to

the door, clutching her tea, watching Will watering the plants and debated telling him. If she told him then it didn't matter how much Luke called or if he threatened to turn up. But she couldn't hurt him. It was her guilt and her problem. She needed to deal with it.

She decided to get off the tube two stops early at Westminster so she could calm herself with a walk along the river. She crossed Westminster Bridge and turned onto the South Bank, which heaved with weekend crowds. People poured in and out of the Aquarium and the galleries, and hung around on the Embankment eating Pret sandwiches and taking photographs. Harmony weaved through the crowds. Ordinarily, she'd have walked with a spring in her step; she loved this part of London. It was unique with its historic buildings and famous landmarks nestling comfortably beside utilitarian pieces of modernist architecture. It was even more beautiful at night. She and Will used to come here to eat fish and chips and look at the lights strung like pearls beside the river, their reflections rippling silently in the oily nighttime blackness of the water. Those were happy times. When nothing mattered but the two of them. When love was straightforward.

His flat was in a huge concrete and glass building beside Blackfriars Bridge that loomed over the river. When she walked into the reception area the dark grey of the exterior was replaced with a shiny chequerboard floor and wall-to-wall mirrors. There were two lifts, and she pressed the button and waited, tapping her foot as she did so in an attempt to ease her nerves. His flat was on the top floor, and by the time the lift got there she worried she might throw up. Had she made a terrible decision to come to his place? Maybe a pub would have been better. Or the park. A park would have been ideal.

'Don't be silly,' she whispered aloud. 'He's a lawyer and a friend of Ian's, not a bloody axe-murderer.'

When he answered the door he smiled at her as if nothing was untoward. He leant forward to kiss her mouth, but she turned her head, deflecting his kiss so it landed on her cheek. His smell filled her and she had a sudden flashback to the afternoon they'd spent together, the clash of their bodies, the frenzy and desire, the way he'd clung to her, buried his face in her neck. Her stomach heaved; any attraction she'd felt had vanished.

She walked past him and into the flat. 'I'm not staying long.'

He closed the door and she heard the click of the lock. She pushed her shoulders back and lifted her chin.

'You look lovely. I've not seen you without make-up before.'

'There are lots of things about me you haven't seen.'

He laughed. 'Yes, I suppose there must be.'

She followed him into the main room, which was twice the size of her and Will's flat alone. There were two full-height windows that overlooked London as far as the eye could see and glazed double doors that opened onto an empty concrete roof terrace. Harmony walked up to the central window and took in the panorama, a sea of roofs and glinting towers and famous buildings.

'Not a bad view, is it?' he said, from behind her. 'It's at its best at dawn.'

She turned to face him.

'I bought this flat after my wife died. I couldn't sleep in our house without her so I sold it and bought this.' He smiled at her. 'What would you like to drink?'

'I'm fine, thank you.'

Her eyes scanned the room. The walls were brilliant white with abstract paintings in muted black and greys. The floor was polished concrete with a high sheen in a swirl of charcoal greys. There were no rugs to soften the effect and the furniture was sparse: a large white corner sofa, a glass coffee table and a couple of sixties-style chrome-and-black leather seats. There was a stainless steel kitchen area with an ornate faceted metal ceiling light that hung over the island unit and a solid steel-and-glass dining table to one side. The whole place was spotless – no clutter or books, no ornaments, nothing on the kitchen surfaces apart from an expensive-looking coffee machine. She tried to keep herself relaxed, but as she looked around the sterile, soulless room, her skin prickled with unease.

He told her to sit down so she did, perched on the edge of the sofa, knees pressed tightly together, hands in her lap. She watched him open the fridge and get out a bottle of champagne.

'I don't want a drink.'

'Just a small glass?'

'No.'

He popped the cork on the champagne anyway and the noise echoed. He poured himself a glass then put some music on. Her mouth and throat felt dry as she began to worry how vulnerable she was. She was painfully aware that nobody knew where she was, and as she looked out of the huge window and the far-reaching view over London, her head began to spin as if she had vertigo.

'I need you to accept this is over and that anything we had is finished,' she said. He sat down beside her. Too close. His knee touching hers. She pulled herself away. 'You can't call me, or text or email.'

'I don't have a choice.' Suddenly there was a dark desperation about him; his eyes flicked back and forth over her face as if searching for something.

'Of course you do.' She was aware her breathing had become quick and shallow. She tried to take a fuller breath to calm herself. 'Luke, listen to me. I made a mistake. I was in a bad place and I never should have done it.'

'There are no such things as mistakes. There are things you do and things you don't do. We were not a mistake. You and I have something special.'

'You and I have nothing, Luke.'

'We have a connection.'

'We don't have a *connection*, for God's sake!' she said with exasperation. 'We had sex against a wall in a lock-up on an industrial park.'

Luke took hold of her arm below her elbow. 'Leave him and be with me.'

'Christ,' she said, shaking her head. 'You really mean that, don't you?'

'Yes.'

'You don't even know me!'

He stared at her, his face blank, his mind visibly whirring. 'Come with me,' he said then, leaning forward to put his glass on the coffee table. He stood then walked away from her and disappeared into another room.

'Luke?' she called after him. He didn't answer her. She swore quietly then followed him to the doorway. 'I don't understa—'

She stopped speaking and stared. What the hell was she looking at? She stood, mouth ajar, and tried to make sense of it. It was his bedroom, large and white-walled like the main room, with a neatly made bed and a bedside table with nothing on it but a stainless steel lamp and a photo frame. But her eyes were drawn to the wall directly behind the bed. Hanging on it was a large canvas. A blown-up photograph.

A photograph of her.

'Where did you get that?' she breathed.

The canvas was at least a metre in width and half a metre high; it was the photo Will had taken on their wedding night on one of the disposable cameras they'd put out for their friends. It was one of his favourites, taken just after they'd made love. She stared at it, mesmerised, fear mounting with every breath she took. As she stepped closer she saw the photo frame by the bed also had a picture of her. She walked over and picked it up. It was her profile picture from Facebook.

Luke leant against the wall. His arms were crossed, eyes dead, mouth set. She noticed to the left of him there was a chest of drawers and on it were a dozen or so more photographs.

All of them were of her or Will.

A cold sweat crept over her body. One of the pictures showed her walking down the steps at work. It was winter, and there was a thin layer of snow on the ground. She wore a woollen hat and gloves and her long navy trench coat. The quality of the picture was grainy, as if it had been enlarged.

'You photographed me?' she whispered, weak with growing horror.

She looked back at the canvas above his bed, the face of a young woman so besotted with her new husband, the scent of sex fresh on her skin, her eyes full of him. She heard his voice telling her to smile, laughing as he stroked his hand down the inside of her thigh, telling her he loved her, that he would always love her.

Oh, God, she'd been so stupid.

She reached up to the smaller version of it, the one in a silver frame on the chest of drawers. 'You took this from our flat.'

'Yes, when I came for dinner and you went to talk to him in the kitchen.' There was an eerie flatness to his voice that startled her.

'But . . . but why . . .' she stuttered. 'Why have you got these?'

'He'll hurt you, Harmony.'

She pushed her fingers against her temples and moved them in small circles, trying to relieve the pressure that was building. She looked back at the photographs. Looked at the ones of Will. Will walking into the wine shop. Will laughing in a café, the picture taken from outside on the street. Will opening their car door. Then she noticed a yellowed Polaroid tucked into the frame of another photo. Two boys, about thirteen or fourteen, both in short-sleeved shirts, school ties loosened at the neck, arms looped around each other's shoulders, matching grins on their faces from ear to ear. One of the boys she recognised immediately – her husband, his crop of white-blond unruly hair catching the sunlight, his ruddy cheeks smeared with dirt, that smile of his luminescent even then.

The other boy was skinny with clear, pale skin, dark hair, shorter than Will, his good looks feminine, with high chiselled cheekbones and delicate pink lips. They were outside on a games field, rugby posts in the background, other boys sitting about on the grass behind them, talking, watching sport, picking at blades of grass. She put the Polaroid back and as she did she heard Will's voice. His desperate anguish as he'd stood up from the dinner table and asked why Luke had come. The look on his face at that lunch when Luke walked through the French windows, a mix of alarm and distress.

It was as if a blindfold was removed from her eyes.

'This isn't about me, is it?' she said. 'It's about Will.'

'It was. At the beginning. But I fell in love with you, Harmony. I didn't expect to but I did. I didn't think I was capable of loving another woman. Will took my life away. Falling in love with you gave me it back.'

'I don't understand . . .' Her words drifted to nothing as she tried to untangle her thoughts, went back over everything that had happened, every conversation, every look, trying to work out how she hadn't seen any of this.

'We argued the night she died.' He leant his head back against the wall, closed his eyes. Harmony noticed his fists were clenched. 'She told me I was impossible to live with. Said my head was too messed up. She wanted to leave me.' He turned his head to look at Harmony. 'She was pregnant,' he said. 'Eight months pregnant with our daughter when she died. I lost them both. I lost everything.'

Harmony felt her stomach turn over. She tried to swallow. 'But that's not Will's fault,' she managed to whisper.

'It's *all* his fault. Will lives a life he doesn't deserve.' Luke pushed himself off the wall and walked towards her. 'He doesn't deserve you. He doesn't deserve your love.' He smiled at her, a smile that made her flinch, so out of place. 'I lied when I said I didn't believe in love,' he said. 'Love is all we have.' He lifted his hand to stroke the side of her face and she recoiled from his touch. 'I can give you the love you need, Harmony. I'll be there for you in a way he never can be. Our love is our salvation.'

'I don't love you. It was never even close to love, Christ almighty, Luke. I don't even know you.' She shook her head with incredulity. 'It was sex. Just sex, for God's sake.'

She turned on her heel and walked out of the bedroom, back into the living room.

'So that's what you are?' he suddenly shouted, following her. He grabbed her arm, his fingers digging into her. He yanked her around to face him and she saw his eyes had frozen over, cold and hard. 'Some cheap dirty whore who has sex with men she doesn't know?' His lips curled into a sneer. 'You're a fucking whore?'

His venomous words, piercing and angry, cut into her like blades. She stared at him, the wind taken out of her, sharply feeling the bite of fear. 'Don't speak to me like that,' she said quietly.

'Is that what you do? You go around flirting with men, seducing them?' His rage grew with every syllable and she remembered what Will had said about his fiery temper that could erupt from nowhere. 'Sleeping around with anybody who catches your eye?'

'Let go of me—'

'Is this a game to you?' He dragged her towards the coffee table and bent to pick up the bottle of champagne. 'The drinks? The flirtatious glances? The fiddling with your fucking necklace while you flutter your eyelashes?' He lifted the bottle close to her face, pushing the icy glass, wet with condensation, against her cheek.

Adrenaline pumped through her. She flicked her eyes towards the door. Would anybody hear if she called out.

'Is this a game?' he repeated.

'Of course it's not a game.' Harmony swallowed and tried to lean away from him. Everything in her body screamed at her to run. 'You're scaring me. Put the bottle down. It's not a game. I don't think that. I—'

'Be quiet!' he shouted.

Then he drew his arm back and for a moment she thought he might bring the bottle down on her, but instead he hurled it hard against the wall. It smashed loudly, broken bottle and champagne spilling down the wall and onto the polished concrete floor where it made a pool of fizzing liquid and shattered glass.

Harmony watched, terrified, as his hands flew to his face, his fingers clawing his scalp, again and again. 'Will betrayed me. He abandoned me. This is all his fault.' Then he cried out as if wounded, then dropped to the floor, crouching, bouncing on the balls of his feet. Then his fury began to fade and he folded his arms over his head as if sheltering from falling debris. She stood frozen to the spot and stared at Luke, who was shaking, cowering on the floor in front of her, battling whatever demons raged inside him.

'I'm sorry,' she managed to whisper, heart hammering with fear, knees feeling like they might buckle at any moment. 'But it's not Will's fault. It's mine. Whatever happened at school, he was just a child. But I'm not and I shouldn't have let this happen. Will was just a child.'

Luke lifted his head, his face drained of colour, drained of fight. 'We were all just children.' His eyes were glassy and unblinking, focused on something far away. 'Leave me alone now,' he said.

For the briefest of moments, she wondered if she should leave him in this state, but then she glanced at the mess of glass and champagne on the floor, thought of the photo of her on the wall in his bedroom, recalled the way the red mist had descended over him.

'I'm sorry,' she said, as she turned and fled.

A few hours later, with an overnight bag in the boot of the car, she drove along the Talgarth Road, heading out towards the M4. She couldn't stop thinking about the look in Luke's eyes, that eerie mix of hatred and hurt. She relived the crash of the champagne bottle as it hit the wall. She tried not to think of him following them, of the pictures he had of her and Will in his empty, cold bedroom, but it was difficult to think about anything else. She knew she should tell someone but she didn't dare. She would have to confess her infidelity and if Will found out about her and Luke she was convinced it would be the final straw, that her marriage would collapse, and she was determined to do what she could to try and save it. There were issues they'd have to work through – those hadn't gone away – but the episode with Luke had focused her mind; she and Will had too much to lose.

When she joined the M25 she found it gridlocked. The traffic was solid and unmoving. Harmony swore and craned her neck to see how far the line of stationary cars stretched. It seemed to go on for miles.

'Must be an accident,' she said to herself, wiping her brow and lying back against the headrest. 'Of all the nights.'

An hour passed and she'd only moved two miles. She kept glancing at her phone, imagining she heard it ring, imagining it was him, calling or texting. She would have to get a new number, a new email address too, maybe even change their landline number. She wondered how she would explain that to Will.

Up ahead, some way away, she saw the blink of flashing blue lights and heard the distant sound of sirens. 'Come on,' she whispered. 'Hurry up and clear the traffic.'

She eventually crawled past the accident, a multi-car pile-up with a couple of cars so badly crushed they no longer looked like cars. Three serious-faced policemen waved the queue through a single lane. Fire engines and ambulances lined the hard shoulder. She wondered how many people had been hurt, and how many families would be receiving horrific news that a loved one had died, their lives altered forever from this moment. She thought of Luke then, of his pregnant wife dying, imagined the look on his face when they told him, the news shattering him. Tears sprang in her eyes as she imagined how she would feel if she received a similar phone call about Will.

The journey, which should have taken a little over an hour and a half, ended up taking over four. By the time she pulled up outside Gill's house it was well past midnight. Just being near the house, seeing it, knowing Will was inside, reassured her. She unclipped her seatbelt then got her phone out of her bag to text Will. When she turned it on, she braced herself for missed calls and texts from Luke, but there were none and she breathed a sigh of relief.

I'm parked outside. Are you awake?

She pressed send and waited. Out of the corner of her eye she saw a movement in the window upstairs. The curtain drew to one side and the shadowy outline of her husband looked down at her.

'Oh Will,' she breathed. 'Thank God.'

Tears of relief welled in her eyes.

He opened the door and she fell into him, throwing her arms around him and holding him tightly. His familiar shape immediately comforting, making her feel safe and secure. He kissed her on the top of her head, her shoulder, her neck. A weight lifted off her and she breathed in deeply, drawing his scent into her. When she exhaled it was as if she'd been holding that breath in for eternity.

He pulled back from her and looked down into her face as she gazed up at him. He tucked a few strands of hair back from her face and brushed his fingers lightly down her cheek.

'You're coming back to me?'

'Yes,' she breathed. 'If you still want me.'

He smiled and gave a soft laugh. 'Are you serious? Still want you? Of course I want you.' He paused, then held up his hand. 'Wait there,' he whispered. 'Don't move, OK?'

She nodded and watched him run into the kitchen. When he reappeared he was holding his camera, unclipping the lens as he returned.

'You can't take a photograph now. I look hideous. I've been in the car for hours,' she protested gently, as he lifted the camera and began to fiddle with the focus.

He smiled at her. 'All these years I've photographed you in the moments that matter and they've been my favourites. Let me take a photo of you now.' He pressed the button a few times. She laughed and he pressed.

'That's the one,' he said, looking at the viewing screen. 'That's the one when you came back to me.' He lowered the camera, face falling. 'I didn't take any photos of you when you were pregnant. That was wrong of me. I'm sorry.'

Her smile faded, she didn't know what to say; it would have meant so much to have a photograph of her with her baby inside her.

He took her in his arms again. 'I didn't see how important that was to you, to us, but I do now.' He pressed his lips against her hair. 'If you still want a child with me, I'd like to try.'

She tensed and he leant back from her to look at her face. He smiled at her and she knew that he meant it, that it wasn't some empty platitude.

'What's changed?'

He shrugged a little. 'Maybe talking to my mother. Maybe worrying I'd lost you and realising that was the worst thing that could happen. I did a lot of thinking. Admitted that I wasn't my father, and that I wasn't a terrified boy anymore, that I could be strong and look after people I care about.'

'I know you don't want it though,' she said. 'And I understand that. I do. You wouldn't have done what you did if you weren't absolutely certain.'

He shook his head. 'I panicked. Convinced myself I wasn't able to look after anything. Even you. You're always the one looking after me, but when you lost the baby you became so vulnerable. The way you looked at me changed, like you needed me to do something, and I had no idea what it was and that scared the shit out of me.' He kissed her again, tightening his arms around her. 'I mean it about trying for a baby.'

Harmony stepped back so their arms fell away from each other. 'Really?' she said.

He nodded. 'Yes. I want a child with you. I want a father-child relationship I can be proud of. I want to get it right, where my own father got it so wrong.'

'But what about the vasectomy?'

'I spoke to the hospital this afternoon. They said a reversal is straightforward enough and because it's such a short time since it was done it's almost certain sperm production will come back. Something to do with a low chance of epidermis blockage.'

Harmony smiled. 'You mean epididymal.'

'Do I?' He furrowed his brow. 'What did I say?'

'It doesn't matter.' She shook her head and took hold of his hand. 'But let's talk tomorrow. I'm shattered.' She had a memory of sitting in her study, staring at the phone in her hand, as Luke plagued her with texts.

'Would you like a bath? I could jump in with you. Like the olden days.'

She smiled and nodded. 'That sounds nice.'

They walked up the stairs quietly so as not to wake his mother, then Will went into the bathroom. Harmony took her bag into the spare room and looked at the bed, the sheets and pillows ruffled where he'd been lying. She was looking forward to climbing into it with him, laying her head on his chest, absorbing everything that was safe and familiar about him.

She went into the bathroom and found he'd run a bath. He closed the door behind her and slid the lock home. She undressed and slipped into the water. He turned the light off, leaving the room gently lit by the glow of the streetlights. Will undressed and got into the bathtub behind her and she lay back against him. It was quiet and dark and the warm water enveloped them.

'This is lovely,' she murmured.

He moved his hands back and forth through the water so it made a gentle lapping sound. The feel of his skin against her was magical. He rubbed his hands down her arms from shoulder to fingertip, then pushed his fingers through hers to clasp her hands. He leant forward and reached for the flannel that hung on a hook on the wall and submerged it in the water. He took the soap and rubbed it against the flannel and began to rub her skin, carefully and softly, the light from outside the window glinting on her wet, smooth shoulders and chest. She turned her head and kissed him, touched the tip of her tongue lightly to his. Then she climbed wordlessly out of the bath and laid a towel on the floor. She took his hand and he climbed out and they kissed. He stepped back from her and took in her body, wondering, as he often did, at how beautiful she was, and it felt comforting to have his eyes on her, as if she'd truly come home.

Afterwards, they lay with their limbs entwined like pieces in a jigsaw.

'I was shopping this afternoon,' he said softly. 'So I could cook Mum some supper, and there was an elderly man in the queue in front of me. He was dressed in a suit with a green waistcoat and a tie, but it was pretty grubby and crumpled. In his basket was a single portion of reduced shepherd's pie, a Battenberg, and a can of cider.' He stroked her shoulder lightly. 'It was sad. Really sad.'

'Why?'

'I don't know, I suppose the thought of this old man dressing himself smartly in a suit he doesn't clean, buying out-of-date food for only himself each day. It was one of the loneliest things I'd ever seen. I convinced myself I was going to end up like that.'

'You won't end up like that.'

'I was so scared you weren't coming back to me.'

She kissed his chest and stroked his hand. 'Well, I did come back. And I'm here, right where I want to be, and I'm not going anywhere. So you'll have to share your Battenberg.'

CHAPTER TWENTY-FOUR

Harmony was in the kitchen with Gill having a cup of tea while Will nipped out for some guttering to replace a section he'd noticed was cracked.

'It's lovely to see you both,' Gill said, stroking the purring cat which was curled up on her lap. 'Will seems much happier – sunnier – this morning.'

'We both are,' Harmony said. 'It's been a tough few months.'

She glanced again at her phone which lay face up on the table, but there had been no phone calls or texts from Luke since she left his apartment. The relief was immense, and waking up beside her husband that morning had felt like waking up to a new life.

'You will make sure you eat properly though, won't you? You're looking a little pale.'

A little later Gill went upstairs and left Harmony in the kitchen. She stared out of the window at the rain, the wind driving droplets against it, which collected in rivulets that helter-skeltered down the glass. She went through to the living room and cast her eye over the bookshelves. She pulled out a copy of *To Kill a Mockingbird*, a favourite she'd read countless times, and sat on the sofa to read.

Her phone rang, making her jump. Panic hit her instantly. She grabbed for it, ready to turn Luke's call off, but saw her sister's name instead. She smiled and shook her head and chided herself for being so jumpy.

'Hey Soph,' she said. 'How are—'

'I don't know what on hell is going on, but I've just had some man on the doorstep demanding to know where you are. He said you're having an affair with him?'

Harmony's heart stopped.

'Hello? Did you hear me?'

How dare he go to her sister's house? She crumpled her face up and swore. She got up and closed the door to the living room so Gill wouldn't overhear. 'What did he say?' she asked. She walked to the window and peered out through the rain to check for Will's car.

'Oh my God, it's true?' Harmony could hear her sister's disapproval beneath the shock. 'He said Will found out and turned violent. He's worried about your safety and wanted to know if I knew where you were and that you were OK.'

'Did you tell him?'

'No, I didn't tell him. I said I had no bloody idea where you are, which, as a matter of fact, I don't. But even if I did, I wouldn't have told him; there's something not right about him. He scared me.'

'I'm sorry,' Harmony whispered. A cold sweat crept over the back of her neck and her head swam as if she were drunk.

Sophie sighed. 'The man seems unstable, Harmony.' The irritation in her voice had abated. 'How does he even know where I live?'

Harmony was bombarded by flashes of the photos he had of her and Will in his apartment. She wondered how long he'd been following them. Just the thought of it gave her the shivers. 'I have no idea.'

'And who is he?' She paused. 'Do you love him?'

'No! God, no. It's over. It was nothing. I lost the plot. It was one afternoon – not that that makes it any better. It should never have happened.' Harmony dropped her head into her hand; she'd been naive to think this would just go away. 'Are you angry with me?'

'I'm not angry. I'm surprised, that's all. I didn't think you'd ever do something like that.'

Harmony didn't reply; there was nothing she could say.

'If it's over, why did he tell me you want to leave Will?' Sophie asked. 'Is he right? Do you?'

'No. Not at all,' Harmony said. 'But I've got myself into a real mess and I'm not sure what to do.'

'Do you want to tell me what's going on?'

Harmony told Sophie what had happened, everything from meeting him at the party through to the afternoon they spent at Will's studio, and the attempt she'd made to end it at the restaurant. She told her about the barrage of phone calls and texts, but not about going to his apartment and the rage he'd got into; it would only worry her more.

'You have to tell Will.'

'No,' Harmony said, shaking her head. 'I can't. He'll be so upset. I can't do that to him. It's not fair. And what would it achieve? If this situation has shown me one thing it's that I want to make my marriage work. I know it sounds dishonest, but I don't want to hurt him. It will always be there between us. I regret every second of it and I don't want it to ruin my marriage.'

'He's going to find out. That man has no intention of letting this lie. He's delusional. He thinks the two of you belong together.'

Harmony heard Gill calling her. 'I've got to go,' she said. 'I'll call you later.'

Gill opened the door and popped her head around it to offer her a cup of tea.

'No, thanks,' she said, forcing a smile and trying to keep her voice level.

Harmony sat on the edge of the sofa. She knew Sophie was right. She couldn't risk Luke telling Will and he would. She knew that now. He would tell him a pack of lies, poison Will with his conviction it was a full-blown love affair rather than the regrettable and sordid mistake it was.

She had to tell him.

As she tried to think of the best way to break it to him, tears rolled down her cheeks. It wasn't long until she heard the front door open and close. Will was home. She ran out of the living room and threw herself into his arms.

'What's happened?' Will's question was thick with worry. 'What's wrong? Is Mum OK?'

She stepped back and looked up at him, her eyes sore from crying. 'She's fine. But, oh, God. Everything is wrong. I need . . . to tell you . . . something,' she said through sobs. She walked back into the living room and he followed. 'Can you . . . close the door? I don't want . . . your . . . mum to hear.'

He sat beside her on the sofa and took her hand. She looked down at his hand on hers. Large, soft hands, with a light dusting of blond hairs across the tops of them, short nails, the edge of one thumbnail bitten into an irregular shape. She stroked his skin with her other hand and shook her head. Two tears fell onto his jeans. The ache in her chest was unbearable.

'Hey,' he soothed. 'It's OK. Whatever's happened, it's OK.'

She felt as if she was part of a firing squad, rifle aimed at a blindfolded innocent, her finger hovering on the trigger.

'I had . . .' She sniffed and wiped her eyes with her sleeve. 'I got involved with someone.' She took a deep breath and watched his face fall. 'It happened once.' She lifted her hand to the side of his face and rested the flat of her palm against him.

'I don't understand.' His brow furrowed in confusion.

'It should never have happened. But it did. I finished it, but . . .' She hesitated and tears began to fall again. 'He won't stop calling me.' This was even harder than she imagined it would be. 'He even went to Sophie's—'

'You had an affair?' Will stood up and walked over to the fireplace and gripped the mantelpiece with one hand.

'It wasn't an affair—'

'Who is it?'

She didn't answer.

'Do I know him?'

She closed her eyes, dropped her head and nodded.

'Who?'

'Luke,' she whispered.

'What?'

'It's Luke.'

She looked up at him and saw the horror on his face and her heart lurched.

'How? Why?' he whispered. 'Luke?'

She could see him concentrating, as if he was trying to translate a foreign language.

'Luke Crawford? Who I was at school with? But you don't know him. I mean, you've only just met.'

'I don't know why I let it happen. I was . . .' She hesitated. 'All over the place. It was a mistake. I felt alone, and . . . confused. I . . . was . . . I was so angry with you. About the vasectomy and the way you were when I had the miscarriage. I felt abandoned by you. And . . . and . . . I was flattered by his attention. I wasn't thinking straight. It meant nothing. Do you understand that? It means absolutely nothing.'

'Of course it means something.'

He moved back to the sofa and sat down, pushed himself into the corner, keeping distance between them.

'This didn't.' She rubbed her eyes dry and took a few deep breaths.

Will rubbed his face. 'Where?'

'What?'

'Where did you fuck him?'

Her stomach turned over. She looked at him in shock, surprised at the tone in his voice, the harshness of his words.

'Tell me where you fucked.'

'Please don't do this.'

'Tell me!'

'How will it help?'

'Did you fuck in our bed?'

'No,' she said. 'Of course not.' She felt wounded by his question, shocked he would think she'd do that. But as she sat there, looking at his emotionally battered face, shoulders hunched, dazed and confused, she realised how ridiculous this was. Why was sleeping with Luke in their bed any more awful than sleeping with him at the studio or in the back of a car or some bed and breakfast off the M25? She was sickened by her own hypocrisy. Her eyes prickled. 'At the studio.'

Will swore under his breath.

'There's more, though,' she said, her tears now abated, a heavy shroud of numbness settled over her. 'You were right. He blames you for something. I've no idea what. And he says he loves me. Won't leave me alone. I told him I don't want to see him. I told him I love you, but he won't listen. He turned up at my sister's and told her a pack of lies. He's messed up. He's got it into his head that he and I should be together.'

Will stared straight ahead.

'Will?' His face blurred as her eyes welled with fresh tears.

He stood up and, without a word, walked out of the room. Harmony heard him pick up his keys then leave the house, the front door slamming behind him and reverberating around her. A moment later the car engine started and the car pulled away with a screech of acceleration.

*

Harmony sat at the kitchen table and watched the hands of the clock march slowly around, willing him to come back. When Gill asked, she said everything was fine and that Will just wanted some space. Gill looked worried so Harmony tried to reassure her, despite feeling anything but reassured herself. She held her breath when the phone in the house rang, terrified it was going to be the police saying he'd been in an accident. By six o'clock she began to think about people he might have gone to. She phoned Sophie and Frank, and sent deliberately vague texts to a couple of Will's other friends, asking them to let her know if he happened to show up. Then she telephoned Emma.

'If he turns up at yours, you'll call me? Even if he tells you not to?'

'Yes, of course. We're in tonight. Ian wants to watch some hideous war film. Anything but talk to me.' She paused. 'Hey, it's going to be OK. I'm sure Will will be back soon.'

Harmony closed her eyes. 'I hope so.'

She hesitated before calling Luke. Cold dread filled her at the thought of Will confronting him. But she knew that there was every chance that he might have made contact with him. She dialled Luke's number.

'Luke?'

'Yes.'

'Is Will with you?'

'No.'

'I told him what happened. He's left in the car. That was hours ago and he's not come back. I thought he might have come to talk to you.' The churning in her stomach was unbearable.

'Where are you?'

'Jesus, Luke. I'm not telling you where I am and if you go to my sister's house again she'll have you arrested,' she said with a flare of anger. 'How did you even find out where she lived? Did you stalk her too?'

'You told the taxi driver her address the evening we had a drink after work.'

Harmony swore. 'Just call me if he turns up.'

There was silence from Luke.

'Please,' Harmony said, trying hard to keep her voice calm.

Still silence.

'Luke, please tell me you'll call the if you see him.'

'Yes, and will you let me know when he shows up with you?'

'What?'

'I'm not a monster, Harmony. If something happens to him behind the wheel of a car because he's upset about what happened between us, whatever you think about me, I'd never forgive myself. It's happened before, remember? Not to mention I'd quite like to know he's not about to appear here and kick the shit out of me.'

Harmony lied to Gill and told her Will had been called to a client whose wine had been stolen. It was a tenuous lie and one that Gill didn't believe for one moment.

'Do you need to get back to London?' Gill asked her. 'We could call a cab to take you to the station.'

Harmony hesitated. She was fairly sure he'd come back to his mother's house and wanted to be there when he did. 'Do you mind if I stay? I've got my laptop here and work I can be getting on with. If you don't mind?'

'It will be nice to have your company.' Gill stood to leave the kitchen but paused at the doorway. 'Are you all right? You seem very distracted.'

'I'm a bit worried about Will. We had an argument. I'd have thought he'd be back or called at least.'

'Good gracious, I've been worrying about that boy for the whole of his life.' Gill smiled kindly. 'He'll be fine. He always is.'

They had soup and buttered toast for supper, which they ate while watching a costume drama Gill loved but Harmony found hard to concentrate on. When they finished she carried the empty bowls back to the kitchen and washed them up, staring out of the window as the night settled over Gill's back garden. It was tidy and well-kept but it lacked the flair and excitement of their garden at the rectory. It was as if Gill's passion had gone, as if she didn't have the time or energy to create anything special, but instead merely went through the motions of gardening. It was easy to think their garden had been the place Gill escaped to on those occasions when her husband's behaviour was too much to bear. On the other hand, perhaps gardening was a hobby Will's parents had enjoyed together, and without him it didn't hold the same allure. There were always several sides to a story. She'd often wondered if this was why she felt safe with science, where there were right and wrong answers. Rules and theories. You worked on a theory until you had a rule. Grey areas unsettled her; she liked absolutes.

When she'd dried the bowls and put them away, she called the flat and Will's mobile again. But still no answer from either.

'I think I'm going to go to bed,' she said to Gill, poking her head around the living room door. 'Is there anything you need before I go up?'

Gill was stroking the cat, who purred so loudly Harmony could hear it from the doorway. Gill glanced up and gave a brief smile. 'No, thank you. I've everything I need right here.'

At eleven-thirty her phone beeped a text. She grabbed at it. It was Luke.

Is Will back yet?

No

She wasn't sure what else to say.

She lay awake for most of the night, as a confusing mix of feelings and emotions jostled in her head. She wanted to know where Will was. She was terrified he was lying dead or dying with the car wrapped around a lamppost somewhere. She hated how he drove when he was angry, and hearing him screech off like that was hideous.

She must have dozed off as she woke with a start as soon as she heard the front door open.

She looked at her clock; it was four-thirty.

'Will,' she breathed. She leapt out of bed and ran to the stairs.

It was him and she felt weak with relief. He looked tired, deep grey bags beneath his eyes, his skin pale, clothes rumpled and smudged with dirt. She put her arms around him, one hand against his head, held him close to her chest. They walked into the kitchen.

'Where did you go?'

He wasn't able to look her in the eyes. 'I drove a bit. Walked a lot.' He leant heavily against the work surface. 'I had some thinking to do.'

'I'm so sorry, Will.' Harmony sat at the table. 'Truly. I love you so very much but I understand if you can't be with me.'

'I love you too. I don't think I knew what that really meant until yesterday. All this time I've been coasting through life, hiding stuff from you – from myself, even. There was so much I should have told you, but I hid it, and hoped it wouldn't interfere. But the stuff I kept inside has held me back and stopped me being truthful to both of us. I've been living a lie. But when I thought about you with another man, when I thought about you leaving me, I saw my world fall apart.'

'I was so angry and hurt, but that's no excuse. What I did was wrong. I should never have used it as an excuse to betray you like that.'

'My father used to take great joy in telling me how unfair life was. "Life isn't fair, William," he used to say. "Life is ugly. Get used to that." I used to think he was a prick for saying it, but I know what he meant now. Life isn't fair. I wasn't fair to you and you weren't fair to me.'

'Can we get through this?'

He took hold of her hand. 'Yes, I think we can. I hope so. I'd like to try.'

Harmony lifted his hand and kissed it. But then her face fell. 'But what about Luke? What if he calls again? He hasn't left me alone. He's insane.'

'You don't need to worry about him anymore. I'm here now.'

They went upstairs. While Will was in the bathroom, Harmony grabbed her phone.

He's back. Now leave us alone.

CHAPTER TWENTY-FIVE

Alastair Farrow settled down on the sofa to watch the television. His wife had got up to take the empty plates through to the kitchen, so he grabbed the remote and started to flick through the channels. There was no way he was watching some reality crap about orange-skinned nobodies he'd never heard of trying to bonk each other. Christ, her taste in television – no, in all things – sickened him. He trawled through until he found a repeat of *Have I Got News for You* on Dave then tucked the remote beneath a cushion to hide it from her. He swilled his whisky gently, listening to the ice cubes clink against the glass, and began to laugh along with the show.

When the phone rang he checked his watch and muttered under his breath. Who the hell could that be? It was nearly ten o'clock. He heard his wife answer with that irritating sing-song voice she put on for the telephone, and a few moments later she came into the room.

'There's someone on the phone for you,' she said.

'For me? What do they want? If it's someone trying to sell something you can tell them to piss off.'

'He isn't a salesman, he said he wants to talk to you. He said his name is Will English?'

'For crying out loud,' snapped Alastair. He took a heavy breath and shook his head. 'What's wrong with that idiot?' He drank some whisky and turned back to the television. 'You can tell him to piss off anyway. I'm not interested in talking to him.'

'He sounded quite insistent.'

'I don't care!' shouted Alastair, not taking his eyes off the television. 'He's a pillock.'

'Alastair?'

'Jesus,' he muttered. 'Did he say what he wants?'

'No, he just said it wouldn't take long and he's sorry to disturb us this late.'

'Is that all?'

She nodded.

Alastair thought for a moment or two, remembering the things Will had said to him in the pub. He didn't want to hear any of that crap again. It was a part of his life he didn't need to revisit.

'I don't want to talk to him. Tell him to write me a letter or something. In fact, don't say that. Tell him to go fuck himself.' He chuckled quietly at the thought of his wife passing that message on, and drained his whisky.

'Perhaps you could tell him yourself?' she suggested. 'It might be better coming straight from you. He's got a very nice voice,' she said, as if this might persuade him.

He banged his glass down on the side table. 'Jesus, woman, it's ten o'clock on a Sunday night!'

'You talk to him and I'll fetch you another drink. How about that?'

Alastair Farrow stood up and straightened his clothes. 'I'm not happy about this at all,' he grumbled as he passed her.

She walked over to the side table and picked up his empty glass.

'What the fuck are you doing calling me?' he said, as he grabbed the phone.

'I need to see you. I didn't say what I wanted to say last time. I lost control and I'm sorry about that. You need to listen to me. You're going to tell your wife you have to talk to me then you're going to get into your car and drive to an address I'm going to give you.'

'Ha!' Farrow exploded with laughter. 'Don't be ridiculous.'

'Don't say another word. If you do I will tell your wife what you did at school. I'll show her. I have a photo of what happened that afternoon. Of you and what you did.'

'You're lying.' Alastair turned to check where his wife was. He lowered his voice. 'I know you're lying.'

'I had my camera that day. You threw it into the bushes. You remember that? Well, I went into the bushes and got it back and took a photo. It's a good one. No denying who it is and I have no qualms about sending it to your wife and your kids' school and your boss. I'll put it on Facebook and make sure everybody you know has seen it. Do you hear me? All I want is five minutes of your time and you'll never hear from me again. I need some . . .' He paused. 'Closure.'

Closure? Who did this guy think he was? Peddling politically correct American therapist claptrap like that. He was even more of a pathetic prick than he first thought.

Farrow looked up to see his wife coming out of the kitchen with a glass of whisky in one hand and a large gin and tonic in the other. She handed him the whisky as she passed. He waited until she was back in the living room before replying. 'You're blackmailing me,' he hissed.

'All I am asking is you give me five minutes of your time. A quick, calm chat. Then we can both forget all about it.'

'Where is this bloody place?' he asked, keeping his voice low.

'Not far. Under an hour.'

Farrow shook his head and rolled his eyes. 'Address?' he snapped. He tore a piece of paper off the pad by the phone and grabbed the pencil that lay beside it, wrote the address down, then slammed the phone into its cradle.

'You should never have picked up that bloody call!' he shouted.

'It's some idiot I was at school with. He's an utter lunatic and now I've got to go and talk to him.'

She ignored him and laughed at something on the television.

'Did you hear me?' he yelled.

She looked up at him. 'Please don't wake the children.' Then she turned back to the television and drank some of her gin.

'Don't wait up for me.'

She didn't look away from the screen.

Alastair Farrow knocked his second whisky back in one then took his car keys off the table in the hall. As he unlocked his car, he looked out over the cul-de-sac. He hated living here. Hated the dull tweeness of it. It was a dead-end street populated with dead-end people and nothing like where he imagined he'd be at this age. He'd always imagined himself with a large pile somewhere, a couple of staff, an indoor swimming pool and a holiday home in Spain. His neighbours to the left were clearly out for the evening, no car in their driveway, and all the lights off. Stupid idiots. Why not leave a sign on the door telling all and sundry there's nobody home? He made a mental note to speak to them about it in the morning. It wasn't good to encourage attention from burglars in the Close. Burglaries always happened in clusters. Burglars were a lazy bunch.

He climbed into his company car, which was just about the best bit of his excuse for a life, and clipped his seatbelt. It was a four-year-old BMW and he kept it immaculate. The children weren't allowed anywhere near it; they and their sticky fingers were only allowed in the rubbish-strewn Galaxy. Just looking at the crisp crumbs, books, plastic toys and accumulated child detritus in that heap turned his stomach.

As he turned on the engine he realised how utterly ludicrous this was. A gold-plated farce. Raking up the past like this was pathetic. Will English was a wimp; he always had been. He'd deal with him quickly, get the photograph, burn it and get on with his life. He pulled the piece of paper out and then tapped the address into his SatNav. Fifty-two minutes. If he put his foot down he'd do it in forty-five. Three minutes with the idiot. Then forty-five home. He checked the clock on the dash. Nine minutes past ten. He'd be back by half past eleven for a large whisky and a bit of internet porn before bed.

The monotone voice of the SatNav told him he was nearly there. He put the indicator on and turned into a small business park. It was dark and set back from the road with a large pair of metal gates open against an overgrown hedge. There were a number of garage-type units. One of them, number three, the number English had given him, had its door ajar, throwing a stripe of fluorescent light across the forecourt. He parked up and turned off the engine. Then he pulled down the visor and checked his appearance. He ran his hands over his head and straightened his shirt collar before getting out of the car.

'Hello?' His voice echoed off the walls of the prefab building. A police siren sounded over the noise of the traffic on the street beyond. He walked towards unit three. 'Hello?' he called again. 'English?'

'In here.'

As soon as he stepped inside he saw it was some sort of photographic studio, with painted breeze-block walls and lights on stands, and cloth backgrounds hung from metal clips. The door closed behind him with a thud.

He turned and saw a man with his back to him sliding closed the bolt on the door.

'You're not Will English.'

'No,' said the man, who was well dressed in an expensive suit with a foppish haircut framing his pretty-boy face. He smiled. 'I'm not.'

'Who the hell are—'

The man walked over to Farrow and the next thing he knew he'd taken a punch to the stomach. The pain shot around his body. Farrow bent double, too winded to call out. He tried to stand upright, tried to catch his breath, but then there was a kick to his head.

When he came round he was lying on the floor and the left side of his head throbbed. He tried to get up, but found his hands were tied behind his back. Both his wrists and ankles hurt. He looked down and saw his feet were also tied with a couple of brightly coloured bungee cords. Where the hooks met they pushed into his skin. His mouth ached and he realised with horror that he'd been gagged. Fear took hold and he began to panic. He kicked his legs in an attempt to free himself, wriggled back and forth. The man who'd locked him in, who'd punched him, and who, Alastair assumed, had tied him up like this, came into his sights. He crouched beside him and stared down at him. His eyes were dark and cold, but his clothes and the way he held himself were at odds with his menacing look; he looked more like a management consultant than a mugger.

The man grabbed Alastair by his arm, hooking his hand through the crook of his elbow, and yanked him to his feet. He gestured to a chair a few feet from him.

'Sit down.'

Alastair glared at him and shook his head as he retched at the stench of the rag stuffed in his mouth.

'Sit.' The man held up a Swiss Army knife, the blade open, glinting in the light.

Farrow didn't move.

The man lifted his hand and brought the knife down across Farrow's face, over the scar that ran down his cheek. The pain was excruciating and Farrow tried to cry out but the sound was muffled by the gag.

'Did that hurt as much as last time?' hissed the man. 'Does that turn you on?' He stepped closer, until his mouth was next to his ear. 'Does that make you want to fuck me?'

And then Farrow knew who it was and his legs buckled beneath him.

Luke Crawford grabbed hold of his shoulders and sat him on the chair. Alastair's face stung and he was aware he was bleeding profusely. Crawford spent a few moments tying him to the chair with more bungees that he got from a large holdall. He closed his eyes and thought back to that day. That little shit, that skinny runt – Bible Boy, Puke Crawford – humiliating him in front of his friends. He'd seen their faces when he'd looked at them, his face sliced open; they hadn't known whether to laugh or scream. One of them – Toddy, was it? – had clamped his hand over his face to cover a smirk. Rage had balled inside him as he'd looked back at that crazy scrap of a boy with his mad eyes and lunatic temper. Standing tall and strong, telling him to leave pathetic Will English alone. They'd all had so much fun with him, pressing his buttons, watching him fly off the handle, sending himself straight to the end of Drysdale's cane. But that cut. The river of blood that had flowed. His face, he knew even then, would be scarred forever, and there he was, that little shit, bony fists clenched at his sides, knife gripped tightly, facing him like David against Goliath. He'd grabbed him, knocked the knife out of his hand and growled words he couldn't remember. A red mist descended. Anger like he'd never felt. The boy needed to be taught a lesson. You didn't fuck with Alastair Farrow.

The act itself had been quick. The others watched in a semi-circle around them. Silence had fallen over them like a mantle. The only sound he could hear was a soft whimpering from Crawford. He'd hated himself, sickened but at the same time filled with such rage, a rage he couldn't control. He couldn't explain it. Now it seemed heinous, toxic, but then his instinct overwhelmed him, this need to dominate, to punish, to show everybody who had the power. When he pushed himself away from Crawford, blood from his face covering both of them, the boy had slumped on the ground like a beaten puppy. He watched with contempt as Crawford struggled to pull his trousers up to cover his skin that looked ghostly white against the deep browns of the woodland floor. Farrow turned away. He still remembered the revulsion he felt. Still remembered how he had used every piece of strength inside him to muster his bravado. He straightened his shoulders. Faced the others. Out of the corner of his eye he saw a figure about a hundred feet away. Will English. They locked eyes just before the boy fled. That look on his stricken face, a picture of disgust, horror and reproach, would stay with him forever.

Crawford finished tying him to the chair and stood up, running his hand through his hair to neaten it.

'I am going to take the gag off your mouth. If you yell or shout, even just one syllable, I will stick this through your throat without a second thought. Do you understand me?'

Alastair stared at the penknife in his hand and nodded. Luke raised the knife and came closer to him. He held his breath, preparing for the pain that might come. He felt a sawing motion as Luke cut through the tape that held the rag in place, tugging his skin where it stuck to him. Luke pulled the gag from his mouth and Alastair flexed his jaw. He considered calling Luke's bluff and shouting for help, but there was a look in his captor's eye that kept him quiet.

'You know,' Luke said, voice flat and soft. 'People who rape children are the lowest of the low.'

'Rape?' Alastair stuttered. 'Jesus Christ, I did no such thing. I was teaching you a lesson. Teaching you some respect. That's how it was done back then. You know that.'

Luke laughed then, the type of laugh you might hear down the pub with the boys – an unbridled laugh of amusement. He lifted the blade. 'This is the very same knife I cut you with that day. You left me at the foot of that tree, bleeding and sore, violated, alone and petrified. And you know what I did after you'd all gone? I searched for this knife. I stayed there, until it was too dark to see, until I found it. It took a long time. It had travelled some way when you smacked it out of my hand. But it was my friend's knife, his most beloved possession. It had a message from his father, who wasn't the nicest of men, but you know how these things are. Will loved that knife and I wanted to find it for him. When I found it, feeling with my hands in the undergrowth, I felt as if I'd won the lottery. In the end though, I decided to hang on to it.'

Luke advanced on Alastair.

'Stay away from me!' cried Alastair, fear and anger melding into one indistinguishable rush of emotion. 'Stay away or you'll pay for it.'

'I've already paid for it – every day of my life since that afternoon.'

'You'll go to prison. If you kill me, you'll go to prison. Is that what you want?'

'Like you went to prison?' Luke looked at him and smiled, his eyebrows raised. 'Not everyone gets punished for the crimes they commit. You should know that better than anyone. And anyway, a bit like you did, I've got it covered. I'm not going to go to prison. Someone else is.'

'Enough now,' Alastair was panicking. A paralysing fear had begun to creep over him. He wanted this to stop. 'What do you want? You don't have to hurt me. Is it money? Do you want money?'

'Money?' Luke said with a smile. 'No, I don't want your money. I've plenty of my own.'

'Then what?' Farrow thought of Will, of what he'd said in the pub, of wanting to hear remorse. 'You want me to say sorry? Is that it? I'll say it then. I'm sorry. OK? I'm really, really sorry.'

'Your apology means nothing to me.'

As he spoke Luke Crawford walked over to him and lifted the blade. Calmly and methodically, he drew it down the other side of his face. Farrow yelled out and as he did so Luke grabbed him by the throat and brought his face close to his. 'Shut the fuck up,' he spat. 'That's what you said to me that afternoon. Do you remember? You said *shut the fuck up*.'

Alistair Farrow began to whimper. 'Please don't hurt me. I have a family.'

'I know all about your family. They seem nice enough. In a dull, suburban kind of way.'

'Don't hurt my children,' he whispered. He thought of them all asleep in their beds. Would Diane be wondering where he was? Would she have called the police by now? Or would she be snoring in bed, blissfully unaware of the danger he was in?

'I'm not going to hurt anybody. Except you.'

Farrow began to scream then. Luke's hand was over his mouth in an instant. Pressing against him, squeezing so hard he feared his jaw might shatter.

'Do you know what happened to me after you defiled me and left me in the woods to limp back to school alone in the dark?' Luke asked him then. He loosened his grip on his face and lowered his hand, lifting a single finger as a warning not to scream. 'I told my housemaster – I know, telling tales, that kind of behaviour would have got me into serious trouble, but I figured you couldn't do any worse to me – and the man sent me straight to the head. Drysdale said I was lying. He said that lying about things like that, spreading muck about respectable members of the school was akin to treason. But I insisted. So I was sent to the nurse and told to sleep on a camp bed in her office. Nobody sat with me. They turned the lights off and left me alone in the dark. No windows, no lights, pitch black. It was like lying in a coffin in the ground. I lay awake all night feeling dirty and confused, my body throbbing with pain, desperate for someone to tell me I was going to be OK. I was terrified, abandoned and broken, a child ruined. Ruined, as it turns out, forever.'

As he spoke, spitting the words out like poison, he dangled the penknife back and forth.

'I tried everything I could to get on with some sort of life. I was driven. Everything I did I did so I could put what happened behind me. I studied, kept fit, worked hard. Searched the world for someone to love so I could salvage my life. I thought that would make it better. If I had my own family to love and look after, to protect from animals like you, I could prove to the world and myself that life could be good. But I was wrong. You ruined me. You stole my life.'

Luke came up behind Farrow, pulled his head back and stroked his fingers gently down his exposed neck. 'My wife died because she couldn't deal with me. She tried to help but she couldn't.' He bought himself close to Alastair's ear. 'You know why nobody can help me? Because of you,' he whispered, his breath hot on Alastair's skin. 'Because of you I can't even help myself.'

Alastair tried to shake his head. 'Why are you doing this?' he rasped. 'What have you got to gain from killing me?'

'It's not about what I have to gain. It's about having nothing left to lose.'

Alastair Farrow struggled against the bungee cords that held his feet and hands in place as Luke bent to rummage in a holdall at his feet. He came out with some grey gaffer tape, picked up the piece of rag and pushed it back into Farrow's mouth, then wrapped the tape twice around his mouth and head as he pulled back and forth in desperation, panic engulfing him.

Then Luke leant close to his face. 'Do you remember what else you said to me that day?'

Farrow stared up at this man, his crazed eyes locked onto his, his panic levels surged again. There was an eerie calm to his voice that chilled the dead, stale air around them. He looked up at him, those eyes burning with hatred, that mouth twisted into a bitter snarl. Fresh fear gripped him as he fought against the cords that tied him, tugging and twisting like a snared rabbit desperate to free itself.

Luke leant forward and whispered close to his ear, his breath hot, words creamy with intent. 'You said, *This will teach you.*'

CHAPTER TWENTY-SIX

Harmony was tidying the cushions on the sofa when she noticed the dark saloon pulling up and parking on the road outside the building. Two men got out of the car, both wearing sombre suits and serious expressions. They exchanged words before walking away from the car. She craned her neck and saw them climbing the steps to the main door.

She jumped when the doorbell rang.

She went to buzz them into the building, smoothing her hair as she did. 'Hello?' she said, as she opened the door.

'I'm DC Fletcher,' said one of the men as he approached. His grey suit was crumpled, his white shirt greying on the edges of his collar. He was older than he'd seemed from the window, with deep, craggy lines, a large nose that had been broken on more than one occasion, and a small scar through one of his eyebrows. He flashed his identification at her and she leant forward to read it.

'Is everything OK?' she said.

'Does Will English live here?'

'Yes,' she said, looking from one to the other. 'He's my husband.'

'Is he in?' asked the other, a younger man with sandy hair and matching eyes and the sallow skin of a heavy smoker.

'He's in the garden.' She turned and gestured unnecessarily to the back of the flat. 'Shall I call him?'

'If you wouldn't mind,' said the older man patiently.

Harmony nodded. 'Would you like to come in?'

The two men came through the front door and she directed them to the living room. They made the room seem small and overcrowded. She went to the back door and called for Will. He was on his hands and knees, wearing shorts and a T-shirt, a sheen of sweat coating his sun-reddened face, weeding the bed to the left of the lawn. They'd both been too tired to think about work, so Will had phoned Frank first thing and told him he wouldn't be in, and Harmony had called in sick. Alice told her to take care and that she was happy she was finally looking after herself. They'd ended up leaving Gill's just after midday, with Harmony driving so Will could sleep, though she'd found it hard to keep her own eyes open on the monotonous stretch of motorway. They'd both gone to bed when they got back and had a few hours' sleep, and when Will woke he went straight into the garden. He told her he wanted to make the most of the last few hours of sun, but she suspected he was still trying to come to terms with the idea of her with Luke. He'd need time; she knew that.

'The police are here,' she said to him in hushed tones. 'They want to talk to you.'

Will looked surprised. He stood up and dragged his arm over his damp, earthy brow.

'Do you know why?' he asked, as he walked up towards her.

She shook her head. 'They didn't say. Maybe something to do with Luke?'

'Why would it be to do with him?' he asked sharply.

She shrugged and lowered her eyes. 'I don't know? All the phone calls and texts. And . . .' She hesitated. 'And, well . . . I went to see him. To tell him to stop calling me. And there were all these photos in his flat.'

'What photos?'

'Photos of us. You and me. Taken without us knowing. I should have told you . . .' She paused, unsure why on earth she hadn't told him about the photographs. 'He's not well, Will. He needs to see someone who can help him.'

Will nodded and headed towards the house, brushing earth from his shorts and smoothing his sweaty T-shirt as he went.

Harmony glanced up at the sky, which was the blue of a robin's egg with a few white clouds hanging as if suspended by invisible threads. A group of children walked past on the other side of the wall. They were laughing and joking. She heard a snippet of their conversation, two boys discussing football, then a ball bouncing and their happy voices faded as they walked away.

She followed Will down the corridor. The two men straightened their shoulders. 'Will English?'

'That's right. How can I help?'

'I'm DC Fletcher and this is DC Jones. We'd like to invite you to the station to ask you a few questions.'

'Can I ask what about?'

'A man's been reported missing. His wife said a man called the house last night, around ten p.m. and said his name was Will English. Her husband took the call then left to meet him. He hasn't been seen since and hasn't turned up for work, and there's no answer from his phone.'

'And this woman said it was me who called? That's definitely what she said?'

'Yes,' said the older man.

'But I didn't. It has to be a different person with the same name.'

'If you wouldn't mind coming with us, we can discuss this at the station.'

Will turned pale as a corpse and fear swamped Harmony.

'Will? What's going on? Do you know anything about this?'

He shook his head. 'Nothing at all.' He turned to the policemen. 'Who is it who's missing?'

'The man's name is Alastair Farrow.'

Harmony gripped her hands behind her back in the hope the policemen didn't notice how much she was shaking.

Will opened his mouth to speak, but nothing came out. His eyes flicked back and forth. She could see his brain turning over.

'Couldn't he be at a friend's or sleeping off a heavy night, or something? He hasn't been gone long?' The words left her mouth before she could stop them.

'It's out of character. The wife says he never misses work. He was in a state when he left the house. We tend to follow things up. Better to make a few simple checks at this stage.'

'Do you need me to come with you now?' Will said then.

'Yes, please.'

Will took a breath and nodded. 'Would you mind if I wash my hands and change into some clean clothes? I'm pretty dirty from the garden.'

DI Fletcher hesitated for a fraction of a second before nodding.

Will left the living room and went into their bedroom.

'Will you excuse me?' Harmony asked.

'We'll wait in the hallway,' the older man said.

Harmony followed the men into the hall. DI Fletcher checked his watch. The other man opened the front door. She was filled with the sudden urge to flee, to get Will and run, down the corridor, out of the kitchen, over the garden wall and away.

Will had changed his shorts for a pair of jeans, and taken his T-shirt off which lay at his feet. He was bent over the basin, using his cupped hand to wash under his arms and behind his neck.

'You need to tell me where you were last night,' she whispered. 'When you were gone yesterday. You were gone for hours. Where were you?'

He turned the tap off then reached for the towel which hung over the edge of the bath and patted his face and neck dry. 'I didn't call Alastair Farrow last night and I didn't meet him.'

'I called people. Left messages. People know you were missing.'

'You think I've done something wrong?'

'No,' she said, shaking her head. 'No, of course not.'

He rubbed his face and shook his head, then sighed. 'Look, I went to my father's grave, OK?' His brow furrowed, as if hearing those words surprised him.

'What?' She followed him out of the bathroom and into their bedroom.

He took a clean T-shirt from his drawer. 'I sat beside it. For most of the night. Before that, I drove to my parents' old house. I snuck in over the fence at the bottom of the garden and walked around. Sat in the places I had done as a child – in the hollow in the copse, on the swing – thinking about things. About you and Luke. About how everything was fucked up and how much I blamed my father for things I did wrong. And then I realised it was all such bullshit. It hit me like bricks. Blaming other people – my father, the school, Alastair Farrow – was a cop-out and I have to start taking responsibility for the decisions I make.' He paused. 'I'd been blaming all these things for my decision to have the vasectomy, for my fear of having children, for keeping things from you. Giving myself all these excuses. But you have to take responsibility for your actions, don't you?'

She braced herself as an unwelcome image of her and Luke came into her thoughts. 'Yes, blaming others for our mistakes is too easy.'

'Anyway, that's when I decided to go and see him. His grave. Mum and I had talked and she said some things that really stuck. It got me thinking about how unhelpful it was to carry so much anger around. I drove to the church and sat by his headstone and ended up telling him I was sorry. Not to him, sorry about our relationship. Our missed opportunity. I told him we were trying for a baby and I was going to be a good father,' he said. 'Then I lay down next to his grave and closed my eyes and, for the first time in my whole life, I felt close to him.'

For a moment she didn't move, but then she smiled and stepped forward to put her arms around him.

'I didn't phone Alastair Farrow last night,' he said quietly.

She held him tighter. 'I know.'

CHAPTER TWENTY-SEVEN

Will sat in the interview room at the police station and tried to keep calm.

'And where were you last night?'

'I took the car out. Drove around a bit. My wife and I had a fight.'

'Did you go and see anybody?'

'No. Well, not really.'

'Not really? What do you mean by that?'

Will rubbed his face hard. 'I went to my father's grave.'

There was a knock on the door of the interview room. A woman opened the door.

'Can I have a quick word?' she said to the two men. DC Fletcher leant forward and switched off the recorder then both men excused themselves.

When they came back in, they wore serious expressions, and the air about them had altered. 'There's been a development,' DC Jones said, taking his seat. He waited for his colleague to sit down, then both men fixed their gaze on Will.

DC Fletcher leant forward, clasping his hands in front of him. 'A body has been found. This morning by a security guard. Turns out the body belongs to Alastair Farrow.'

'What?'

'And he was found on your property in Battersea.'

'I don't understand—'

'William English, I'm arresting you on suspicion of the murder of Alastair Farrow. You do not have to say anything, but it may harm your defence . . .'

The man's monotonous voice faded to nothing as Will's mind settled on Farrow. He recalled the hatred in his eyes that day in the pub, how he'd stared at him coldly, remorselessly, truly believing he'd done nothing wrong. A voice in Will's head wanted to tell the police they needn't worry. That if Farrow was dead, it didn't matter; he was a nasty piece of work who deserved it.

Did his lack of compassion make him a bad person?

What followed came in a blur. Will was led to the custody sergeant. He was searched. His clothes swapped for a tracksuit. DNA samples taken. Then more questioning.

He declined a solicitor.

'Are you sure?'

'I've nothing to hide.'

DC Fletcher opened his folder and picked up his pen. He pressed the button on the recording system, said the date, then checked his watch and said the time.

They covered the basics: name, address, contacts, work details. The detective didn't look up, he merely asked the questions and paused, pen suspended, waiting for Will's answers. Will found it difficult to think. His mind was foggy, drifting away from the room, trying to understand how Farrow had ended up dead on the floor of his studio.

Who had called Farrow's home and pretended to be him? It had to be Luke. But surely he wasn't a killer? Maybe it was someone in the pub. An enemy of Farrow. He had a vendetta and used Will's name as a disguise. It crossed his mind that perhaps he – Will – was psychotic and had killed Farrow but had no recollection of it, like a sleepwalker? Maybe the memory of being at his father's grave was an elaborate fantasy constructed by his subconscious mind. Was that even possible?

'Can you answer the question?'

Will narrowed his eyes and forced himself to focus on the man in front of him.

'I know you've answered some of these already, but your co-operation would be appreciated. Can you confirm how you know Alastair Farrow?'

Will nodded. 'Sorry, yes. We were at school together. But we weren't friends.'

'You met with him recently?'

Will began to wander again. He saw himself driving through the outskirts of Camberley. Turning into the car park. Felt the warm buzz of the pub as he opened the door.

'Answer the question,' DC Jones said firmly.

'We went for a drink.'

'And this was following contact you'd made with him . . .' The man looked back through his notebook, licking the tip of his finger to flip through the pages. 'Through Facebook?' He said the word Facebook as if it was something he'd never heard of.

'Yes.'

'And it was your idea to meet?'

'I think so . . . It might have been him.' Will trawled his brain to remember which of them had suggested meeting up. Why couldn't he remember? He closed his eyes and thought hard, trying to sift his mind for the answer. 'It's hard to remember whose idea it was.'

'If you weren't friends, why did you contact him?'

'Um, well, another boy . . . a man . . . from school . . . we bumped into each other at a friend's house. I just . . .' Will shook his head. 'It's hard to explain. I think it was nostalgia. I was having a few problems with my marriage . . .' Will stopped talking as he watched the man scribbling. What was he writing down? That he was having problems with his wife? Why?

'We've spoken to a Mr Mike Cherry—'

'Who?'

'The landlord of the Dog and Duck, the pub you and Alastair Farrow met at.' He paused and sat back in his chair, crossing his arms and lifting his chin. 'There are several witnesses who saw you fighting. When we spoke to the landlord, he said you attacked Farrow and threatened him.'

'No, it wasn't like that,' said Will. 'We had a row, but I didn't threaten him.'

DC Fletcher consulted his notes. 'Did you or did you not say: "I could fucking kill you?"'

Will had a flash of losing his temper and going for Farrow. He turned his hand over and stared at the scar which struck through his palm.

Everything was clear now.

He was going to prison for a murder he didn't commit, the murder of the only person in the world whom he'd ever truly wanted to kill. Will almost laughed out loud at the irony. He placed his hand palm down on the table and pressed it hard against the wood. 'I can't remember the exact words. But I didn't mean—'

'And did you grab him by the neck?'

Will didn't answer.

'Can you answer the question, please. Did you grab Alastair Farrow by the neck in the Dog and Duck pub?'

'Yes.'

'What was your argument about?'

Will recalled his feelings towards Alastair that night, the rage that caused him to jump up and lunge for him, the overwhelming urge to put him down like a rabid dog.

'The man was a bully,' he said at last. 'Alastair Farrow bullied me and I wanted him to apologise.' He hesitated. 'At least, I think I wanted him to apologise. I'm not sure what I wanted.' Will's mind was hazy. He took a long, deep breath which he let slowly out.

'So you wanted Alastair Farrow to say sorry for things he'd done to you at school?'

'I suppose so. Yes. I wanted him to least acknowledge that what he did was wrong.'

'And did he?'

Will looked at the man whose pen was poised. When Will didn't answer he looked up and they locked eyes. 'Did he apologise?'

Will held his gaze for a moment or two as he was hit by an overwhelming urge to vomit. He shook his head slowly then looked down at the table. 'No,' he whispered. 'He didn't. He said he had nothing to apologise for and that the bullying was no more than mucking about.'

'And you left in such a state you left your credit card behind the bar?'

'Yes. I cancelled it the next day.'

The man turned to a new page in his notebook. 'The premises where the victim was found. What do you use it for?'

'I used to run my photography business from it. I don't use it now.'

'Why not?'

'I couldn't make it work. Not enough business.'

'Who knew the code to the door?'

'The keypad?'

The man nodded.

'Just me and my wife.'

'So only you or she could have unlocked the door using the code?'

'Was it open?'

'Yes, it was. With no sign of forced entry. Whoever went in there with Alastair Farrow knew the code.'

Will's heart pummelled in his chest. Everything pointed to him. But how? He thought hard, tried to sort through the chaos in his head.

Where did you fuck him?

In his mind's eye he saw Harmony's face fall, her eyes shining with tears, head shaking back and forth. Will's head pounded. He squeezed his eyes shut and pressed his knuckles against his temples.

'Why did you call Alastair Farrow's house yesterday evening?'

'I didn't,' Will said.

'His wife said she spoke to you. Then Alastair Farrow spoke to you. Records show the call was made from your studio.' The man flicked through his notes. 'At four minutes past ten.'

Will shook his head.

The man stayed quiet.

'I didn't kill him.'

'Do you know of anyone who might have wanted to kill Alastair Farrow?'

Will closed his fist over the scar on his palm. 'Yes. Luke Crawford. Farrow bullied him too and he . . .' Will stumbled over his words.

'He what?'

'Alastair Farrow sexually assaulted him.' Will hesitated. 'Raped him. I witnessed it. I watched it happen.'

Will winced as he heard an echo of his voice crying out to Farrow. *I didn't do it! Don't hurt me. It was him, not me. It was Luke.* Alastair Farrow had looked at him with scorn, had shaken his head, blood running from the cut on his face, dripping from his jaw. Will pictured Farrow nodding at his friends. Watched two of them drag Luke over to him, Luke's feet desperately scrabbling against the ground, his arms flailing, trying to wriggle free. Will had frozen – petrified – and watched Farrow advance on Luke, his face, neck, and shirt blooded as if someone had thrown a tin of scarlet paint over him. Will saw Luke's face smeared with terror. He muttered *I'm sorry, Luke* over and over, too scared to move, to get help, to intervene. Farrow held his hand over Luke's mouth to muffle his shouts and tried to force him onto the ground. Luke must have bitten him because Farrow yelled and hit Luke so hard that he spun and fell into the dark, loose earth. Will watched as Farrow pulled him up while yanking his belt open, grasped Luke's hair with his hand, pulled his head back so hard Will feared his neck would snap.

'He works at a law firm in the City. Luke Crawford.'

DC Fletcher wrote something in his notebook and showed it to DC Jones, who nodded.

Will scraped his fingers through his hair. 'I don't want to say anything more without legal representation,' he said. 'I'd like to call someone. I can still ask for that, can't I?'

'You can.' The man sat back, closed his file, and formally terminated the interview.

Will was taken back to the custody cell and given a glass of water and a limp ham sandwich from a vending machine. He lay on the bed, hands behind his neck, and stared at the ceiling. He thought about Farrow again, about his wife and red-faced children, his balding head, the smug look he'd given Drysdale in his office that afternoon and the colluding smile Drysdale had given in return. Will turned over and hid his face in the crook of his elbow.

He'd tried for so long to forget the horrific details of that day and what followed. But lying there, alone in custody, those memories were crystal clear in his mind. He recalled waking the day after the attack on his friend. He'd sat bolt upright and looked across the room to Luke's bed. With horror he saw it hadn't been slept in. The grey blanket was tucked around the mattress, smooth, not a single wrinkle, as if it had been ironed on. Will dressed quickly then hared along the corridors, down the stairs, across the courtyard to the huge, intimidating refectory where the boys were gathering for breakfast. There was no sign of Luke. Will sat on the end of one of the long wooden tables and craned his head as each new group of boys came in, desperate to see Luke among them. Careful not to be spotted by any masters or kitchen staff, he pocketed two slices of bread and an apple to give Luke when he found him. All day he looked out for him. At lunchtime he snuck back to the woods, heart pounding, sweat creeping over his skin, in case Luke was still there, too injured to move. After supper, while he was sitting at his desk in prep, his housemaster, Mr Fraser, came in with an apologetic look on his face. His voice was tinged with regret as he told Will to go immediately to Drysdale's office. Will still recalled the weight of his hand squeezing his shoulder, trying to reassure him.

'Tell the truth and you'll be fine, lad.'

When he'd opened the door to Drysdale's office the man had looked terrifying, larger than a giant, his torturous cane resting on the desk in front of him.

'Sit down,' he barked.

Will sat on the chair opposite the desk.

'There's been an incident,' Drysdale said. 'Involving a boy – a friend of yours, I believe – Luke Crawford.'

Will's heart started racing. *Please be OK,* he thought. *Please be OK.* He'd crossed the fingers on his left hand and slid them under his thigh.

'He's accusing one of the prefects of a very serious crime.'

Will stared at him.

'Of course,' Drysdale said. 'We know he's lying.'

Will began to shake his head.

'And we all know he's lying because this type of thing doesn't happen at Pendower Hall. Farrow is one of our most respected members of school. He's a stellar pupil, on track to do great things. His father was at this school and is a valuable benefactor. Alastair Farrow is everything a Pendower boy should be and he has assured me he hasn't laid a finger on the boy.'

Will began to protest.

Drysdale rose to his feet and leant on his desk, glaring at Will with blazing eyes. He reached for his cane, picked it up, and came round to Will's side of the table.

'Boys like Crawford are easily confused. He's a liar and always has been. In this situation, we know very well who's telling the truth and who isn't.' Drysdale leant close to Will's face. His breath sour with stale coffee and cigarettes. 'If Crawford was, for argument's sake, telling the truth, the reputation of this school would suffer. Now, I know you don't want that any more than I do, do you, English? Of course you don't. But Crawford insists you were there, so I am forced to ask you.'

Will stared at him, tongue-tied, unable to speak.

'If you were, as he says, there, you would've seen that nothing untoward happened, wouldn't you? If you do the right thing, if you tell the truth, then I'll spare you the caning for missing prep and playing silly buggers with the Crawford boy. If you lie, if you repeat this accusation, I will make your life a misery. Do you understand? You'll be outside my office every day for the rest of the year during afternoon break and I'll suggest to Farrow that he might like your services for a bit of errand running. You and I know your father, and his church, would be most unimpressed to hear that his only son was involved in a scandal so sordid.' Drysdale leant even closer to Will and laid his cane across Will's lap, tapping his thigh lightly a few times. 'You know what the right thing to say is, don't you? I know you know what really happened. Pendower Hall doesn't need any muckraking. It won't do any of us any good at all. You appreciate this, English?'

Will's eyes stung with tears.

Drysdale flicked his cane against Will's legs again.

Finally, weak with fear, Will nodded.

'Wonderful. I knew we'd get to the truth,' said Drysdale calmly, turning to place his cane back on the desk. 'And I'm glad we have an understanding.' He walked over to the door of his office and opened it.

'Farrow! Crawford!'

First Farrow came in, his face bandaged, his exposed eye piercing Will like a sharpened spear. Farrow positioned himself to the right of Drysdale's desk as Luke walked slowly in. When Luke saw Will his face lit up. Will felt a surge of relief. Luke had been crying, his cheeks were even more sunken than usual, and his arms hung limply, but he was OK, he was alive. Luke started to mouth something at Will, but Will looked away, glancing first at Farrow, who glared daggers at him, then Drysdale, who'd sat down in his chair, hands on his chest, fingers drumming.

He heard Drysdale's voice demanding Will tell his made-up truth.

Will knew what he should do. He should tell the real truth. Luke's truth. He should tell Drysdale what happened beneath the Judas tree, what he saw with his own terrified eyes. He should stand up for his friend. But in Will's world telling the truth never did any good. When he told the truth bad things happened.

Life isn't fair, William, he heard his father's voice say.

Life is ugly.

'Luke is lying,' Will said. 'I was there. Farrow was mucking around and Luke cut him with my penknife. That was what happened. Luke is lying about the rest.'

'No, Will! You know that's not right. Please! Blood brothers, remember? I'll watch your back, you watch mine? You said—'

'Shut up, Luke!' Will screamed, clamping his hands over his ears, tears burning his cheeks. 'I hate you, don't you understand? I hate you and I wish I'd never met you. I *hate* you!'

Then he'd pushed back from the chair, so hard it fell over, and ran from the room, ignoring Luke's cries and Drysdale's shouts for him to get back that instant.

It was the last time he saw Luke Crawford. Until Sunday lunch at Emma and Ian's, that was, when Luke strolled back into his life and turned it upside down.

CHAPTER TWENTY-EIGHT

It was Frank's message on the landline voicemail that galvanised her. Will had been in custody now for approaching forty-eight hours. She felt desolate, worn out from trying to face the very real possibility that her husband was going to prison for murder.

'Harmony, dear, it's Frank. I've called a couple of times, but must have missed you. I hope you're bearing up. I've made a cottage pie. It's a bit large. Enough for eight, really, but maybe you could eat portions of it over a couple of nights. It'll freeze well, of course. Anyway, I'll bring it over on my way to work in the morning. If you're not in I'll leave it on the doorstep wrapped in a few carrier bags, with a packet of custard creams as well. And, oh dear, I just *know* he didn't do it. As if he ever could. Keep strong and bye for now.'

'You're right, Frank,' she said aloud, as she put the phone down. 'He didn't do it and at the moment the man who did is walking free.'

She picked up the phone, grabbed the sticky note that was stuck to her computer screen and dialled the number. The lawyer Will had appointed answered the phone with efficient brusqueness.

'Why they haven't arrested Luke Crawford?' Harmony demanded.

'He has an alibi. He was with someone who corroborates his story from eight until four in the morning. The police have questioned him, but there was nothing to hold him for, I assume.'

'But he did it,' Harmony said, shaking her head and gripping the phone. 'I know he did it, so why isn't he a suspect?'

'As I said, he has an alibi.'

'What has he told them he was doing?'

'He was entertaining a client. They went drinking then picked up a couple of prostitutes, apparently.' Her distaste was obvious.

'He's lying.'

'That's beside the point. He has an alibi and there's no evidence pointing to Mr Crawford. Worryingly for us, however, there's an awful lot of evidence pointing to your husband, including,' she said, with a loaded pause, 'the fact he has no alibi whatsoever. This wandering around the countryside for twelve hours with no witnesses does not look good at all. Luke Crawford and this client . . .' She paused and Harmony heard the rustling of papers from the other end of the phone line, ' . . . a Mr Barratt-Jones were—'

'Who?' Harmony barked. Her heart started pounding.

'Barratt-Jones.'

'Ian?' she asked. 'Ian Barratt-Jones?'

'Yes,' said the lawyer. 'Do you know him?'

'Yes, I bloody do,' said Harmony, suddenly incensed. 'And he's bloody lying.'

As soon as she put the phone down, Harmony grabbed her keys from the hook and ran out of the flat to the car. As she drove she drummed her fingers against the steering wheel. Ian was Luke's alibi? Why? Why would he lie to protect Luke?

She turned off the M40 and took the road that led to the village where Emma and Ian lived, her mind seething.

'Answer the door!' Harmony shouted, banging on the door of Oak Dene Hall with the flat of her hand.

She knew they were in; she'd seen Emma cross in front of the kitchen window when she pulled up. Harmony banged again on the door. 'Emma! Let me in. I need to talk to you!'

Emma hadn't returned any of her phone calls since the police arrested Will and now she knew why. Harmony kicked at the gravel in frustration, then marched up to the kitchen window and peered in. She saw a flash of one of the children and swore under her breath. She went back to the front door and began to hammer on it again. 'Emma! I'm not bloody leaving!' Harmony paused but still her friend didn't come to the door. 'I just want to talk to you,' Harmony said, no longer shouting, resting her forehead against the door, suddenly feeling alone and desolate. Then she turned and sat down on the step, her head in her hands, as she did so the door opened and she jumped to her feet.

'Harmony?' said Emma. 'What are you doing here?'

She was dressed in tracksuit bottoms and an old sweatshirt, with no make-up to cover the skin around her eyes which was pink and puffy. Harmony couldn't ever remember seeing Emma without make-up. Even when they were younger, make-up was always done first thing in the morning.

The two women stood either side of the door frame, neither of them moving. 'I need to speak to Ian,' Harmony said.

'He's not here.'

'Can I come in?'

Emma shook her head, but Harmony saw the hesitation in her eyes.

'Please?'

Emma wavered.

'I promise I won't stay long.'

At last, Emma stepped to one side and allowed Harmony in. The house smelt of Pledge and floor cleaner and freshly brewed coffee. In the kitchen, the surfaces shone, not a speck of dust or an out-of-place piece of paper anywhere to be seen. The sound of children's television from the den broke the silence.

'Would you like a drink?' Emma asked, without making eye contact.

'Will didn't do it.'

Emma turned away from her to fill the kettle. She turned the tap off, but kept her back to Harmony and put her hands on the edge of the sink and gripped it.

'He didn't kill that man,' Harmony said again.

Emma turned around and crossed her arms. 'I don't know what to say, Harmony.'

Harmony felt the sting of tears and her stomach knotted. 'Say you believe me.'

'The court will have to—'

'Fuck the court!'

Emma flinched, then turned to put the kettle back on its base and flicked its switch.

'It was Luke Crawford.'

Emma shook her head, there was a stoop to her shoulders that aged her.

'Luke killed him.'

Emma closed her eyes. 'He didn't.'

'Because he was with Ian the night that man was killed? Why didn't you tell me Ian was Luke's alibi?'

'I don't know. I didn't think it was relevant.'

'Not relevant?' Harmony cried. 'Of course it's relevant! My husband is in custody for a murder he didn't commit and the man that did it is going to get off because he was supposedly with your husband!'

Emma visibly winced and her eyes shot to the floor.

'And we both know he's lying. We spoke that night. You told me you were with Ian. You remember?'

'No, you're mistaken.' Her eyes gave her dishonesty away, darting from one side to the other. The kettle reached boiling point noisily and clicked off. 'I was here alone.'

'No, you told me you were both here. You said he wanted to watch a war film.'

'No, you're wrong. I—'

'Stop it!' cried Harmony, slamming her hand down on the work surface. 'Do you know what you're doing? My husband will go to prison for *murder*.'

Emma crossed her arms around her body again, her fingers gripping at the sides of her sweatshirt. She shook her head. 'He won't. If he didn't kill him he'll get off. They won't send someone to prison without evidence. If he's innocent, he'll get off.'

Harmony laughed bitterly and looked at the ceiling. 'Don't be so naive! People go to prison all the time for crimes they didn't commit. Why are you lying about where Ian was?'

'I'm not. Ian was with Luke that night. Corporate entertaining.' She said the word *entertaining* as if it caused her physical pain.

Emma locked eyes with Harmony, her body tensed in challenge.

Harmony didn't understand. Why was she lying? Why would Ian protect a work colleague – his lawyer, for God's sake – over one of his oldest friends?

Then the mist cleared.

'Oh my God,' she breathed. 'Luke has something on Ian.'

Harmony knew she was right when Emma's face fell in panic.

Emma glanced through the kitchen door to the hallway, then squared her shoulders, her voice came out well-rehearsed and monotone. 'Ian and Luke went out. Ian was entertaining Luke. It was business. They stayed out late.'

'You're lying,' Harmony said. 'I know you are; I've known you all my life. I can tell.' Harmony took a step towards her, but Emma stepped backwards. 'Do you know what Luke did to that man? He tortured him to death. He beat him and cut him and kicked him in the stomach and head and genitals until he broke almost every bone in his body.'

Emma threw her hands up to cover her ears and squeezed her eyes shut like a child.

'Do you really think Will could do that? You've known him for twenty years. He can't even kill a bloody wasp. It was *Luke*.'

Harmony couldn't help her voice rising. Frustration and contempt erupted inside her. 'Why are you covering for him? My husband's sitting in a cell, right this minute, while yours is out gallivanting on some golf course and that cold-blooded murderer is wandering about free.'

Emma tightened her arms around her quivering body. 'Please,' she whispered. 'You need to leave now, or I'll . . . or I'll . . . I'll call the police.'

'And what?' Harmony shouted. 'Tell them more lies? Try and get me locked up as well? You could try breaking and entering? Maybe tell them I stole some jewellery. Say I hit you. Why not!'

'Don't—'

'You know . . .' Harmony had to stop speaking to allow a lump of emotion to subside. 'You know he's stalking me.'

Emma's face contorted in confusion. 'Stalking you? Who is?'

'Luke Crawford. He's been following me. And Will. I went to his apartment and saw photos he's taken. All over his apartment. Photos I didn't know he was taking.' She paused. 'He and I had an affair.'

Emma stared at her in confusion.

'That's right. An affair. Christ,' she said then, still unable to believe what was happening. 'I can't even call it that. We had sex. One afternoon.'

'But how—'

'How did we have sex? Will and I had an argument. I was angry. Then Luke and I met up and we fucked.' Harmony saw Emma flinch at her words. 'We fucked and it was a massive fucking mistake, which I regretted immediately because as soon as it happened I realised I still loved my husband and that I'd been an utter idiot. I told Luke it was over. Will and I started to try and fix our relationship.' Harmony took a deep breath and laughed bitterly. 'We were actually going to try for a baby. Can you believe that?' She rubbed her face. 'But no, Luke didn't like that. He blames Will for something that happened when they were children. He

306

wouldn't leave me alone. Texts and calls *all* the time. He turned up at my sister's and fed her a load of bullshit. Emma, I am scared. I'm scared because I know Will didn't kill that man. And I *know* Ian was here with you that night, which means I'm pretty sure Luke is a murderer, and I am scared for my own damn life. He's a murderer, Emma, and you're protecting him.'

Emma dropped her eyes to the floor.

'So that's it? You're happy to risk my life and let Will go to prison for something he didn't do?'

'You don't understand.' Emma spoke so quietly Harmony could barely hear her.

'No, you're right,' Harmony said with angry frustration. 'I don't understand. Please, *please*, explain it to me.'

'There is nothing at all to understand.'

Both women jumped at the sound of Ian's voice.

Harmony turned to see him looming in the doorway, and was immediately shocked by how exhausted and dishevelled he was.

'I thought you weren't here.' Harmony stared pointedly at Emma.

'I wasn't. Now I am.' Ian walked over to the large American fridge-freezer and got out a bottle of beer. 'So did I hear you right? You and the dashing lawyer have been having a bit of *fun*?' He said the word in a way that made Harmony's skin crawl.

'Why are you lying? Why are you protecting him? And don't say you're not because I know you are.'

'You know I am?' He retrieved a bottle opener from the cutlery drawer and opened the beer. He drank straight from the bottle, chucking the bottle top onto the kitchen worktop. 'How do you know? Were you there?'

'I rang Emma the night it happened – when you were supposedly out with him – and you were here. You were going to watch a film. It was a war film.'

'Emma got the wrong end of the stick. She was confused. I probably said something like I wish I was watching a film instead of going out and she misheard.' He sat down heavily at the table, his beer clasped in his hand, his gaze seeming to lose focus. 'I was with Luke, drinking champagne, enjoying some whores at a Holiday Inn.'

Harmony looked at Emma, but she'd turned her back on them and was looking out of the window that overlooked the driveway.

'Luke and I were together all night. And there's bugger all you can do about it.' He lifted his head and looked at her. 'Do you understand?'

Harmony knew she was wasting her time. It was there, clear from the stoop of Emma's head and shoulders, the way she gripped the side of the worktop, and the unwavering conviction in Ian's dishonest words.

'You disgust me,' she spat. 'Both of you.'

Then she turned and walked out of the kitchen and into the hallway, hoping she'd make it out of the house without collapsing. She fumbled with the latch on the front door, then pushed it open and stumbled down the steps. She stopped before she reached the car and stood still in the middle of the enormous expanse of new, clean gravel, and realised she had never been so scared in her life.

CHAPTER TWENTY-NINE

Harmony followed Sophie into the house. She was numb and riven with fear. She didn't know what to do or how to help Will. Not to mention the thought she was terrified of Luke showing up. Every noise made her jumpy, her brain was in overdrive and full of worst-case scenarios. And they weren't pretty.

Her sister's kitchen was quiet and tidy, with Ella Fitzgerald playing softly in the background. Harmony had an image of her mother, as she used to be, before the illness had ravaged her beyond recognition. She remembered how the soothing tones of Ella would float through her bedroom wall. How she'd climb out of bed to creep along to the sitting room and peer around the doorframe in the hope of catching her mother dancing, arms spread, twirling, lost in the music she loved.

'Where are the boys?' Harmony asked.

'George is at football, Matt's at a friend's and Cal's at his girl-friend's house.'

'A girlfriend? Really? Is she nice?'

Sophie nodded. 'She's lovely, actually. Bright, pretty, strong opin-ions, and seems to really like him. God knows why. She even laughs at his jokes, including the dreadful ones.'

'He's a great kid, he deserves someone lovely.'

'You look shattered.'

'I feel bulldozed, to be honest.'

Sophie put her arms around her and gave her a hug. 'You know what we should do?' she said with a soft smile.

Harmony shook her head.

'Come with me.' Sophie opened the back door and took Harmony's hand. They wove their way through the assorted sports paraphernalia that littered the terrace and onto the lawn. Sophie sat down and patted the ground beside her. 'How about a bit of cloud-staring?'

Harmony burst into tears and laughed at the same time. She and Sophie lay back, their legs out straight, holding hands. Harmony searched the sky for animals. They used to do this with their mum if they'd had a bad day, if someone had been mean to them or they'd been upset by a teacher or embarrassed themselves somehow or – towards the end of her illness – when one of them was feeling particularly sad or scared. She'd kiss them and give them a chocolate biscuit then whisper: 'How about a bit of cloud-staring?' Then they'd lie on the grass holding hands, like a paper chain of people, and silently scan the sky until they found a creature lurking in the clouds, maybe a running fox or a jumping hare, then they'd point and cry out with such excitement that soon the bad thing was forgotten.

'Luke Crawford reminded me of Dad,' Harmony said.

'How?'

Harmony searched the clouds, but there were only large amorphous shapes that offered her nothing. 'The mystery, maybe. The excitement I felt reminded me of what Mum said to me about him, how she felt when she was with him. That shortness of breath, the thumping heart. And he had the same hands.'

'The same hands? You can't possibly remember Dad's hands.'

'No, I don't, but Mum said he had long, elegant fingers, like a concert pianist.'

Sophie snorted. 'He was a waste of space, not a bloody concert pianist.'

Harmony turned her head to look at Sophie. Her sister was beautiful in profile, her nose small and neat, her skin clear, with fine, even creases around her eyes, and long eyelashes that were tipped with blonde. 'Why do you hate him so much?'

The sisters had never discussed this. It was as if they'd come to an unspoken mutual agreement whereby Sophie was allowed to loathe him and Harmony was allowed to love him. Harmony had no reason to love him other than her desperate desire to do so. As a child she had idolised him and chosen to adopt her mother's rose-tinted memories rather than her sister's hateful ones.

'We shouldn't talk about it; you love him and it's not right for me to bad-mouth him.'

Harmony smiled. 'You've done nothing but bad-mouth him since Mum died.' She turned her head to look up at the clouds again. 'Please tell me.'

Sophie was quiet for a while before she sighed heavily. 'He broke my heart,' she said at last. 'Mine and Mum's. I loved him so much. He was my world.' She hesitated. 'He left the day she found out about the breast cancer.'

'Surely you've remembered that wrong,' Harmony said. 'The same day?'

'I was with her. She was crying. There was a typed letter in her hand. It must have been from the hospital. She sat me on her lap and I cuddled her and told her it would be OK. When he came home she handed him the letter and I watched his face. Everything went dark, like he was cross with her.' Sophie paused. 'That night I heard him shouting. I sat in the corridor outside their room and I heard him say we were suffocating him, which I didn't understand then, I thought he meant actually suffocating. Then I heard him tell her he didn't want to spend the rest of his days looking after her. That he was a free spirit not a nursemaid. He started screaming at her, telling her to stop crying, to stop laying on the guilt. It scared me, and when I heard him coming out of their room I ran back to bed and hid beneath the covers. He was gone in the morning.'

'Poor Mum,' said Harmony. 'I can't imagine how desperate she must have felt.'

'He took his toothbrush, his passport and all the money in the joint account, and just left us. I used to sit there sometimes, watching her sleep, her face pale from vomiting, those drugs attacking her body along with the cancer, and think about how he'd broken her heart. How he'd left me to look after her, left me to try and be both a mother and father to you. I gave everything up when she died: my exams, my friends, my life. I wanted to be an architect. Did you know that?' She turned her head to look at Harmony.

'I had no idea. I thought you weren't interested in exams. I thought that's why you left school.'

'No, I left school to look after you.'

'I'm sorry you had to do that.'

'Don't be sorry.' Sophie looked back at the sky. 'It's not your fault. And it was worth it; you did so well. I'm very, very proud of you. As proud of you as I am of my sons.'

Harmony squeezed her hand and Sophie squeezed back.

'I called him the day after she died. Dad, I mean.' Sophie's voice was soft and distant. 'I found an old number for him and talked to a woman who knew where he lived. I was terrified before I phoned. I remember shaking so hard I could hardly dial the number. The first time he answered I put the phone down as if it had bitten me. Then I plucked up the courage and rang him back and told him that she was gone and that Nan didn't really want us to move in with her and could we come and stay with him.'

'What did he say?'

Sophie didn't answer.

'Tell me.'

'He said he wasn't interested in us. That as far as he was concerned he wasn't our father.'

Harmony was quiet for a moment or two. 'Why didn't you tell me?'

Sophie looked at Harmony, her eyes glistening with a film of tears. 'I didn't want to hurt you. I knew how important it was for you to love him. It gave you strength and I didn't want to take that away from you.'

A large white cloud crept across the sky, changing shape imperceptibly from one nothing to a different nothing.

'What do you think Mum would say to me now?'

'She'd tell you Will didn't do it. She'd say you were a daft idiot for sleeping with that nutter and then she'd tell you she loved you more than all the grains of sand in the world.'

Harmony smiled. 'I'd forgotten she used to say that.' She thought of her mum sitting on the edge of her bed and stroking her forehead before she turned the bedside light off.

I love you.

How much?

So much.

How much is so much?

More than all the grains of sand in the world.

Is that lots?

Gazillions. It's the biggest number you can think of plus a million.

Then she'd kiss the very tip of her nose and tuck the sheets snugly around her.

'I miss you, Mum,' Harmony whispered at the clouds.

They lay there until the grass grew damp and the sun set below the houses at the end of the garden.

'Do you want to stay here tonight?' her sister asked as they walked into the house.

'No, I'm OK. I want to get up early in the morning and do some gardening. I want it to look nice in case Will comes home.'

'He will come home. I know he will.'

When Harmony finally fell into bed, after staring at rubbish on the television until her eyes grew sore, she shuffled over to Will's side and pulled his pillow into her. She loved the way it smelt so strongly of him, a musty manliness mixed with his deodorant and shampoo.

She woke in the middle of the night with a start, thinking her phone had rung, that it was Will calling. But the phone registered no missed call; she'd imagined it, the ringing only a dream.

'Please come back to me,' Harmony said, her voice loud against the dark. 'I miss you so much it hurts.'

She slept heavily and when she woke it took a few moments for her to work out where she was. The bedroom seemed alien and it was only as the fug of sleep lifted that things began to appear familiar. She put her dressing gown on and went into the kitchen to make some tea.

The doorbell rang, making her jump. She glanced at the clock on the wall; it was half past seven. It rang again. Then again.

'Oh my God,' she whispered under her breath, as a sudden fear gripped her. 'Luke?'

Her stomach knotted. She pulled her dressing gown tighter around her body. She wouldn't answer it, she'd pretend she wasn't here. But the ringing was incessant. She crept through the living room and peered carefully through the window.

It wasn't Luke.

It was Emma.

Her heartbeat slowed as the panic left her. She went to the front door and buzzed her in, then opened the door to the flat. The two of them stood and stared at each other. Emma looked tired, as if she hadn't slept since she'd last seen her, and was dressed in the same tracksuit and sweatshirt.

'I'm sorry it's so early,' she said. 'I wasn't sure what time you left for work.'

'I'm working at home today. I can't face the office at the moment.'

'Oh. Right.' Emma's fingers pulled at one of her sleeves and her foot tapped nervously.

'Do you want to come in?'

Emma hesitated, then stepped into the flat.

They sat at the table in the living room. Harmony didn't speak. She had nothing to say. She sat as if made of stone and stared at Emma.

'I told the police Ian was lying,' Emma finally said, in a weak whisper. 'I told them he was at home with me that night. I told them to talk to the supermarket where he bought some beer and crisps. He was there around eight. They'll have him on their CCTV.' She took a deep breath. 'He wasn't with Luke Crawford. He was with me. I lied for him.'

Harmony covered her face with her palms and let the words sink in. Relief crept over her so that she found she was shaking uncontrollably. Just like that, she was going to get her husband home. She became aware of Emma on the other side of the table. As she looked at her, relief was replaced by anger.

'Why did he do it?' she demanded. 'How could you do this to us? I can't even begin to understand what you did. You're supposed to be my best friend.'

'Ian was involved in something at work. He . . .' She broke off and sniffed loudly. 'He was stealing from the company, and not just petty cash. He was stealing hundreds of thousands of pounds. I had no idea. That was why he was being secretive and drinking. It wasn't another woman at all. It was because he was about to be found out. All I know is we would have . . .' She stopped herself. 'He told me we would lose everything and he would go to prison unless I lied about him being home that night.'

'You were willing to send Will to prison? For murder?'

'I had no idea Will was involved,' she said quickly. 'Neither Ian or I knew anything about that. I didn't even know there'd been a . . .' Emma paused for a moment. 'A murder,' she said in a hushed tone. 'All I knew was Ian telling me we were up shit creek and if we didn't tell everyone he was out all night with Luke, we'd lose the house, our savings, the children would have to leave their school, and he'd go to prison.' She looked at Harmony. 'Ian had been stealing money from the bank. Siphoning it off. Luke was involved. He'd told Ian about this scheme, said everyone was doing it, that all Ian needed was a good lawyer to cover his tracks. He was paying Luke a lot of money in fees, but of course,' she whispered, 'Luke made sure nothing could be connected to him. That's why Ian was in such a state. The idiot wanted to get out, but was in too deep, and when Luke threatened to expose him unless he helped, well, he panicked. Ian had no idea why Luke asked him. It was only when I heard your message on the answer phone, when you told me Will had been arrested for something that happened that night, that I realised it might be linked.'

'But even then, when you knew Will was involved, you knew he was sitting in some shitty cell with a murder charge hanging over him, you didn't say anything.'

'We didn't know what to do. We kept going over it. We had some vicious rows. But we sort of convinced ourselves it was fine, that the two things were unrelated. Ian told me Will would get off if he was innocent.'

'What do you mean *if*?'

'Honestly, I never doubted him. We should have told the police, I know that, but Ian was in such a state. I—'

'Don't even go there!' shouted Harmony, shaking her head at Emma's audacity. 'I can't talk about this anymore. It's too upsetting. Luke *killed* a man then tried to frame my husband and it nearly worked because my best friend *lied*.'

Emma's face crumpled and she tried to reach out for Harmony. 'No, Emma.'

Emma didn't move. 'I'm so sorry, Harmony. I . . . didn't . . . I know you must hate me.'

Harmony looked at her desperate friend and the hardness she felt towards her receded a little. 'I don't know how I feel,' she said. 'Right now, I'm just relieved you finally told the truth.'

'Will he be OK now?' Emma asked. 'They'll arrest Luke? You'll be safe and they'll let Will come home?'

'I hope so,' Harmony said. 'I hope to God they will.'

CHAPTER THIRTY

Luke set the alarm for five in the morning. It was his favourite time of day. The air was fresh and London was only just beginning to wake properly. He put his dressing gown on and made himself a strong coffee, so strong it was almost as thick as soup. He drank it down in one then turned the tap on and rinsed the cup. He dried it carefully then opened the cupboard and placed the cup neatly beside the others.

He went into his bedroom and opened his wardrobe. He unwrapped a suit from its dry-cleaning bag and took out a brand-new shirt. Then he opened a drawer, retrieved the wooden box and opened the lid. He stared at the Swiss Army knife and stroked his finger over its polished red handle. He took it out of the box, opened the blade of the knife, and stared at the cold message Will's father had had etched into the shining metal.

He remembered the first time Will had shown him the knife. They'd gone to the woods and made spears out of ash branches, chatting happily while one of them carved a point on one end of his stick and the other smoothed his with a stone. Then they swapped. They'd pretended they were pirates, marooned on an island, surrounded by cannibals.

'Don't let them see you,' Luke whispered to Will as they hid in the bushes and watched the cannibals walking across the field to play rugby. 'If they catch us, they'll *eat* us.'

And the two of them had run in the opposite direction, leaping over fallen tree trunks, scrabbling up slopes, heading to their favourite place, to the Judas tree, and scaling its branches, whooping from the leafy canopy like wild things as they brandished their sharpened spears.

Luke reached for the photograph and slipped it into his inside jacket pocket with the penknife. Then he looked around his bedroom. He'd taken the rest of the photos to the dump in West Norwood. It felt odd to see them lying on the piles of household waste in that big stinking hangar, cars reversing in and out, people depositing all manner of things, things that had once meant something, that had once had purpose but were now disposable. He saw the satisfaction on their faces as they dusted off their hands and climbed back into their emptied cars, feeling freer, feeling cleansed.

He drove out of London and headed onto the M4. His head was strangely clear. Alastair Farrow was there, of course, but not at the forefront. He wasn't sure at what point he'd decided to kill him. He thought back to the night his wife died, to the row they'd had, his temper flaring uncontrollably, the look of hurt on her face as he'd screamed at her to leave him alone. Her begging him to stop shouting. Telling him she couldn't take it anymore. That she couldn't help him. Tears scorched her face. Her beautiful rounded belly, his precious child cosy within, stretching the fabric of her dress. Then later a knock on the door. Two sombre-faced policemen. His world ceasing to turn. He'd sat on the floor of their kitchen, destroyed, memories of what happened at school stabbing him like sharpened spears.

He remembered a few months later, sitting alone in silence on the sofa in his new apartment, tears falling unchecked down his cheeks, struggling to draw breath. He needed to know where they were and what they were doing. Alastair Farrow and Will English. Those two boys responsible for this. Farrow, the monster who violated him, damaged him, defiled him, then left him in the woods alone, and Will, his best friend, the boy who'd untied him from that fence, the boy who pledged his loyalty in blood, then betrayed him like Judas Iscariot.

Both men had been easy to track down. Will English had a photography business in south-west London. Luke had pored over its website until he'd memorised every word, every image, every detail on it. Trading had recently ceased. There was an apologetic voicemail message from Will, pathetic in its plaintive humour, making light of the difficulties creatives face, with a second-rate quip about the recession. Then there was a wine shop and a little-used Facebook account with no privacy settings. A beautiful wife, pictures of whom filled the gallery on the photography website. There were other people in the photos too.

And a wedding.

Ian and Emma Barratt-Jones, July 2001.

There was a picture of Will's wife in the line-up, beaming, arms linked with the bride. They were good friends. A quick Google search and he discovered that Ian Barratt-Jones, a City banker, had come fourth in a tournament at his golf club in Oxfordshire. From there it was easy. The man was arrogant and stupid and sucked up the attention of the glamorous, wealthy lawyer he met at the golf club bar. Luke had learned long ago it was good to be prepared. Ian was ideal, naive as well as greedy, and more than willing to risk his family, their security, everything he should have protected, for a quick, illegal buck. Luke knew from the off he'd do anything to stay out of prison. People like that were useful. Getting to Will, destroying Will's life, had been in his mind from the start. Why should Will get to live happily ever after? It should have been Will whom Farrow hurt. Luke had stood up to him. Faced him. Will had buckled. Rolled over. Watched in silence as the monster meted out his punishment on Luke. And then, in Drysdale's office, when he could have saved him, he delivered his final crushing blow and betrayed him.

He hadn't expected to feel anything for Harmony, but he'd been touched by her honesty and passion, the way she'd battled with herself as she betrayed her husband. There was an innocence about her that was intoxicating, and for a while he was convinced he might be happy with her, that perhaps she was his last chance at something resembling a life. But in the end her loyalty to Will was too strong. The irony in that was bitter; her rejection, the cold look in her eye when she turned her back on him, mirroring the expression on Will's face all those years before.

Everything fell into his lap like a shower of gifts from the gods. In a way it was too easy, discovering that Will had met up with Farrow and caused a scene and threatened him in front of witnesses in a pub; being with Harmony as she put the code into the lock; then her calling to say Will had disappeared. Will and his stupid night walks – rambles, didn't he call them? – that lasted for hours. Of course Luke had no idea how long he'd be gone, but it was worth the risk. That idiot Ian agreed to give him an alibi without batting an eyelid. What poetic justice that was! Will sent to prison for killing Farrow because a friend betrayed him. It was perfect.

Luke checked in his rear-view mirror and moved across into the slow lane in preparation for coming off the slip road. He drove carefully along the country roads. He slowed when he saw the signpost, then put his indicator on.

Pendower Hall.

Just seeing the name made his skin crawl. He remembered being driven away by his aunt, a lady inaptly named Grace, a virtue of which she had none. His parents sent her with a message for him from the outpost in Kenya. She was to pass on their deep displeasure at his expulsion. He had humiliated and disappointed them. He was to stay with Aunt Grace and attend the local comprehensive. He would continue to see them once a year when they returned to England for Easter, but as far as they were concerned he was on his own. His aunt had apologised to Drysdale for inconvenience caused.

'My brother is hugely ashamed by all of this,' she said shrilly, her thin lips barely moving. 'This child is the black sheep of our family flock. We've tried *everything*.'

Luke pulled up in the car park behind the main school. It was early, the boys and staff were still getting up, making beds, eating breakfast. He passed a couple of caretakers, who nodded their heads in respectful greeting. He nodded back and continued to walk. The school hadn't changed. Everything was the same, even the smell coming out of the kitchens, greasy, institutional, spewing from the ventilation pipes at the back of the building.

He squeezed between the gap in the railings that used to be his and Will's route out and walked into the woods. It was peaceful, with only the sounds of songbirds in the beech trees above his head, their branches thick with brilliant green leaves, last year's brown ones fallen at his feet, a carpet of softness slowly breaking down, throwing up that mulchy smell that brought memories rushing so vividly back to him.

When Luke reached the Judas tree – the pride of Pendower Hall – he stood still. He looked up at it. Studied it. Every bit of bark, every twist in every branch, each leaf, each twig. The perfect tree to climb. Their favourite tree, where they would come to play, happy in its comforting boughs, hidden from the rest of the world, a mean world they didn't need when they had each other. He listened to the breeze blowing through the leaves, rustling above him, as if the tree were speaking to him.

Apologising, understanding, waiting.

There was nothing left for him. It was time for him to take control. His life never really got going; cut down in childhood, never allowed to grow. He was tired but he didn't feel sorry for himself. Self-pity was something he'd never succumbed to and this gave him great satisfaction. Self-pity would have been easy. Perhaps, he thought, as he stared up at the tree, self-pity might have been his salvation. Perhaps it was his continuous quest to beat them all, to come out on top, to show them they hadn't broken him, that now left him with no other option.

He took his shoes off one by one, placing them in a neat pair, before taking his jacket off and folding it beside them. He wasn't scared. He was calm. There was a tranquillity about him that was unfamiliar. He imagined he was floating in the middle of a huge ocean, the waves lapping at his face and body as he bobbed on the surface of the water, the sun warming his face. He bent down and opened the bag he'd brought. He took out the rope and the knife. Then he pulled himself up onto the first bough and climbed the tree easily, just as he'd done years earlier, following Will up into the branches.

He tied the rope then opened the knife and admired its shining blade one last time. He held open his palm and drew the blade along the line of the scar that crossed it. Blood flowed like cherry juice and he watched it, transfixed for a moment or two, as it fell in drops on the earth below. Then he threw the knife down into the undergrowth and closed his eyes, the bell for morning lessons ringing out across the courtyard, resounding in the branches and leaves of the tree that held him.

EPILOGUE

The late November rain was falling heavily from the charcoal sky. Cars drove along the New King's Road with their wipers working overtime. Headlights lit the four-thirty dusk and the pavements were covered in a sheen of wet with water flowing in rapids along the side of the road and into the drains.

Will and Harmony walked carefully, avoiding the deeper puddles, and trying not to snag anyone with the umbrella they shared. They kept their heads low to fend off the bite of the cold. As they reached the covered area outside the Chelsea and Westminster hospital Will stopped to shake the rain off the umbrella and close it before they pushed through the revolving doors into the warmth of the hospital's foyer.

'That's better,' he said, as they walked through the airy reception area towards the lifts. 'I've never seen so much rain.'

She smiled up at him. 'You look terrified,' she said, and reached up to kiss his cheek.

He forced a smile back in an attempt to mask his nerves.

'Don't worry,' she said. 'It's going to be fine.'

He pressed the button to go up and glanced at Harmony. Her hand was on her stomach, resting lightly on its roundness. A picture of Luke, dressed in his suit, shaking hands with him in Emma and Ian's garden, flashed into his head. These unwanted images would always be there, however much he fought to keep them at bay.

It was two older boys, sixth-formers, who'd found his body. The boys had been bunking off prep for a cigarette and stumbled upon him. Will had heard enough detail for him to picture the scene: Luke hanging from the Judas tree, bare-footed, hand cut across the palm.

The image would haunt him forever.

The story had made the national news and triggered a police investigation into abuse at the school when Luke and Will had been pupils. Will had found no satisfaction or release while raking over those days with the police, but there was an element of uneasy relief when Drysdale and a handful of ex-members of staff found themselves facing prosecution. He'd followed the trials closely. He hadn't wanted to appear in court so sent a statement to be read on his behalf. His was circumstantial evidence, more linked to the atmosphere and culture of the school than specific events. It was hard reliving those dark days. In the end he was left feeling empty as the full extent of the rot was revealed and Will discovered there were numerous men whose lives had been torn apart as children. He knew he'd got off lightly. The policewoman who'd talked to him had shown him a photograph that was found inside Luke's jacket at the scene of his death. It was the Polaroid of the two of them taken in the summer before it all went wrong. Luke had wanted to send it to his parents to show them who Will was. They'd asked one of the other boys to take it, then hooked arms around each other's shoulders and grinned. Luke had loved the photo so much he'd decided to keep it. Knowing he'd had it on him when he took his life was heartbreaking.

The receptionist called Harmony's name and he followed his wife into a small dimly lit room off the main waiting area. She removed her coat and a nurse asked her to climb onto the bed and lift her sweater over her bump and unzip her trousers.

The sonographer smiled and introduced herself then pulled the top of Harmony's knickers well below the swell of her stomach and tucked green paper towel into them.

'This will feel cold to start with. Sorry.'

'That's fine.' Harmony smiled at her.

She squeezed a large dollop of gel onto Harmony's tummy. Then she took hold of the ultrasound scanner and pushed it hard against her, moving it around in the gel, while staring at the screen.

Will noticed Harmony wince. 'Does it hurt?' he asked.

'No,' she whispered back. 'A bit uncomfortable. I drank a pint of water before I came out and haven't peed.' She looked at the woman, who stared intently at the screen. 'Apparently, it makes the picture easier to see.'

'That's right,' the woman said with a nod, her eyes still fixed ahead.

Will looked at the screen but found it hard to see anything that resembled a baby. To him it was just a mass of shapes in black and white. Then there was a deep, fast, beating sound and the sonographer centred on that part of Harmony's stomach, pushing the scanner deeper into her, making her wince for a second time.

'Are you sure it doesn't—' Will began.

'This is the baby's heartbeat,' the woman said.

Will looked at the screen again and saw a tiny black mass pulsing in time with the sound they could hear.

Harmony reached for his hand.

'And there's the baby's head.' She paused and moved the scanner. 'The spine.'

'I can't see it,' he said, leaning towards the screen and squinting.

'Don't worry, most people can't.' She pointed at the screen with her fingers. 'This is the face. The nose, the lips.'

Just then the baby opened its mouth and seemed to yawn.

'Oh my God,' said Harmony, a small laugh escaping her lips. 'That's amazing.'

It was a peculiar feeling. One of dread and excitement. *This is it*, he thought, as he stared at the indistinct face of the child on the screen.

His chance to make amends.

Luke's child.

He thought back to when she'd told him. She'd been devastated. He sat on the sofa and stayed quiet as she dropped to her knees at his feet, took his hands in hers, and apologised over and over.

'If you want me to . . .' She couldn't finish the sentence. 'I will though . . . I will understand. If you want me to do that . . . I'm sorry, Will. I'm so sorry.'

He'd sat in the garden, at the wrought-iron table, tracing his fingers over the filigree patterns in the rusting metal. Harmony was pregnant. The pain inside him was intense. He wanted her to be carrying his child. Could he ask her to get rid of it? He heard his mother's words in his head: 'You selfish, selfish boy.' She was right, he knew that. He'd learned a lot about himself in the last seven months. He thought back to Drysdale's office, of how he'd watched the light seep out of Luke's eyes when he'd failed to stand beside him.

He was responsible, not alone, but in part, for the jigsaw puzzle of Luke's tragic life. He knew that if ever there was a chance for atonement this was it. This was his opportunity to make amends for those things he'd done wrong, the selfish decisions he'd made again and again over the years. He could be a father to Luke's child and give it all the love and support that had been denied Luke himself. He finally had the chance to prove his own father wrong, that life isn't always ugly, and that sometimes it can be fair.

'Is the baby healthy?' Harmony asked. 'There's nothing we should be worried about?'

'Everything looks fine,' the sonographer replied with a reassuring smile. 'I've got a few measurements to take but otherwise all good.' She turned to them both. 'Do you want a picture of your baby?'

Will smiled at Harmony, who gripped his hand as if her life depended on it, then leant forward and kissed her forehead.

Then he turned his head and nodded.

AUTHOR'S NOTE

An idea for a book can come from anywhere. From an overheard snippet of conversation. From a newspaper article. From an exchange you witness between two strangers in a supermarket. Sometimes, of course, an idea will spring from personal experience, from something close to home, something that affects you or your loved ones directly.

A few years ago my husband received a telephone call from the police while he was at work. It was a call which threw him completely off balance for a period of time. As the woman took a moment to explain who she was he experienced a familiar and unwelcome wave of nausea that he had not felt since childhood. Though he had no clues as to the reason for her call, he described to me later how his world seemed to close in as she introduced herself, how his conscious awareness of the situation diminished and he became an almost third-party observer of the call. Waves of buried memories and emotions swept through him. Even before she'd finished giving her his name he experienced a strange conviction that he knew what the call was about. 'Does this relate to what went on at my school twenty-five years ago?' When she asked how he knew he replied that he had been expecting this call for years but hadn't realised it until that moment.

My husband was sent to a tiny boarding choir school when he was eight years old and stayed until he was thirteen when he left to go to his local grammar school. His parents wanted what they believed was the best for him. He was awarded a full bursary and they felt this opportunity would give him a privileged start to his education. Little did they know that the very fabric of their chosen school was infected by child abuse. Thankfully my husband wasn't one of those sexually abused, but the violent and oppressive atmosphere of the school stayed with him for many years. He didn't know, nor could he have understood, what was happening to his less fortunate classmates, but he had an uneasy awareness of the hidden malevolence. Nearly three decades later, two members of staff were being investigated following allegations made by men who'd been victims of their abuse, and the police were seeking witnesses and other victims from the time.

What both upset and fascinated me was the Pandora's box of emotions that was opened by that phone call. My husband began to look up the names of boys he'd been at school with. He became obsessed with discovering what they'd gone on to do, whether they'd married, had children, whether, essentially, they'd survived their ordeals and managed to find happiness. Tragically, most had never recovered and this hit him hard. It was sobering to talk to him about these boys, these innocents, damaged beyond repair. I became preoccupied with the idea of damaged childhood, not necessarily damaged by abuse, but by an array of incidents: the death of a parent, a father withholding affection from his only son, a child witnessing cruelty, bullying – from both the bullied child and bully's point of view. I didn't want to write about sexual abuse – principally because I had touched on it with my first novel – but the subject of bullying came back to me repeatedly. I started toying with the idea of two boys, one who actively denies his past, papering over his painful memories, focusing instead on his adult relationship as his salvation. Then a second boy, more ruined, unable to find peace, with a desire for revenge that consumed him. It was then that the characters of Will and Luke began to take shape. I saw them clearly even before I knew what route my story would take, these two boys, their troubled childhoods indelibly marked by a single, brutal event, both affected differently, both using alternative ways to cope. I imagined them growing up, one carrying guilt into his adult life, the other anger. And how, if I pushed them together years later, their pasts might wreak havoc on their presents. As the story began to take shape, I started to think about what each of them had to lose, what was at risk. For Will it was his wife, Harmony, his 'anchor in the storm'; his salvation. To threaten his marriage was to threaten to destroy his survival of the past. And there emerged the third key character in my story; Harmony and the dangerous love triangle she finds herself caught up in.

At the beginning Harmony was a fairly neutral character, stable, calm, balanced, but as the themes became clearer, I gave Harmony her own demons from childhood to battle. Though loved by her mother and sister, Harmony had experienced grief as a child and also abandonment. On the surface she seems fine, well-adjusted, rational, but the fallout from her past – the fault lines – were there. Childhood is the most precious and fleeting of times, as is the innocence that goes hand in hand with it, so fragile, so breakable. Any emotional damage to a child will leave scars, some deep, some not so. Trauma in childhood can have far-reaching impact on adulthood. It can influence the decisions people make, tamper with their ability to cope in certain situations, affect how they interact with others, how they deal with the things life throws at them. The inescapable truth is we are all a unique and individual tapestry of our past experiences. Everything that happens to us becomes inextricably woven into what makes us who we are.

What struck me as I began to research the book was the number of times people said things like 'that's just what went on' or 'it was different back then' or 'oh, the headmaster knew'. Blind eyes turned again and again. Children betrayed. Very quickly betrayal as a theme pushed to the front of the book. The exploration of betrayal. What broken trust does to different people. How easily one person can forgive a betrayal and how violently another might yearn for revenge. Or redemption. The concept of betrayal worked its way into the veins of *The Judas Tree*. And betrayal hurts the most where there is love. The stronger the love, the harder the bite of betrayal and the deeper the scar left behind. Love and betrayal link all the stories in the book in different ways: between lovers and spouses, between children and parents, between friends. When betrayal occurs, there are only two options; forgive or don't forgive. And with an absence of forgiveness comes anger, comes blame, comes guilt, and sometimes, revenge . . .

Amanda Jennings, March 2014

ACKNOWLEDGEMENTS

This book was originally published by Cutting Edge Press in 2014. It was called *The Judas Scar*. My acknowledgements from 2014 were as follows: My heartfelt thanks and appreciation go to my agent, the incomparable Broo Doherty, who from day one has taken care of me, and always makes me laugh, even when I don't feel like it. To Paul Swallow for his belief in this book, his incredible passion, and his generosity when it comes to cupcakes. To those friends and family who read various versions of this book, but especially Charlie Jolly for his encouragement, Tiina Verran for her early suggestions, Cosima Wagner and Lou Botham for their expert proof-reading skills, and Sian Johnson who read far too many drafts of this book and offered insightful advice throughout. To Sean Costello for editing with a sensitive and skilful touch and being such a pleasure to work with. To those people I love on Twitter – authors, readers, book bloggers and like-minded souls – who offered support, distraction and laughter whenever I needed it. I have been blown away by the generosity of so many of you. I owe you much. Special mention to Tammy Cohen and Elizabeth Forbes for always being on the end of a phone. I am privileged to have amazing friends, both old and newer, you are my life-blood. Thank you. And then to my family, my three inspiring daughters who make me proud every day, my wonderful parents and sister, and of course, my husband, whose strength and integrity know no bounds and without whom I'd be lacking my very best friend. I love you all.

For this newer edition, renamed *The Judas Tree*, I would like to thank HQ Stories for republishing this book so it can hopefully find a new audience. I am very fond of this book and very grateful for them to give it a second chance. I'd like to thank my editor Kate Mills, Rebecca Jamieson, Sally Partington, and also Graham Bartlett for helping me with the police bit. Any errors here are mine. Since this book was first written I have had the most magical writing journey. I am blessed with amazing and loyal readers, with fabulous friends in the writing community, and, of course, the same thanks goes to the friends and family I am so fortunate to have. Thank you. All of you.

Craving more from Amanda Jennings?

The Haven is a hypnotic, dark thriller about a dream life that becomes a devastating nightmare . . .

It was meant to be paradise . . .

Wanting an escape from the constraints of conventional life, Kit and Tara move to Winterfall Farm, an isolated smallholding on Bodmin Moor, with their daughter and a group of friends.

At first living off-grid and working the land seems too good to be true, but when their charismatic leader, Jeremy, returns from the city with a young runaway, fractures in the group begin to appear.

Jeremy's behaviour becomes increasingly erratic. Rules are imposed, the outside world is shunned, and tensions quickly reach breaking point with devastating consequences . . .

The Haven is available now.

Ready for a thrilling psychological suspense
novel about lost love and buried secrets?

Don't miss *The Storm* . . .

Amanda Jennings

DOESN'T EVERY MARRIAGE
HAVE A DARK SIDE?

THE
STORM

'Twisty, malevolent, gripping'
LISA JEWELL

Available now!

Looking for an emotional family drama,
packed with suspense, obsession, and deceit?

Try *The Cliff House* . . .

Amanda Jennings

'Beautiful and sinister.'
The Times

'Dazzling'
Lisa Jewell

HER OBSESSION.   YOUR HOME.

THE
CLIFF
HOUSE

'Perfect summer holiday reading.'
Daily Express

Available now!

ONE PLACE. MANY STORIES

Bold, innovative and
empowering publishing.

FOLLOW US ON:

@HQStories